ALL THOSE EXPLOSIONS WERE SOMEONE ELSE'S FAULT

ALL THOSE EXPLOSIONS WERE SOMEONE ELSE'S FAULT

JAMES ALAN GARDNER

A TOM DOHERTY ASSOCIATES BOOK

New York

This is a work of fiction. All of the characters, organizations, and events portrayed in this novel are either products of the author's imagination or are used fictitiously.

ALL THOSE EXPLOSIONS WERE SOMEONE ELSE'S FAULT

A Tor Book
Published by Tom Doherty Associates
175 Fifth Avenue
New York, NY 10010

www.tor-forge.com

Tor® is a registered trademark of Macmillan Publishing Group, LLC.

The Library of Congress Cataloging-in-Publication Data is available upon request.

ISBN 978-0-7653-9263-3 (trade paperback)
ISBN 978-0-7653-9265-7 (ebook)

Our books may be purchased in bulk for promotional, educational, or business use. Please contact your local bookseller or the Macmillan Corporate and Premium Sales Department at 1-800-221-7945, extension 5442, or by email at MacmillanSpecialMarkets@macmillan.com.

First Edition: November 2017

Printed in the United States of America

0 9 8 7 6 5 4 3 2 1

To Sigung Bob Schneider, and Pat York:
Absent friends

Eruptions

STOP ME IF YOU'VE HEARD THIS ONE BEFORE

A vampire, a werewolf, and a demon walk into a bar . . .

OH WAIT

I don't know which Earth you're from. You probably don't either. There's this strange idea that Earths can be numbered, starting at 1 then up through the integers. It's not true. The integers don't work, nor do the reals, nor even the complex numbers. The set of all possible Earths is a gnarly, twisted, unordered thing—so contorted and uncountably infinite, not even the word "fractal" does it justice.

Each Earth has its own rules. Some allow magic; others don't. Maybe your Earth does, maybe it doesn't . . . or maybe you don't know. We thought magic was impossible on our version of Earth until April 16, 1982.

On that date, after centuries of hiding in the shadows, the Elders of the Dark finally realized their condition wasn't a curse; it was a marketable asset.

Versions of the following ad appeared in the *Wall Street Journal*, the *Financial Times*, the *Nihon Keizai Shimbun*, and a dozen other money-oriented publications around the world:

Power and an End to Aging
Cost: 10,000,000 US Dollars
Demonstrations and proof given to serious inquiries
Binding contracts to protect your interests
For further information, contact . . .

In each case, the contact information referred to a law firm with impeccable business credentials.

The ad was initially assumed to be a hoax or PR stunt. Days passed, and the only attempts at contact came from reporters; they received "No comment." But millionaires are mortal (at least they were when the ad appeared) and a few were close enough to death—from cancer, heart ailments, or plain old age—that they were willing to take a chance.

They made phone calls.

They attended confidential meetings.

They saw with their own eyes that vampires, werewolves, and demons were real . . . and that the powers of the Dark were transferable.

Every qualified buyer who responded to the Dark Invitation was offered the Dark Pact: a lengthy contract promising the end of aging and disease, plus magic-powered mental and physical vigor, in exchange for the specified sum and other unusual but completely legal commitments.

A few of the oldest and sickest took the deal. They got what they paid for.

THE DARK SPREAD

When colleagues and competitors saw the results, the trickle of customers became a flood.

Within five years, a high percentage of the elite had embraced the Dark. Those who hadn't . . . well, they were mortal, weren't they? Tick. Tock. Attrition happens. By the dawn of the twenty-first century, the price of membership had soared and "super-rich" was synonymous with "Darkling."

Other synonyms: "Van Helsing" became equivalent to "terrorist." "Exorcism" became "hate crime." When CEOs become vampires, Congress outlaws stakes.

(In case you're naively wondering, the churches didn't raise a fuss. Organized religion *loved* the Dark. Nothing proves the power of faith like what a crucifix does to a vampire. Besides, the Dark used their power and wealth to support open-minded ministries. That line about a camel going through the eye of a needle has never been a hard-and-fast principle; it's more of a talking point to begin negotiations.)

YOU MAY ALSO BE WONDERING

How did the newly born vampires procure blood?

Consider: How do rich people procure anything?

They buy it. From less rich people.

Under normal conditions, a vampire only needed about a liter of blood a day. Many people would gladly sell that much for cash. As it turned out, you could buy blood more cheaply than a first-rate bottle of wine.

The obvious name for such payments was "blood money," but that sounded so vulgar. Soon the acceptable term became "trickle-down."

SO THE DARK TOOK OVER

In the next twenty years, the Dark conquered the world—delicately. They were vastly outnumbered by normal humans, but that was how they wanted it. Darklings wanted to remain in an exclusive club.

Being Dark was special. Being Dark was cool. Being Dark made you stronger and *better* than the plebes. Unlike old movies where the monsters tried to make everyone else like them, our world's monsters did their damnedest to keep the riffraff out.

Only the rich and the powerful were allowed to become Darklings. CEOs. Heads of state. The movers and the shakers. Almost all the elite in every country of the world eventually purchased the Dark Conversion. Holdouts were marginalized, cut off from influence. It's hard to compete when your opponents use magic and otherworldly powers to sabotage whatever you do.

By the dawn of the twenty-first century, the Dark controlled the show. Money and privilege flowed uphill; you-know-what flowed down. The Dark Pact forced Darklings not to abuse their powers so outrageously that the "peasants" would rebel, but apart from that, the Dark got its way.

THEN ONE NIGHT IN AMERICA'S HEARTLAND . . .

I got this story directly from a Darkling. It's not a deep secret—not one of the Taboo Truths that'll get a Darkling beheaded if word spills out to non-Darklings—but it's still not a story they spread around. It doesn't show the Dark in a deferential light, and Darklings really, really, really crave deference. They'd get angry if they knew I was passing this on, even to someone from an alternate Earth; but the Darklings are mad at me for so much already, one more offense won't make a difference.

So there was a roadhouse: some sawdusty place surrounded by wheat fields, with no neighbors to complain about the noise. People went there to drink and hook up and let off steam. I imagine pool tables, dartboards, and a jukebox . . . neon beer signs above the bar, and not new ones from glittery boutiques but old originals with the flickers and a grungy-thick coating of cigarette smoke.

But I'm just making that part up—the person who told me this story didn't care about human decor. Humans weren't real to him; nothing mattered but the Dark.

The Darklings in this story were a vampire, a werewolf, and a demon. All young: maybe twenty. Second generation. This was the summer of 2000, and the Darklings involved were children of parents who'd gone Dark in the eighties. These kids had grown up knowing that Mummy and Daddy would buy them the Dark Conversion when they came of age; they'd gone to private schools filled with kids in the same position; and they'd come out the other end with skewed opinions of their own worth.

The vampire was called Lilith. That doesn't tell you much; lots of second-gen girls got named Lilith, after the biblical mother of all monsters. Darkling parents at the time thought their kids should have Dark-inspired names, so we ended up with a bunch of Vlads and Shivas and Bathories.

This Lilith was a typical young vamp. By the time she'd gone through Conversion, she'd gotten the nose job, the boob job, the teeth, and all the rest. The work was tastefully done—big money wants to look patrician, not trashy—so Lilith was beautiful but bland. She looked like someone you'd hire to model sweaters. Her only distinctive feature was her hair: dyed a literal rainbow of colors, red-orange-yellow-green, with a selection of more natural tones thrown in. It must have cost a fortune and taken days to create—but being a vampire, she was physically dead and her hair would never grow out. Dye your hair once and it lasts for years.

The person who told me this story said the werewolf was known as Blood-Claw. I don't believe for a second he actually went by that; if he'd tried, other wolves would have immediately challenged him to claim the name, and whoever won the fight would be way too Alpha to end up in a shitkicker Midwestern bar. (Whatever names they're given at birth, most werewolves use names like Ronnie and Trish. No one ever fights to be Trish.) But let's pretend for the sake of this story that he really was known as Blood-Claw, and it wasn't just a fantasy name he used in front of the mirror.

Like most werewolves, Blood-Claw was big. He probably played football in high school, and would have made the team even if Daddy hadn't paid for the uniforms. This particular night wasn't near the full moon, so Blood-Claw had on his human face. I imagine him wearing a wifebeater and maybe a cowboy hat—but since he was a Darkling, the hat would have been from the priciest men's boutique in Dallas and the wifebeater would have been vicuña. Beneath the shirt, he had real muscles, serious bodybuilder meat . . . but his pecs weren't created through hard work or exercise. If the Dark Conversion makes a man into a werewolf, his human body bulks up fast, so he looks like the cover of *Men's Health*. His jaw gets steely, his back gets straight, and his chest grows the perfect amount of hair—enough to be manly but not to comb.

The final Darkling to enter the roadhouse was a demon: a six-foot-tall praying mantis. Some people say the Dark Conversion is a wish-fulfillment thing; what you become is shaped by your innermost power fantasies. Others say it brings out the "real you"—the truth of your deepest soul. Don't ask what kind of person would have a giant insect as either a heart's desire or a true identity. But always, without exception, Darklings are thrilled with what they become. "Hurray, I'm now a bug! Eat your heart out, Gregor Samsa!"

The mantis's name was CeeCee. Make of that what you will.

SO THIS VAMPIRE, WEREWOLF, AND DEMON WALKED INTO THE BAR . . . More precisely, Blood-Claw kicked open the door with a bang.

Conversations stopped dead. A beer pitcher broke. The jukebox began playing Elton John. (You may not have vampires in your world, but I *know* you have Elton John.)

Blood-Claw stepped into the room and glared at the crowd belligerently. Behind him, Lilith slouched in; she sniffed and wrinkled her nose. CeeCee skittered in last, forelegs raised and rubbing together as though the insect were sharpening knives. Its head swiveled through a disturbingly large arc, scanning the room with its huge compound eyes.

Every human froze. No one reached for a gun, even though plenty of the patrons were carrying. Darklings give off an aura called their Shadow; much of the time it just causes uneasiness, but it can be cranked up on demand to cause debilitating fear. I've felt that fear myself—the same feeling as in nightmares, where you can't move a muscle. Your lungs refuse to breathe, but your heart pounds like it's trying to punch its way out of your rib cage.

Every person in the roadhouse recognized what the newcomers were. Vampires and werewolves look ordinary most of the time, but when they want you to know what they are, you do.

"Listen up," Blood-Claw said. "My girl Lilith is thirsty."

Lilith didn't look thirsty. She looked bored and bad-tempered, like someone who hates where you've brought her and wants to make sure you know.

Blood-Claw threw two hundred-dollar bills onto the nearest table. "This is for anyone who'll give my girl a drink."

He waited. Silence. Except for Elton John. (Decide for yourself which song he sang. "Don't Let the Sun Go Down on Me"? "The Bitch is Back"? Consider this a Rorschach test.)

In response to this silence, Lilith gave a deeply irritated sigh. The mantis rubbed its forelegs even faster. Blood-Claw said, "Come on, people. Two hundred bucks, and she'll only take as much as a fucking blood donation. We'll even buy you orange juice after."

No one spoke. Lilith rolled her eyes and said, "Tsk!"

"Look, assholes," Blood-Claw said to the room, "this is a free country, with a free market, and that's the market price for what my girl needs. You give, we pay, and the wheels get greased. That's how it works, that's how it's always worked, and that's how it's going to work tonight. If you fuckwits think you can gouge us on the price, you don't understand the system."

"It's not about price," said a voice in the back. "It's about not taking your bullshit."

Everyone in the bar whipped their heads around.

OVER IN THE CORNER WITH HIS BACK AGAINST THE WALL SAT A MAN IN HIS EARLY TWENTIES

His head was shaved bald. He wore a white dress shirt and a blue pin-striped vest, like someone who'd come to the bar straight from his job in an uptight office. Rage rolled off the man like surf; once Blood-Claw focused on him, the scent of aggression filled the werewolf's nostrils. The smell of an ape's anger was different than a wolf's, but it provoked the same reaction. If someone issues a challenge, a werewolf can't help responding.

"You," Blood-Claw said. "Do I smell a volunteer?"

"Go fuck yourself," the bald man replied.

Blood-Claw smiled. Lilith had come alert, dropping her pose of petulance. CeeCee stopped the compulsive claw-rubbing and shifted its head from side to side, like a weaving cobra.

The bald man wasn't alone at his table. He had a companion who'd been sitting with his back to the door. The companion was another young man: dark hair, broad shoulders, thick-rimmed glasses. He put his hand on the bald man's arm. "Let's not make trouble."

"I'm not making trouble. They are."

"We aren't making trouble either," Blood-Claw said. "Just arranging a deal: cash for corpuscles. It's yours, Baldy."

"Stick it up your ass," Baldy said.

Blood-Claw grabbed the two hundred dollars and started across the room. Chairs scraped the floor as people got out of his way. In moments, the werewolf was towering over the two men and their table. "You got some mouth on you, Baldy," Blood-Claw said.

"Don't call him that," the dark-haired man said. "His name is Alex."

"I don't need you defending me," Alex snapped. "You always think you need to defend me."

"He doesn't need to defend you," Blood-Claw said. "He needs to keep his fucking head down." The werewolf lifted the hundred-dollar bills and let them fall—one, two—onto the table. "Here you go, *Alex*. Payment in advance."

"No," Alex said. "I don't accept. Let your bitch bite somebody else."

Lilith crossed the tavern with the speed of a sucker punch. If you've never seen a vampire move, you have no idea how fast *fast* can be. I've heard it called a "burst phenomenon"—vampires can't go ultra-quick for more than thirteen steps, and once that's done, they're tapped out until the next sundown . . . but if you think you're safe when they're on the other side of the room, don't blink.

"What did you call me?" Lilith asked.

"I thought vampires had good hearing," Alex answered. "Or is the blood roaring in your ears?"

"Alex," his companion said. "Taunting them is stupid."

"Stay out of this," Alex said. He stood up and raised his voice so everyone could hear. "These 'people' think they can pay me for blood. They can't. I refuse. If anything happens, it's against my will, and that means it's a crime—by human law and the Dark Pact."

"Yeah, like you're an expert on the Pact." Blood-Claw put his hand on Alex's arm. "Come out back with us, Baldy. This is way past the volunteer system now. It's going to happen, one way or another."

"No." Alex tried to shake off Blood-Claw's grip. The bald man was pretty big himself: six feet tall, in good shape. Maybe he hadn't been a star on his high school football team, but he likely won a few medals on track and field day. He was a young, fit guy, and considering how quickly he had flipped into Mouthy Hothead mode, he was probably accustomed to bullying the people around him.

Bullying humans, not Darklings. There aren't many billionaires in the wheat fields. Lilith, Blood-Claw, and CeeCee were the first Darklings ever to come through that neck of the woods: joyriding across the butthole of America, getting their kicks from making mortals lick the dirt. Who knows how often they'd played out similar scenes in similar roadhouses? Bullies just love to bully bullies.

When Alex tried to shake off Blood-Claw, it didn't work. The werewolf held on like a lug wrench. "Seriously," Blood-Claw said, "this is going to happen. We're heading out back, and you're coming with us."

"No," Alex said. He spoke to the crowd. "I'm refusing. You all hear me."

"He'll change his mind," CeeCee said. The mantis's voice was low and hissy, even if its words didn't have many sibilant sounds. In movies, demon voices are sent through audio processing to make them sound inhuman. Real demon voices are barely sounds at all—they're vibrations that bypass your ears and go straight to your reptile brain. You don't hear them, you feel them. And they're terrifying.

"This human will change his mind," CeeCee said. "In a few minutes he'll return, alive and intact. He'll tell you he reconsidered and voluntarily offered his throat."

"I won't," Alex said.

"You will," CeeCee replied. The mantis set out toward the back door. Human eyes had trouble following; the demon's carapace was brilliant green and yet the moment it touched any shadow, it seemed to fade out of existence. The mantis flared back to bright visibility when the shadow was past. Visible, vanished, visible, vanished, until it reached the back door. "Let's go," it said to Alex.

"No."

"Yes," Blood-Claw said. He yanked Alex's arm, jerking the big bald man off-balance and dragging him a step toward the door.

"No," said Alex's companion. He got to his feet: not fast, not slow. The man was bigger even than Blood-Claw. Despite the glasses, he didn't look bookish—a farm boy who'd worked from dawn to dusk tossing hay bales. He had the plaid shirt, the cheap jeans, the farmer's tan: Unlike the Darklings, he'd spent his life soaking up fresh air and sunlight. "Let's all calm down . . ."

"Shut up, Cal," Alex snapped. "Just stay the fuck out."

"Alex . . ."

"I mean it. Back off. I can handle this."

"Sure," Blood-Claw said. "You can handle us."

"I can keep saying no," Alex told him. "Whatever you do, I'll keep saying no, and when you're finished, I'll press charges."

"Sure you will."

The werewolf yanked the bald man's arm again. This time Alex didn't resist, but said, "I'm under duress," over and over as Blood-Claw dragged him toward the back.

Lilith looked at Cal. She raised an eyebrow as if asking, *Are you going to give us trouble?* Cal clearly considered it . . . but even as Alex was dragged away, the bald man's eyes were on Cal, saying, *Don't you dare butt in.*

So Cal didn't move. Lilith sneered at him and said, "Glad you know your place." She reached down with one finger and flicked the hundred-dollar bills toward him. Then she left to go have a drink.

OUT BACK, THE NIGHT WAS CLEAR

A big Midwestern sky without a speck of cloud and a yellowish half-moon shining down across the fields. If you turned your back on the roadhouse, all you'd see would be wheat: a thousand acres of grain, and a sky with a million stars. The air smelled of pot; what else would you expect behind a fleabag roadhouse? But whoever had been smoking up ran off when the mantis appeared. Now the soft Great Plains wind slowly sighed the stink away.

Lilith was the last out the door. By the time she arrived, Blood-Claw had passed Alex to CeeCee, who held the man's arms and legs with four of its six appendages. Pincers scissored tightly; the mantis's upper arms were lined with spikes for ripping prey. They hadn't done much damage yet, but Alex's shirt had been torn. If you possessed the nose of a vampire or werewolf, you would have smelled blood trickling from the little nicks on Alex's arms.

Lilith walked up to Alex. She took his chin in her hand. She wasn't as tall as the bald man, but she was not a short woman. She stared into his eyes. "Say yes."

"No."

Her face moved closer. "Say yes."

"Not going to happen."

She gave his jaw a shake and squeezed hard. "Say yes."

"No." The way she was squeezing his face, he had trouble getting the word out, but his intention was clear. Lilith let go in disgust.

Alex exercised his jaw; it obviously hurt. After a few moments, he said, "You can't use your powers on me. That's against the law."

"Oh, the law," Lilith said. "I'm trembling."

"It's also against the Dark Pact," Alex said. "If you break that, you're fucked."

Blood-Claw rolled his eyes. "You have no idea what's in the Pact." This was true. The contents of the Pact were one of those Taboo Truths: never to be divulged, on pain of death. Spokespeople for the Dark claimed that the Pact forbade all Darklings from using their powers to "exploit" mortals. In practice, however, there seemed to be plenty of loopholes. Perhaps the Pact's only true rule was, "Don't get caught."

Still, the Elders of the Dark publicly disapproved of using magic to bludgeon mortals into submission. It made the Dark look bad; it *hurt the brand*. And damaging the Dark's reputation had more deadly repercussions than breaking human law. The Elders ran a tight ship. Every Darkling knew that.

THE MANTIS DEMON TOOK ITS TURN

"Let me handle this," CeeCee said. Slowly, carefully, the mantis turned Alex around. Alex struggled, trying to break free, but CeeCee had the advantage in both the number and strength of appendages. Fighting only drew more blood as the demon's rough pincers scraped the man's skin.

When Alex and the mantis were finally face-to-face, CeeCee leaned in and stared. Just that: multifaceted insectile eyes looming less than an inch from Alex's human ones. Intimidation, pure and simple—a giant bug playing on primitive human fears. As it stared, it twitched its mandibles, close enough to brush Alex's face. Softly, softly, it chittered, "Say yes."

Alex leaned his head back as far as he could . . . but he didn't look away, nor did he close his eyes. After a moment, he forced his mouth into a smile. "I get it," he said. "You're just *asking* me to head-butt you. If I attack in any way, you get to fight back."

The mantis said nothing.

"I'm smarter than that," Alex said. "I'm smarter than the three of you put together. I don't give a fuck what powers you have. I have brains."

Lilith gave a "Tsk" and rolled her eyes. "Can I just bite him, for fuck's sake? I'm getting a headache."

"Wait," Blood-Claw said. "We'll see how this idiot's 'brains' measure up to the Big Gun."

Lilith gave another "Tsk" and leaned against the wall of the roadhouse. She turned her back on the others and stared sulkily over the wheat fields. "Whatever."

"Turn him around," Blood-Claw told CeeCee. The mantis maneuvered around to Alex's back, then turned the man to face the werewolf.

"What now?" Alex asked, trying to sound bored. He didn't quite manage it.

"Look," Blood-Claw said, "we've tried asking politely . . ."

"No, you haven't. You tried buying me off. Maybe you can't tell the difference, but humans can."

Blood-Claw made a face that said, *I'm tired of this shit.* But here's a crucial thing: He still didn't ask politely. Not even sarcastically. I don't know what would have happened if Blood-Claw had asked, *Please, may my girlfriend have some blood?* Probably Alex still would have told them to fuck themselves, but none of the Darklings even tried.

That's what you have to understand. This story is a legend that Darklings share among themselves; heaven knows how much they've embellished it to their tastes. Remember though that to the Dark, the three Darklings are the heroes. They're the ones being reasonable. Alex is the incomprehensible villain.

But never once in this story do the Darklings just say *please.* Like crossing running water, it's something they flat-out don't do.

THE HALF-MOON SHONE DOWN FROM THE SKY

It beamed like half a searchlight on the guard tower of a prison. And maybe on your Earth, were-beasts only Change when the moon is full. On my world, however, were-folk transform when they want. It's harder at some times than others, and the exertion can be draining. Still, they can wolf out on demand . . . and it's terrifying.

Lots of humans think they know what it's like when a werewolf Changes. The muzzle grows . . . fur sprouts . . . clothes rip . . . bones crack as they rearrange. It's gross, but not too scary.

Seeing a werewolf Change for real—oh, that's different. The Change = Terror. It's that simple. Because it's magic.

You're not just witnessing something that looks and sounds and smells like someone being torn apart. You're struck by an overwhelming enchantment that shocks every cell in your brain.

You can't control your response. No human can. Courage is irrelevant—courage can't toughen your skin against bullets, and it can't keep you from shitting yourself when a werewolf transforms in front of you.

You can even close your eyes; most people do. It doesn't make a difference. The terror still gets in.

That's what happened to Alex. Blood-Claw Changed in front of him. Knowing what would happen, CeeCee let go at the last moment and stepped away before the excrement was released.

Alex screamed. Then the piss and the shit: an outburst from every orifice. Vomit too, after Alex collapsed to his knees . . . but first, the bloodcurdling shriek.

AND *BOOM*, CAL WAS THERE

He must have been waiting inside the back door, listening for a cue to charge in. The farm boy just missed seeing Blood-Claw's Change, so he was in full possession of his senses—apparently not fazed by the sight of an eight-foot-tall wolfman towering in the moonlight.

Blood-Claw had taken on his feroform. When were-beasts Change, they can choose to become a full-fledged animal, or else they can choose their feroform: half animal/half human. The hybrid form combines the benefits of both other possibilities—huge claws, for example, but also opposable thumbs—plus it's taller and heavier. Enough to match a grizzly inch for inch and pound for pound.

Cal, the farm boy, didn't waver. "Back off. This is over."

Lilith said, "You're kidding, right?"

"No. Get out."

"FUCK!" Alex screamed, even louder than he had when he saw the Change. "Cal, I told you!" he said, tears running down his face. "I told you to stay away!"

"You know I couldn't," Cal replied.

"But you should have! I didn't want you to see . . ."

"It doesn't matter."

"It does to me!" Alex was down on his knees, dripping with his own urine. He wiped his face with the back of his hand. "I could have done this alone. I don't need a fucking Boy Scout to hold my hand when I cross the street. Don't you get that, Cal?"

"Oh, for fuck's sake!" Lilith said. "Do this after we're gone. I'm thirsty!"

"The answer is still no," Alex said.

"Tough shit."

Lilith moved toward Alex—not in a fast vampiric blur, but stomping with anger. Cal stepped between her and Alex. She yelled, "Get out of the way," and slammed her palm against Cal's chest with enough force to knock down a moose.

She bounced back and landed, ass in the dirt. "What the fuck?" she screeched. Then she said, "That cocksucker hit me. You saw it, right? He hit me."

"Big mistake," CeeCee said. The mantis brandished its claws and began weaving its head in that cobralike motion.

"See what you've done?" Alex said to Cal.

"It had to happen sometime," Cal said, half to himself. "I guess tonight's the night."

He reached up and took off his glasses. At the very same instant, Blood-Claw lashed out with a strike intended to rip out Cal's intestines. The wolf's talons tore across Cal's belly, shredding his shirt to ribbons . . . but they had no effect on what lay underneath.

"Hey," Lilith said, "this freak is wearing blue underwear."

CeeCee stabbed Cal in the back with sharp mantis pincers, then raked down with its chitinous spikes. Cal's shirt ripped off completely, freeing what he wore beneath.

"A cape?" CeeCee said. "What kind of a moron wears a cape? Oh, FUCK!"

I'LL LET YOU FILL IN THE NEXT 12.7 SECONDS FROM YOUR FANTASIES OF "DIRTBAGS GETTING WHAT THEY DESERVE"

Some hours later, Lilith, Blood-Claw, and CeeCee were found battered but alive in the ghoul-and-zombie quarter of Marrakesh. The three were reckless enough to consider going back for revenge—not on Cal, of course, but on the more vulnerable patrons of the roadhouse.

Luckily for all concerned, the Darklings didn't know the roadhouse's location. They'd spent weeks idling through the Midwest, indulging themselves and raising hell. By the night in question, they'd stopped paying attention to where they were. They couldn't even agree on the state.

Oklahoma?

Nebraska?

In all the infinite versions of Earth, the farm boy with the cape must show up first. He's the only one who shines brightly enough; until he breaks the ice jam, the rest can't make their entrance. Even beings as old as time—warrior gods, Champions Eternal—have to stay in the shadows, like chess pieces locked in the box. Crisis after crisis may shatter and remake the world, but humans must cope on their own until the superpowered Boy Scout takes the field.

Only then may the curtain rise. The floodgates open and the genies in crazy costumes come streaming from their bottles.

But the farm boy and his kind weren't genies at all; they were human. Even the ones not native to Earth were human in their hearts.

Ordinary humans with superhuman powers. Inevitably, they were called the Light.

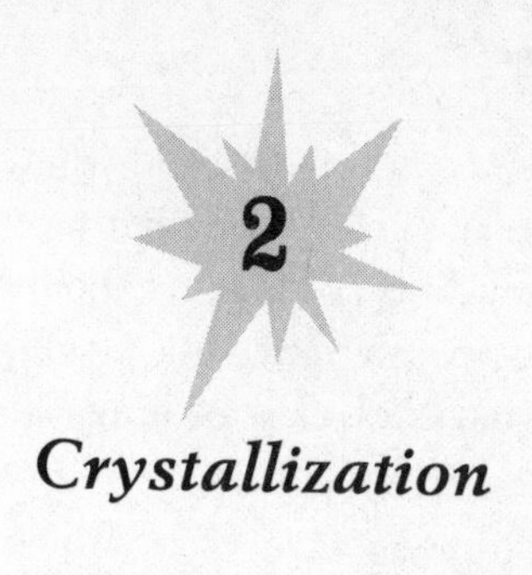

Crystallization

MY SECRET IDENTITY

My birth name is Kimberlite Crystal Lam. (Blame my father. He's a geologist.) By the time I could talk, I had normalized into Kimberley, for the same reason my parents stopped being Letao and Xiaopu and became Michael and Beth.

I'm third-generation Chinese-Canadian. Twenty-one years old. A third-year student at the University of Waterloo; that's in the smallish city of Waterloo, Ontario, an hour west of Toronto. I'm following in my father's footsteps by studying earth sciences, specializing in geology.

Let's just address the clichés head-on. Yes, I'm four foot ten, I wear thick glasses, and I hate getting less than 90 percent on any test. But also: When I arrived for my first year at UW, I reinvented myself as Kim. I cut my hair very short, bleached what little remained, and bought clothes that kept people guessing where I stood on the spectrum of male, female, and none-of-your-damned-business.

Also: In my last year of high school, I had begun my search for who I really was but hadn't yet recognized the full scope of my options. I decided to call myself Kimmi. I grew my hair long, dyed it L'Oréal Ultimate Black #1, and wore clothes very, very different from the hiking boots, overalls, and shirts from Mark's Work Wearhouse that now fill my closet.

Kimmi spent all her spare time with Darklings. One Darkling in particular: Nicholas Vandermeer. He hadn't yet gone through the Dark Conversion, but it loomed in his future like the Rocky Mountains as you drive west from Calgary—visible in the distance, getting closer all the time, with no way to avoid what's coming unless you crank the wheel hard and get off the highway.

I thought he might do that for me. I thought he might not give in to becoming Dark. I was wrong.

There. That's my backstory. Everything else is window dressing.

8:30 PM, DECEMBER 21

It was the last night of UW's fall term. I'd finished my exams and all my end-of-semester assignments. I had nothing to do until classes started again in January . . . but like a tiger walking back and forth in a rut, I'd gone to the lab to look at thin sections under a microscope.

Thanks for asking: A thin section is a slice of rock that's been shaved down and buffed until it's thinner than paper. At that thickness, most minerals are transparent and you can play tricks with polarized light to learn cool things.

No, really, I'm serious. Rocks and minerals are cool. I didn't go into geology just to get a job, nor did I do it because the Vandermeers made their money in mining and petroleum so I had some pitiful idea that I could win Nicholas back by becoming a lithological genius. I didn't even do it to please my father. But he's the reason I love geoscience. He's a geologist-in-residence at Banff National Park, and he taught me how awesome our planet is: the geosphere, the hydrosphere, the atmosphere . . . all the amazing stuff that surrounds us. How can anyone not want to learn everything about it?

So I scoped out rocks on my own free time. I wasn't hiding in the lab just to shrink away from the world.

Seriously. I do like rocks. The Freudian substitution is just a bonus.

I HAD SOMEWHERE TO BE AT NINE

So at 8:45, I locked up the microscope and headed into the tepid winter night.

Outsiders sometimes think that Canadians all live in igloos, but Waterloo seldom gets much snow until well into January. We'd had a few minor flurries over the past two months, but not enough to stay on the ground. That night, the air was a notch above freezing, and I was still dressed for fall: a gray zip-up hoodie and cheap black knit gloves with the fingertips cut off so I could text.

I carried better gloves in my backpack. I also carried a scarf because the hoodie gaped at the throat, and if the breeze picked up, my neck got cold real fast. But the gloves and the scarf were only for emergencies. My home is in Banff, Alberta, up in the Rockies. Waterloo is two time zones east, nine hundred kilometers farther south, and more than a thousand meters closer to sea level. Compared to Banff, Waterloo winters were piddly wee puppies that could give you tiny nips, but only if you let them.

Albertans refuse to admit that Ontario ever gets cold.

THE CAMPUS WAS EMPTY—NO ONE IN SIGHT

A few unlucky souls were stuck in the gym, writing the last exam on the last night of the exam period. Apart from that, everyone else had gone home—as in "home for Christmas." The only reason I hadn't headed back to Banff was because I was a keener. (That's Canadian for a student who's excessively keen. The kind who's never late and always sits in the front row.) I'd booked my flight home three months in advance, at a time when I didn't know my exam schedule or if I'd be last-minute scrambling to finish some project. To be safe, I'd scheduled the trip for December 23, which left me loose for another two days.

The sky was black and clear, decked with thousands of stars. A perfect night for the winter solstice: the longest night of the year. For added appeal, the moon would start eclipsing at 1:00 AM, hitting totality around three. My roommate Miranda was so excited, she planned to stay up and see it. She'd trash-talked the rest of us for refusing to join her. "You call yourself science students? Do you know how long it will be until the next lunar eclipse on a solstice?"

I actually knew how long, but didn't have the nerve to answer. Miranda intimidated the heck out of me—and remember, I used to hang with vampires.

Let me correct that. It wasn't *me* who hung out with vamps—the fang-banger was Kimmi. I'm not Kimmi anymore. And since I get this all the time from people who knew me back then, let's clear the air. I didn't become Kim as a wounded reaction to Nicholas rejecting me. Kimmi was just a closet that I hid in for a while. I became Kim because that's who I was when I stopped hiding.

Outward representation of internal reality. Just more premeditated than how a lot of other people live.

UP THROUGH THE MIDDLE OF CAMPUS

Past the J. R. Thomas Centre for Mathematics . . . through the shadows between Elizabeth M. Cochrane Chemistry Hall and the S. Lorenzo Gotti Biology building . . . around "P-Cubed," the Patricia Park Physics Institute . . .

You get the idea.

J. R. Thomas and the rest? Every one of them was a Darkling. As far as I can tell, they didn't have anything to do with math, chemistry, etc. They just wanted their names on UW buildings, and they outbid the competition. It was graffiti tagging for rich people, except they used plaques instead of spray paint.

One building on campus had escaped the Darkling vandalism. Engineering 3: a name the building was given before the Dark Invitation changed everything. As with everything else on campus, the name of Engineering 3 had been bought and paid for in the past few years, but by a super-intelligent guy who called himself the Inventor.

No one knew his true identity, but everybody agreed he must have been one of the thousands of engineers to graduate from Waterloo. The Inventor had made billions of dollars from patents in energy storage, smart materials, and much more—things that could be used by anyone, but first had to be dreamed up by a super-enhanced brain. His inventions were part of a burgeoning field called Cape Science or Cape Tech. The Inventor himself was called a *Spark*: a term we were forced to use after some damned Darkling trademarked the word "superhero."

The Inventor had spent a hefty wad of cash to protect Engineering 3 from a Darkling name change. Presumably he did it out of nostalgia for the place where he'd learned his trade. Also, to give the finger to non-engineer Darklings who wanted their names above the door.

So E3 had no bronze plaque; no *in honor of*; no full-length painted portrait of a Fortune 500 vampire or were-jackal. E3 had nothing but classrooms and labs, pretty much as they'd always been.

As a science student, I was required to trash-talk engineers and curl my lip in disdain, but on this particular issue, I envied them.

UW MAPS DEPICTED THE CAMPUS AS DIVIDED INTO SEPARATE BUILDINGS

The maps lied. Many buildings had accreted into lumpy conglomerates by means of tunnels, overpasses, and extensions. Some connections were planned from the start, and joined so smoothly you couldn't tell when you left one building and entered another. Other connections were obvious afterthoughts, hodgepodged together like a clutter of plugs and extension cords jammed into a power bar.

Hence the Engineering Link. It's where E3 merged with the Simon and Janine Hunter-Chan School of Chemical Engineering and also with the Vlad T. Kallikandros Center for Systems Design. The result was Escher architecture: a convergence of corridors, stairways, and ramps of varying widths, heights, and angles. To add to the fun, vending machines had been planted in the exact center of the Link, because nothing improves traffic flow like a crowd of engineers lined up for Doritos.

One of the Link's stairways always seemed to be cloaked in shadow. The effect was just psychological—the campus's Health and Safety Department would have done something if the lighting were truly dim. But the stairs were narrow and deep, bounded between grim gray walls. Standing at the bottom, you felt like you'd fallen down a well.

I was climbing those very stairs when I heard the Darklings coming.

FOOTSTEPS ECHOED THROUGH THE EMPTY HALLS

I pictured engineering students: maybe guys returning from an off-campus pub after celebrating the last night of the term.

I don't get hassled often, not even by drunk engineers. But once in a while, someone gets all Precambrian about the way I look. With the campus so empty and abandoned, discretion seemed the better part of valor.

I slipped as fast I could back to the bottom of the shadowy stairwell. With luck, the group would pass by overhead and never notice me. The footsteps drew nearer, moving at a purposeful pace. I held my breath, but peeked to see who they were.

Now that I think of it, that's foreshadowing. I was a hider, but also a peeker. Huh.

I SAW A PARADE OF DARKLINGS

Two were-beasts, then two demons, then two vampires: paired off, one male and one female of each, as if Noah were assembling an ark whose walls would leak blood.

The were-beasts were in feroform. Male polar bear, female black panther. Both were huge—eight feet tall, with their heads approaching the ceiling of the modest corridor. But they weren't decked out for a fight. They were clothed in casual wear and wore backpacks.

Backpacks are standard gear for were-beasts. A were's feroform is so much bigger than its ordinary human size that it needs two sets of clothing. Then it needs a backpack to carry the extra outfit. Were-beasts could, of course, go naked, but remember who Darklings are. They are *not* going to show the world their primary and secondary sexual characteristics when they could buy something chic from the Armani Wyr★Wear line.

Behind the beast-folk walked two demons. The male was a classic bogeyman: human shaped but murky, like the darkness at the back of an alley. If you've ever had a nightmare of being chased by someone you can't quite see, you know what a bogeyman is. You can't pin down why he's frightening—he doesn't have weapons or claws. He's just something that wants to *get* you . . . and if he does, whatever happens next will be awful.

The bogeyman was bad, but the female demon was worse. She wore a white wedding gown draped down to her toes, plus long silk gloves and a veil over her face. Her body was fully concealed, not a millimeter visible; even her hair was completely covered by the veil.

And that was good. I knew, I just knew, that a single glimpse of the woman herself would break me. I could tell that my dread was caused by the demon's Shadow, but knowing my fear was due to magic didn't matter. The were-beasts could rip me to ribbons and the bogey could hurt or kill me, but this bride could corrupt who I was.

I shrank farther into the shadows. But I couldn't look away.

The last two Darklings were vampires. They looked human, their eyes and teeth normal. If not for my time as Kimmi, I wouldn't have known what they were.

But vampires move too fluidly—like butter across a griddle. Living creatures move with muscles that are under control of neurons. The neurons work together, all trying to fire in sync, but inevitably they don't. A microsecond here, a millisecond there, and the discrepancies mean our movements are never completely smooth.

Vampires, on the other hand, aren't alive. Their hearts don't beat, and their neurons don't spark. They shouldn't be moving at all; they should be rotting in their graves. But magic lets them walk with perfect precision. A vampire is how a mind moves when it simply ignores its body. Once you notice, it's disturbing—deep in the Uncanny Valley.

So two vampires, two demons, two were-beasts glided along. Not speaking, not looking around. Almost robotic.

If they sensed me, they made no sign. They passed by with the air of people who had something important to do.

THE DARKLINGS SURELY NOTICED ME

The were-beasts must have smelled me. The vampires must have felt the heat of my blood. Either they were all so focused they weren't paying attention, or else they sensed me and just didn't care.

And why *should* they have cared? They weren't doing anything villainous, they were just walking down a hall. Probably they were even legitimate students. Waterloo isn't a big Dark school—Darklings usually study law and finance, not tech—but we had about a hundred and fifty Darklings on campus, counting undergrads, grads, and professors. The six who passed me had as much right to be there as I did.

On the other hand, it was the long dark night of the solstice. The moon was full and scheduled for a total eclipse. If the Darklings were on the move, in silent procession, on a campus devoid of other people . . .

It just didn't bode well.

THE SMART MOVE WOULD HAVE BEEN TO LEAVE

But I've mentioned my time as Kimmi. I sort of had a thing about Darklings.

So I was up those stairs in a flash, as quiet as falling snow. (When you're a hider you learn to tiptoe, even in hiking boots.) I reached the top of the stairs in time to see the Darklings enter a room down the hall. The last vampire closed the door behind him. A red light lit up above the door: the kind of light that's always accompanied by a sign saying DANGER, DO NOT ENTER WHEN LIGHT IS ON.

I knew the rooms down that hall were all labs: high-ceilinged spaces with big, chunky machines and roaring ventilation systems. By contrast, our labs in the science buildings were smaller and more sedate. (We preferred precision to brute force.) We also kept our laboratories closed, but whenever I walked through E3, every lab door was open, spilling decibels into the world.

Not tonight. The labs were silent. Everything was shut down for Christmas.

I crept along the hall, past labs with signs like HIGH-PRESSURE HYDRAULICS and TRIBOLOGY. But when I got to the Darklings' lab, it had no ID. Just that red warning light. A small window was set in the door at eye level (well, somebody's eye level, not mine), but thick black paper covered the other side of the glass.

I heard nothing from the lab. If I hadn't been interrupted, I would have pressed my ear to the door. Before I could do that, the corridor filled with singing.

"HOW BEAUTIFUL ARE THE FEET OF THEM THAT PREACH THE GOSPEL OF PEACE . . ."

Handel. From the *Messiah*. I'm no cognoscente of music, but I recognized the tune because Miranda had been belting it out all month long. She claimed she didn't know when she was doing it; one moment she'd be hearing it in her head, and the next she was singing out loud.

And I mean *loud*. Before microphones, opera sopranos had to be heard at the back of theaters while accompanied by hundred-piece orchestras. Ever since, they've been trained to deliver arias at volumes that would scare a trumpeting elephant.

Which Miranda often did. In the shower. Sometimes at six in the morning.

When I heard Handel echo through E3, I knew Miranda hadn't been able to resist the acoustics of the empty building. Silent, vacant corridors = reverberation. I should have been glad that Christmas put her in a mood for the *Messiah*. Otherwise, she might have been trilling one of those high-pitched coloraturas that make non-opera-lovers want to blow up La Scala.

One thing for sure: I couldn't stay where I was. The Darklings in the lab might wonder, "What's with all the noise?" and open the door to see. I didn't want to be caught trying to eavesdrop. As quietly as I could, I trotted in Miranda's direction so I could shush her before the Darklings got upset.

I met her at the intersection of my corridor and hers. I waved my hands. "Shh, be quiet."

Miranda stopped and asked, "Why?" She made no attempt to keep her voice down.

If you whispered to Miranda, "Hush, we're being stalked by a moon-maddened werewolf," she'd say in her normal opera-volume voice, "Don't be ridiculous, that's against the law."

LET ME TELL YOU ABOUT MIRANDA

She was a goddess.

Not literally. Our world has real goddesses—you can watch them on YouTube—and Miranda wasn't actually divine. But she'd still fit in with Bastet, Athena, et al.

She had Nordic blond hair: long and genuine, not L'Oréal. (I love dye, but I envy those who don't need it.) She was six feet tall with flawless Nordic skin. Not too thin, not too full, perfect posture and teeth. I don't know if her voice was great by professional opera standards or only impressive to lowbrows like me, but I'll bet Miranda could walk into any concert hall and get a role as a Valkyrie just on looks alone.

She also knew how to dress, even how to accessorize. And how to use makeup so she didn't look made up at all.

Miranda Neuhof: the ideal woman, as defined by the media and thrown in the faces of short, queer Asians.

If life weren't unfair enough, Miranda also had a brain. Ish. Selective intelligence: She'd made the physics honors list for three years running, but didn't have an ounce of common sense or moderation.

Miranda came from old money. She shared much in common with Lilith, that vampire from the roadhouse. I don't know how much of Miranda's perfection was innate, how much came from surgery, and how much was the result of expensive "optimizations"—everything from private tutors to human growth hormone and "maximum potential" treatments sold on the black market by superintelligent Sparks.

Unlike Lilith, Miranda wasn't a Darkling. Miranda's parents inherited fortunes, but they refused to join the Dark. Their refusal was pure pigheadedness—I'd met Miranda's mother and father, and they would argue about anything, just to be contrary. While the rest of the Neuhof clan had eagerly embraced the Dark Invitation, Miranda's parents said no. Vociferously. The arguments grew into a family feud, and now Miranda hated Darklings more than anyone else I knew.

BACK TO MIRANDA ASKING WHY I'D SHUSHED HER

"Darklings," I whispered.

Her eyes turned steely. "Doing what?"

"Six of them went into a lab and locked the door."

"Which lab?"

"Umm." If I told her where the Darklings were, she might go and bang on the door, demanding to know what they were up to.

"Look," I said, "it's past nine. Richard and Shar are waiting. We have to get over there."

WHY RICHARD AND SHAR WERE WAITING

Shar was another of my roommates. Housemates. Whatever. Shar, Miranda, and another girl named Jools shared a townhouse with me off campus.

Richard was Shar's boyfriend. He was a fourth-year engineer who worked ten hours a week in a lab elsewhere in the wing. The fact that he had a lab job tells you that Richard was pretty darn smart—competition for on-campus work can be hellishly fierce.

Richard's expertise was pumps: anything from the giants used to pump oil across the country to the cute little babies that keep you alive during surgery. I estimate that Richard spent 85 percent of his waking moments working or thinking about pumps. That left 10 percent for Shar, and 5 percent for everything else.

This suited Shar fine. She wasn't what you'd call emotionally invested. She saw Richard as a convenience, and both seemed content with the arrangement. When Richard graduated in April, he'd leave for a high-paid career of pumps, pumps, pumps. He and Shar would hug good-bye, then never think about each other again.

Until then, Shar played Supportive Girlfriend. On the night in question, this meant that she dragged our household to Richard's lab to cart equipment. Giant metal pipes? Obsolete computers? I hadn't been told what the job entailed. Shar had only said the professor who ran Richard's lab was giving him a load of surplus pumpy goodness, and Richard needed extra hands to haul it away.

So we intended to lug a mess of machinery out of a lab on a night when the campus was empty. This didn't exactly scream "legitimate." But even Miranda had agreed to help. None of us believed Richard had the balls to steal stuff so blatantly—not even a stash of lovely, lovely pumps.

Besides, Shar had promised us cookies when we were finished. Shar made really good cookies.

BRING ON THE PUMPS

Miranda pressed me for more information about the Darklings, but I just headed toward Richard's lab. Fortunately, we didn't have to pass the room where the six Darklings had gone; I doubt if I could have walked by without a furtive glance. I managed to stonewall Miranda's questions until we reached our destination, but that didn't mean she dropped the subject. The moment we entered the lab, Miranda told Shar and Richard, "Kim saw Darklings up to no good but won't tell me where. No cookies for Kim till we get the story."

Typical Miranda, laying down rules for somebody else's cookies. Something else typical: No one objected. Shar merely said, "Darklings? What were they doing?"

"Nothing," I said. "Just walking down the hall."

Shar looked at me dubiously. She was good at dubious. Shar did dubious better than anyone else in the world except my mother.

Ashariti Chandra: born in Sri Lanka, dark-skinned and generously big. I don't want to call her a mama bear, since that's condescending and besides, she's two months younger than I am. Also, she'd hate being called motherly. Shar's own mother was the opposite of maternal—a professor cross-appointed between applied math and economics. Mama Chandra used computers to model financial systems, and she was good enough to be in demand at universities around the world. Shar and her mother had bounced hither and thither on visiting fellowships from Colombo to Brussels to Chicago to Shanghai, finally coming to rest at UW. Shar's father had traveled with them for a hop or two, but then he'd gotten fed up playing househusband and had stomped back to Sri Lanka after a quickie divorce.

Since then, Shar had been her mother's keeper: cooking, cleaning, and organizing because Mom didn't want to be bothered with anything except GDP and exchange rates. It must have been tough for eight-year-old Shar to run everything on her own; on the other hand, Shar was smart and had a take-charge personality that fit quite well with domestic domineering. Besides, it meant she could go for days eating nothing but her own home-baked cookies, and Mom didn't even notice.

Shar still looked like someone who ate a lot of cookies, but she no longer ran her mother's life. Quite by surprise, Mom had remarried when Shar was in her first year of university, and five months later, Shar had moved in with Miranda, Jools, and me. Her only explanation was, "Friction at home." She'd smiled when she said it, and she didn't seem upset, so I didn't think it was anything too severe. Maybe her new stepdad just had a mind of his own and didn't like to be "managed."

Richard, on the other hand . . . he practically *expected* Shar to order him about. Richard Chan was third-gen Chinese-Canadian like me, but his ancestors hailed from Hong Kong so he spoke broken Cantonese instead of my own inept Mandarin.

Richard was cute in a meerkatish way, all bright-eyed and perky. He was one of those people who can't tell when you're joking, so he laughed at anything he thought might be meant as funny. Eager to please, that boy . . . which may have been another reason Shar kept him around.

I OUGHT TO DESCRIBE THE PUMP LAB

But the place was just a jumble of pipes and multi-ton equipment, all painted that shade of pistachio that seems compulsory for heavy machines. The lab also had more than a dozen computers humming away. (No one at Waterloo ever turned off computers. All across campus, there'd be thousands running through the whole Christmas break.) Circuit boards lay haphazardly on workbenches, some with Post-it notes saying where the boards came from, while others were completely unlabeled. I guess you weren't a real engineer unless you could identify what a circuit did just by looking at it. And paper was stacked everywhere, a lot of it dating back to the days when computer output was run off on whacking huge line printers in continuous perforated sheets. The printouts were piled on tables and floors, forming a bedrock on which subsequent papers accreted like ooze on the ocean floor.

I wonder if anyone has ever written a paper on the stratigraphy of laboratories.

I'd visited Richard's lab several times and never once asked him what any of the equipment was for. I knew all too well that he'd eagerly explain it. At length. With wiring diagrams. Until my heart quit beating just to make it all stop.

"LOOK," I SAID, "CAN WE FORGET ABOUT THE DARKLINGS AND GET THIS OVER WITH?"

"Right," said Richard, who'd weighed the relative importance of Darklings versus pumps and come to the only proper conclusion. "I've parked my parents' minivan at the loading dock. The back's cleared out, so it should hold everything."

"I assume," Miranda said, "you have the proper paperwork to take this stuff away . . . cuz if the campus police show up, I don't want to spend the night in jail. Been there, done that."

(Yes, Miranda was no stranger to the legal system. Not that she'd ever been convicted—her family could afford obscenely expensive lawyers—but you can't take part in dozens of anti-Darkling protests without occasionally getting swept up in mass arrests. Even when you look like Miranda.)

"This is totally legit," Richard said. "My prof was just going to trash everything, but some other guy hogged all the space in the e-waste drop-off, so there wasn't room for our stuff. We've got two new test beds arriving in January, so like, this is an *emergency*. Taking away this junk is doing everyone a favor."

Miranda and I shared dubious looks. "So no paperwork?" she said.

"Not to worry," Shar replied. "We'll use Kim as lookout. A better use of Kim's presence than carrying things."

She was right—I was more suited as a lookout than as muscle. But I didn't like the suggestion that I couldn't carry my fair share. On behalf of short people everywhere, I was going to protest, but I got interrupted by our last roommate, Jools, storming through the doorway.

Jools: "How the hell can anyone find anything in this place?"

JOOLS WAS THE ILLUSTRIOUS JULIETTA WALSH

But she wasn't a Julietta, nor a Juliet, nor even a Julie. Jools had to be Jools; nothing else fit.

Our Jools: a jock. Almost as tall as Miranda; not as supermodel beautiful, but good-looking in an athletic healthy-as-a-horse way.

Light-skinned. Brown hair and eyes. Given to wearing bicycle shorts and skirts, even in winter, because she knew her legs and ass were taut. Also because she didn't give a damn about the cold—tonight, on the winter solstice, her legs were bare and she wore sandals.

Jools came from Alberta like me, but from Edmonton: hundreds of kilometers farther north than my home in Banff. If you think I'm a stick-in-the-mud when it comes to dismissing coolish weather, Jools was a big honking log-in-the-mire. When she came to Waterloo, she didn't even bring a winter coat—just a jacket in the bright orange and blue of the Edmonton Oilers.

Jools was hockey-mad. In her first year, she'd even made Waterloo's varsity team. They'd kicked her out when her marks started sliding—this is Canada, not the States, and school comes first—but Jools still played with an ultracompetitive intramural team that practiced at three in the morning because that's when ice time was cheap. Getting up that early (or staying up that late) didn't improve Jools's grades. Since the four of us had met in our first year, we'd all helped Jools as much as we could, but we'd finally hit the ceiling. Jools was in biology, Miranda in physics, Shar in chemistry, and me in earth sciences. None of us knew enough about one another's subjects to contribute anything useful.

Jools had squeaked out a pass the previous year, but I suspected that she'd bombed her Christmas exams. Too much hockey. Too much beer. Too much throwing herself at guys. Plus every other flavor of self-sabotage she could think of. Jools had decided she was a fuckup, and was doing her best to prove it.

Shar and Miranda were too self-involved to notice. Otherwise, they'd have held an intervention so fast we'd all have gotten whiplash. Me, I'd tried some heart-to-heart talks, but I'd messed them up. (I suck at dealing with emotions. Anyone's.) So when Jools said, "Don't worry," and "I'm fine," I mumbled dumb nothings and let her get away with it.

Kim: not a confronter. Miranda marched in protests, Shar was a take-no-excuses life-boss, and Jools punched her hockey opponents until they bled. I just obsessed over rocks and high marks.

But that was about to change. Five seconds after Jools walked in, we heard the explosion.

BANG, THEN _BOOM_, THEN A SHUDDER THROUGH THE FLOOR

I'd heard explosions before. I'd accompanied my father to watch mining operations; I'd stood beside park rangers in Banff as they set off preemptive avalanches; in my second year, I'd waited with forty other students as a highway construction crew blasted out a road cut, after which we had six hours to pick through the rubble for geological treasures.

Controlled demolitions have deep, measured voices. You feel them more in your feet than your ears, because the point is to move solid matter, not fill the air with wasted energy.

The explosion in E3 began with a bang, like one of those specialty fireworks made for maximum sound—the kind where you see the flash first, then hear the noise, loud and sharp enough to make you jump. The *bang* was still echoing when we heard a secondary *boom*: blunt thunder that rattled metal throughout Richard's lab. Finally, the ground shook, earthquake style. The rattle of metal increased, the lab door thumped shut, and something in the wall went *crack*.

I gauged it a four on the Mercalli earthquake intensity scale. I wasn't in danger of being knocked off my feet, but I still grabbed a workbench for support.

"What the fucking hell?" Jools said. She stopped and her face went wary. "You're all feeling this too, right?"

No one answered. The shaking subsided. The room went still.

"Those damned Darklings," Miranda said.

"What damned Darklings?" Jools asked.

"Kim saw some down the hall," Miranda replied. "What the hell have they done?"

I said, "It might not be them."

"Who else could it be?" Miranda demanded. "There's nobody else in the building." She turned toward Richard. "Do you have a phone here? An official university one?"

"Probably. Somewhere." He looked vaguely around the lab. Odds were, there really was a phone buried under the clutter, but who used landlines anymore?

"Find it," Miranda said. "Call nine-one-one. Don't use your cell—you want the on-campus emergency line, not a generic one."

"Okay," Richard said reluctantly.

Miranda turned to the rest of us. "Let's see what those bastards have done. Kim, you lead. You know where they are."

"I should go with you," Richard said.

"Call first," Miranda told him. "Getting help is the main priority. Fire trucks, ambulances, everything. Do it!"

She strode toward the door. The rest of us followed, leaving Richard morosely searching for the phone.

I LED MY ROOMMATES TO THE DARKLINGS' LAB

The door was shut, but the explosion had shattered the little inset window, spreading nuggets of safety glass across the floor. Copper-colored gas spilled out through the hole. Strands of the gas ran down the face of the door like one of those high, thin waterfalls in Venezuela. When the gas reached the floor, it spread across the terrazzo in a wispy brown pool.

"That doesn't look good," Jools said.

"Could be worse," Shar replied. "The vapor is clearly heavier than air. It will stay close to the floor, and we won't have to worry about inhaling it."

Thus Shar proved she was in chemistry. Every chemistry student I know delights in stories about people mishandling chemicals—grisly tales of acid burns and blinding. Chemists radiate contempt for first-year students who break the teeniest, tiniest rules of lab safety. But at the very same time, chemists believe the rules don't apply to themselves. "I never waste my time with latex gloves or the fume hood. I just pour carefully." As if *genuine* chemists have nothing to fear because chemicals know who's boss.

Shar went straight to the lab door. It was locked. She stuck her bare hand through the window (despite the scary brown gas that immediately surrounded her fingers), then felt around inside until she found the doorknob. She popped the lock and withdrew her arm.

Miranda asked, "How does your hand feel?"

Shar flexed her fingers experimentally. "Stings a little; nothing serious. We'll be fine if we minimize exposure."

"Gloves," Miranda commanded. "Everybody," she added with a stern look at Shar. "If you have a scarf, wrap your face."

"Yes, Mom," Jools said. She had neither gloves nor a scarf; she shoved her hands into her jacket pockets. Shar, on the other hand, had plenty of winter gear. Just as Jools and I made a show of saying, "Cold? This isn't cold," Sri Lankan Shar outfitted herself with approximately twenty-five layers of thermal insulation. Jools made a face, then grudgingly began bundling up. I did the same, fetching my full gloves and scarf from my backpack. I may sneer at Ontario winters, but not at weird brown smoke. The corridor was beginning to smell like burnt plastic.

"Okay," Miranda said when we all looked ready. "This is purely a rescue mission. Whoever's inside, we drag 'em out, nothing more. And we do it fast, before we become the next casualties."

"If we're talking about Darklings," Jools said, "do they really need our help? They're supernaturally tough."

"Most are," I said, "but tough doesn't mean invulnerable. A small-sized explosion they could probably laugh off, but a big one will kill them just like humans."

"Trust Kim to set us straight about the Dark," Jools said. "You're such a fangirl. Fanperson. Fanentity. Whatever."

"Enough," Miranda said. "We're in crisis mode." She laid her hand on the doorknob. "Ready?" Without waiting, she threw the door open.

GASEOUS BROWN GUCK GUSHED OUT IN A HEAP

The coppery vapor was heavier than air and had been spilling through an eye-level window. Conclusion? The gas must have filled that great big lab from floor to window height. When Miranda opened the door, the effect was like that dorm prank where someone leans a big garbage can full of water against somebody else's door. Open the door and *SPLOOSH!*

The *sploosh* was gaseous, not liquid, so it wasn't an actual flood. Instead, copper clouds billowed and flopped out into the hall. With them came a stink like nothing I'd ever smelled. Not just sharp like acid; not just thick like the manure local farmers spread on their fields; not just rank like the spoiled meat Jools threw in the trash, then let sit. It was all those and more: It hit every scent receptor in my nostrils, then cranked the volume to eleven. I smelled every smell I could possibly smell—the good, the bad, the flowers, the rot, the warm bread, and the vomit. All at maximum intensity. It was the olfactory equivalent of a blinding white light shone directly into my eyes . . . and remember, my scarf was covering my nose.

In contrast, the lab had no actual illumination. All I saw was blackness, like the depths of a cave when you turn your lights off just to see how pure darkness can be.

THE DARKNESS CONFRONTING US WAS A BLINDER WALL—MAGIC

I'd seen such walls before. Kimmi had encountered a few, back when she spent so much time with Darklings.

Blinder walls were standard enchantments for privacy. Converting to the Dark didn't just make you a vampire, were-beast, or demon. It also gave you the power to cast magic spells.

The creation of blinders was the first spell most Darklings learned. A blinder wall privatized a room. No sound or light escaped through the wall, ensuring that no one outside could spy on what happened within. A top-notch wizard could even shut out clairvoyance and other scrying magic, but that was difficult and invited escalation. Better blinders encouraged others to develop better intrusion spells, etc., etc.

The blinder wall in front of me definitely wasn't top of the line. After all, we'd heard the explosion, so the blinder wasn't strong enough to suppress the sound of the blast. Either the blinder was weak, or the explosion had been so huge it could be heard despite being muffled.

I reached out and touched the blackness. It felt like nothing at all. The wall blocked my nerve impulses, just like it blocked light and sound. If I reached through, somebody could chop off my hand and I wouldn't know until I'd pulled the stump of my wrist back to where the pain could finally flow to my brain.

I really hoped that hadn't happened. I didn't pull my hand back.

Instead I took a breath and forced myself to step into the blackness. For an instant, I sensed precisely nothing. Then momentum carried me through the blinder and I saw what it had been hiding.

A RIFT/GATEWAY/HOLE IN REALITY

The portal that hovered in the middle of the lab was archetypically yonic in shape . . . or if you prefer, it was a football standing on end: taller than it was wide, with sharp points at the top and bottom. Copper gas spilled in torrents over the rift's bottom lip. The stinking vapor splashed to the floor as a continuous cascade, then swirled outward in all directions. The world beyond the rift gave off enough light for us to see that brownish mist filled the place—no solid ground or other features, just that unending fog giving everything a rusty tint.

The six Darklings I'd seen were floating in the mist. They seemed weightless, turning slowly at different heights and angles. Their eyes were closed, their bodies relaxed. I could see the were-beasts breathing, so I assumed all six were asleep, not totally dead.

Flickers of light danced around them, like fireflies but all colors. Reds and blues, whites and blacks, golds and silvers. Moving sparkles brushed against the Darklings' bodies and wove about them like the birds making Cinderella's dress; patterns and orbits of light like an atom's electron clouds.

Where the lights touched the Darklings, they left no burns or wounds, but they bristled with power. The longer I watched, the lights seemed less like fireflies and more like bees: calm for the moment, but with dangerous potential.

ALL THIS TIME, I'D BEEN HOLDING MY BREATH

The vapor in the room came up to my thighs, despite the constant spillage into the hall. My nostrils felt chafed; if I inhaled, I knew the gas would sting all the way to my bronchia. I folded my scarf several times and pressed it to my mouth, hoping the multiple layers of cloth would filter more toxins. "What do we do?" I asked through the scarf. "Go through the rift and get the Darklings? Or just leave them in there?"

Miranda had pulled a woolen toque from the pocket of her coat. (She always carried that toque but never wore it—she liked to pretend she was prudent, but when push came to shove, Miranda would rather her ears freeze than wear an unflattering hat.) She covered her mouth with the toque and said, "Do you want to barge into an unknown world with a poisonous atmosphere? I don't. And the Darklings don't seem to be in distress."

Shar said, "We can't just walk away." No effort to cover her mouth or filter the air. Chemists!

"These Darklings opened a rift and jumped inside," Miranda said. "Whatever they're up to, they chose it."

"Hey," Jools shouted. She'd gone around to the other side of the rift and was out of sight behind it. "There's a weird machine back here. Kind of like a movie projector. It's shining a light into the back of the hole. I think it's transmitting energy to keep the portal open."

"Is there a plug?" Shar asked.

"A cable into a wall socket."

"If we pull the plug," Shar said, "the hole might close."

I said, "Then the Darklings won't have a way out."

"We don't have to do a thing," Miranda said. "The situation is stable and nine-one-one is on the way. Let's leave this to professionals with gas masks."

The portal chose that moment to pulse: a drumbeat so loud, I felt it in my chest. The rift opened wider. Its top shot upward, almost reaching the ceiling. The copper gas spilling into our world became a gusher.

"Fuck," Miranda said.

"You jinxed it, dude," Jools told her. "You said things were stable."

Shar asked, "*Now* do we pull the plug?"

Another pulse: *boom!* This one I felt through my entire body—a shock wave that popped my ears. Chunks of concrete rained from the ceiling. The rift's pointed top had spiked through the roof, and the pierced section of roofing material broke into pieces. Objects in our reality apparently couldn't stand the touch of another realm of existence.

Shar and Miranda yelled in unison, "Pull the plug!"

"Give me a sec," Jools replied.

But Fate wasn't in a giving mood.

THE SPARKLES INSIDE THE PORTAL WENT BERSERK

If the little flames were bees, then the rift was their hive. Somehow they knew it was threatened. Before Jools could pull the plug, the sparkles zoomed out in an angry swarm.

As the flames entered our world, they expanded to globes of fire—still small, like ping-pong balls, but moving hard and fast.

Hundreds of burning balls in hundreds of brilliant colors flew from the portal and attacked.

The first wave of flame balls went for Jools. After that, the swarm must have decided we were all potential threats. The alien ping-pong bees broke into squadrons, one for each of us. They bore down in a rage, like furious stars.

I threw up my arms to protect myself before they burned my eyes. It made no difference—the fireballs passed through my flesh. I felt no touch of contact, but their heat seared my skin and kept on moving. Fire blazed directly inside my forearms. I screamed and squeezed my eyes shut.

Not that it did any good. Blinding flames forced through my eyelids. My eyeballs were replaced with scalding suns. The suns pressed onward, through my eye sockets and into my brain.

PURE ANIMAL PAIN

I hurt so badly, I couldn't think. Obliteration.

Yet something remained in my head: images plucked from my memories. They weren't like normal imaginings, but full sound-and-color re-creations, as if I were actually reliving the past. The feeling of being shoved against a locker . . . insults yelled at me . . . getting frisked in a store while dozens of people watched, because someone thought a queer Asian kid *had* to be a shoplifter. The images flicked through pain after pain, each memory lasting less than a second. So many humiliations. So many bruises. The flame-bees invading my brain fast-forwarded through my life's "worst of" album in search of rock bottom.

Eureka: Memory found. Then relived, as if I were truly enduring it once more.

I was Kimmi. My view was framed by ultra-black hair, much longer and heavier than my current brush cut.

Kimmi stood in the Vandermeer home, in the study used by Nicholas's sister, Elaine. Elaine was a vampire—all the Vandermeers were. Each had undergone the Dark Conversion alone, but for some reason, every last one of them had come out the other side as a vampire. "The Vandermeer Vamps," Nicholas called them.

This scene had happened the night after Nicholas decided to join them. After he sent me the email saying, *I have to do this, Kimmi. Good-bye.*

Elaine sat behind her desk. She was a Darkling, but not "dark": not a Goth like me. I wore a long black dress and corset under my black Chantilly blouse, but Elaine only wore black in the rims of her glasses. They made her look like an optician's ad—one of those fashion models who look fabulous in glasses, but give the impression they never wear them in real life. Elaine didn't need glasses; vampires can read four-point type in total darkness. But she wore them anyway, for the sake of gravitas. She also wore a white blouse with demure bits of frill, plus a tan jacket and skirt that were likely from a couturier so high-end I'd never heard of him.

The room was bright, though unnatural shadows clustered in the corners. Anyplace where Darklings spend time begins to go dark. Paper withers. Spiders lurk.

Elaine folded her hands on the desk. She looked me in the eye, with just enough vampire charisma that I couldn't look away. "This isn't a good idea, Kimmi. Talking to Nicholas would be awkward and embarrassing. Also futile."

When this had happened for real, I'd tried to protest. In this forced relived memory, I couldn't speak. Trapped in the nightmare.

Elaine continued, her voice softly reasonable. "Breaking up with you by email was inconsiderate." She paused. "But at least it allowed him to choose his words carefully. Nicholas let you down as gently as he could. You were a training experience, nothing more. Our kind encourage that kind of play in adolescence, but when we reach adulthood, we put away childish things. He'll tell you that himself if you confront him face-to-face. You can't possibly change my brother's mind, but things may become unpleasant. Surely you want to avoid that. Do you need to add to your pain?"

I had argued, trying not to cry. But in this merciless reenactment, everything I did sped past in a blur. My mind clung to every word and gesture from Elaine but paid no attention to myself.

Elaine didn't blink, not once in the whole conversation. Her green eyes never took on the red that would indicate the use of vampiric power. She could have imposed her will on me; she could have made me her slave. But she didn't. She simply waited and watched as I crumbled—as Kimmi, who had been so strong, shrank to nothing.

When I'd finally shriveled completely, Elaine screwed down the lid of the coffin. She rose from her chair and came around the desk. She stood very close. "All right, Kimmi. All right." She put her hand on my shoulder. "I'll talk to Nicholas. I'll ask if he's willing to see you. I'll tell him you're desperate. That's right, isn't it? You're desperate?"

I said yes.

"It might make a better impression if you prove how desperate you are."

I said I'd do anything.

SHE WANTED BLOOD; OF COURSE SHE DID

I wasn't stupid. I could see how things would go. I would let Elaine drink; then either she'd laugh and call a servant to throw me out, or else she'd leave and come back a few minutes later, saying how sorry she was, but Nicholas refused to see me.

She wouldn't help. I knew that. But I still said yes. Maybe I hoped she'd kill me.

That's basically what happened. Elaine, almost clinically, took Kimmi in her arms and ended Kimmi's life. Not literally—a living body remained, with only a modest sip of blood actually removed. She didn't even drink from my neck; once she had me in her grip, she asked me to lift my arm, pull back the sleeve, and put my skin to her mouth.

She bit. She drank. Afterward, she wiped her lips.

Nothing illegal happened. Nothing detectable. But the Kimmi

in me died with Elaine's teeth sunk in my arm. After Nicholas's cold "It's over," this was the last nail in Kimmi's coffin.

I wasn't actually dead. This is all just metaphor.

But it didn't feel that way.

THAT WAS HOW IT WENT IN REAL LIFE

Now, the alien fireballs in my brain made me relive it. Begging Elaine to help me. Offering what she wanted.

But this time when I spoke, my words had no sound. I could feel my lips move, but all I heard was the rustle of Elaine's clothing, and her footsteps on the carpet as she walked toward me. Inside, I was already weeping. I knew what was coming, and everything in my soul yearned for a way to stop it.

Suddenly, I wasn't in my head anymore. I saw the scene from above, as if floating on the ceiling of Elaine's study. I'd escaped the pain as well; whatever the flames were doing inside my brain, I'd broken free into a safe bolt-hole.

Perhaps I was dead. I might have truly died, there in that lab, there in that dream. Or maybe astral projection isn't just for Darklings and Sparks; maybe ordinary people can do it under extraordinary conditions. One way or another, I floated above the scene. I saw myself start to cry. I saw Elaine reach out to take me.

And my disembodied self said, "No."

WHEN DO WE EVER GET SECOND CHANCES? WHY THE HELL WAS I WASTING THIS ONE?

I swam through the air, back into my body. My consciousness slipped into place and locked home.

I silenced my former self. I cut off her pleading, "Just bite me, then go get Nicholas." It took all my effort, like doing one more push-up when you have nothing left . . . but I said to Elaine, "Get fucked. This is over."

I planned to walk out the door. Before I could do that, the scene shattered into a million pieces.

I FOUND MYSELF BACK IN THE LAB

Had it just been an illusion? Or honest-to-goodness time travel? I didn't know. In a world with magic and superpowers, reality gets hard to pin down.

All around me, multicolored flame balls still swarmed like angry bees, but they no longer affected me. Dozens shoved against my arms and face but couldn't get in. They didn't burn my skin. Their light didn't even hurt my eyes, despite intense flares right in front of my pupils.

Bees? No. Now they were just fruit flies. I waved them aside.

Miranda and Shar stood exactly where they'd been. They were cringing, surrounded by their own furious fireballs. Teardrops ran down their cheeks. I wanted to snap them out of whatever they might be reliving, but before I could move, the portal gave another thunderous pulse.

The rift had grown gigantic since I'd last seen it. Now it spanned half the width of the lab and reached so high that I couldn't see how much of it extended out through the building's roof. With another few pulses, the gash in reality would engulf the whole room, and swallow us with it.

I ran behind the rift. Its rear surface was opaque and swirling with colors, like the sheen of oil on water. A cone of light shone out of the darkness, feeding into the back of the portal, just as Jools had said—like a movie projector illuminating a screen. I could easily follow the cone backward to its source. I did so, staying out of the light.

I almost tripped over Jools.

SHE LAY ON THE FLOOR IN FETAL POSITION

The coppery gas enveloped her. Every breath she took was a wheeze, filling her lungs with poison. I wanted to lift her out of the mist, but I knew I wasn't strong enough. *Unplug the machine,* I told myself; that was the best way to save her.

I continued to follow the cone of light until I reached the portal projector. It was the size of a fridge, but made from a transparent crystal material that reflected the light swirling on the back of the rift. Inside the crystal case were a host of components that looked like mock-ups from a Saturday morning kids' show: a lemon wired up with the old penny-and-nail trick; a brain, upside down, in a jar of murky liquid (yellow-green, like water in an aquarium that's lost the battle with algae); a ray gun clutched by a robot hand that repeatedly pulled the trigger. And those were only the first items to catch my eye. Other, maybe stranger components lay deeper within the machine's guts.

I knew a Mad Genius machine when I saw one. This was Cape Tech created by a Spark so supersmart he or she had gone insane from cosmic "insights." Or perhaps the people who became Mad Geniuses were crazy to begin with—the Light played no favorites with the people it made super, giving powers to both the sane and the deranged. Perhaps unbalanced minds were especially suited for hyper IQs; the world had a disproportionate number of Mad Geniuses compared to more run-of-the-mill supervillains.

But however unhinged the machine's technology was, its power supply was conventional. A heavy-duty cable ran out the machine's back, connecting it to an outlet in the wall. The plug was the size of a loaf of bread, made of surprisingly slippery plastic. I had to take off my gloves and use my bare hands to get a grip on it. I grabbed the plug, planted my foot against the wall, and played tug-of-war until the connection grudgingly yielded.

The plug came out. For a moment, nothing happened. Then something went *CHUNK* inside the projector.

AT THAT INSTANT, MIRANDA LET LOOSE A SCREAM

It was a cry that could only have been made by an opera singer. The fireball-bees, still swarming around me, jolted as if struck by mallets.

The portal began to close: no thudding percussion, just slow diminution, like a tire deflating. Still, it sent the flaming ping-pong balls into a panic. The ones near my face abandoned me and sped to Jools, doubling the crowd around her. Hundreds burrowed into her body like scavenger insects invading a carcass.

From the other side of the rift, Miranda called, "Can anybody hear me?"

I sighed with relief. Miranda hadn't screamed because she was hurt—she'd broken free. "People heard you in Australia," I said. "But welcome back. How are you feeling?"

"I'll live. But Shar's still surrounded by fire things. A bunch are inside her."

"Jools too," I said. "But I unplugged the machine that kept the portal open. The rift is shrinking now. Let's get out of here."

"Fine. I'll deal with Shar. Can you drag Jools to the door?"

"Sure," I said, hoping it was true.

I TURNED MY ATTENTION TO JOOLS

She lay on the floor, submerged in coppery fumes and wheezing like she ought to be in an oxygen tent. Ping-pong fireballs whizzed frantically through her, as if they knew the rift was closing and their time was growing short. Each ball had a different color, so I could track when one shoved into her eye socket and when the same one came out the back of her skull. I put my hand over her eyes, but it made little difference—the flames didn't seem able to pass through my hand anymore, but they could go around, zipping into Jools's ears, her temples, or under her chin, flying so quickly I couldn't block them fast enough.

Forget it, I told myself. *Just get Jools outside.*

I tucked my hands under her armpits and tried to drag her. She barely budged. I thought of all the times Jools had told me, "Shut your damned books and get some exercise." Other times when Miranda had invited me to go to yoga. And even Shar went to the gym on occasion—she always said, "If I'm going to be big, I might as well pump iron."

So, yeah, I thought, *I'm a weakling by choice.* That made me angry enough to heave harder. Jools started to move.

Jools wasn't bulky like Shar, but she was no lightweight. Wispy girls can't give and take body checks, or skate at high speeds in ungainly hockey equipment. As I struggled to keep her in motion, I muttered, "Come on, Jools, wake up. Whatever the fireballs are doing inside your head, Miranda and I got past it. She'll never let you live it down if you don't beat it too."

It made me wonder what Jools was seeing. Did all of us have awful memories like mine with Elaine? If the fireballs couldn't find anything bad enough, would they invent some experience so dire you went catatonic? I didn't know, and I had no intention of asking my roommates what they'd gone through. They might actually tell me. Then they'd ask me the same question.

"Jools!" I snapped. "Wake up! You're late for practice. Wayne Gretzky will be at the rink. And beer: free beer."

Jools's eyes snapped open. "What? Oh, fuck, that really sucked." Her voice was so hoarse I could barely hear her.

JOOLS'S BEVY OF FIREBALLS ROSE UP IN A BLAZING CLOUD

They shot toward the portal, abruptly desperate to get back home before the rift closed. I watched them zip across the threshold, then Jools started coughing, as if her lungs were trying to escape through her windpipe. She was still on the floor, still breathing the gas. Now that she wasn't completely deadweight, I wrapped my arms around her chest and tried to raise her head above the vapors.

After a moment, Jools swallowed her coughs enough to stagger to her feet with my help. Our heights were too different for her to drape an arm around my shoulders, but she leaned against me as I got one arm around her waist and started walking her toward the door.

Behind us, the portal continued to shrink, emitting less and less of its rusty brown light. The lab darkened; with the blinder wall still in place all around the room's perimeter, I wasn't sure where the exit was. The rift began rumbling with the same drumlike thuds I'd heard before, but now in a continuous roll that made my heart feel like it was fibrillating.

I turned my head for one last look at the Darklings, still on the portal's other side. They seemed peaceful, despite being mobbed by sparkles. Perhaps inside the rift, the fireball-bees gave you happy dreams instead of traumatic ones. I hoped so, because it looked like the Darklings might be locked in the rift universe forever.

I told myself, *It's what they chose.* I kept heading for the door.

MIRANDA AND SHAR CONVERGED WITH US

Shar was awake. She and Miranda walked with their arms around each other's shoulders, like drunks propping themselves up. "How are you doing?" I asked.

"Fucking awesome," Miranda growled.

"I'm surprisingly well," Shar said.

"You puked on my shoes," Miranda told her.

"And now I feel cleansed," Shar said. "I had a terrible dream, but I—"

Her voice cut off as she and Miranda stepped into the blinder wall. I hoped they were in the right spot to go through the door; with the light fading, it was hard to orient myself. The portal had shrunk to a rusty sliver, and the only other illumination came from stars shining through the broken roof. I gritted my teeth and moved forward, wondering what would happen if I hit the lab's wall rather than the doorway. Would I get trapped in the blinder, unable to move or think?

At the very last instant before we entered the blinder, Jools gave a sideways tug to correct my course. I didn't resist, despite doubting that Jools's sense of direction was any better than mine.

We came out safely on the other side, just brushing the doorframe. I didn't want to think about how I would have ended up without Jools.

Half a second later, the room exploded behind us.

THE SHOCK WAVE THREW US FORWARD

We were tossed across the corridor and into the opposite wall. Hard. But we were lucky—the blinder wall suppressed much of the explosion's force, or we might have been flattened to paste. The blinder itself didn't survive the blast. I don't know if it popped like a bubble or ripped into tatters, but by the time we struggled to our feet, the wall of blackness was gone.

So was any good evidence of what had happened in the lab. One glance through the door showed an unholy mess. All the time I'd been inside, I hadn't examined the lab in detail—the big, glowing portal had monopolized my attention, and the gas obscured everything else. Now I just saw chaos: papers scattered and burning, machinery blown to pieces, tables and chairs knocked helter-skelter.

Had the closing of the portal caused this devastation? Or had the Darklings planted a bomb to destroy the evidence, keyed to detonate if the portal disappeared?

The wreckage looked worse where the rift projector had stood. According to rumor, Mad Genius tech had a habit of obliterating itself—partly so no one could copy it, partly to hide that it was ever there, and partly because the stuff was so damned unstable it could blow up spontaneously like nitroglycerin past its best-before date.

One way or another, the excitement was over. The four of us staggered down the corridor and around a corner, to where the toxic vapor was only a finger-thin layer on the floor. We leaned against the wall and listened to Jools cough her lungs clean.

*Suspect Terrane**

BELATEDLY, ALARMS STARTED RINGING

Why so long after the crisis was over? My guess was that the Darklings disabled the safety systems in their own lab, and the coppery vapors took their own sweet time diffusing elsewhere. Eventually though, the fumes reached a toxic-gas sensor in one of the other labs and the ruckus began.

These were *serious* alarms: so loud, they hurt my eardrums. We couldn't possibly stay in the building with all that painful noise. My roommates and I covered our ears and ran for the exit—straight into a campus policeman who'd arrived to check out the fuss.

THE POLICEMAN "DETAINED" US

No surprise: When people stagger out of a building where an "incident" has occurred, police will request that you stop and give a statement. Inconveniently but with reason, the cop declared it unsafe to talk on the building's doorstep. Not only were alarms clanging away at deafening volume, but Richard had actually succeeded in calling 911. So the cop knew about the explosion—the first one, not the second. Firefighters were on their way, plus more police, ambulances, and (probably) news crews. To avoid getting caught in the furor, we were escorted to Police HQ.

The cop never said, "You're under arrest," nor did we ask if we were. We let that stay nebulous, for fear of crossing a line we'd all regret.

* A geological region substantially different from adjacent regions because it originated elsewhere and was brought in by a moving tectonic plate.

AN IMPORTANT FACT

UW's campus cops aren't private security. They're full-fledged police, officially authorized by the province. They can investigate crimes and throw you in jail. They're more chill than regular cops, because our university isn't a high-crime area: no knife fights, no gangs. But our campus police are still the real deal. On our way to the station, Miranda whispered, "First sign of trouble, ask for a lawyer."

Duly noted. She was the voice of experience.

In the station, we were led one by one into a room where a detective took our statements. He was gray-haired and grandfatherly, despite being twice my height and five times my width. Polite, even friendly, in a heavyweight wrestler way. He was just in shirtsleeves, no jacket, as if we were having a casual chat around the kitchen table.

I told the truth pretty much as I've written it here, except more incoherently. Since that night, I've had time to process everything that happened. In the police station, I was still high on adrenalin and yipe-yipe-yipe. My clothes reeked from the copper gas.

The detective stayed deadpan, despite my talk of portals. Our world has had Darklings for more than thirty years, and the Light for over a decade. Bizarre shit happens.

On the other hand, every crook in the world invents far-out lies to blame their crimes on supernatural weirdness. "I was mind-controlled!" "Possessed by demons!" "A supervillain broke it, then ran away!"

I don't envy the police their jobs. Someone says, "This was done by otherworldly forces," and almost always, it's bullshit. But one time out of a thousand, if you don't take it seriously, a million people get eaten by alien sludge worms.

And really, I was in the same boat as the cops: I had to decide what to believe. Did I really want to make an official statement about fireball-bees and the rest? I would have loved to leave parts out. (I *did* leave out Elaine. I just said that the flames got inside my head and they really hurt.) But what if I left out too much? If this was the start of a major crisis and I hid some crucial detail, it would be like seeing a suspicious package and not reporting it. So I spilled.

The detective took notes without calling me a liar.

THAT WAS ROUND ONE

We all were interviewed. Richard too—he arrived at the station soon after we did. When the "chats" were over, the five of us sat in the small front lobby while the police decided what to do with us.

None of us spoke. Miranda glared when any of us opened our mouths.

A paramedic arrived and, once again, we were taken away one by one, this time to a different back room where we were examined. Pulse, blood pressure, etc. The woman told me I didn't seem to be in immediate danger, but I should go to a hospital ER as soon as possible. "You were exposed to an unknown gas. You need to get tested."

That made sense, but the police showed no signs of letting us leave. They began a second round of interviews, starting with me. That annoyed me. Did they think the queer little kid with thick glasses would be easiest to crack?

Two detectives this time: the grandfatherly one and a younger man. The new guy was in his midthirties and wore a high-priced suit. (I hate that I pay attention to the cost of people's clothes, but I picked up the habit from the Vandermeers and I've never managed to shake it.)

I assumed that detective number two was from off campus: maybe Waterloo Regional Police, maybe provincial, maybe even the Mounties. The university does its share of government research. An explosion in one of our labs might attract high-level attention.

Especially when Darklings are involved.

Or should I say "allegedly" involved? Detective number two used that word a lot. "These alleged Darklings . . . this alleged portal . . . this alleged blinder wall . . ."

The friendly atmosphere was gone. The younger detective soon laid out his version of the "truth" and badgered me to confess. "Is it not true, Miss Lam . . ."

(I hate being called *Miss*. I said, "It's just Kim." But apparently paying attention to a person's preferences was a violation of standard interrogation procedures.)

"Is it not true, Miss Lam, that Miranda Neuhof is a fanatic anti-Dark radical?

"Is it not true she persuaded Ashariti Chandra, a dean's-list chemistry student, to manufacture a bomb?

"Is it not true that the four of you detonated the bomb yourselves, then concocted a story intended to foment anti-Darkling unrest?

"Is it not true that you yourself have anti-Darkling leanings, having been jilted by a young man from a prominent Darkling family?"

I wanted to ask, *Is it not true that you know way too much about us, way too fast?* It was no surprise the cops would find Miranda's arrest record—basic operating procedure must be to run everybody's name through police databases. But my relationship with Nicholas? We kept that hush-hush. First, to prevent his family from finding out; then, when they *did* find out, because the Vandermeers themselves wanted zero publicity.

They weren't happy with Nicholas dating a nobody. They also saw me as a vulnerability: someone who might be used by the Vandermeers' enemies. So I'd never posted a word about us on Facebook, Tumblr, or wherever. Trust me, I've had experience keeping secrets. But in less than an hour, a detective in Waterloo found out about a clandestine relationship that had happened three years earlier on the opposite side of the continent.

WTF. Seriously. WTF.

I WAS ABOUT TO ASK FOR A LAWYER, WHEN A KNOCK CAME AT THE DOOR Detective number two looked pissed at the interruption. He locked eyes with the older detective and jerked his head toward the door. The older man quietly stood and answered the knock; after a whispered conversation, the older detective turned to me. "Thanks for your help. You're free to go."

"What?" said the young guy in outrage.

The older man just held the door open for me. "Have a good night, Kim. You take care."

Through the open doorway, I could see a young woman with "second-generation Darkling" written all over her. If you scraped off the makeup and put her in denim, she'd look eighteen, but she wore a maroon business skirt suit and cosmetics that aged her by a decade. She stood uncannily still; or perhaps the uncanniness came from her Shadow manipulating my emotions. One way or another, she had an air of authority. I could tell why even a seasoned police detective deferred to her.

The Darkling stared at me expressionlessly. I got up and left the room. As I passed her, I felt like a mouse under the gaze of a cat. She waited for me to walk by, then went into the room with the two detectives and shut the door.

THE HALLWAY WAS DARK AND QUIET

To my left lay the route back to the front lobby where my roommates waited. To my right . . .

I found myself looking toward the lobby again—as if time had skipped a beat when I glanced the other way. I turned my head right . . .

Skip. Lobby.

Huh.

My sense of direction said the right-hand part of the hallway had to extend some distance back into the building. This hall was the only access from the lobby to the rest of the station. I assumed the police station had offices, washrooms, a lunchroom, all the usual. Those rooms had to be farther back.

I looked again. Skip. Lobby. This time a chill of fear bloomed from nowhere: *Really seriously, don't look. It's dark, it's scary. Go back to the light.*

So now I knew: an Ignorance spell.

Also called a No-See-Um spell, Avidya, and (in tribute to Douglas Adams) Someone Else's Problem.

Like blinder walls, the Ignorance spell was so basic that even brand-new Darklings could learn it. I'd experienced it before, thanks to Derek Vandermeer, Nicholas's older brother. Derek was a show-off and a bully, but he'd taught me a lot about magic—mostly by subjecting me to various spells and explaining how they made me his dancing monkey.

An Ignorance spell forced people to ignore you. Their eyes simply skipped past where you were. Usually, they didn't notice the blind spot: just a moment of inattention. If circumstances made the gap obvious and someone persisted in trying to look, emotional aversion kicked in. Something like the way that children shied away from the dark stairs to the basement.

So a Darkling had to be standing in the hallway to my right, and they didn't want to be seen. Was the Darkling working with the woman in maroon, or was it spying on her? I figured the odds were even either way. Darklings showed solidarity against outsiders, but behind closed doors, the Dark were competing predators, divided into factions, clans, and rivalries that shifted with every breeze.

My safest move would be walking away: letting the Ignorance win. That's what Kimmi had done when Derek used the spell. Kimmi wanted the Vandermeers to like her. She let Derek make her look like a fool.

But I wasn't Kimmi. I was Kim, and grouchy as hell from all the repetitions of "Is it not true, Miss Lam?" Something inside me said, *Fuck this crap,* and I snapped my eyes right with all my willpower.

Oh, look. My old boyfriend Nicholas.

HE STILL LOOKED SEVENTEEN

It's strange how it hit me, him looking so young. My mental image of Nicholas had aged as I did. I didn't have a precise picture of what he'd look like, but I imagined him as a third-year university student, not a high schooler. Now, here he was, still a teenager. My never-entirely-abandoned fantasies of reconnecting with him instantly turned creepy; it would be like robbing the cradle.

I say Nicholas hadn't changed, but that was only my first impression after a glimpse down a darkened hallway. A moment later, I realized he was a ghost.

Slightly transparent. Gray-white skin. Stringy hair with the texture of dead grass. His hair used to be blond, but it had bleached to the same gray-white as his skin. He wore a nondescript white shirt, but only the collar was distinct. Below his neck, Nicholas's body faded, growing more and more vaporous until it vanished completely at waist level.

I felt so bad for him. He had believed the Dark Conversion would give him more: that he'd become a vampire like the rest of his family, lethally charming and powerful. As it was, Nicholas was reduced to an ashen half person, hovering with his head the same level as mine.

It was the same height as when we'd been together. Nicholas was a ghost and didn't need to touch the ground, but consciously or not, he chose to position himself at exactly the same height as when he'd been in his wheelchair.

NO, I HAVEN'T MENTIONED THAT BEFORE

It was and wasn't important. It was everything and nothing.

You know how that goes? How something can be the central fact of a person's life, yet almost irrelevant to who he is?

Anyway. Riding accident. Age six.

You really don't need to know more.

BEFORE YOU ASK

No one had attempted to cure him, either with magic or super-technology. Nicholas's injuries were complex; invasive treatment would have been risky.

Besides, his family took for granted he'd embrace the Dark Conversion the day he turned eighteen, the earliest age allowed. Nicholas would be reborn, presumably without his "condition."

Mr. Vandermeer Sr. decided it didn't matter if Nicholas had to use a wheelchair for eleven years. A brief inconvenience was trifling compared to the infinite remainder of his life.

Yes. That's how Darklings think.

I DON'T THINK NICHOLAS RECOGNIZED ME AT FIRST

Then he gaped as if he'd seen a ghost.

I'd changed since the last time he saw me. Leave it at that.

HE SAID, "KIMMI?"

"No. Kim."

He said, "Oh."

I SAID, "YOU FINALLY GOT OUT OF YOUR CHAIR."

"Yes. I'm a Darkling now."

"With powers and everything."

"Yes."

"You can hover," I said. "Can you fly?"

"I can do lots of things."

"Ghost things."

"I can haunt like a boss."

He was trying not to gawp at me. I was trying not to gawp at him.

I said, "Your Ignorance spells need work. Mortals shouldn't be able to beat them."

Oh good, Kim . . . start criticizing him. But he didn't seem upset. He just said, "Look, we can't talk here."

WITHOUT WAITING FOR ME TO RESPOND, HE FLOATED OFF DOWN THE HALLWAY

A door opened at his approach. It creaked when it moved—haunted house stuff. I wondered if Nicholas had actively used a power, or if doors just naturally opened for him, even if they were locked. Probably the latter. When Darklings are around, the world is infected by their presence. The environment writhes in response to their Shadows.

Nicholas went through the doorway, and I followed. We entered an unlit room: somebody's office. Vertical slats of moonlight came through venetian blinds, and a chocolate smell hung in the air—someone had left a box of Turtles open on the desk. It was probably a Christmas present; the last night of term sees a lot of Secret Santa action. I usually like Turtles, but my stomach had gone fluttery. The smell threatened to make me sick.

Maybe Nicholas felt the same fluttering nervousness. He quickly went around behind the desk, putting it between him and me.

He took the corner wide, as if he were still in the chair.

I closed the office door behind me. Alone in a moonlit room with the Ghost of Christmas Past.

NICHOLAS SAID, "YOU'VE CUT OFF YOUR HAIR."

"Not all of it."

"Most. And you've dyed it. What color?"

"You can't tell?"

He looked away. "I don't see colors anymore."

"I'm sorry," I said. Some Darklings gained the ability to see in pitch blackness, but lost their color vision. I said, "My hair is basically white. I spray on color when I feel like it. At the moment, it's light pink."

"Oh. Interesting." He was staring at me again. I wasn't wearing my coat—I'd taken it off in the lobby—so Nicholas was getting the full effect of the new me. No more Goth in a push-up corset. "Is this because I . . . we . . ."

"No," I said. "It has nothing to do with you. It's who I am. Why are you here, Nicholas?"

His jaw tightened. His flesh was so white that even in the dark, I could see he had no beard stubble. As smooth as a thousand-count sheet. I remembered the first time he'd given me whisker-burn. The memory made my stomach ache with loss.

"I can't tell you why I'm here," Nicholas said. "It would be bad for you to know."

"You could tell me, but then you'd have to kill me?"

He smiled slightly. "Nah, I'd just wipe your mind clean."

"You can do that?"

He nodded.

"Is that what you're going to do when we finish talking?"

Nicholas didn't answer.

I said, "You probably suck at mind wipes as badly as you do at Ignorance spells."

He laughed a little. "You must have natural resistance—some mortals do. Either that, or I'm unconsciously pulling my punches because it's you."

"Bull. You didn't even recognize me."

"I knew you might be in the building," he said. "I heard someone say 'Kimmi Lam.'"

"Really. Kimmi?" All my current IDs said *Kim*—student card, driver's license, health card. Of course, my passport and birth certificate said *Kimberlite*. No one should have been able to find the name *Kimmi*.

"What's going on, Kimmi?" Nicholas asked. "How did you end up in a police station?"

"It's Kim," I said, "not Kimmi. And you have to know something about what's happening, or you wouldn't be here. Unless you make a habit of invisibly invading police stations a thousand miles from home. You still live in Calgary, right?"

"Officially. But I travel on family business."

"This is connected with family business?"

"No," Nicholas replied. "And I'm not saying anything more on the subject."

"Then I'm not saying anything more either."

Silence. Prolonged.

I sighed. "This isn't how I imagined things would go if we met again."

Pause. "Me neither."

"You really spent time imagining it?"

He gave a rueful smile. "Oh, Kimmi . . . Kim. I imagined a hundred scenarios." Nicholas blurred for a moment, then became a Hollywood version of himself—tall and strong, standing casually on long muscular legs. He wore tennis shorts so I could see his legs and even his manly bulge.

I giggled.

"You're supposed to be impressed!" He slumped back to his bedraggled ghost form. "I knew you wouldn't be."

"Sorry."

"I can take other shapes," he said. "They'd scare the piss out of you. Seriously."

"Even with my natural resistance?"

"Don't tease. I mean, come on, you *must* have natural resistance. You're talking with me like normal, despite my Shadow. Other commoners—I mean anyone who isn't a Darkling or a Spark—my Shadow's effect is intense."

I didn't answer. I knew full well that Nicholas's Shadow might terrify most people—not just provoking the usual unease, but outright panic. Some Darklings are like that. But I felt nothing except pity. Pity for a boy who looked like something the cat had killed and who hadn't been able to talk to real, live humans since he'd Converted.

Perhaps the pity showed on my face. He suddenly looked offended. "I should go."

"Why?"

"Because my Shadow will get to you eventually. It gets to everyone. If you start screaming, the police will come and catch you back here."

"So what?" I said. "The police have been ordered to let us go. By that Darkling woman. Do you know who she is?"

Nicholas shrugged. "She's likely with the government."

"But what department? What agency?"

"You know as much as I do."

He turned away toward the window. A pair of venetian-blind slats spread wider apart to give him a better view; he didn't touch them, they just spread on their own. His eyes raised up toward the moon. "I really have to go," he said. "Sorry for all this."

"Why?"

"You know. Darklings and coincidences. The universe loves to orchestrate surprises for us."

I nodded. Darklings and Sparks experience coincidences at a much higher rate than normal humans. Supposedly, it's because the forces of Dark and Light play hell with probability—they just love to create drama. So: sudden confrontations. Flukes, reversals, and bombshells. The Dark and the Light use lesser folks like me to get a rise out of *important* players like Nicholas.

Oh well, I thought, *at least I wasn't killed and crammed into his fridge.*

Not yet, anyway.

"I have to go," he said again. This time he really did leave. He passed straight through the glass of the window, as unhindered as the moonlight.

AT LEAST HE HADN'T SAID, "NICE SEEING YOU."

At least he hadn't said, "Why don't you give me your number?"

At least he hadn't shaken my hand good-bye.

Then again, he was a ghost; maybe he *couldn't* shake hands. Or maybe when I felt his icy touch, I'd lose my mind with fear and my hair would turn white for real.

Heh.

I STOOD ALONE IN THAT DARK OFFICE AND ASKED ALOUD, "DO I STILL LOVE HIM?"

The answer was no. Kimmi had loved him. Kimmi was gone.

Almost.

As for my current self, I had no idea whom Kim might love. It hadn't happened. Kim had sometimes said, "Oh, he's cute. Oh, she's hot." But love? Kim didn't go there.

Not yet.

I didn't love Nicholas, but I was caught on him, the way the strap of your purse can get caught on a doorknob as you're trying to race out of a room.

I GOT BACK TO THE LOBBY WITHOUT BEING SPOTTED

I might have looked rattled, but no big—being interrogated could do that. Then I imagined Jools saying, "You look like you've seen a ghost," and I almost broke into hysterical laughter.

I choked it down. Cool and composed. None of the others raised a peep. A uniformed cop stood with them in the lobby; she'd just announced we were free to go. The others leapt to their feet, eager to get out of the station. Jools tossed me my coat. "Let's bounce."

With a deadpan expression, the policewoman said, "Thank you for coming in. Have a good night."

"Merry Christmas," Richard said. Shar hustled him out the door.

4

Daylighting

WE STOPPED ON THE SIDEWALK AS SOON AS THE STATION ENTRANCE WAS OUT OF SIGHT
We leaned back against the building, as if we'd just finished a race and needed to catch our breaths.

"Wow," Richard said, "I was afraid they'd lock us up."

"I think they wanted to," I said, "but they were ordered to kick us loose."

"Ordered by who?"

"A Darkling woman. A vampire, I think. Didn't you see her?"

"I didn't see anyone," Richard said.

I looked at the others. They shook their heads.

There were only two ways for that woman to reach the interrogation room: She could have gone through the lobby past my roommates, or come from the back of the building past Nicholas. She might not have seen him because of the Ignorance spell, but if I could beat the spell, a Darkling could too.

Maybe the woman was so distracted she hadn't noticed. Or maybe she and Nicholas had an "understanding" even though he'd denied knowing her.

"Tell us about this vampire," Miranda said. She glanced back at the station. "No, I take that back. No talking till we get home."

"We can't go home," Richard said. "We still have to pick up the stuff from my lab."

Miranda snorted. "You won't get into your lab. The building will be locked down. Crawling with crime scene investigators."

Shar took Richard's arm. "There were explosions, my sweet, and a toxic gas release. The authorities won't let anyone inside until they're sure it's safe." She glanced at Miranda. "That includes crime scene investigators. No one in or out except safety inspectors."

"Fair point," Miranda admitted.

"I still have to pick up the van," Richard said. "If I don't, my parents will kill me."

"Dude," Jools said, "it's been, like, two hours. Your van's been towed."

She was likely right. UW was ruthless when it came to towing cars. An unattended van at a loading dock would be long gone.

"Maybe the tow trucks are off for Christmas," Richard said.

"Forget the tow trucks," Miranda said. "Worry about the police. What do you think they'll do with a van illegally parked near a crime scene? There'll be sniffer dogs all over it."

Richard moaned. "Sniffer dogs!"

"Let's not jump to conclusions," Shar said soothingly. "E3 is only a few minutes away. We'll check if the van is still there." She glanced at Miranda. "And if it's gone, you can say, 'I told you so.'"

"I never say, 'I told you so,'" Miranda lied. But she turned toward E3 and set out at full speed. I had to hurry to keep up.

THE CAMPUS SEEMED EVEN MORE DESERTED THAN BEFORE
No lights in any building. Not a single car on the ring road. Nothing in the nearby parking lot except three university trucks parked side by side. They'd sit there unneeded till January.

The sky was clear, with cold, hard stars and the full moon rising. *Good night for a ritual,* I thought. Melodramatic events like the solstice and eclipse made magic more effective, if, say, you were trying to open a magic portal. To a science student, the solstice and eclipse were just astronomy, but to the Dark, they were powerful mystic woo-woo.

But why did the Darklings want a portal in the first place? And how was the Mad Genius machine involved? That was Cape Tech, not magic. The two didn't go together.

And the million-dollar question: How was Nicholas involved?

He was a Vandermeer, first, last, and always. He wouldn't travel all the way to Ontario and snoop around a police station except to serve Vandermeer interests. Mind you, they had a lot of interests—political, commercial, and sorcerous. His family had a serious hard-on for power in government, business, and the factions of the Dark.

Something big, dark, and nasty was unfolding in Waterloo, and the leaden hand of coincidence had dragged me into it.

My knee-jerk reflex was to say, "This sucks." Isn't that how you're supposed to react when you're snarled in somebody else's mess?

But actually, I was grinning. The game's afoot, bitches! Tally-fucking-ho.

I could feel a new Kim coming on.

RICHARD SAID, "WHY DO YOU KEEP LOOKING AROUND?" He was talking to Miranda. She said, "I expect to be jumped any second."

"By who?"

"Darklings."

Richard surveyed our surroundings. We were on a broad sidewalk that ran beside the ring road. Fifty meters of open lawn separated us from the nearest building: no trees, no bushes, nowhere to hide. Richard said, "I don't see any Darklings."

"You wouldn't, would you? Until it's too late."

"Why would Darklings jump us?"

"To keep us quiet," Miranda said. "Why do you think they forced the cops to let us go? They couldn't attack us as long as we were in the police station."

"Wow," Jools said. "Paranoid much?"

Miranda glowered. "Just wait till someone puts a bag over your head."

"Why would they?" Jools asked. "We've told the cops everything—at least I did. It's too late to shut us up. And if the five of us get whacked, the police will go ballistic, not to mention the media and every student on campus."

"What if we're found back home, dead from poisoned Kool-Aid?

With a suicide note saying we bombed the lab to get Darklings in trouble, but when the cops wouldn't believe us, we decided to end it all."

Jools thought for a moment. "They'd have to plant evidence: the materials for making a bomb, stuff like that. Also a trail of where we bought what, and witnesses who'll say they saw us. Lots of room for mistakes and loose lips."

Miranda said, "The Dark could just brainwash us. Use their powers to make us confess. Hell, they might make us truly believe that we planted a bomb."

"Risky," Shar said. "Some heroes of the Light can detect psychic tampering. Can you imagine the backlash if Dark manipulation were discovered?"

"Why would Sparks even think to check us for tampering?" Miranda asked.

"Why would Darklings bother to brainwash us?" Shar countered. "The damage to that lab . . . how much would it cost to repair? Perhaps a hundred thousand dollars? To a Darkling, that's pocket change. Someone could pay off the university, and everyone would pretend the explosions never happened."

"Now you're talking," Jools said. "Forget brainwashing. Toss me enough cash, and I'll confess to anything."

"Not me," Miranda said. "I would never—" She froze midstep.

So did the others. As did I: as if my body had turned to stone.

I WAS CONSCIOUS AND CLEARHEADED

I just couldn't move.

Fucking magic. *Nicholas, you dick, let me go!*

I couldn't be sure it was him, but it didn't matter. Whoever was responsible, I had to break free.

I pushed and pulled. It was like being trapped in cement. I could breathe, but only a little.

Sips of air weren't nearly enough to handle the panic flaring inside me. Claustrophobia. Immobility. I go crazy at being confined.

The one constant in my life.

WHEN I WAS TEN, I WAS KIMBERLEY

Back then, I didn't ask questions about who or what I was. Kimberley was *conventional*. So of course, I had a best friend; her name was Hannah.

Hannah's parents enrolled her in judo. Soon enough, she did that thing done by every new martial arts student. "Hey, I learned something cool. Want to see?"

Kimberley was so naive, she said okay.

Next thing I knew, I was in a submission hold—all scrunched up, too cramped to breathe. I wanted to cry, "Stop, you're hurting me!" but didn't have enough air.

Hannah kept asking, "Do you give?" and I couldn't even tell her I surrendered. I was panicked, frantic, and smothered. I thought I was going to die.

Something snapped inside me. I went berserk.

I don't know how I got free—Hannah had just learned the technique, so maybe her grip was a little off. But suddenly I was out of the hold, and scratching, biting, screaming, out of control.

Most kids hold back when fighting, even if they're desperate. I didn't. Something extreme inside me knew no restraint.

Eventually, Hannah's parents pried me off her, but I don't remember that. I don't remember anything but the frenzy.

Afterward, Hannah had to go to the hospital. I had to go to counseling. We never spoke again.

NOW ON THE SIDEWALK, I HAD NO ONE TO ATTACK

I couldn't even thrash around—my body refused to respond. But mentally, I was feral, writhing and wild.

Again, something snapped inside me. A barrier broke. The world changed.

NIGHT BECAME DAY

The dark campus flooded with light, as bright as a football field lit for a night game.

The sky remained black and scattershot with stars, but the ground lost all shadow. The buildings cast no shadows on the dead winter grass. No shadows either from the five of us on the sidewalk. I could see through every window in every building; every office was lit as brightly as the aisles in Walmart.

Every window. Every building. Three hundred and sixty degrees.

I saw simultaneously in all directions: north, south, east, west. Up and down too. It wasn't like looking through a fish-eye lens—I saw clearly, without distortion. It should have been overwhelming. Instead I felt a sudden relief, as if my head had been clamped in a vice since the day I was born, but at last I'd been released. As if all my life, I'd watched my surroundings on the tiny screen of a phone, but finally I'd thrown the damned thing away and looked at the world directly.

My panic eased immediately. I still couldn't move, but the feeling of openness banished the sense of being locked in.

My new perception felt natural: the way I should have been seeing all along. But of course, I realized it was a superpower.

It's hard to feel helpless when you realize you've become one of *them*.

MY SUPER-SIGHT DIDN'T JUST SHOW THE PLAIN VANILLA WORLD
I also saw things that were previously invisible.

Five thick gray tentacles stretched through the air in front of me. They looked like the arms of an octopus, except that instead of suction cups, the tentacles oozed with raw red pustules. Each one of us there on the sidewalk had a tentacle embedded in our skull. My new sense of sight meant that I could actually see the top of my scalp where a tentacle passed through the hair and bone without hindrance. If I concentrated, I knew I could track the tentacle all the way into my brain.

But instead, I aimed my vision in the opposite direction. My viewpoint moved like a tracking shot in a film, following the tentacle back to its source . . . except that my "camera" wasn't limited to seeing straight ahead but showed a full 360 degrees with perfect lighting. As my viewpoint moved away, I could see myself recede in the distance: another out-of-body experience like back in the lab, but this time I felt fully in control.

I could see more clearly than ever before in my life. As Kim, I wore bottle-thick glasses. As Kimmi, it had been contacts. But the new whoever-I-was saw better than 20/20 with no artificial aids.

(*Sorry, Mom,* I thought. My mother is an optometrist. Her definition of being a good parent is strongly bound up with my eye care. If I could suddenly see without glasses, she would say she was happy, but she'd feel bereft.)

ALL FIVE OF THE GRAY TENTACLES LED BACK TO A BLACK LEXUS

It was parked and idling on a nearby service road. The parking spot was mostly hidden behind a building, but the car had a clear line of sight on the short patch of sidewalk where we stood. Anyone going from the police station to E3 would have to pass through the car's field of vision. We'd been grabbed as soon as we came into view.

The tentacles passed through the windshield of the car as easily as they passed through the skulls of my roommates and me. *Ectoplasm,* I thought. *Nicholas, you dick!*

But I was wrong about who was responsible. My new sense of sight could penetrate the windshield as easily as the tentacles could. I thrust my viewpoint inside and saw who was really attacking us.

THE CAR HELD ONE MAN, ONE WOMAN, ONE OTHER

The driver was male, apparently human, and tough looking: the kind of bruiser that Darklings hired as "special assistants." Ex-military or ex-cop. Good at Getting Things Done. He might have been a full-blown Renfield—made faster and stronger by drinking Darkling blood—or he might have been unaugmented: less powerful but free of the physical and mental aberrations that Renfields inevitably developed. Either way, he was a hard man (as the British say) but not so thuggish that he couldn't be house-trained. Darklings needed employees who behaved themselves at soirees.

I took one look at the man, then ignored him. He was only the help.

On the car's passenger side sat a demon connected to the ectoplasm tentacles. His skin was elephant gray, but speckled with weeping red pustules. The five biggest buboes were the roots of the gray tentacles: two sprouting from his forehead like long phallic horns, two more growing out of his cheeks, and the last going all beanstalk from the point of his chin.

The base of each tentacle leaked oily wet goo that dribbled down the demon's face and spilled off his jaw onto his clothes. With supreme bad planning, the demon had chosen to wear a cream-colored suit. The goo made greasy stains on the fine linen.

Too bad. This tentacle-sprouting douche had paralyzed us with demon magic. He deserved a lot worse than an inflated cleaning bill.

A WOMAN SAT IN THE BACK OF THE CAR

She leaned forward, one hand on the demon's shoulder, as if eager to be part of what he was doing. Her hand was gloved; in fact, she was covered from head to toe. The woman's clothes matched the wedding outfit worn by the "bride" I'd seen in E3—long gown, elbow-length gloves, chiffon veil fully covering face and hair. But this outfit was black instead of white. Not a bride: a widow.

Instinctively, I had known that the Bride's face was monstrous. The same instinct told me the Widow was worse. I didn't know what seeing her face would do to mortals, but it would be terrible beyond comprehension.

Instinct also told me that the Widow and Bride were sisters; maybe even twins. They had gone through the Dark Conversion together, emerging as a complementary pair. Now the pair bond had been severed. The Widow burned with rage—so much that her sense of loss seemed like a heat haze around her. I could *see* it. I couldn't tell if that was due to my special powers of perception, or if the Widow's boiling emotion literally distorted the world.

One thing I was sure of: after what had happened to the Bride in the E3 lab, the Widow was now on the warpath. She'd commanded her demon companion to thrust his tentacles into our brains.

We were frozen and at the Widow's furious mercy. I hated to think what she planned next.

THE PUSTULE DEMON SHUDDERED

The movement drew my attention back to the demon. Four of his gray tentacles stretched unhindered through the windshield, but the fifth—the one attached to the demon's chin—had become enveloped in strands of violet. They resembled the stringlike creepers that bindweed uses to strangle other plants. The violet strands came from outside the car, weaving rapidly up the tentacle until they reached the demon's face and thrust themselves into his skin.

His body jerked. His mouth opened in a scream. I couldn't hear his cry—my perception gave sight, not sound. Still, I could see the inside of the demon's mouth lit bright violet as the strands invaded the bones of his jaw. Some strands ran down his throat, while others stabbed through his soft palate and dug toward his brain.

The tentacle growing from the demon's right cheek flared with violet fire. The gray ectoplasm shriveled like burning plastic, and in less than a second it was gone, leaving a scorched black crater where it had been attached to the demon's face.

Another scream I couldn't hear. The demon's eyes fluttered, as if he was close to passing out.

The Widow clutched his shoulder, shaking him and trying to keep him conscious. More violet fire appeared, this time around the tentacle on the demon's other cheek. The demon's ectoplasm flashed in spontaneous combustion. He slumped, held up only by the seat belt.

MY CONSCIOUSNESS REELED BACK TO MY BODY AS IF IT WERE ON A BUNGEE CORD

My point of view zoomed back on a straight-line path. As it cut through the corner of the building that had hidden the car from sight, I had a brief glimpse of wires and pipes running inside the wall, then an open area with books and desks, then more wires and pipes, then back outside. My vision sped above the frozen lawn before docking back into my body with a bump, like a boat coming to rest against a pier.

But I hadn't been alone on my trip back from the Lexus. My path ran side by side with a brilliant beam of violet, retracting at the same speed as my vision. At the moment when my viewpoint nestled back into my body, the violet slithered home into Shar's forehead.

She said something in Sinhalese—perhaps along the lines of, "Wow, I have superpowers!" She smiled broadly and said in English, "*Ex*cellent."

THE LEXUS SPURRED INTO LIFE
The night was quiet enough to hear the engine, even at that distance. The car never came into sight, but I could hear it drive away—sedately, not racing. It did nothing to draw attention to itself or its passengers.

JOOLS SAID, "WHAT JUST HAPPENED?"
"Goddamned magic," Miranda replied.

"A psychic attack," Shar explained. She began to fuss over Richard, who seemed more dazed than the rest of us. He was close to drooling.

Poor Richard. He could strain my patience, but I felt bad for him. He'd missed out on the portal, the fireballs, and everything.

I thought about the onset of the pustule demon's attack: my panic at being immobilized. Richard must have felt the same, but he'd had no liberating vision to ease his hysteria.

"What?" Richard said in a muddy voice. "What?"

"Don't worry, sweet," Shar said. "Darklings attempted to violate our minds, but it's over."

"What do you mean, don't worry?" Miranda demanded. "They attacked, then just stopped? It doesn't make sense. Unless they tampered with our minds, and we just don't feel it."

"They didn't tamper with our minds. I intervened."

"You?"

Shar just gave Miranda a cat-versus-canary smile.

"Bullshit," Miranda said.

"No," I said, "she did. I saw it."

Miranda turned to me in surprise. "What?"

"Open your nose," Shar told Miranda. "The attack smelled like phenol, correct? But you can't smell it now, because I neutralized it with sodium hydroxide."

Silence. Richard said, "You did what now?"

"It smelled like phenol," Shar said. "You must have noticed."

"What's phenol?" Richard asked.

"C_6H_5OH," Jools said. "Also called carbolic acid. A volatile white crystalline solid."

We stared at Jools in surprise. "Don't look at me like that," she said. "Why shouldn't I know about phenol? We used it in first-year chemistry. Remember?"

Of course I remembered first-year chemistry. It was where the four of us had met. By chance, we'd been assigned to the same lab bench: Miranda and I were partners, and we worked beside Shar and Jools.

That was two years ago, and I still vaguely recalled the name *phenol*. I did *not* remember its formula or what it had smelled like.

And if *I* didn't remember, it was astounding Jools did. I'm sure that's why Miranda and Shar were staring at her. But me, I stared at Jools for a different reason. Her head had flared with a bright green light when she recited phenol's vital statistics.

AFTER A MOMENT, MIRANDA SHRUGGED AND TURNED BACK TO SHAR "Explain what you said about phenol. I didn't smell anything."

"It stank to high heaven!" Shar replied. "And since phenol is a weak acid, I projected the thought of neutralizing it with sodium hydroxide."

"NaOH," Jools put in. "A hella strong base."

"That one was easy," Miranda said. She was right. Jools hadn't glowed.

"The point is," Shar said, "my strategy worked. You can't smell phenol anymore, and we're no longer under attack. In fact, all we smell is saffron." She inhaled deeply and smiled. "It's strange because saffron is chemically unrelated to either phenol or sodium hydroxide. But I like saffron. It's soothing."

"So you smelled a weak acid," Miranda said, "and you thought back a strong base. Now all you smell is a spice. Which I don't smell, by the way. And you believe that you somehow defeated a Darkling attack? It makes no sense!"

Shar gave Miranda a patronizing look. "I'm sorry if I can't explain why it worked, but it's like . . . like how you recognize people. You don't follow a checklist: tall, blond, overplucked eyebrows, it must be Miranda. When you see someone, you just know who it is instantly."

"Automatic processing in the brain," Jools said. "Below the level of consciousness. Face recognition is centered in the fusiform gyrus, but with participation from several other cerebral regions."

This time, we outright gaped. Miranda said, "Jools, what the fuck?"

"I'm in biology," Jools said. "I know things."

"No you don't."

"Thanks a heap."

"Shar," I said, "did you smell anything special when Jools said *fusiform gyrus*?" I'd seen another green glow shine out from Jools's head, and I was putting two and two together.

Shar shrugged. "All I smelled was ale."

"No way," Jools said, "I was doing shots, not beer."

I TOOK A DEEP BREATH AND STARED

Which is to say, I looked carefully in every direction at once. No one in sight. "I know what's going on," I said. "I think Shar does too."

She nodded.

"Well, enlighten the rest of us," Miranda grumped.

"Okay," I said. "Someone hold up some fingers behind my back."

Jools shrugged and put her hand behind my back. She held up two fingers.

"Two," I said. She changed her hand. "Four," I said. "None. Five. One. Three. One."

"Fuck me," Jools said.

Miranda put her hands over my eyes. "Keep going."

"Two," I said. "None. Four. Five. One. Three."

"Fuck me raw," Jools said.

Miranda lowered her hands and looked at Shar. "What do you smell?"

"Vanilla. Quite strong."

"I don't smell anything," Richard said.

Shar patted his cheek. "The smells aren't real, sweet. Try to keep up."

"THIS IS . . . THOUGHT-PROVOKING," MIRANDA SAID

"It's fucking awesome," Jools corrected.

"What?" Richard said. "Just because Kim can guess . . ."

"Kim isn't guessing," Shar said. "What's happened is—"

Miranda cut her off. "No talk. We're out in the open. Anyone could be watching."

Nobody was—I could see like noon in all directions. But I didn't know whether my strange new perception could see through an Ignorance spell. I decided to say nothing as Miranda continued. "Whatever has happened, we don't do anything till we have privacy. No tests."

Jools said, "You're no fun."

"I mean it," Miranda said. "We go and pick up the van . . ."

"Dibs on picking it up first!" Jools said.

Miranda glared. "We see if the van is still there. If so, we drive home. Or even better, into the country where we can experiment without being seen."

"Experiment? What do you mean?" Richard asked. He looked worried, as if Miranda meant trying a fivesome.

"Experiments," Jools said. "Like this."

Without warning, she grabbed my waist and hoisted me like a male dancer lifts a ballerina. She held me high for a couple of seconds; I forced myself not to fight her. Finally, she set me down with a sigh.

I glowered, but couldn't help asking, "Well?"

"I could have held you up longer, but I don't think I can toss you into orbit."

"Praise be," Miranda said. "Now can we please just chill until we're sure we're not being watched?"

"Can't wait," Jools said. "Let's pick up the van." She gave me a wink, then trotted toward E3.

THE REST OF US FOLLOWED

Shar took Richard's hand. They soon lagged behind. When they were well back, a beam of violet shot from Shar's forehead and hit me in the back of the skull. I said, "Hey! I can see that. Eyes in the back of my head, remember?"

"Don't worry," Shar said. The beam didn't go away.

"Stop it," I said. She didn't. "I mean it, Shar, cut it out right now." In my mind, I added, *Or I'll see if I can shoot lightning up your ass.*

Shar made a face and the beam disappeared like a flashlight being shut off. "You're always so defensive," Shar said. "I was just curious what you saw. A demon with sores on his face and a woman dressed in black?"

My mouth dropped open. "You saw them? In my mind?"

Shar nodded.

I said, "Fuck me raw."

Tectonic Collision

RICHARD'S VAN HADN'T BEEN TOWED

It was parked where Richard had left it, with the van's front touching the dock and its rear hatch toward us. E3 has several loading docks, but Richard had chosen the least accessible—on an alley off a side road off a service road off the ring road, with the surrounding buildings cutting off your view unless you were right in the mouth of the alley. Richard seriously hadn't wanted his van to be seen.

Yeah, sure, his late-night equipment removal was totally legit.

On the plus side, I couldn't think of a more sheltered place to test what we could do. Only a few windows overlooked the alley. I scanned them and saw no one. No security cameras either—Waterloo students are so well behaved, there's never been a reason to TV up the campus.

"This is perfect," Jools said. She clutched her hands in a begging pose and pouted at Miranda. "Please, Mom, please, can we try a few widdle experiments?"

Miranda eyed the area. I knew she hated giving in, but she had to realize she couldn't keep Jools in check much longer. Besides, Miranda could play the ice queen all she wanted, but I would have bet she was bubbling like a vat of champagne wondering what she could do herself.

"Okay," Miranda said. "Let the Sparks fly."

JOOLS SPRANG INTO ACTION

She jumped, hit one wall of the alley, bounced off on an upward trajectory, and somersaulted in midair to land hands first on top of the van. She let momentum carry her forward, doing a handspring to her feet. From there she kept going across the van toward the opposite alley wall. With a leap, she caught the top of the wall and pulled herself up to E3's roof.

"Ta-da," she said, bowing. "Eat your heart out, Jackie Chan."

"Wow!" Richard said. "I didn't know you could do that."

"I couldn't," Jools said. "I hated gymnastics in high school. But that was then, this is now."

"How did you know all that was possible?" Miranda asked.

"I didn't. When I took the first jump, I was hoping I could fly. But then the moves came so naturally . . ." Jools shrugged. "Automatic processing in the brain. Something inside me knew what I could do and how to do it."

I hadn't seen her glow green at any point during her moves. Did that mean she wasn't using superpowers? The tricks Jools had done weren't superhuman—as she said, they were pure Jackie Chan. But Jackie carefully choreographed his stunts, with prearranged props and rehearsals. He also got multiple takes. Jools had just winged it.

"Jools," I said, "what's the fine structure constant of the universe?"

"7.29735257 times 10^{-3}. Approximately."

This time she glowed. Interesting.

Miranda muttered, "I want to edit that number on Wikipedia, then ask the question again."

"WHAT ELSE CAN YOU DO?" SHAR ASKED

"You name it," Jools said. "I feel so damned strong and clearheaded. Not super-*duper* strong—I don't think I'm off the charts. But human-max in everything. I could win Olympic gold in weight lifting, sprinting, fencing . . . even that weird thing with the skiing and the guns. And chess. And violin. And car repair. Hey, I think I can finally knit!" She grinned. "I am so going to rule League of Legends."

Richard grumbled, "I'm not following any of this."

"We're Sparks now," Shar told him.

"We are?"

"Well, *we* are," Shar said. "Not you, sweet."

"Why not?"

"We had an origin," Miranda said. "In that lab. We were exposed to"—she raised her fingers and made air quotes—"'otherworldly forces.'" She grimaced. "Is anyone else embarrassed to become super from something so dumb?"

Richard said, "You're Sparks and I'm not? That sucks!"

Shar patted his arm. "If you're careless, maybe you'll have a lab accident of your own someday."

"I've had plenty of lab accidents. Just not the good kind."

"Blah blah blah," Jools said. "Aren't you guys going to check what you can—"

My superpowered sight caught movement at the mouth of the alley: the barrel of a weapon poking around the corner.

"Gun!" I shouted, and threw myself behind the van.

MIRANDA INSTANTLY SURROUNDED HERSELF WITH A GOLDEN BALL OF LIGHT

The ball seemed perfectly spherical, with a handsbreadth of clearance above Miranda's head and below her feet. So yes, her feet were off the ground, lifted above the pavement.

Shar also sprouted an aura. Instead of gold it was violet, and instead of being a sphere it was more like a suit of armor: only as wide as my thumb and tailored to Shar's body. It moved when she did.

I thought, *Two different types of force field.* I wondered if I had one myself. Nothing had flicked on around me, so it didn't seem likely.

Jools had jumped off the roof as soon as I yelled. Now she hit the asphalt with a breakfall roll that brought her up to her feet right beside me. We both crouched behind the van.

Richard, with mere human reflexes, just said, "What?" Then, "Oww." A feathered dart hit his thigh, piercing his jeans and burying itself in his leg. He reached down and pulled it out. "What the . . ."

His face went slack. He crumpled to the ground.

I SHIFTED MY VIEWPOINT OUT OF MY BODY . . .

Wait. Clarification.

I've talked about out-of-body experiences, but that's too mystical. I'd become a Spark, and Sparks are creatures of science. Call it weird science or pseudoscience, but it's the absolute opposite of magic: the counterweight on the reverse end of the balance.

So when my viewpoint leaves my body, it's not astral projection. It's remote sensing. No different than seeing through the lens of a distant camera.

Except my camera transmits its images telepathically instead of by electronics.

And the picture is a full 360 degrees.

As bright as day, even in the absence of light.

And the camera doesn't really exist.

But apart from that, there's nothing weird about how I see. Just imagine I have detachable virtual eyes: Spark-o-Vision.

I LOBBED MY VIRTUAL EYES TO THE END OF THE ALLEY SO I COULD SEE AROUND THE CORNER

Three Darklings lurked out of sight: a skeleton in a powder blue tracksuit; a were-bat in feroform, wearing nothing but urban-camo jeans; and Lilith, the vampire who had once barged into the wrong Midwestern roadhouse.

Uh-oh.

I KNEW IT WAS LILITH BECAUSE I'D MET HER ONCE IN PERSON

She'd attended a party at the Vandermeers'. That's when I heard the story of Lilith in the roadhouse. Nicholas's brother, Derek, told me the tale. Lilith was a celebrity in the Darkling world, and Derek wanted me to be impressed.

He even introduced me to her. I don't know why; from the look on her face, I could tell she considered me just another dispensable blood-cow. When Derek introduced me, Lilith barely glanced in my direction.

But I took a long look at her. Derek said she hadn't changed a bit since that night in the roadhouse: young and surgically beautiful, with her hair in dozens of colors.

Even Kimmi felt Lilith's allure. But Kimmi also wanted to scream and run and hide. Lilith's Shadow projected a chill that stood out even in a room full of Darklings. Nicholas told me later that he felt it as strongly as I did. He'd lived around Darklings all his life, but back then, he was still human and Lilith scared him shitless. His hand trembled on the controls of his chair, and he nearly drove over someone in his haste to get away.

We fled to his room. He was under orders to stay at the party, but he disobeyed and left. Very softly, whispering even though we were alone, he said, "There's something very wrong with her. The others can't feel it—they're Darklings themselves. But I think Lilith is abyssing."

DARKLINGS ARE POTENTIALLY IMMORTAL

They don't age, they don't get sick, and they can heal from almost any damage. Only beheading, incineration, and other such trauma will kill them (although specific Darklings may have quirky vulnerabilities, like certain werewolves and their problem with silver).

In practice, though, Darklings don't live forever. They may live a very long time, but sooner or later, they "abyss": go bestial, catatonic, or delusional, sometimes turning so monstrous that they commit atrocities in front of non-Darkling witnesses.

Usually, the decline is a slow progression. First, little slips of the tongue (saying "cattle" instead of "people"). Then, carelessness in hiding inhuman behavior (not making enough effort to conceal bloodstains on one's clothing). Then, a genuine inability to understand how normal people live (offering raw deer intestines as a tip to a bellboy). One way or another, Darklings lose touch or control.

Of course, they all believe they're too strong to succumb—that's why people continue to pay for the Dark Conversion despite the potential downside. And the Elders of the Dark are living proof that

Darklings can live for centuries without losing their minds. Even so, every year a handful of Darklings abandon all sense of restraint.

When that happens, the Elders protect the Dark's reputation by whatever means necessary: reeducation, punishment, or worse. Particularly serious problems are resolved with quiet finality by a group called the Dark Guard.

Because if the Dark doesn't handle their own rabid dogs, the Light forcefully takes up the slack.

NICHOLAS HAD BEEN AFRAID LILITH WAS PLUNGING INTO THE ABYSS

Her Shadow was hyperprojecting, even at a social event. It seemed she was burning out.

Three years had passed since then, and Lilith was still alive—as alive as a vampire can be. That was surprising. Also surprising that she'd turned up at the University of Waterloo.

With a tranquilizer rifle in her hands.

Which she'd fired at Richard without warning.

And which she was hastily reloading.

BUT I SMILED

Lilith had targeted Richard first. I supposed since he was a guy, Lilith considered him the biggest threat.

Let this be a lesson about gender assumptions.

I LOOKED MORE CLOSELY AT LILITH'S COMPANIONS

The skeleton in the tracksuit seemed nothing but bones. He'd left his jacket unzipped so we'd be in no doubt: no flesh on his ribs, no organs in his chest. Only ligaments held him together—ligaments and magic. I assumed he had demonic powers, but I couldn't guess what they were. Mythology and folklore are full of bone demons, all with different ways to do you harm. Besides, Mr. Skinless might not match any historic precedents; many Darkling demons are brand-new one-offs.

The demon's face was covered with mud: a pale clay caked on his bones and smeared over his nose hole to close the gap. His mouth and eye sockets were highlighted with thick black circles. I couldn't tell if he'd put them on as war paint, or if the mud and the circles were a permanent part of him. He'd drawn a swastika on his forehead with red lipstick, and it seemed to glow, but maybe that was only a trick of my Spark-o-Vision.

The were-bat was like any other you've seen: huge leathery wings, a furry body, and a face only a chiropterologist could love. When I say "bat," you might be picturing something small. Nuh-uh. Imagine a grizzly bear with wings. Wicked claws. Sharp teeth. But somehow as light as a bird, hopping airily up and down in anticipation of carnage.

Lastly, Lilith, a vampire. She wasn't as brutally frightening as I remembered from the party, but I put that down to my newfound status as a Spark. The Light confers resistance to a Darkling's Shadow; Sparks aren't completely immune to Shadow influence, but we're far less susceptible than normal humans.

So I could look at Lilith without cringing. Even so, what I saw made me wince. Her incisors had grown long enough to protrude over her lower lip.

Your world may not have vampires—at least not out in the open—so maybe you're fang-naive. Most of the time, vamp teeth look normal, but when vampires are aroused, they get a fang-on.

Yeah. Ew.

It isn't just when a vampire craves blood: The fangs come jutting out at any sight of cruelty. Even worse, vampires don't feel sheepish when it happens. One of Nicholas's cousins told me, "Kimmi, everyone feels the same. Human, vampire, whoever. Everybody gets turned on when someone else takes a hit. They're down and you're not, which means you're ahead. Everyone gets off on the thrill. With us, it just shows."

That's how the Dark think. On one hand, they're certain they're special. On the other, they believe that secretly, everyone feels the same ugly urges they do. "We're not different, just more up-front. That makes us better."

I SAW ONE LAST THING: LILITH'S TRANQ GUN

I have experience with tranquilizer rifles. Since my father worked for Banff National Park, I hung around the park HQ. The rangers showed me the tranq rifles they used when bears wouldn't stay out of town. I wasn't allowed to fire the guns, but I was shown how they worked and was taught the dos and don'ts.

Naturally, I asked what would happen if you tranqed a human. The rangers joked about shooting idiot tourists, but then answered my question seriously. "Kimberley, people vary a lot in sensitivity to sedatives. A dose that barely slows one person down might kill somebody else." So darting Richard was reckless. Even now, he might be overdosing.

That's what Kimberley learned from the rangers. Years later, Kimmi learned more about tranq guns from Derek Vandermeer. What he told me had more bearing on Lilith.

Why would a vampire own a tranq gun? To hunt humans for blood. Vamps tranq the homeless in alleys, or shoot people walking alone. Attacking hand to hand is dangerous, if only because a vampire might get caught up in the moment and rip out someone's throat. Tranqing a victim keeps the situation controlled, and you still get a thrill from the hunt.

Best of all, you don't have to pay for the drink. You'd be amazed how Darklings resent paying trickle-down. "Why should I give my hard-earned cash to filthy parasites? Those deadbeats don't have to work to make blood: Blood just happens, even to the laziest human alive."

Paying for blood was rewarding indolence. It wasn't about the money, it was the principle of the thing.

"HEY!" MIRANDA SHOUTED

"What the hell do you think you're doing?"

Lilith heard the shout and looked up from loading the rifle. The were-bat took an eager step forward; with the lift from his wings, he bounced as if he were walking on a trampoline. The skeleton laced his fingers and stretched, as if cracking his knuckles before getting down to work.

"Answer me!" Miranda said. She couldn't see the Darklings because they were still around the corner. "Who are you and what do you want?"

"There's no point explaining," Lilith called back. "Shut up and let us finish."

"You want to dart us all?" Miranda asked.

"That's the plan," Lilith said.

"Get a Plan B."

"Got one," Lilith said. She turned her eyes toward the skeleton and the were-bat. The skeleton gave a Jolly Roger grin. The were-bat flexed his claws. "But," Lilith told Miranda, "you'll wish you'd stayed with Plan A."

SOMETHING FLUTTERED AGAINST MY HEAD

Like being brushed by a moth. My Spark-o-Vision snapped back from around the corner to home base, where a tendril of violet had just penetrated my skull.

I tried to jerk away. More violet strands appeared, reaching out from Shar's forehead, holding my head like being clamped in an MRI machine.

"Don't fight," Shar said. "Go back to watching the Darklings. I want to see."

"Darklings?" Miranda said. "We're being attacked by Darklings?"

"Shh!" Shar said. "I'm trying to concentrate. Kim, would you please stop resisting?"

I couldn't have stopped struggling even if I'd wanted. Claustrophobia: that judo-hold panic I'd felt with Hannah. I threw myself at Shar, ready to scratch, bite, and gouge, but that violet shell surrounded her and my fingernails skittered off like scraping on steel.

"Stop it!" Shar snapped.

A blob of violet came gulping down the tendril that connected her head to mine, like an embolism squeezing through an artery. When it reached me, I could feel it injected into my brain . . .

Then I went dead.

IMAGINE WHAT IT'S LIKE TO HAVE NO EMOTIONS

Peaceful? No.

Numb? Getting closer.

Violated? Oh, yes. But with your emotions dead, it's not an outrage, it's just an adverse position in game theory.

The game theory response: retribution. Possible strategies: anything, no matter how extreme. My first move should obviously be to stomp Richard in the throat and crush his windpipe. If Shar's force field prevented a direct assault, I'd have to hurt her indirectly.

I took a step in Richard's direction. I stopped when Miranda yelled, "Gun!"

LILITH HAD FINISHED RELOADING

She'd thrust the muzzle of the rifle around the corner again. She fired almost immediately, perhaps hoping we wouldn't have time to react.

That was a miscalculation. The moment the dart left the rifle, a strand of violet snatched it from the air. The strand reversed the dart and slammed it hard into Lilith's leg, exactly where the first dart had hit Richard.

Shar was Buddhist. She believed in karma.

LILITH WASN'T THE ONLY ONE WHO'D MISCALCULATED

Shar had split her powers between her force field, her suppression of my emotions, and her trick catching the dart. She was new to being super and had spread her strength too thin. Her grip on my brain weakened and a flicker of anger managed to rise inside me. I dispassionately fed that anger with all the energy I had.

It was like trying to lift something far too heavy, but I fought with all my strength. Something broke—I actually heard a crack.

Like an earthquake fault slipping when the pressure becomes too great, my emotions surged back with a lurch.

Shar slumped to the ground, unconscious.

I NEARLY KICKED SHAR IN THE HEAD

She was down. She was helpless. I wanted to hurt her so badly.

But I remembered how matter-of-factly I had planned to kill Richard. Was that really who I was underneath everything else?

Vomit stung my throat. Horror at myself replaced my fury at Shar. I wanted to crawl into a hole . . . to completely shrink out of the world . . .

When you're a brand-new Spark, be careful what you wish for.

I SHRANK TO THE SIZE OF A HOUSEFLY

That horror and self-loathing? It popped like a bubble.

A boggled mind can only hold so much.

THERE ARE TWO WAYS TO LOOK AT WHAT HAPPENED

(I've thought about this a lot.)

Maybe I was destined to be a shrinker from the moment the Light entered me. Maybe wanting to shrink from the world triggered a power I already had.

But maybe my thought about shrinking determined what my power would be. Sparks are apparently malleable after they're imbued by the Light; for a while, internal and external conditions can influence the final result. If I'd thought, "I want to disappear," perhaps I would have become invisible. "I want to run away" might have turned me into a speedster, able to run as fast as lightning.

I've learned a lot about the Light since becoming a Spark, but I still don't know why our powers take the shape they do. It isn't totally random: You'll soon see what happened to Miranda. But if I were tall instead of short, would I be able to grow ten stories high instead of shrinking down to nothing?

I don't know. But temperamentally, I'm not suited to be a giant. I'm low profile, not "Hey, look at me."

Character is destiny, and the Light multiplies that by a billion.

MY SPARK-O-VISION CHANGED SCALE WHEN I DID

The pavement around me previously seemed smooth. Now, it was as craggy as a rockslide, with huge fissures between lumps of black asphalt. The minivan towered above me, as tall as the walls of a canyon. The buildings were distant mountains, far off but enormous.

Jools was beyond a colossus. She'd been standing right next to me, taking cover behind the van. Now, her leg was a skyscraper; I was shorter even than the sole of her sandal. If Jools took a step in my direction, she'd squash me so flat I wouldn't leave a smudge.

On the plus side, my clothes had shrunk too. I wasn't standing naked under a heap of empty overalls while trapped at the bottom of a hiking boot.

You might ask, was I seriously worried about nudity *when I had shrunk to the size of a bug?*

Yes. I was a science student, and I knew I was far below the minimum size where warm-blooded creatures can survive. The smaller you are, the greater your surface area relative to your volume. The higher that ratio, the more heat you lose to cold air. The smallest mammal is the bumblebee bat, about three centimeters long; any smaller and mammals can't sustain their body heat, even in the tropics.

I was half a centimeter tall, and Waterloo wasn't close to the equator. Even with clothes on, I'd likely die of hypothermia.

But at least I wouldn't die in the buff. Em-bare-ass-ing.

I DIDN'T KNOW HOW LONG BEFORE I FROZE

But if Jools so much as shuffled her feet, the cold would become irrelevant. I had to scurry someplace I wouldn't get stepped on, and the obvious refuge was under the van.

I tried to bolt to safety. I took a single running step.

HERE'S WHAT I DISCOVERED ON THAT VERY FIRST STEP

No matter how small I shrink, I'm as strong as normal.

Don't try to invent a scientific rationale—you'll only hurt your brain. Just smile and nod. "Yes, Kim, whatever you say." Because it's true.

I weighed less than a gram. My urgent running step was powered by leg muscles that usually propelled a hundred thousand times more mass.

I shot up like a rocket. That's not a figure of speech. I launched off the ground with a *stupid* amount of thrust. By the time air resistance stopped me, I was high above the alley, with a bird's-eye view of the scene. My vision was still scaled to the size of an insect, so it seemed as if I were up at an airplane's cruising altitude.

I was, of course, falling . . . but just barely. I was almost as light as a feather, so the breeze buoyed me up. Eventually I'd settle to the ground like a snowflake. For the moment, however, I floated, gazing down on the action below.

AROUND THE CORNER, LILITH LOOKED PISSED OFF

The dart in her leg didn't faze her. A single dose of tranq juice couldn't possibly knock out a Darkling. Besides, vampire blood doesn't circulate—vampire hearts don't beat. So the sedative from the dart would mostly stay at the site of injection. It would take many hours to diffuse through the rest of her body and have any tranquilizing effect.

Lilith gestured to the were-bat and skeleton. "Go."

THE WERE-BAT TOOK TO THE AIR

With a single flap of his wings, he rounded the corner. As far as he knew, he'd been out of sight until this moment, so he paused in the alley's mouth, his wings spread wide, deliberately casting an intimidating silhouette. To add to the effect, he pumped power into his Shadow and loosed a screech like a hawk that needed oiling.

Miranda rolled her eyes. She turned off her force field, lifted her hand, and made a "bring it on" gesture.

The bat plunged forward. With his wings outspread, he could barely fit into the narrow alley, but that didn't slow him down. He dived headfirst at Miranda; his open mouth showed dozens of sharp white teeth. He looked more shark than bat. For all I knew, he could sprout additional fangs on demand—some were-beasts have tricks like that. They seem like simple maulers, only able to bite and scratch, but then they sneak out a magic power that takes you by surprise. Breathing fire, teleportation, nasty impossible stunts.

But this bat was going straight aggro, aiming to chomp Miranda's face. She waited until he reached point-blank range. Then she opened her mouth and sang.

THE NOTE SHE SANG WAS A CONE OF GOLDEN LIGHT

It emerged from Miranda's mouth as bright as molten metal. It shot straight into the bat's face.

The force of the sound wave crumpled the bat's snout and flattened his huge pointed ears back against his skull. Such a focused sonic blast would have hurt almost anything, but a keen-eared, light-boned bat had to be categorized under "Targets: Ideal." Its fur nearly peeled back from its face.

The bat's nosedive was stopped by the sonic hammerblow. Before the bat could bounce backward, Miranda moved shockingly fast and grabbed the Darkling by the fur under his jaw. She heaved him up and over her head, sending him crashing into the van behind her.

By then, Jools was in position to take over. She caught one of the bat's legs in both her hands, and swung. The Darkling's wings provided some drag, but Jools still slammed the bat downward into a face-plant on the pavement. The resulting crunch should have been sickening; really, it should have been. But I didn't have time to think about my delight at the sound of a guy being hurt, because suddenly, I was struck by a *boom* of thunder.

It was the backwash of Miranda's blast echoing off nearby buildings. Think about that for a moment: In the time it took for a wave of sound to travel a few dozen meters, both Miranda and Jools had pounded on the bat. Super-fights happen *fast*—much faster than I can describe them. Also note that my own speed of mind was fast enough to watch what my super-roommates did and to analyze each movement.

But that clarity vanished when the thunder banged into me. The shock wave tossed my featherlight body head over heels.

IT TOOK SEVERAL SECONDS FOR ME TO STABILIZE

Air resistance finally stopped me. By then, the bat lay unmoving on the asphalt.

Were-beasts can recover inhumanly fast, but at least we'd proved we had game. The remaining Darklings weren't blind to the fact. They'd stayed back around the corner and didn't have a good view, but they couldn't miss the thunder of the sonic blast.

"Sparks," Lilith hissed. "You're Ssssparkssss."

"Sssurprissse," Miranda said.

JOOLS CROUCHED OVER THE WERE-BAT

Maybe Jools was checking the bat's health. Still breathing? Not bleeding too much? But more likely, she was determining whether to whack him a bunch more times to make sure he was out.

She didn't have the chance. Without warning, the skeleton demon appeared out of nowhere behind her back.

I THINK HE WAS SHADOW-WALKING

You might have heard of the trick: Step into a shadow here, step out of a shadow there. I'd known several Darklings with that power. Since shadows didn't show up in my Spark-o-Vision, I can't be sure of what Skinless actually did, but let's say he entered the darkness back where he was, then emerged from the shadows cast by the van.

He was quiet and quick. No sooner had he arrived than he jumped onto Jools's back and wrapped his hands around her throat. Then he started to cackle: a high-pitched eerie laughter that gave me goosebumps. His laughter went on and on, without pausing for breath, as it echoed off the walls of the alley. The skeleton began to glow with a dull gray light, the same shade as his dirty bones.

Jools reacted immediately. She grabbed the hands around her neck, trying to pry off his bony fingers. It didn't work; either Skinless was too strong or Jools couldn't get a decent grip. When she realized she wasn't making headway, she turned her back to the van and thrust hard backward.

The skeleton smashed into the van with a sound like wooden wind chimes meeting a fender bender. The impact left a dent in the van's rear panel, but the demon's cackling only got louder. Skinless seemed amused by Jools's attempts to hurt him. She turned and ran backward, crashing the Darkling full speed into the alley's brick wall. The collision had no effect: no break in the cackling, no break in the choke hold.

JOOLS KEPT BASHING THE DEMON INTO THE WALL

But a memory sparked in my brain. My Grandpa Tang collects Chinese prints—everything from views of a single budding branch to village scenes full of visual jokes. My favorites were always the monsters: the ghosts, the hopping vampires, the crazy-eyed demons. When I was little, I could stare at those for hours. (I know where Kimmi got her thing for Darklings.)

I remembered a woodcut of a corpse riding a man in exactly the same pose as Skinless on Jools: piggyback, with skeletal hands on the victim's throat. Grandpa Tang gleefully translated the picture's caption for me. "Once the nightmare fixes its grip on a victim's neck, no strength under heaven can make it let go."

THE FIRST LAW OF DARK AND LIGHT SAYS NO POWER IS UNBEATABLE

No attack gets through every defense; no defense withstands every type of attack. The law applies equally to magic and super-science. It doesn't mean that every power has a tricky weakness—sometimes the defense against an attack is just a whole lot of armor. But the law guarantees that nothing is 100 percent unstoppable.

On the other hand, some powers *are* invincible in narrow contexts. Bogeymen simply can't be seen when looked at directly. Antaei can never be defeated as long as they stay in contact with bare earth.

These are magical trump cards that Darklings possess in special circumstances. Such powers don't violate the law, because there are obvious ways to beat them. Look at the bogeyman in a mirror. Lift an Antaeus off the ground. Mythic powers inevitably come with mythic vulnerabilities; exploit the vulnerability, and you win.

So what was the defense against strangler demons? "Simple," Grandpa Tang told me. "They flee at the sound of sacred gongs."

That was a slam dunk in ancient China, but since the UW campus didn't have any Taoist temples, Jools was in trouble. As long as Skinless was locked on her back (hands on her throat, legs around her waist) she absolutely couldn't throw him off.

Jools needed help. Miranda could give it. She moved toward the demon and opened her mouth, obviously intending to belt out another sonic blast. Jools was thrashing too much to allow a clear shot, but Miranda shouted, "Stand still, damn it!"

Easier said than done. Jools was having a Hannah moment: struggling for air and freedom. Me, I'd be so crazed, I wouldn't be able to think. Jools had more presence of mind. She began to slow down . . . but then the issue became moot.

Lilith flared with blood-colored light and pointed at Miranda. "KNEEL!"

IT WAS THE VOICE

The Voice: a power of magical command with which vampires dominate other creatures. It's mind rape, pure and simple. It's also illegal as hell, not just by human laws, but by Darkling ones too. In 1994, three Elders of the Dark swore in a binding public statement that the power would never be abused. Any vampire caught using the Voice had to face an open tribunal; if they couldn't justify themselves, they'd be executed.

Then Sparks arrived in 2001. In an equally binding statement, the Elders swore that while Voicing a Human or Darkling was still totally out, heads wouldn't roll if you Voiced a Spark.

Still, most fights don't reach the point where the Voice comes out of its holster. The Light and the Dark get into punch-ups all the time, but only on the level of bar brawls, not open attempts at murder. It's like rival sports fans smacking each other under the bleachers: Fists are fair game but weapons aren't.

Using the Voice means *shit just got real*.

"KNEEL!" LILITH COMMANDED

The word exploded from Lilith's mouth as a fountain of bloodred light. Until that moment, I'd imagined the Voice as merely verbal. Spark-o-Vision let me see the magic behind it: a hyper-powerful Submission spell. The spoken word was merely the trigger, like saying, "Abracadabra." The Voice's real power lay in the ensuing bolt of arcane energy. It spiked into the victim and crushed the person's will.

Lilith's bolt sped toward Miranda as fast as an arrow. But the word had been spoken first—the "KNEEL!" that pulled the trigger. In the fraction of a second between hearing that word and the arrival of the magic, Miranda's ungodly fast reflexes let her throw up her force field.

The protective golden sphere inflated around her with the speed of a car's airbag. When the red bolt struck, the sphere shuddered. Flecks of crimson splattered across the sphere's exterior like blood marks on an egg yolk. The ball stayed intact, but so did the flecks: permanent points of corruption in the golden surface, like acid burns on skin.

Miranda inhaled sharply, as if she'd felt pain from the bloody splash. She raised her head to retaliate, but Lilith was already shouting another "KNEEL!" A new red bolt flew out of Lilith's mouth, hammering once more against Miranda's force field. More red splashed across the gold, like mud beginning to cover a windshield.

Miranda sucked in her breath; she was hurting. Again, Lilith ordered, "KNEEL!"

MIRANDA WAS ON PURE DEFENSE; JOOLS WAS CHOKING; SHAR AND RICHARD WERE UNCONSCIOUS

Me? I drifted above the fray.

All right, Kim, enough avoidance. Get down there.

I unzipped my hoodie and grabbed its bottom hem with both hands. I raised my arms and flapped. The coat caught the air and gave me a serious forward push.

As light as a fly, as strong as a human. What does F=ma tell us? Huge force and tiny mass means *insane* acceleration, even if my "wingspan" was minuscule.

Zoom.

NEITHER COATTAILS NOR THE HUMAN BODY ARE DESIGNED FOR AERONAUTIC PRECISION

My first stroke sent me veering toward the nearest building. If air resistance hadn't slowed me down, I would have smacked into the brick wall. But my mass was so negligible, the air drag braked me like an anchor. Imagine throwing a feather: It leaves your hand at high speed, but stops in a fraction of a second. I wasn't as fluffy as a feather, so I traveled several meters before I stopped. Still, air resistance was my friend, ensuring that one bad flap didn't send me shooting for miles.

My next flap was better aimed. Thanks to that old "automatic processing in the brain," a single flap was enough to make me an ace.

How amazing is that? How suspiciously unbelievable. But at the time, I didn't question it.

The super-dog who didn't bark.

WHO TO SAVE FIRST?

Jools seemed the closest to dying. But how could I save her?

The jacket of the skeleton's tracksuit waved in the breeze, exposing his rib cage. Easy enough to fly between his ribs and into his chest. Once inside, I could revert to normal size, at which point one of two things would happen: Either his bones would be too strong for me to break, and I'd be squeezed out between the ribs like a hard-boiled egg through an egg slicer; or else I'd rupture Mr. Skinless's thoracic cavity into a million pieces and kill him.

I'D KNOWN DEMONS; I'D TALKED WITH THEM; I'D DANCED WITH THEM

I didn't know Skinless, but still. He was an intelligent being who once had been human. True, he was trying to kill Jools; but surely I could cool off a jerkwad dudebro without actually murdering him.

I got an idea.

ONE FLAP OF MY COATTAILS TOOK ME DOWN TO ALLEY LEVEL

Jools was still on her feet, but her thrashing and bashing Skinless against the wall had slowed to a dizzy reel. The demon never stopped cackling—it was obviously part of his demon shtick. That meant that his mouth was wide open. Another flap and I flew inside.

I came to a stop against a molar. With that as a point of comparison, I could see I was now the size of a fingernail clipping—much smaller than before. How did that happen? And when? I must have done it instinctively: maybe to lighten myself on the wind, maybe to fit into Skinless's mouth. One way or another, it meant I wasn't just stuck with two settings, housefly-size and normal. I could vary my height as need be.

I pictured growing to thumbnail size and it happened, no fuss, no bother. I adjusted my height so I straddled the molar: one foot on either side as I stood on the adjacent teeth. I squatted like a weight-lifter preparing to pick up a barbell. It brought to mind the only time I'd let Shar talk me into going to the gym. (Cookies had been involved.) I'd been so pathetic, I could barely pick up the barbell's bar, never mind adding extra weights. I *hate* being bad at anything, and I was certain all the jocks were looking at me disdainfully. Which I also hate.

All that hate came back to my mind as I squatted above the tooth. My anger made my adrenaline surge. I dug my fingers under the tooth's body and heaved with all my strength.

My normal human strength.

Focused on a single molar.

Which wasn't firmly rooted, because skeletons don't have gums.

I reefed out that molar like plucking a daisy with a steam shovel.

The tooth left its socket so easily, it took me by surprise. I fell backward and lost my grip; the tooth flew out of my hands and hurtled toward the roof of the mouth. The tooth hit Skinless's hard palate and kept going, embedding itself deeply. When it finally came to rest, its roots dangled down like a pair of white stalactites.

SKINLESS HOWLED

Instinctively, he raised a hand to his jaw in the classic "I've got a toothache" position.

Bzzzt. Wrong. The demon's "you can't dislodge me" magic only worked as long as he kept both hands on the victim's throat.

Jools must have heard the skeleton's cackling change to a howl. She retained enough strength for one last move: She leapt and came down back-first on the pavement, with Skinless between her and the asphalt. A classic wrestling slam, with the demon's head hitting the pavement first, and Jools's whole weight landing on top of it.

The crunch of bone must have been gruesome. I wasn't paying attention—Jools's move sent me caroming inside the demon's head like a pinball. *Zing-zing-zing* off the skull bones, then I shot out some orifice; I think it was an earhole but I was too dizzy to be sure. By the time my senses cleared, both Jools and the demon were sprawled unmoving.

The skeleton's skull was starred with cracks, like a windshield struck by a rock. To a mortal, such damage would be fatal; to a Darkling, likely not. As I've said, if attacks don't kill Darklings outright, they can usually recover. It might take weeks or months, but Skinless would eventually bounce back as good as new.

With Jools, I couldn't tell. Her neck was badly bruised from the choking, and she wasn't breathing. I shifted my vision inside her throat and saw that her windpipe was crushed. The damage was so bad I could instantly discern it. That meant it was god-awful, because my knowledge of anatomy was woeful. (I'm a geologist, okay? I do rocks, not icky squishy organisms.)

I didn't have a clue how to help Jools survive. Fly into her throat? Reestablish the airway by pushing through the ruins of her esophagus? Or perhaps I could perform a tracheotomy, punching through her neck below the wreckage and making a hole Jools could breathe through.

What if I did it wrong? What if I killed her?

This was crazy. I had superpowers. Why was I so useless?

JOOLS FLARED WITH A BRILLIANT GREEN LIGHT, LIKE A FIREWORK IGNITING IN HER THROAT

She took a shuddering breath. The air rasped in her throat, barely getting through because the passage was still blocked by windpipe debris. The green light flared again, and the next breath sounded clearer.

I sighed with relief. High-speed regeneration. Some Darklings could heal that quickly, but the power was rare—maybe one Darkling in a thousand. In Sparks, I didn't know the percentages. Kimmi had read voraciously about the Dark, but never felt the tiniest interest in the Light.

Kimmi, you were a dumbass. In more ways than one.

But Jools would be okay. She seemed deeply unconscious—maybe her healing didn't work if she was awake—but she wouldn't die.

Okay. Deep breath. Time to deal with Lilith.

I HADN'T BEEN BLIND TO THE FIGHT BETWEEN LILITH AND MIRANDA

My 360-degree vision continuously takes in everything around me. However, I can focus my attention selectively, and I'd been centered on Jools. Now I shifted to Miranda and Lilith, to see how their duel was going.

Not well. Lilith's Voice had spewed bloodred corruption over almost all of Miranda's force field; only tiny patches of gold remained. I could guess what would happen when the last patch vanished. Miranda was already doubled over, as if the weight of Lilith's "KNEEL!" was forcing her to her knees.

"KNEEL!"

"KNEEL!"

"KNEEL!"

The Voice kept lashing out, one Submission spell after another. Each spell required mystic energy to fuel it; Lilith was burning her reserves at a terrible rate. Yet she didn't seem to be tiring.

How had she amassed such a huge store of magic? Back in the roadhouse, she'd been nothing special. Darklings grow stronger with age, but that takes decades, even centuries. They can take shortcuts, but the means are forbidden: pacts with unearthly beings or stealing life force from fellow Darklings. Increases in strength can only be bought at great cost—loss of sanity, coherence, control.

No wonder Lilith was abyssing. I flapped my coattails and flew toward her.

SHOULD I PULL ANOTHER TOOTH?

That would require entering Lilith's mouth, which meant exposing myself to the red bolts of magic shot by her Voice.

No way.

Where to attack instead? Her eyes? Ew. Lilith might be lethally insane, but I couldn't stomach the thought of gouging her eyeballs.

What else?

I CIRCLED TO THE SIDE OF LILITH'S HEAD

I shrank as small as the point of a pin, and flew straight down her left ear canal.

If you're a poet and you need a symbol for thick, creepy darkness, you could do worse than a vampire's ear canal at midnight on the winter solstice. But with Spark-o-Vision, I saw the place lit as brightly as a gym. Lilith's eardrum was a huge climbing wall just waiting to be conquered.

YOU HEAR "EARDRUM" AND PICTURE A TAUT FLAT SURFACE, LIKE A KETTLEDRUM

No. I was looking straight at the eardrum, and it was much more complicated. The top third was thin and pinkish; the rest was thicker and grayer, with a toothpicky bone down the middle. Spark-o-Vision told me the bone was attached to other teeny bones deeper in the ear. The "drum" part caught vibrations and transferred them to the toothpick, which sent the vibes down the chain until they reached the auditory nerve.

So the toothpick bone had KICK ME written all over it.

I GREW A FEW ORDERS OF MAGNITUDE

I ended up lying on the floor of the canal, propped up on my elbows. And yes, I got earwax all over my pants and hoodie. Vampire earwax. One of my first accomplishments as a Spark: getting waterproofed by undead dubbin.

I felt Lilith's head shift. She must have sensed me like something stuck in her ear. But the feeling wasn't enough to stop her using the Voice; further distraction was required. I figured slamming my boots on that bony toothpick would do the job.

I was not wrong.

I STOMPED BOTH FEET AS HARD AS I COULD INTO THAT FLIMSY LITTLE BONE

I still hadn't gotten my head around the concept of "normal human strength in an eeny-weeny package."

WE GEOLOGISTS KNOW ABOUT STRESS

Shear stress, normal stress, tectonic stress—the pushes and pulls that turn flat beds of rock into bizarrely tilted folds.

Stress isn't just force, it's force divided by area. If you press your hand against a wall, not much happens. If you press a thumbtack against the wall, the same force gets focused on the tack's tiny point. Result? The tack pierces the wall.

Result of kicking the toothpick? Pretty much the same. The bone snapped like dry spaghetti, and my feet burst through the eardrum.

For a moment I lay there, gooey with earwax, my legs dangling out the other side of the drum.

Then Lilith gasped in agony.

GASPS ARE SHARP INHALATIONS

And there's a channel called the eustachian tube, connecting the esophagus to the inner ear. When you sneeze, you feel the pressure from your lungs push against the inside of your eardrums. If you inhale sharply, it creates a suction in the same region. When there happens to be a featherlight object in the vicinity . . .

Yeah. I was sucked feetfirst through the hole in the eardrum and down into Lilith's throat.

I SAW BLOODRED LIGHT BENEATH ME

I was heading for Lilith's larynx—the source of those awful red bolts that were battering Miranda. It looked like a chamber of magma, and me, I was barreling down into the volcano.

Luckily, the red light was only afterglow. Lilith was no longer shouting, "KNEEL!" She was screeching, "Ow, Jesus, fuck!" and clutching her ear.

The air power of her screech sent me shooting back up her throat. Then she sucked in another breath. More cursing, more gasps. I tumbled ass over teakettle up and down her windpipe, caught in the hurricane from her lungs.

Instinctively, I tried to stop myself. I grabbed at her windpipe's wall as I caromed off. But stress is force over area, and my fingers were thumbtack points. As I dug them into Lilith's flesh, I simply gouged out fistfuls of esophagus, like filling my hands with hamburger. At least it wasn't bloody—most vampire tissues have no blood. But bone-dry burger is its own kind of gross.

Apparently, Lilith could feel the damage. I imagine a hot tearing rasp in her throat.

She coughed hard. Up I came on a bronchial gale.

I WAS SPAT OUT LIKE AN ANCHOVY ON A WAVE OF SALIVA, MUCUS, AND YOU-REALLY-DON'T-WANT-TO-KNOW-WHAT-ELSE-IS-IN-A-VAMPIRE'S-THROAT

As usual, air resistance slowed me, but I still shot a heroic distance out of Lilith's mouth, thanks to the supernatural strength of her lungs.

That worked out well. I was clear of the blast zone when Miranda finally returned fire.

A VOLLEY OF GOLDEN SOUND THUNDERED OUT OF MIRANDA'S MOUTH
Quite the night for oral emissions.

Miranda sang an angry boom that knocked Lilith clean off her feet. Lilith hit the pavement ass-first and slid scraping backward for several meters. It must have given her a major case of road rash.

I flapped away hard, expecting more fireworks. They didn't arrive. Lilith lay on her back, eyes open but body unmoving. Miranda had doubled over, hands on her knees and panting heavily. Her blood-pocked force field was gone; she must have put every drop of her power into that single thunderous shot. Now, she had no strength to deliver a coup de grâce.

Still panting, Miranda said, "Can we . . . stop fighting . . . now? Maybe just . . . talk?"

"No," Lilith replied. Her voice was a whisper—I must have damaged her throat. I felt guilty, but also relieved: She couldn't use the Voice again. The Voice might be a spell rather than a sound, but magic is bound by rules. If Lilith's physical voice stopped working, so did her magical one.

Or so I hoped. And so it seemed.

But Lilith had one trick left, even more extreme than the Voice. She flared with red brilliance, like lava bursting in a fountain straight out of Mount Etna.

I'D READ ABOUT THIS: THE BLOOD BURN
Also known as the Inferno or the Pyre. They were different names for the same phenomenon: a vampire igniting all the blood in her body.

Like a poker player going all in, Lilith had converted all her stolen corpuscles into arcane energy. She would burn through that boost in about sixty seconds. In the meantime, however, her speed and strength would be amped to the max.

She wouldn't think. She wouldn't feel pain. She'd reduced her world to a single goal: feeding.

Like a missile that's spent all its fuel, Lilith was simply a payload plunging straight toward her target. She'd crash into a coma unless she drank blood right away. She'd stop at nothing to get it, and precious little on Earth was strong enough to hold her off.

LILITH'S FANGS STABBED OUT OF HER MOUTH

This wasn't the creepy arousal I'd seen before. This was full throat-ripping extension.

Lilith spun her legs gymnastically, helicoptering so fast that the momentum pulled her up to her feet. I'd never seen anyone move so quickly. Few mortals had, and almost none had survived.

Lilith charged toward Miranda. This wasn't the burst phenomenon that vampires are famous for—Lilith was too feral to remember she could do that. But she was so cranked, she didn't need fancy tricks.

Lilith shot toward Miranda like a bolt from a crossbow. That's not poetry; it's just the literal truth.

MIRANDA'S REFLEXES WERE SUPERFAST

I'd already seen how quick Miranda had become. Even so, she barely had a heartbeat to react. As Lilith streaked along the alley in a blaze of bloodred fire, Miranda leaned toward the pavement and sang a single golden note. It lifted her off her feet like a rocket's blast. She soared straight up into the air.

Even so, she barely escaped. Lilith launched herself too, her fingertips turned to claws. They raked out and gouged, catching the edge of Miranda's coat as she rose. The coat was a ski jacket filled with eiderdown; feathers exploded in a cloud of white that filled Lilith's face and blinded her. She hissed and clawed at the down, scratching her cheeks in the process. By the time Lilith could see again, Miranda was flying well out of reach—no longer singing to stay aloft, simply glowing as golden as the sun.

LILITH BEGAN TO FALL

She gave Miranda a last furious hiss. Then she looked downward, to the bodies of Jools, Richard, and Shar lying on the ground. Lilith bared her fangs in anticipation of a feast.

Miranda noticed, and switched from escape mode to attack. She followed Lilith down, singing shot after shot of focused sound. But the golden power of those blasts was as pale as diluted lemonade, and I couldn't hear their echoes at all. Miranda was running on empty.

Lilith wasn't fazed by the puppy-weak blasts raining down on her. Her blood-maddened attention was fixed on the targets below.

I HAD NO PLAN, BUT I FLEW TOWARD HER

Without thinking, I'd grown to the size of a wasp. It seemed to be the sweet spot that let me fly fastest, given all the trade-offs between weight, air resistance, and coattail propulsion. By the time Lilith hit the pavement, I'd caught up with her.

I could have killed her on the spot; I just had to enter her ear, then grow. End of story. Not even a vampire can survive having her brain squished out of her skull. In fact, I realized I could be an unstoppable assassin. Shrunk to a pinpoint, I could slip past any sensors. Unseen, I could sneak into anyone's body and wreak havoc: heart attacks, strokes, aneurysms. Then I could escape microscopically. With practice, I could make my kills look like natural causes . . . maybe even create delayed effects by starting little bleeds in the brain that wouldn't cause death until I was somewhere else for an alibi.

I could murder anyone, anywhere, anytime. I could take down world leaders during televised speeches; I could dispatch any Darkling or Spark, hero or villain; if I wanted, I could casually kill innocents on the street.

The prospect made me sick to my stomach. I could be far worse than Lilith with her simple thirst for blood. It would be trivial to kill her, but then what? Where would it stop?

So don't judge me for letting her live, or for any other monster I haven't slaughtered. Do you think I don't realize how much tragedy I could prevent? Leaving maniacs alive is a promise of horrors to come.

But.

When I shift my vision to look at myself, I see a perfectly normal person who happens to have powers. I don't see the apex predator of this entire plane of existence.

I cling to that. I have to.

I COULDN'T KILL LILITH IN COLD BLOOD

But I couldn't let her kill anyone else either. I darted at her eyes, hoping I'd distract her like an irritating gnat. If I could hold her attention long enough, her blood boost would burn out. She'd collapse. Problem solved.

So I whisked in front of her like a kamikaze bug. I planned to shrink out of sight a heartbeat later, before Lilith could grab me.

Lilith's hand shot out so fast I could barely see it. She snatched me out of the air and squeezed. Hard.

If I'd been a real insect, I'd be nothing but squashed guts. Surprise: All of Lilith's amplified strength couldn't pulp me. I felt nothing but the coldness of Lilith's undead skin. She might as well have tried crushing a diamond in her bare hands.

Two seconds of squeezing. Two seconds of Blood Burn wasted. Then she threw me away in disgust.

She hurled me toward the van. I smashed headfirst through the back window like a pellet of buckshot. I sailed the full length of the van and bounced off the front windshield, making a collision star in the glass.

I FELL ONTO THE DASHBOARD, AMAZED I WAS STILL ALIVE

I hurt; I expected bruises. But as far as I could tell, I had no major injuries, despite the equivalent of a high-speed car crash without wearing a seat belt.

Still not believing it, I turned my vision on myself: the first time I'd seriously looked at Kim 2.0.

My skin wasn't skin; it was rock.

The rock looked much like my normal skin, which was why it hadn't caught my attention. But the color was a little more sandy, and its sheen appreciably more glossy. In geology speak, my luster was vitreous to adamantine. When I zoomed my vision in close, I could see that every exposed surface of my body had changed into small flat crystal faces, like the facets of a well-cut gem.

Whoa.

Some Sparks are only a teeny bit super: able to breathe underwater or change color like a chameleon. Me, I'd hit the jackpot. Perception, shrinking, and stone-skin armor.

Part of my brain started asking, *What* kind *of stone? What hardness? What mineral formula?* But another part realized that was only my mind's way to avoid dealing with Lilith.

Grimacing, I sent my vision to see what she was doing.

LILITH WAS ABOUT TO SINK HER FANGS INTO RICHARD

She held him high, his feet barely touching the ground. Lilith had lost her human intelligence, but she was Darkling enough to pause and savor her victory. She flared her fangs . . . aimed for Richard's throat . . .

. . . and got bodychecked by Jools.

A blood-amped vampire is hellishly strong. A normal human might simply bounce off, like hitting a wall. But even before Jools became a Spark, she could deliver a body check that *worked.* Now she was even better: more strength, speed, and accuracy, plus an instinct for using leverage in her favor. She struck Lilith perfectly, knocking the vampire off her feet and making her drop Richard in surprise.

That was the good news. The bad news was that Jools didn't have nearly enough raw muscle to stop Lilith for more than a heartbeat. Jools could distract her by using surprise, but that advantage ended instantly.

Lilith whipped back onto her feet in a fraction of a second. Hissing with rage, she threw herself at Jools, all fangs and claws and fury.

JOOLS WAS PREPARED

Take the world's great martial arts: kung fu, Brazilian jujitsu, boxing, whatever. Add every technique from bar brawls, combat zones, and those underworld arenas where people fight to the death. Whatever punch, kick, or elbow smash you can think of, Jools could do it as well as any human ever. That was her gift—not to be super, but human max in *everything.*

(From time to time, I catch myself saying, "Poor Jools didn't get real superpowers." Then I contemplate how astounding Jools's brain must be. Not just because she can pluck textbook facts out of nowhere, but because she can survey seven billion possible responses to a given situation and choose the very best. And her brain does it fast enough that Jools still moves at top human speed.)

It was still a close call. Lilith lunged so inhumanly fast, she almost caught Jools in her claws. But as Lilith charged forward, Jools twisted sideways just enough to evade Lilith's outstretched arms. Jools grabbed one of those arms and pulled, accelerating Lilith that much more.

Jools tripped her as she sped past. Lilith lost her balance and fell, landing nose down several paces away. She skidded, grinding her face along the pavement for a meter before she came to a stop.

"Go home, Vampirella," Jools said. "You're drunk."

Howling, Lilith scrambled to her feet. Her face looked as if it had been buffed by a cheese grater. But a blood-amped vampire doesn't feel pain. She came back at Jools even faster than before, and this time Jools didn't dodge quite quickly enough. She tried for the same kind of grab-trip-throw, and succeeded in making Lilith do another face-plant; in the process, however, one of Lilith's claws caught Jools on the cheek, ripping a bloody gash from Jools's ear down across her lips.

Jools's flesh sagged below the cut. A chunk of face hung off like stripped wallpaper.

The smell of blood drove Lilith mad. She leapt to her feet with her eyes set to "bugfuck."

LILITH WAS CLOSE TO RICHARD'S PRONE BODY

She jumped over him, frantic to get at Jools and her welling blood. As Lilith passed Richard, my attention was caught by the dart in his thigh.

Ooo. Idea.

FLAP-FLAP WITH THE COATTAILS

I bat-out-of-hell'd through the van back toward the window where I'd come in. I was nearly there when I realized how precise I had to be in order to exit through my entrance hole. Robin Hood splitting the arrow—the hole was exactly my size, and here I was flying at high speed, imagining I could thread the needle perfectly.

Being made of rock, I wouldn't get hurt hitting the glass. But I was still leaping before I looked: not the safe, strategic person I'd been since Kimmi died.

Of course, when I got to the hole, I just shrank a little and passed through easily. The new Kim was good at this stuff, even if the old Kim was slow to figure that out.

I SPED TO THE END OF THE ALLEY

Lilith had dropped her tranq gun when she went Voicy-berserk. It lay beside a box containing ten darts filled with sedative, plus two spare canisters of pressurized gas propellant.

I grew back to normal size, then picked up the rifle. It wasn't identical to the guns the park rangers had shown me, but it wasn't too different. I ejected the gas canister that was already in the rifle, since I didn't know how much charge it had left. I loaded up one of the spares, then put a new dart into the gun's chamber.

BY THE TIME I'D READIED THE RIFLE, JOOLS'S LUCK HAD TURNED SOUR

No human can beat a blood-amped vampire forever, especially not when bleeding profusely. Lilith had somehow grabbed Jools in a face-to-face bear hug. Jools had one arm trapped in Lilith's grip, but the other was free. Jools had jammed the free arm against

Lilith's throat and was just barely holding Lilith's head out of biting range.

Lilith snapped, her fangs protruding as far as they would go. Jools's face continued to bleed; Lilith's tongue extended hungrily, trying to lap blood like a dog drinking from a bowl.

Lilith's arms wrapped so tightly around Jools's spine, Jools was bent back in a V. Some of Jools's ribs must have been broken; maybe vertebrae too. Moment by moment, Lilith tightened her clench, threatening to crush Jools into two separate pieces. Blood gushed from Jools's face like toothpaste squeezed from a tube.

As for Miranda, she had landed and taken up a position behind Jools. She sang over Jools's shoulder, full force into Lilith's face. The sonic barrage helped push back Lilith's head, keeping her a finger's width away from Jools's blood.

But the strength of Miranda's blasts and Jools's arms weren't enough: little by little, Lilith was closing the gap. She couldn't have much time left—another few seconds and she'd use up the boost from going Inferno. But if she got even a drop of new blood, she wouldn't collapse. She'd return to normal, strong enough to keep fighting.

That would be bad.

I LIFTED THE TRANQ GUN AND LOOKED DOWN THE BARREL

My lovely Spark-o-Vision showed me a new trick: a zoom with crosshairs.

Mind. Blown.

My sphere of perception collapsed down flat, showing a close-up of Lilith with a white + sign on top of her—exactly like first-person-shooter games where the screen shows where you're aiming. Richard once called such visual aids "annoying cheats for n00bs": even if a real weapon had telescopic sights, a targeting laser, and all the rest, nothing could guarantee you'd hit where the crosshairs indicated. They were a lie. They weren't real life.

Well, Richard, I thought, *I'm not real life either. I'm a gorram Spark.*

I CENTERED MY NOOB CROSSHAIRS ON LILITH

Everything slowed, like the bullet-time effect from *The Matrix*.

I thought, *This is getting ridiculous. Slow motion? Really?* The universe was crazy eager to make me the ultimate killer.

I pulled the trigger anyway. Meh, it was only a tranq gun.

THE DART FLEW STRAIGHT AND TRUE

Well, straightish and trueish, subject to deflection by gravity, the slight winter breeze, the eddies of air in the alley, and the itty-bitty wobbles from imperfections in the dart. My powers must have compensated for all those deviations, because the dart zipped flawlessly over Jools's shoulder and hit Lilith in the eye.

Earlier in the fight, I'd decided to leave Lilith's eyes alone. Not anymore—the situation was too dire for me to be squeamish. Or maybe it was just the difference between ganking an eyeball with my bare hands and shooting it from afar with a dart.

Either way, out, vile jelly. Sploosh.

LILITH SHRIEKED

Not the roar of a wounded predator. Lilith shrieked like a stricken child, bewildered by what had just happened. She dropped Jools and staggered away, clutching her eye.

She whimpered.

Shit.

JOOLS FELL

Her legs wouldn't hold her. They were as limp as rags.

Miranda possessed just enough strength to put herself between Lilith and Jools. Then she slumped, exhausted.

The alley was so quiet I could hear the faint pop when Lilith plucked the dart from her eye.

Then she erupted. Since my first sight of Lilith, she had hissed, howled, shrieked, and gone through a zoo's worth of noise. What was left? A terrifying bellow, like the T. rex in *Jurassic Park*.

It was answered by a screech at the top of human hearing. The were-bat, woken by the clamor, lurched to his feet.

I snatched another dart from the box.

LILITH WHIRLED TO FACE THE WERE-BAT

But even in her bestial state, she recognized the bat wasn't a target. Vampires say fellow Darklings don't smell like food—Darkling blood doesn't have the "vitality" to keep vampires alive.

Make of that what you will.

Lilith turned away from the were-bat. Gooey fluid dribbled out of her punctured eye. Lilith's face had been rasped by her impacts with the pavement. Her wounds had no blood to shed, but her skin was tattered and her nose cocked sideways; when she bared her teeth, I could see that several had broken off. The fangs, however, were still intact. A vampire's canines are almost impossible to damage.

Lilith stalked toward Jools and Miranda. No running now: Lilith had precious little energy left. But she still had enough to rip out a jugular. Jools and Miranda looked too tired to resist.

BEHIND LILITH'S BACK, VIOLET LIGHT CLAMPED AROUND THE WERE-BAT'S HEAD

It encased his skull like a helmet. His eyelids fluttered; he leapt.

THE BAT SLAMMED HIS CLAWS INTO LILITH'S BACK

He raked down, tearing deeply into her flesh. The violet glow that encompassed his head never wavered.

Lilith wheeled, all teeth and talons. The next few seconds were like a cartoon fight, where all you see is a roiling cloud: Once in a while, a hand or a foot pokes briefly out of the cloud, and strings of $%&! curse words appear. As soon as the fight was raging, the glow around the bat's head vanished, but by then, the bat had to keep fighting or die.

I almost felt sorry for him. Almost.

I DIDN'T CATCH THE MOMENT WHEN LILITH WENT CATATONIC

The bat missed it too. He kept fighting for several seconds after she went limp. He bit, slashed, and buffeted her with his wings. At last, he realized she was no longer conscious. He stepped back and Lilith crumpled, a sad tumble of flesh.

She was completely burned out. She wouldn't wake until someone forced blood down her throat.

As the bat stood panting and bewildered at what just happened, I put one foot against the box of remaining tranq darts and gave it a shove. The box slid down the alley. The sound of it scraping along the asphalt attracted everyone's attention.

"Tranq darts," I said.

I'd loaded a dart into my gun. I shot the were-bat in the belly.

Half a dozen violet tendrils reached toward the box. Each grabbed a dart. Together they rose like cooperating snakes and slammed all six darts into the were-bat's chest. His mouth plopped open as if he wanted to speak; then he teetered and collapsed.

Tendrils caught him before he smacked into the ground. They lowered him gently to the pavement.

I LEANED WEARILY AGAINST THE WALL OF THE ALLEY

Miranda leaned against the van. She said, "Fuck."

Jools said, "Fuck," or at least she tried. Her lips were too torn to manage the "F." She pushed the flap of her face back into position. "Fuck."

Shar sat up. She said something in Sinhalese. I imagine it was basically, "Fuck," but she likes to pretend she's genteel.

From atop the E3 building came a round of slow applause. Clap. Clap. Clap.

Rapid Uplift

ON THE ROOF STOOD A MAN DRESSED AS ABRAHAM LINCOLN
He had the stovepipe hat and a black old-fashioned suit, with a starched white shirt and a black bow tie. The man himself, however, seemed the physical opposite of Lincoln: short rather than tall, dark-skinned rather than white, round-faced rather than gaunt, and grinning broadly unlike the familiar deadpan photos of Honest Abe. If not for the clothes, I might have compared him to Gandhi rather than Lincoln. He had that birdlike stature, with an air that blended cheerfulness and gravitas.

The man's face was painted with patterns of small dots. White dots made spirals on each cheek, while black and red dots surrounded his eyes like a mask. The overall look suggested an octogenarian wise man dressed for some formal occasion—but a happy occasion, not a somber one.

Beside him stood a basset hound, exceptionally mournful even by basset standards. Its tail drooped; its ears almost touched the ground. It was brown, black, and white, with mottled freckles on its snout. It wore an oversize collar that glowed with a soft orange light in my Spark-o-Vision. The collar was a band of interlocking metal plates, each the size of a postage stamp. Each plate had a different color and luster: some shiny, some dull, some textured like woven fabric.

The collar had the look of Cape Tech: a super-science gadget made by a Spark. I wondered what the collar did, and why you'd put it on a dog. Then again, why not? The man was likely a Spark—his odd clothes and painted mask were strong hints, not to mention him being on the roof instead of the ground. If you were a Spark, why *wouldn't* you trick out your pet with a superpowered collar? At the very least, you'd want something to keep the dog safe in a firefight.

And maybe a weapon or two. Because Sparks.

THE MAN CROUCHED AND PUT AN ARM AROUND THE DOG

A moment later, both man and hound stood beside us in the alley. The teleportation had been silent and instantaneous. I hadn't even seen a glow.

"You folks okay?" the man asked. He glanced at the fallen Darklings. "Looks like you had quite the party."

"A real bash," Jools said, but the "B" sounded like a "V." She pressed harder on the flap of skin that Lilith had slashed loose. Her face was slick with blood, but the wound was slowly knitting itself shut. "How much did you see?" she asked.

"Only the last few seconds," the man said. "Otherwise, I would have helped."

"Helped us?" Miranda asked. "Or them?"

"Don't get snippy," the man said. "I'm with the Light, not the Dark."

"You're a Spark?" Miranda asked.

"He's Grandfather," Jools said. "Don't you recognize him?"

"He's your grandfather?" Shar asked in surprise.

"No, he's *everyone's* grandfather," Jools said. "The Y-chromosomal Adam. The last common ancestor of all *Homo sapiens.*"

"Nonsense," Miranda said. "Our last common ancestor was, what, a hundred thousand years ago?"

"Can't say exactly," the man, Grandfather, said. "We didn't count years back then, considering none of us could count past five. But yes, you're all my great-great-granddaughters." He looked at me. "Or whatever."

"Then you can't be a Spark," Miranda said. "They've only been around since July 2000."

"Wrong," Grandfather said. "Sparks might have come out of the closet in 2000, but think of the Darklings—they went public in '82, but the Elders had been around for umpteen centuries. Same with the Light. Us old folk stayed under the radar till Big Blue let the cat out of the bag."

"So you claim," Miranda said.

"That I do," Grandfather agreed. "On the other hand, I might be a delusional old coot driven crazy by going super. Who knows?"

He grinned. The grin was exactly like my own two grandfathers'. When I was little, both loved to string me along with outlandish lies. I've often wondered if they competed, seeing which could make me believe the wildest stories.

The man in front of me radiated a similar mischief. That feeling undoubtedly came from a superpower, and a devilishly potent one.

IT WAS THE FIRST TIME I'D FELT A SPARK'S HALO

Halos are similar to Darkling Shadows: supernatural auras that induce emotions. But Shadows always broadcast fear. It's a constant ingredient, whether the Darkling creates a sense of subtle disquiet or outright terror.

Halos are more varied. One Spark may fill you with hope; another inspires you to improve the world; a third makes you feel guilty for every selfish deed you've done. Some Sparks can suppress their Halos temporarily, which is useful if you specialize in disguise or invisibility. But once a Spark is noticed, the effect of the Halo kicks in.

Grandfather filled me with amiable reassurance. I just naturally liked and trusted him.

So another part of me didn't trust him at all.

THE BASSET HOUND PADDED TOWARD THE WERE-BAT

Miranda said, "Whoa, boy, better stay back."

"Yeah," Jools said, "when you get too close, that's always when the monster wakes up."

Jools's words were less slurred than before. Her face was healing quickly. But the dog ignored her.

"Grandfather," Shar said, "you really should call your dog back."

"He's not my dog, and I don't give him orders," Grandfather replied. "He hates that."

The dog had reached the were-bat. He licked the bat's face; the dog's metal collar flared bright orange.

"The dog is using a power," I said.

"You can tell?" Grandfather asked. "Useful talent."

"What's he doing?" I asked.

"Erasing Mr. Bat's short-term memory." The basset continued licking the bat in long even strokes, methodically covering the Darkling's head. The light from the collar shone so brightly, it made my brain hurt. I shifted my viewpoint back to a less painful distance. "When Invie's through," Grandfather said, "that bat won't remember anything from the past half hour."

"Your dog's name is Invie?" Shar asked.

"He's not my dog, he's my partner."

"Oh, shit," Jools said, with a flash of green. "He's the Inventor."

THE HOUND LOOKED IN JOOLS'S DIRECTION FOR A MOMENT, THEN WENT BACK TO WORK

"Yep, he's the Inventor," Grandfather said. "How did you know?"

Jools tapped her head. "I know things."

"Oh," Grandfather said. "One of those."

"Didn't the Inventor graduate from Waterloo Engineering?" Miranda asked. "I know engineers aren't picky, but they generally don't give degrees to basset hounds."

"Invie's a Spark," Grandfather said. "This kind of shit happens. You grow horns, turn purple, become a dog . . . occupational hazards. He'll revert to human eventually. Maybe. Except Invie *likes* being a dog. It means he doesn't have to make small talk."

"He's erasing that creature's memories?" Shar asked. She was watching Invie closely, as if taking notes.

"Just cleaning off the top layer, so Mr. Bat won't remember what you look like." Grandfather waggled a finger at us. "Next time, you four better get masks."

Miranda made a face. "There won't be a next time. And I refuse to wear a mask."

"You're new at this, aren't you?" Grandfather said. "Guess I'd best explain some facts."

"Such as?"

"Secret identities. Can't let out who you actually are, or Darklings and villains'll make your lives hell. Threatening your loved ones and whatnot."

"Oh, I get that," Miranda said. "I just don't understand how masks can make a difference. On Halloween, I always recognize people in costume if I know them. Even if they completely cover their faces, I recognize their voice or the way they walk. What good is a silly mask? And by the way, I notice *you* don't wear one."

"I got my paint," Grandfather said, pointing to the dots on his face. "That's good enough. I know one guy, all he does is take off his glasses. It's the thought that counts. I mean that literally."

Inside my head, a nasal voice said, *«Anonymity is a projective psionic power possessed by all Sparks. However, it requires an activating focus.»*

I looked around for the source of the voice. Grandfather slapped his knee in delight. "Hey, Invie likes you. Not often he talks to strangers."

«They are Sparks,» the nasal voice said. *«With remarkably high liminality quotients. They must be informed of their new state of being.»*

"What's a liminality quotient?" Shar asked.

"Fancy way to say 'power level,'" Grandfather replied. "Which explains why Invie's willing to talk to you. He thinks you four got mojo."

"Liminality means being in some either-or/neither-nor state between possibilities," Jools said. (Yes, she glowed green.) "What does that have to do with power level?"

Grandfather looked to Invie, clearly waiting for the dog to answer. Invie didn't respond; he gave the were-bat a final lick, then headed for the skeleton. Grandfather sighed. "Here's how I understand it, but I'm no expert. Not like some people present." He gave the basset a reproachful look. "Dark and Light powers, they're both channeled from other universes. Places where physical rules are more negotiable."

"What do you mean, negotiable?" Miranda asked.

"Open to persuasion. Invie says there's a spectrum of universes. At one end, you got ones totally ruled by physical laws. The laws differ from one universe to another—different physical constants, that sort of thing—but the laws are cast iron, and you don't get a whisker of wiggle room."

"And the other end of the spectrum?" Shar asked.

"Willpower," Grandfather said. "Mind over matter, and to hell with rules. You want to win? Be hungrier than the other guy. Nothing counts except ego and drive."

"The Darkling ideal," Miranda said.

"Bingo. Dark powers come from that end of the spectrum. Darklings are conduits between such universes and our own. They channel power from there to here according to their liminality quotients."

Shar said, "Liminality quotient is bandwidth?"

"Close enough," Grandfather said. "Invie seems to think you folks got it in spades."

"Where do Sparks channel power from?" Miranda asked. "The physics end of the spectrum?"

"Nah, Sparks are bang in the middle," Grandfather said. "Mind over matter is part of it: *Wishing makes it so.* But we need scientific mumbo jumbo to cover the physics requirement. We can't just fly because we want to—we need boots that shoot jets of flame. Or maybe we have dinky little wings on our ankles, never mind that they're too small to lift a sparrow. Sparks don't fly by aerodynamics; we fly by wish fulfillment dressed in rocket boots."

"Pseudoscience bullshit," Miranda said.

"Yeah, basically," Grandfather said. "Except you can't ever say so. Like this: I can speak and read and write every language in human history. That's one of my powers. And it makes perfect sense, because I'm the ancestor of every human ever, so naturally I know everybody's language." He winked. "Now if I got all analytical on that rationale, I'd end up losing the power. It only works if you don't look too close."

Grandfather grinned another grin so charming it could smooth over anything. In a low voice, he said, "I can get away with saying shit like that, because one of my powers is getting away with outrageous stuff. But you folks better not question how powers work. This universe where we live—this one right here, right now—it's 80 percent toward the physics-only end of the spectrum. There's room for slack, but the laws of nature impose a friction you have to overcome before you can do anything super. The way you beat the friction is plausible deniability."

Miranda opened her mouth, but Grandfather put his finger to her lips with superhuman speed. "Before you talk, girl, think twice. The moment you say a thing's impossible, it becomes impossible for *you*. Is that what you want?"

Miranda glowered but didn't speak. Grandfather lowered his hand. "Better."

Still glowering, Miranda said, "Explain about masks."

"Plausible deniability," Grandfather said. "Masks don't provide much disguise for normal folks, but for Sparks, they let you channel the superpower of anonymization. Costumes kick it up a notch, and so do codenames. Create a distinctive Spark identity—mask, costume, name—and no one'll recognize you. Guaranteed."

"So it's magic?" Shar asked.

Grandfather waved dismissively. "Magic is Darkling stuff. Sparks do Science with a capital S. In this case, psionic projection: clouding folks' minds. Look at my war paint." He pointed to the dots on his face. "It's not a disguise, it's a focus for the power to work through. Like a magnifying glass that turns sunlight into a heat beam. People who know me in civilian life just don't recognize me with the paint on."

He held up his hands and waggled his fingers. "You want to hear something even crazier? When I'm in costume, my fingerprints change. I've watched it happen. I dabbed on paint with one hand while watching the other. My fingerprints rearranged themselves. It was the damnedest thing."

"That really happens?" Jools asked. "If I put on a mask and rob a bank, my fingerprints won't be the same?"

"Don't go robbing banks, young lady." Grandfather gave her a stern look, then turned it into a grin. "But yeah, that's how it works. And not just fingerprints: DNA, your blood type, the works. Make up a strong Spark ID, and no human, no sniffer dog, no digital face recognition, no magic spell, will ever connect your super-self with your everyday."

«Except,» Invie said, *«through negligence or betrayal.»*

I'D FORGOTTEN ABOUT THE DOG

The basset hound had finished purging the skeleton's memories and had moved on to Lilith. Slurp, slurp. I said, "Negligence? Betrayal?"

"Getting sloppy," Grandfather said. "Like using your powers outside of costume." He gave us an accusatory stare. "Or if you spill your secret to someone. Suppose you got a sweetheart, and you tell 'em you're super. Bad idea: It opens a hole in your protection. Makes you vulnerable."

I couldn't help it. I glanced at Richard, still unconscious on the pavement.

"You four knowing about each other, that's no problem," Grandfather said. "You're Sparks; you got joint immunity. But if you tell who you are to non-Sparks, what if their minds get read by enemies? What if a Darkling makes 'em into Renfields? That kind of shit happens. We Sparks are magnets for weirdness, both in and out of costume. The people you hang with get caught in the craziness, and confiding your secret makes it worse."

I was still looking at Richard. By apparent coincidence—as if anything is coincidence in a Spark's life—Invie finished erasing Lilith's memories at that moment. The dog walked over to Richard, apparently mistaking him for another Darkling.

No one told Invie to stop. When the dog began to lick Richard, I thought Shar looked relieved.

"WHY DO THIS AT ALL?" MIRANDA ASKED

"Mask, costume, it's ridiculous," she said. "I don't want any part of it."

"Not an option," Grandfather told her. He gestured toward the Darklings. "You just had a fight. Did you start it?"

"Of course not," Miranda said. "They attacked *us*."

Grandfather nodded. "And how many other freaky run-ins have you had since you got powers?"

None of us answered. The others had to be thinking of the pustule demon attacking us. Me, I was remembering Nicholas in the police station.

"You want your lives simple," Grandfather said. "Who doesn't? But it doesn't work that way. I know a guy: in his fifties, ran a business, had a family. He got powers but didn't want 'em, so he acted like nothing had changed. Now his wife is dead and his daughter's missing a leg, with a clear line of cause and effect from him staying out of the game."

Grandfather shook his head sadly. "If it was up to me, I'd say live how you want. But Fate smacks you hard for refusing the call. Smacks your loved ones too, and everybody else in sight. Then it just keeps smacking till you give in."

"FOR FUCK'S SAKE," JOOLS SAID, "TELL US SOMETHING LESS DEPRESSING!"

Grandfather rolled his eyes. "Shit, girl, are you stupid? Now you got superpowers."

"Okay," Jools admitted, "there's that."

"And," Grandfather said, "no offense to your fine selves right now, but you can expect to start looking more . . . cinematic."

Miranda scowled. "Like how?"

Grandfather just grinned. Jools said, "I think he means thirty-six triple-Ds."

"Ouch!" Miranda said. "Bite your tongue!"

Grandfather chuckled. "Gaining Spark powers gives you one hell of a makeover. That guy I told you about, in his fifties: Within a week of getting powers, he was rippling with muscles. His face niced up too. Got more regular and less pouchy. He still looked like himself, but like he'd been training hard for a year. All tucked 'n' tightened.

"So expect to see changes. Like belly muscles. God almighty, the Light loves belly muscles. Every Spark—man, woman, or other—gets a six-pack. And great hair. And, uhh, better cheekbones. Isn't that what women always go on about? Cheekbones?"

"Definitely," Jools said. "Thirty-six triple-D cheekbones."

"Fuuuuuuck," Miranda said.

GRANDFATHER LAUGHED

"Don't worry," he said. "The Light is wish fulfillment, remember? You become what you long to be. Most of us get better looking, whatever that means to us personally. A few, though, would rather be scary than sexy. Some even become monsters: flying jellyfish and whatnot. Freud would have a field day."

«Oversimplification,» Invie said inside my brain. *«There are also nonpsychological factors.»*

"Yeah, okay," Grandfather admitted, "it isn't all wish fulfillment. The Light cares about usefulness too. Like maybe some guy loves the idea of shooting fire from his hands. Okay, that's good for attacking. But if he doesn't have defense too, he's mincemeat. So the Light gives him a force field or something, even if he's never fantasized about that."

"You talk about the Light as if it can think," Shar said.

Grandfather shrugged. "I don't know if it thinks as such, but it sure as hell has an agenda."

"Which is?"

"To oppose the Dark. Duh."

"It's just about fighting?" Shar asked. "That's senseless. Conflict never ends conflict; only letting go brings peace."

"*This is the world's most ancient law,*" Grandfather intoned, then chuckled. "Girl, I was sitting beside old Buddha the first time he trotted that out. And nobody's saying the Dark and the Light should claw at each other all the time. But you can't let the Dark have their way unopposed. They screw things up royally if they don't have adult supervision."

Miranda snorted. "Adult supervision means dressing in spandex and punching people out?"

Grandfather grinned. "Pretty much. Otherwise, the Darklings never stop trying to take all the cookies."

INVIE FINISHED LICKING RICHARD'S FACE

«Done,» the basset hound said. *«We must proceed with other business.»*

"What other business?" Miranda asked.

"We got word of a lab explosion," Grandfather said. He jerked his thumb toward E3. "That's why we're here. We operate out of Toronto, but Invie keeps his ear to the ground—eavesdropping on police, the feds, and so on. When interesting news comes down the pike, we investigate. A lab explosion with Darkling involvement? That's right up our alley."

"Adult supervision," Miranda said.

"Exactly. Cuz Darklings automatically cover shit up, always thinking it'll never hit the fan. Invie and me, we stick in our noses to offer a second opinion." He looked at us keenly. "So a lab explosion a few hours ago, and suddenly there's four new Sparks I've never heard of. Makes me put two and two together. You want to talk about that?"

"No," Miranda said.

"Fair enough," Grandfather said. "Never wise to be too trusting. But look, you just got attacked by a team of Darklings. And let me tell you, there's a ton of Darkling chatter between Waterloo, Toronto, and Ottawa. Rich and powerful folk are getting their panties in a knot, squabbling over who's gonna do what where. By the way, did you know it's the winter solstice and there's gonna be a lunar eclipse?"

"Yeah," Jools said. "That had come to our attention."

"The Darklings are saying the walls are thin, whatever that means," Grandfather said. "They're sweating about that and the potential for things getting ugly, but they aren't doing much to police themselves. The Dark never ask, 'What's the right thing to do?' It's always, 'How can we turn this to our advantage?' They put effort into *using* disasters, not stopping 'em. If anyone's going to handle this . . ."

Suddenly, Grandfather changed. I don't know if he used a superpower; he certainly didn't glow. But he went from "kindly grandfather" to "stern grandfather you really don't want to mess with." He said, "Will you four see to this? Cuz if you take responsibility for being guardians of Waterloo, Invie and I will back off. Professional courtesy. But something's going on, and someone has to deal. Are you gonna step up?"

THE FOUR OF US EXCHANGED GLANCES
For a long moment, nobody spoke. Then Miranda said, "I don't think we're ready to commit. We have a lot to discuss."

Grandfather shrugged. "Then discuss. Meantime, Invie and I will keep poking around. See what needs doing."

I said, "How do we contact you once we make a decision?"

"Oh yeah." Grandfather reached into the pocket of his suit coat. He fumbled around, then pulled out four silver rings: plain silver bands with no markings. "Invie makes these," Grandfather said, handing each of us a ring. "We've given them out to Sparks all across the country. Our own private radio network."

"If we put these on," Miranda said, "anyone in on the secret will recognize us as Sparks." She thrust the ring back at Grandfather. "No thanks."

He held up his hand to refuse the ring. "Give us some credit," he said. "They reshape however you like. Change color too. Fit your outfit, fit your mood."

"How do they work?" Shar asked.

"You want to contact anyone who's wearing a ring, just picture 'em in your head. Instant mental connection."

"Does it have voice mail?" Jools asked. "I hate voice mail."

"More to the point," Miranda said, "do these things let you track us or eavesdrop on conversations? Are these basically bugs?"

"Would you believe me if I said no?" Grandfather asked. He gave another of his disarming grins. "I guarantee these rings are more secure than phones or the Internet. Ordinary comms are hacked by everybody and their dog. So to speak."

Miranda grimaced, but I'm sure she realized he was right. Normal modes of communication are monitored by government security bureaus, which are hand in glove with the Dark. Mad Genius supervillains have their hooks in everything too. Only someone like the Inventor has a chance of making something a Mad Genius can't hack. And let's not forget the others who've showed up since the Dark and Light appeared. Aliens. Super-science-using Atlanteans. Extradimensional tourists/pranksters/parasites/slave traders.

If Invie's rings bypassed some or all of that surveillance, they were worth it, even if Invie himself could listen in.

I PUT THE RING ON MY LEFT PINKIE FINGER

A moment later, it changed to show a classical Greek–type head with two faces: one male, one female, looking in opposite directions. *Okay,* I thought, *a little on the nose, but I like it.*

«*Yo, Kim!*» Jools said inside my head. She'd put on her ring and was grinning like a loon. Her ring had become fat and gold with a mass of diamonds set into it.

«*Is that a Stanley Cup ring?*» I asked silently.

«*From 1988,*» Jools answered. «*The last time Gretzky won the cup playing with the Oilers.*»

«*You weren't even alive in 1988.*»

«*YOU weren't alive when the Rocky Mountains formed, but you won't shut up about how it happened.*»

«*Touché,*» I said. «*So when you put on the ring, you asked it to look like Gretzky's?*»

«*I didn't ask, but it's perfect. Wish fulfillment, right?*»

I came close to saying, *Be careful what you wish for.* But that was just reflex, and a bad one. What's wrong with wish fulfillment? Sure, we sometimes wish for stupid things. But too often, people say, "Be careful what you wish for," when they mean, "Don't wish at all."

Stop aspiring. Stay small.

Well, screw that—up, down, and sideways. Wish for every star in the sky. Wish for love. For delight. For doing great things in the world.

Because the wishes that go wrong are the petty, mean ones. For money. Admiration. "Winning."

Ew. Just ew.

End of sermon.

MIRANDA DROPPED HER RING INTO HER COAT POCKET

Shar (who wore half a dozen rings already) put the new one on the thumb of her right hand. Immediately, it changed to a plain gold band, blending in with the others.

"Time for Invie and me to get cracking," said Grandfather. "Touch base with us after you've made your decisions." He winked. "Or your costumes."

"You're heading off to investigate the lab explosion?" Miranda asked.

"Someone has to. And Invie's great at turning up clues." Grandfather tapped the side of his nose. "If there's anything to find, Invie'll find it."

He gave us a wave and touched his hand to the dog's back. They disappeared instantly.

SHAR SAID, "NOW THAT HE'S GONE, MAYBE WE CAN THINK MORE CLEARLY."

"What do you mean?" Miranda asked.

"Grandfather smelled like a garden full of jasmine," Shar replied. "By which I mean he emitted a psionic field influencing us to trust him. *Leave everything to Grandpa. He'll take care of us.*"

"That bastard!" Miranda said.

Shar shrugged. "He may not realize he's doing it. He probably thinks people trust his common sense. But even if he were ranting like a lunatic, most normal humans would respect and obey him."

"Sweet," Jools said. "How do I get a power like that?"

"You already have it," Shar replied. "You're now a paragon at every skill, are you not? If you choose to exert yourself, you can be as charismatic and persuasive as any human in history."

"Whoa." Jools looked thunderstruck. After a moment, she said, "We're fucking scary, aren't we? I mean, seriously, we're weapons of mass destruction. Who the hell would trust someone like me with that kind of clout?"

We all nodded somberly.

Shar said, "But every time I feel unworthy, ten seconds later I'm imagining how much fun I'll have being super."

We all nodded again.

"FUCK THIS," JOOLS SAID

"I refuse to get depressed about being kickass."

"Right, fuck depression," Miranda said. "And fuck those guys for poking their noses into *our* lab explosion. If there's anything to find, we should be the ones to do it."

Jools said, "Last one to the lab buys the beer."

She sprinted out of the alley and was soon out of sight.

But I've already remarked how much faster Miranda is than the rest of us. "Jools can buy her own damned beer," Miranda said. She took to the air and was gone even faster than Jools.

I told Shar, "Don't abandon Richard." I shrank, jumped, and spread my coattails.

I FLEW FULL SPEED TOWARD THE BUILDING'S NEAREST DOOR

I aimed for the tiny gap between the bottom of the door and its frame. Bristly hairs hung down as weather stripping, but I shrank even smaller and zipped madly through the forest like Luke Skywalker in *Return of the Jedi.* The moment I was clear, I grew back to wasp size and zoomed through the halls till I reached the lab.

I stopped short of the door and sent my Spark-o-Vision ahead. Grandfather stood in the ruins while Invie wandered around snuffling at smudges on the floor. Occasionally, the dog licked charred scraps of metal or melted plastic. His collar flickered orange like an irregular strobe light—he was probably gathering data, but don't ask me what. Since Sparks arrived, we've had an embarrassment of new particles, fields, and phenomena. Tachyons are passé; now we talk about upsilon waves, chronon quarks, and smegma radiation. (Seriously, some supersmart Sparks have the maturity of six-year-olds. But when they invent a name, it usually sticks.)

No matter what sensors Invie brought to bear, how much was there to find? I could see that someone had sifted through the room before we arrived. Paths had been cleared through the junk on the floor; debris had been stacked into piles. The place was still a mess, and perhaps something juicy had been overlooked, but the searchers had come and gone, presumably taking all the evidence they'd found.

I wondered who it had been. Local cops? Some secret federal agency? Or perhaps someone unofficial—the Mad Genius who'd made that rift-projecting machine, or the Widow and her friends from the black Lexus.

Maybe even Nicholas.

I HEARD FOOTSTEPS BEHIND ME

Jools came running down the hall. Miranda, glowing gold, floated a short distance in front of her; Miranda could fly faster than Jools could run, but she preferred to denounce racing as "childish" (while making sure to stay in the lead). From the opposite direction, Shar drifted toward me with her feet a short distance off the floor. Richard trailed in her wake, lying unconscious on a levitating bed of violet light.

Before any of them arrived, I couldn't help myself: I flapped to the lab doorway and grew to full size. I leaned against the doorframe and tried to look as if I'd been waiting for the slowpokes to get there.

"Nice trick," Jools said as she jogged the last few steps. "Do you go invisible? Walk through walls? During the fight, I could tell you were helping—I mean, from the way both the skeleton and the skank started screaming. But I can't tell exactly what you do."

I glanced in Grandfather's direction. I told Jools, "Talk to you later."

GRANDFATHER GRINNED

"I figured you four would show up. Have you decided to take over from Invie and me?"

"We're keeping our options open," Miranda said. "Which means keeping an eye on you. Have you found anything?"

«Strong residues of Dark and Light energies,» Invie transmitted.

"The Light may have been from us," Jools said. "And we know there were six Darklings present when this all went down."

«Mere presence is not sufficient for these readings,» the dog said. *«The Darklings must have performed significant magic.»*

"They put up a blinder wall," I said. "Is that enough?"

Invie looked at me with his doleful eyes. *«A conventional blinder wall spell does not produce the amount of energy I'm reading,»* he said. *«An extremely enhanced spell might.»* He sounded doubtful.

"What about opening a great honking portal to hell?" Jools asked.

«No hell energies present,» Invie said. *«Nor traces of other known realities.»*

"We saw a portal," Miranda said. "Not to hell," she added, glaring at Jools. "But definitely to some other unusual place."

Invie's collar strobed fiercely for several seconds. *«No indications,»* he finally reported. *«My sensors can detect evidence of any cataloged universe, but there is always the potential for something new. Alternatively, low-level readings may be masked by the Dark and Light energies. The energies are large enough that they could drown out subtle emanations—especially ones similar to the Dark and Light themselves.»*

"Too bad," Shar said. "It would have been nice to know what we were—"

***«ALERT, ALERT!»* INVIE INTERRUPTED**

«A kraken has been reported approaching Toronto.»

"I don't know the word 'kraken'," Shar said.

"A sea monster," Jools told her. "They used to be legends, until Mad Geniuses started making them for real."

Grandfather said, "Invie uses 'kraken' for anything nasty in the water." He looked at the basset. "Specifics?"

«In Lake Ontario,» Invie answered. *«Massive entity, mostly submerged, on slow approach.»*

"Damn," Grandfather said. "I hate slow approach. It makes me suspicious."

"Of what?" Miranda asked.

Grandfather sighed. "Say a Mad Genius plans something bad elsewhere in the city. He sends a big dumb car-crusher to draw everybody to the harbor. It pulls in police, Sparks, even Darklings trying to make themselves look good by beating on a monstrosity. Meanwhile, the Mad Genius is miles away, making his real play."

"Miles away," Shar said. "Perhaps Waterloo?"

"That's the problem with distractions," Grandfather said. "You can't tell where the real attack'll be. Doesn't matter either: This kraken may be a time waster, but we still gotta deal with it. You have any idea how many people live on Toronto's waterfront? And God knows how many billion dollars' worth of property."

"So you're leaving?" Miranda asked.

"Got to," Grandfather said. "We're Toronto's guardians. Besides"—he smiled at us all with a look of so much grandfatherly affection, I could barely resist throwing myself at him for a great big hug—"you four can handle whatever's happening here."

"How do you know?" Jools asked. "We could totally suck at being guardians. It's not like we have training or experience. Maybe we don't even care about doing the right thing. We're just four random people who received powers by a fluke."

"That's how the Light works," Grandfather said. "It supers up everyday people and trusts 'em to do what needs doing. Surprisingly often, they do."

"Except for supervillains," Miranda said.

"Every family has black sheep. And even villains can come

through in a pinch. This lake monster in Toronto? If things go too pear-shaped, we got bad guys who'll lend a hand."

"Canadian bad guys," Shar said. "Villainous but civic-minded."

"Nah," Grandfather said, "they just love stomping the crap out of things. But we take what help we can get." He lifted his top hat and gave a bow. "Nice making your acquaintance. I'm sure we'll meet again. At which point I trust you'll be suitably attired."

"Fucking masks," Miranda muttered.

"They're important. They have power." Grandfather put his hat back on and swept his finger along the brim in a little salute. "Walk in the Light, granddaughters."

He laid his hand on Invie's head. I hadn't even noticed the dog come up beside him—very odd, considering my power of sight. Could Invie make himself invisible? Or did Grandfather have the power to become the center of attention so that you ignored everything else?

What powers did the two of them have? What made them so nonchalant about facing this kraken? I had trouble picturing either of them punching a giant squid.

But Grandfather was smiling hugely as he and the hound disappeared.

*Ground Truthing**

LEFT ALONE IN THE LAB, WE LOOKED AT EACH OTHER
"What now?" Jools asked.

"I guess we search," I said.

"For what?" Miranda asked. "Not only has everything been smashed and burnt, but somebody clearly rummaged through the room before we got here."

"We'll find something," Jools said. "There's always some clue—like maybe a scrap of paper with GPS coordinates written in blood."

"Helloooo," Miranda said, "that's in stories, not the real world."

"Dude, we left the real world two hours ago. You can fly. Shar reads minds. I know the fine structure constant. And Kim . . ." She paused. "What *do* you do?"

"I shrink." I dropped to the size of a Barbie, gave a bow, then popped back up again.

"Fuck me!" Jools said.

"Do you know how impossible that is?" Miranda asked. "How can it work? Do your atoms get closer together?"

"No," I said, "because my mass goes down too."

"Maybe you're losing atoms," Jools suggested.

"That can't be," Shar said. "Kim's made up of complex molecules. If they lose atoms, they fall apart. Then *Kim* falls apart."

"But maybe," Jools said, "if Kim selectively lost exactly the right molecules in exactly the right proportions—"

"Ahem!" I said loudly. They clearly hadn't paid enough attention

* Getting out into the real world to check a supposition that originally came from lab experiments, computer modeling, or map/photo analysis.

to Grandfather. "I shrink by generating an omnimorphic field that shrinks me, my clothes, the stuff in my pockets . . . everything. Plus anything I'm holding in my hands."

"What the hell is an omnimorphic field?" Miranda asked. "That's sheer and utter . . ."

I put my finger to her lips just as Grandfather had done minutes before. *"I generate an omnimorphic field,"* I said sternly. *"It's an amazing wonder of Science."*

Miranda glared but took the hint. She held her tongue.

"And I," said Shar, "am psionically attuned to the energy flows of the universe. That allows me to make serendipitous discoveries, even in the midst of chaos. Like this lab."

"Oh, for fuck's—" Miranda began, but this time, I pressed my whole hand to her lips.

Shar grinned, then put on a deadpan earnest expression. She closed her eyes and turned in a circle, as if starting to play blindman's bluff.

"And I'm awesome at everything," Jools said with a taunting look at Miranda. "Including searching. I'm the fucking *queen* of searching." She too closed her eyes and started walking.

I took my hand away from Miranda's mouth. Under my breath, I told her, "If we have such high liminality quotients, there may be limits on what we can get away with, but I'll bet they're psychological. We hit the wall when trying for more feels like going too far."

"And if I declare that my sonic powers let me hear where evidence is hiding?"

"You don't believe that," I said. "You disbelieve it so strongly, it can't possibly work. Maybe you've completely set your boundaries already. But I think we've still got wiggle room. Our core identities are solid, but we've still got slack on the details."

Miranda looked like she was going to argue. Then she sighed and laid a hand on my arm. "Kim, you're naturally inclined to be omnimorphic. Some of us are more constrained."

Suddenly, she leapt into the air and shot straight up to the ceiling. Miranda hovered for a moment with her back to what remained of the roof, like someone floating facedown in a swimming pool. She closed her eyes, took a deep breath as if steeling herself for a great effort, then sang a single piercing note. My hands flew to cover my ears, but the note ended as sharply as it began. In the ensuing silence, a single sound persisted: a ringing resonance like a small bell after it's been struck.

I WALKED TOWARD THE SOUND

The ringing didn't fade like the toll of a real bell would. It continued at the same volume, like in a movie where a phone rings endlessly in a dark empty house. As I drew nearer, I felt like the person who answers the phone and immediately gets stabbed from behind. Of course, with my Spark-o-Vision, I could see anyone creeping up on me . . . and suddenly I realized I could Spark-o-View the source of the ringing.

I was close enough to tell that the sound came from a pile of charred metal and melted wires. I threaded my viewpoint through the wreckage, magnifying my sight to get a better look. Something vibrated in the middle of the heap like a plucked guitar string.

The ringing stopped as soon as I spotted the object. Silence, eerie and thick.

The object was the size and shape of a birthday-cake candle. One end had a metallic luster while the other was adamantine—brilliant, jewellike. The metal end resembled polished steel; it changed slowly but seamlessly along the length of the "candle," morphing into the bright clear crystal at the opposite end.

I'd never seen anything like it. It had no glow of power, but I couldn't believe it was made by conventional means. This was either Cape Tech or a magical artifact.

I PULLED MY VISION BACK INTO MY HEAD

I swept aside debris to uncover the mysterious "candle." As I picked it up, Miranda dropped from the ceiling and landed beside me. I held it up for her to see. "From some kind of machine?" she suggested.

"Or magic," I said. "Nothing natural could resonate that long."

"Might have been the effect of my powers," Miranda said. "As it happens, I'm able to instill audible vibrations in materials that contain Light or Dark energies."

I smiled. "Now was that so hard? Everyone is a little omnimorphic."

"You wish," Miranda replied. "I've been thinking of other tricks too."

The metal-crystal object in my hand said, "Hello, my name is Kim." It spoke in my own voice. It didn't sound the way I hear myself in my head, but I've heard enough recordings of my voice to know what I sound like. "So," I said to Miranda, "super-ventriloquism."

"Sound effects in general," she said. "I could simulate the noise of a freight train running through the room at full volume, but I don't want to upset Jools and Shar."

"Now you're getting into the spirit of things," I said. I was about to say more when Shar announced, "Aha!"

SHE STOOD ON A DISC OF VIOLET LIGHT HOVERING HALFWAY UP ONE WALL LIKE A WORKER ON A SCAFFOLD

The wall was made of cinder blocks, originally painted a glossy cream color. The paint was now charred in some places, blistered with bubbles in others, and flaking off completely in many large patches. Shar pointed to an area where the bare cinder block was exposed. Miranda flew up to take a look, but I just stayed where I was and shifted my viewpoint.

A symbol was carved into one of the blocks as deep as the inscription on a tombstone. It was an equilateral triangle, point downward: like a YIELD sign, but instead of a word in the middle, it had the ∞ infinity symbol.

I said, "Oh hell." I was looking at a powder keg.

IT WAS THE MARK OF THE UNBOUND . . . MAYBE

Officially, the Elders of the Dark claim that in 1982, all the Darklings of the world met in a conclave and agreed to issue the Dark

Invitation. The story is a lie: There never was nor will be a time when all the Darklings agree on anything.

The counterstory (told to me by Nicholas) was that a number of ancient vampires, were-beasts, and demons fiercely disapproved of what the majority of Elders decided. The dissenters became known as the Unbound: the bogeymen to the bogeymen. The Unbound were the enemy of conventional Darklings, always lurking in the shadows, conspiring.

Rumors sprang up that the Unbound could liberate new Darklings from the bonds of the Dark Pact—a major attraction for many post-1982 Darklings who hated having their actions curtailed by restrictions. For the right price, the Unbound would supposedly free Darklings from all the magical geasa that prevented new Darklings from going too far.

Of course, that didn't make sense. Why would fierce old tyrants who didn't want to sell the gift of Darkness in the first place then help the nouveau Dark in exchange for cash? But ignoring that contradiction, numerous Darklings began to seek out the Unbound.

Mostly the Darklings trying to find the Unbound ran into stings set up by the Dark Guard: false fronts designed to uncover would-be defectors from the Pact. Executions swiftly followed. Yet rumors persisted that the real Unbound were out there. If they were, your family's business rivals might no longer be bound by the Pact . . . in which case, they would *eat your lunch*.

Nicholas told me that certain Darklings cautiously used the ∞ symbol in an attempt to attract the Unbound's attention. Others used the symbol as a rallying sign, just as swastikas are used as symbols of rebellion by people who've never met a real Nazi.

So what about the ∞ on the wall of the lab? Was it someone just trolling to make the Elders mad? Was it put there by Darkling rebels who identified with the Unbound even if they hadn't actually met one? Or were the real Unbound connected with this somehow? Powerful, ancient entities who didn't acknowledge the Pact or any other restraint.

I hated all those possibilities. But some were worse than others.

I SAID, "CAN WE GET RID OF THAT THING?"
Its presence guaranteed an extreme Dark Guard response. I said, "Let's use a sonic blast to wipe the wall clean."

Miranda glared down at me. "You mean destroy evidence?" She looked at the triangle-∞. "Evidence that will help us avoid blame for the explosion? Because a) this is way too high for us to have reached, and b) I have no idea how we could have chopped it into the wall even if we did get up here."

She had a point. We could have climbed a ladder to get to the symbol's height, but the carving would have taken time and specialized tools.

"To heck with evidence," I decided. "There's never going to be a trial. Look what happened with the police—that woman at the station shut them down. The Darklings have decided to hush this whole thing up."

"That's the best-case scenario," Miranda said. "But if it doesn't happen . . ."

"Then," Shar said, "a team of brand-new Sparks will tell the media, 'Look at that sign on the wall! Those four nice students were innocent bystanders and this is actually a plot by rebellious Darklings.'"

She was right. We couldn't take the symbol down. We had to leave the hornets' nest where it was.

JOOLS SAID, "STOP CONGRATULATING YOURSELVES; I'VE FOUND SOMETHING TOO."
She'd been rooting through debris near a heavy wooden table lying on its side. The table must have been heaped with papers; now the papers were scattered across the floor. The top layer was charred black, but underneath, Jools had found a massive green book that I instantly recognized: the famous "rubber bible," otherwise known as the *CRC Handbook for Physics and Chemistry*.

For decades, the Chemical Rubber Company had published handbooks containing information about everything under the sun: heats of enthalpy, logarithms, protein structures, and a million other things techies needed to know. Now, of course, they've moved their data online, but not so long ago, every scientist, engineer, and STEM student had to have their own CRCs. (Both my mother and father had their own CRCs, and both had tried to give me the books before I left for university. "You'll need this; trust me." "No, I won't, I've got my phone, and if I carry fifty spare batteries, they'll still weigh less than that.")

There was nothing unusual about this lab having a CRC handbook. Thousands of labs must contain abandoned CRCs, left by people who can find the same info faster using the Web. Nor was it strange that such a book had survived the explosion—it was a big honking slab of more than two thousand pages, bound by excellent rubberized covers. You'd have to work hard to ignite that sucker. The copy in Jools's hands had a tiny bit of fire damage on the corners, but it was still mostly intact.

As Jools walked over to join us, she hefted the book and flipped open the front cover so we could see. A name had been written on the endpapers in extravagantly fine cursive writing—the kind of penmanship that takes hundreds of hours to master, looking baroquely ornate while remaining easy to read.

"Adam Popigai," I said. "Never heard of him."

Jools glowed green. "He's a prof in Chem Eng. Degrees from Lermontov, Princeton, and Cambridge. Hired six months ago—he got his picture in the *Daily Bulletin*." She closed her eyes as if seeing the photo. I imagined she was. More and more, I suspected that Jools had a mental Internet connection with one hell of an amazing search engine. Her eyes opened. "Popigai's skin is completely metal."

"So he's either a Spark or demon." Metal skin sounded more like science than magic, but Grandpa Tang's woodcuts included a few cast-iron demons. "Did the *Bulletin* say whether Popigai was Light or Dark?"

"That would be rude," Shar said, which was true. As the official voice of the university, the *Daily Bulletin* would no more say whether someone was Light or Dark than it would casually reveal someone's religion. You just didn't mention such things unless they were very, very pertinent to a story.

"If he's a chemical engineer," Miranda said, "he's likely a Spark. Darklings usually avoid scientific nitty-gritty."

"Unless they're doing alchemy," Shar put in. "With so many Darklings in the government, alchemy research receives an enormous amount of funding. Our chemistry department has hired several Darkling alchemists in an effort to acquire a share of that money. It wouldn't surprise me if Chem Eng did the same."

Alchemy made me think of the "birthday candle" we'd found. The way in which it progressed so smoothly from metal to crystal might indeed indicate it had been made by alchemical transmutation.

I still held the object; I ran my fingers along it, feeling no irregularities, no joints. What was it? What was it for?

The simple answer was that it might be for anything, especially if it was imbued with magic. Theoretically, any object can be enchanted, but it's easier to use high-level wizardry on specially prepared items rather than random old junk that's lying around. If the "candle" I held was created by alchemy, it might be a talisman with extremely powerful effects.

I set it down quickly. I shouldn't have touched it in the first place. My annoying imagination envisioned terrible possibilities of what the "candle" might have done to me.

"LET'S GET OUT OF HERE," I SAID

"Don't you want to keep searching?" Shar asked.

"We've found some interesting things," I said, "and the longer we stay, the more chance of someone showing up. We really don't want to be seen without masks or costumes."

"Masks. Costumes," Miranda said. "Yuck."

"Oh, you'll love whipping up a costume," Jools told her. "That is totally your thing."

Miranda scowled, but Jools was right. Miranda was our fashion queen; clothes mattered to her almost as much as physics and opera. Once she got into outfitting mode, she'd try to make costumes for all of us. "Fine," Miranda said. "Let's head home."

With the still-unconscious Richard floating behind us, we traipsed back to the van.

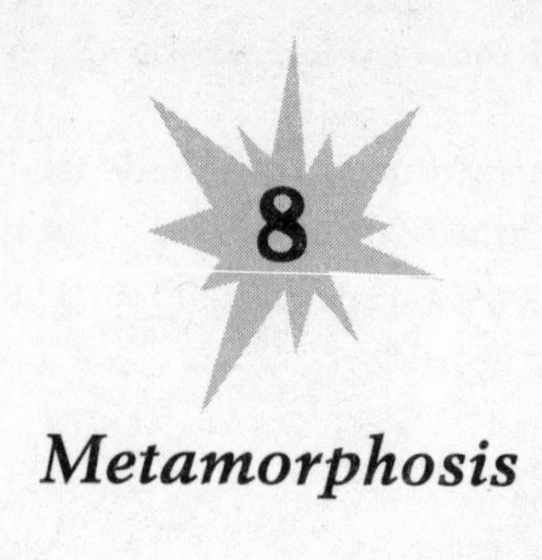

Metamorphosis

LILITH AND THE OTHERS STILL LAY WHERE THEY'D FALLEN
Good: That likely meant no one had witnessed the fight. If we got away fast, and if Invie's tongue had truly erased the Darklings' memories, they'd have no clue what had happened when they finally woke up.

SHAR TELEKINETICALLY DUG THE CAR KEYS OUT OF RICHARD'S POCKET
She handed the keys to Miranda because experience had proved that this was the path of least resistance. Miranda was too well-bred to criticize other people's driving, but if she wasn't driving herself, she sat bolt upright with her fists clenched as if expecting a crash any moment. It was very distracting. Jools got shotgun because she *always* got shotgun, so the rest of us piled into the back.

Shar used her powers to slide Richard into the van's middle seat, leaning him against the windows on the far side, then buckling him into place with the seat belt. She showed no qualms at slinging him around like a human-size backpack. I decided I was offended on Richard's behalf, but really I was just disposed to take offense at anything Shar did.

I hadn't forgotten how she'd messed with my mind. During the fight, I'd had more pressing things to think about, but now that the life-or-death was over, I had ample opportunity to brood. Kim, Kimmi, or Kimberley, I've always been a first-class brooder.

What Shar had done was horrific. Unforgivable! And so typically I'm-the-only-real-adult-here Shar.

Curdling with resentment, I got into the rearmost seat of the van and felt hard done by. I wished I could have huddled there, enveloped in sullen shadows, but my damned Spark-o-Vision made the van's interior look like a beaming summer's day. Despite my sunny surroundings, I did my best to glower.

NO ONE SPOKE AS MIRANDA BACKED THE VAN OUT OF THE ALLEY For some reason, we stayed silent until we'd finally left the campus and got out to the city streets.

Jools let out a noisy sigh. "So *that* happened."

"Yes," Miranda said. "Why yes, it did."

"Fuck," Jools said.

"Well put," Miranda agreed.

"And," said Jools, "we're all going to be thirty-six triple-Ds."

I said, "That'll ruin my mystique."

"Also your nose," Miranda said, "when you fall over on your face."

"I'll fall over," I said, "but my face won't touch the ground."

"I shall find it most annoying," Shar said, "if I have to buy a whole new wardrobe."

Without even thinking, I said, "You know what annoys *me*? When someone stomps around in my brain!"

A moment later, I literally stared at myself in surprise. (I can do that now.) Non-super Kim hated confrontation, but Kim 2.0 apparently wasn't as repressed.

Shar sighed. "I'm sorry you were upset, Kim, but it was necessary. You were losing your head in a dangerous situation. I did what was needed to keep you steady."

"You made me an inhuman machine! Don't you know—"

I stopped myself; I couldn't explain. When you grow up as a studious Chinese girl, do you know how often "machine" is whispered behind your back? How often you're brought to tears, thinking maybe it's true?

One reason I became Kimmi was to demolish my image as a mark-maximizing robot. She was a calculated effort to make myself un-bookish. Now that I was Kim, I felt more genuine, but I'd still assembled my current persona carefully: the look, the style, the trimmings. Going away to university was my chance to get myself *right*.

I knew that I planned my identities in ways other people didn't. I prepared, I made choices, where others couldn't imagine conscious decisions. When you stop following well-trodden paths, you have to make your own.

But I wasn't cold. Never that. "Deliberate" is not "detached."

"Kim," said Shar, "you know I didn't mean any harm. If I went too far in calming you, I just hadn't grasped the strength of my powers."

"Doing *anything* was going too far," I said. "You can't just manipulate someone's emotions."

"The thing is," Shar said, "I can."

"But you shouldn't. It's the sort of thing supervillains do."

Shar didn't answer. Perhaps because I was sitting behind her, she thought I couldn't see her face. But I'd shifted my viewpoint to the front of the van, so I'd have a clear view of everyone. The look on Shar's face was resentful; I could almost hear her saying, *I did it for your own good.*

WITH ARTIFICIAL BREEZINESS, JOOLS SAID, "SO HAS ANYONE PICKED OUT A NAME?"
Miranda groaned. "Do we have to?"

"I've been checking my mental database," Jools said. "So far as I can tell, any Spark who gets a name, mask, and costume . . . it's just ridiculous how thoroughly they maintain their secret identities. Some of these people are like seven feet tall and made of muscle; they must stand out in a crowd like Goliath surrounded by Davids. And what about ultra-hotties like Tigresse? Every guy I've ever met has her poster taped up in his room. Even the guys who are gay."

"*Especially* the guys who are gay," I said.

"Truth. So how come she's never recognized? When she walks down the street, it should be all over Twitter. But nothing."

"Actually," Shar said, "Tigresse sightings *are* all over Twitter. People are constantly spotting her in their local McDonalds."

"Yeah, having lunch with Elvis," Jools said. "But there are hundreds of Sparks in the world, and most are so distinctive you'd spot them from miles away. They never get outed as long as they keep on their masks. What does that tell you?"

"Look," Miranda said, "I have a mask—that one from Halloween, remember?"

"Oh yes," Shar said. "It's lovely."

"But everyone's seen it," said Miranda. "I wore it to that party in Fed Hall. What will happen if I wear it as a Spark? *Hey look, that superheroine is wearing the same mask as Miranda. And she's built the same as Miranda, and her hair is the same color.*"

"That's not how it works," Jools said. "Nobody puts two and two together. Like Grandfather said, it's a superpower: The mask clouds everyone's mind."

Miranda grimaced. "I hate when things don't make sense."

"Dude, you fly by singing," Jools said. "And Kim's omnimorphic, which we all know isn't a real thing. And—"

"Okay, I get it!" Miranda snapped. "We've switched from the real world to Dungeons and Dragons. Fine! But I don't have to like it."

"What's not to like? You can fucking fly!" Jools grinned broadly. I noticed that her teeth looked straighter. "I know it won't all be ponies and teddy bears. The things that pop into my head—I see bad things as well as good. All the horrible, grisly shit Sparks have gone through since they appeared. You want a list of atrocities, I can talk for hours on end. But at least let's enjoy the fun parts. Like picking out names."

Shar said, "Have *you* chosen a name?"

"Ninety-Nine," Jools answered immediately.

"Excuse me?"

"Ninety-Nine," Jools repeated. "Wayne Gretzky's number."

"Who's Wayne Gretzky?" Shar asked.

Jools gaped. "You are never going to be granted Canadian citizenship."

"Wayne Gretzky," I told Shar disdainfully, "is the greatest hockey player ever. One hundred percent Albertan, even if he made the mistake of being born in Ontario."

Miranda said, "Gretzky won't be pleased if some Spark pretends she's him."

"I'm just borrowing his number," Jools said. "Like a tribute band."

"But for your costume," Miranda said, "I'll bet you're planning to wear your Edmonton Oilers jersey: the one with the big ninety-nine on the back."

"Look," Jools said, "I've thought this through. You and Shar have force fields. Kim gets so small no one can find her. But what do I have? I heal quickly, but it *hurts* getting my throat crushed and my face sliced off. So I'm gonna wear my hockey equipment. That way I'll have some padding between me and the bad guys. Hockey gear, hockey jersey, hockey name."

"The Oilers will sue you," Miranda said. "Gretzky will sue you. The NHL will sue you."

"Oh all right," Jools grumbled. "I've got more than one jersey. I'll wear the solid black one. *Ninja* Ninety-Nine."

"And for my costume," Miranda said, "I'll get a T-shirt that reads I'M NOT WITH THE DWEEB."

SHAR SAID, "I INTEND TO CALL MYSELF DAKINI."
"What does that mean?" Miranda asked.

"Dakinis are spirits. Goddesses. They're similar to the Muses in Greek mythology, except they inspire you to enlightenment rather than the arts."

"Actually," Jools said, glowing green, "dakinis play different roles in different traditions . . ."

"I've said what role I shall play," Shar replied. "Calling myself Dakini will remind me to act for the betterment of others. Not to be irresponsible."

She gave me a look. I ignored it.

"WHAT ABOUT YOU, KIM?" JOOLS ASKED
"Have you picked a name?"

"Diamond," I said. That surprised me when it came out—it hadn't been in my mind at all. But once I thought of the way my skin went hard and faceted when I shrank, Diamond was actually quite good.

"Diamond," Miranda said. "I should have known it would be a rock."

"Diamond isn't a rock, it's a mineral."

Jools glowed green. "You can't call yourself Diamond, Kim. The name is taken."

"By whom?"

"A Mad Genius in Australia. Total douchewad. He shows up every few months, kills hundreds of people with his latest crazy scheme, then escapes without getting caught. He's so bad, whenever he comes out of hiding, the Dark and the Light work together to beat him. Even then, it's always a close call."

"So what if there's another Diamond?" The more I thought about it, calling myself Diamond would be perfect. "This douche guy is on the other side of the world. There ought to be room for two of us."

"What if this Diamond guy gets pissed off?" Miranda asked. "What if the next time he goes on a rampage, he decides to hit Waterloo because somebody stole his name?"

I had no answer. It was insane to kill people halfway around the world just because of a name, but Mad Geniuses are called mad for a reason.

Grudgingly I set the name "Diamond" aside. Too bad. Remember, my true name is Kimberlite: the rock that most often contains diamonds. I've never gone by Kimberlite, but I like having it in reserve—a special fallback identity in case I screw everything else up.

I had only told my true name to two people in my life: Nicholas and Hannah.

I SAID, "WHAT ABOUT ZIRCON? IS THAT OKAY?"
Jools glowed green. "Nobody named Zircon," she reported.

"Do you really want that name?" Shar asked me. "Zircons have a reputation for being tawdry. You shouldn't pick a name that will make you feel that way, Kim."

"If you're thinking of the fake diamonds," I said, "they're cubic zirconia—zirconium dioxide. Totally different from zircons, which are zirconium silicate. Real zircons are *amazing*: the oldest things on Earth we can put a date on. We've found zircons 4.3 billion years old. They're tough as hell, resistant to physical and chemical changes, and they're great for radioactive dating. Geologists love 'em."

Shar looked at me a few seconds longer, then shrugged. "All right. Zircon."

"THAT LEAVES YOU," JOOLS SAID TO MIRANDA

"Gotta be Valkyrie," I said.

"Definitely," Shar agreed.

Jools shook her head. "Do you know how many Sparks call themselves Valkyrie? One in Stockholm, one in Berlin, one in Osaka . . . oh fuck, you do *not* want to know what the one in Osaka wears."

"I don't want to be Valkyrie," Miranda said. "Honestly, if you're a blond soprano, do you know how often you get called a valkyrie? I'm sick of it."

"What do you prefer?" Shar asked.

"What about something to do with birds?" Miranda asked. "I sing, I fly . . ."

"Yeah," Jools said, "but I don't see you as Lark or Nightingale. None of those songbird types. What do you think of Screech Owl?"

Miranda glared.

"Screaming Eagle?"

Glare.

"Howler Monkey?"

"All right, forget wildlife!" Miranda said. "What about Aria?"

Jools glowed green. "Hmm. No Arias."

"Aria is nice," Shar said. "Sophisticated."

"Like farting champagne bubbles," Jools said.

Miranda gave Jools one last glare, but she said, "Aria will do unless I think of something better. And we're home."

WE HAD REACHED OUR TOWNHOUSE'S PARKING LOT

It was practically empty. Almost every student with a car had already gone home for Christmas. Most of the townhouses were probably empty too, but how could I tell? To Spark-o-Vision, every house looked like it had all its lights on, as if twenty separate parties were going full swing.

They weren't. The place was quiet. The van's dashboard clock said midnight.

MIRANDA PARKED THE VAN BEHIND OUR UNIT

It was a typical student townhouse, but I'd been spoiled by a much better model: the townhouse where Nicholas stayed while at "finishing school" in Banff. He'd described his townhouse as "cozy," but I called it "posh" . . . and that was before I understood how much money you can spend on something as prosaic as a wastebasket.

(Let me add, I'm ignoring the expense of refitting the townhouse to accommodate Nicholas's wheelchair. Then again, the house's most important accessibility feature was the formidable Ms. Bain: a mute and muscular woman who drank the blood of Nicholas's father once a month, and could therefore carry both Nicholas and his chair as if they were as light as a laundry hamper.)

The townhouse I shared in Waterloo was nothing like the one in Banff. It wasn't out-and-out awful: We'd spackled the holes made by previous tenants and put on fresh coats of paint; we also had a brand-new fridge and stove, thanks to Shar bribing the landlord with cookies. In lieu of cute animal pictures and posters of firefighters, our living room had something we could all enjoy—a wall-size chart of the periodic table. And the boring white broadloom could barely be seen under all the throw rugs plus a Persian carpet provided by Miranda. (That carpet was likely worth a fortune, but I'd never asked the price. Miranda already thought I was obsessed with money, and I didn't want to give her more ammunition.)

THE MOST IMPORTANT THING ABOUT OUR HOUSEHOLD IS ALMOST INVISIBLE

That night, it could only be seen as two coffee mugs in the sink, left by Miranda and me after drinking post-dinner chai. Those mugs were a sign that Miranda and I (and Jools and Shar) all shared the same level of Clean. We were neither neat freaks nor slobs. We could leave mugs in the sink and no one would have a seizure, but we didn't let too much mess accumulate.

That was what truly kept us together. Jools and Miranda might snipe at each other, Shar might treat us like children, and I might run off to look at rocks because I was less than great at socializing. But we were on the same page for housework, and that was precious.

We'd lived together peaceably since the start of our second year. Superpowers are nothing compared to compatible standards of tidiness.

AS SOON AS WE GOT INSIDE, JOOLS RAN UP TO HER ROOM

I suspected she was going for booze, but I resisted sending my Spark-o-Vision to spy on her. I refused to be as intrusive as Shar.

Speaking of Shar, she said, "Cookies are on the counter. Help yourselves." She headed up to her room too. Richard was in tow behind her, still unconscious on that violet platform.

Miranda and I were left alone. She rolled her eyes and said, "Costumes. Sigh." Then she brightened. "Do you need help?"

"No, I'm fine," I said. "I used to be good at dress-up."

But I'd never talked about Kimmi with Miranda or anyone else in Waterloo. To avoid the threat of a real conversation, I shrank and flew up to my room.

MY ROOM . . . OH, MY ROOM

I'd hung the walls with geological maps: one showing the region around Banff; one showing the whole of Alberta; one of southern Ontario (I'd been forced to buy that map for a course); and one covering all of Canada, from coast to coast to coast.

Much as I love geology, I knew the maps were my way of avoiding more personal decorations. Jools had hockey stuff, including a life-size poster of Wayne Gretzky; Shar had two Buddha statues and dozens of photos of Sri Lanka; Miranda had genuine prints by Matisse and Lichtenstein; but I just had maps.

They were placeholders. I'd never figured out what Kim would want to see first thing in the morning and last thing at night.

"COSTUME," I MUTTERED. "GOTTA MAKE A COSTUME." I opened my closet and stared, half hoping that Spark-o-Vision would come to my rescue. If it gave me laser sights when I aimed a gun, why couldn't it point to an ideal outfit? But my eyes refused to rescue me. If anything, they made things worse—they displayed my wardrobe bright and shadow-free, mercilessly revealing that I had nothing "super" to wear.

When it came to clothes, Kim was the anti-Kimmi. Kimmi had always dressed in deliberate costumes; Kim strove to avoid the tiniest costume-y whiff.

Usually, I wore shapeless bib overalls . . . not the cute girly kind, but ones in blue denim made for small fat men. Mario overalls. I mostly wore single-color work shirts, but I also had a supply of T-shirts acquired at various campus events. (Students can measure their time on campus by the number of T-shirts they have. T-shirts build up like sedimentary strata on closet shelves.)

I had no "dressy" clothes. I sure as hell didn't own spandex. And not a single cape! What an oversight.

As for masks, Kimmi had been big into Halloween, so Kim wasn't. Zero in the mask department. I *did* own a decent quantity of makeup—it's useful when you want to keep people guessing. But a "mask" made of makeup would be a pain to apply and clean off, so that was a last resort.

I was still staring morosely at my closet's lack of potential when someone knocked on my door. Without thinking, I shifted my viewpoint out into the hall.

My jaw dropped. Ninety-Nine. An honest-to-goodness superhero.

OMFG.

NINETY-NINE WAS AWESOME

These days, "awesome" doesn't mean very much. We tell kids they're awesome if they can tie their own shoes. But Ninety-Nine literally inspired awe.

Superficially, I saw a young woman in an all-black hockey uniform. I'd seen Jools wear that outfit plenty of times, but my brain refused to connect this amazing vision with Jools. The idea made me laugh—Jools was just my roommate. Ninety-Nine couldn't possibly be the same person.

Ninety-Nine wore black Reeboks instead of skates. She had padding and fiberglass guards on shoulders, elbows, knees, and shins, making her look even more imposing than she was without them. (This heroine *couldn't* be Jools; Jools wasn't that big and majestic.) Ninety-Nine wore a black fiberglass helmet, but she'd also smeared black greasepaint around her eyes in the shape of a mask. On the back of her jersey was the number 99, made with glossy black satin that seemed to shine.

You may think you have a mental picture of what Ninety-Nine looked like. No. Unless you actually saw her, you can't imagine her Halo.

Ninety-Nine was inspiring. Uplifting. One look, and I wanted to be so much more than I was. Why wasn't I working to perfect my body and mind, or inventing new ways to feed the hungry? No, wait, I was a geologist; I knew that was my calling. So I should be studying day and night to develop skills that would let me save innocents from earthquakes, floods, and other natural disasters.

I wanted to be as pure and good and strong as Ninety-Nine. I wanted to help her in every way I could. Then, together, we'd make the universe perfect.

SHE KNOCKED AGAIN

I raced to open the door, eager to stammer out apologies for keeping her waiting. But I couldn't talk. I just stared.

After a moment, she said, "What?"

She waited. I still couldn't speak.

"Have I got a booger or something?" She raised her hand to her nose and searched a bit. When she didn't find anything, she looked at me again. "What? What?"

THAT WAS WHEN I SMELLED THE VODKA ON HER BREATH

Noticing the smell didn't completely counteract Ninety-Nine's Halo, but it took the edge off my hero worship. I shifted my viewpoint straight up through the roof so I couldn't see Ninety-Nine at all: just clear fresh air and the stars. I breathed for a moment, then said, "Take something off before I wet myself."

"Excuse me?"

"Take something off. Your helmet—that should be enough. Anything to reduce the effect."

After a moment, I heard grumbling and the sound of the helmet being unstrapped. I counted to five, then shifted my viewpoint back into my head. The helmet was off and Jools was where Ninety-Nine had been standing.

"Wow," I said.

"Wow what?"

"Your Halo," I said. "It packs a punch."

"Really? What's it like?"

"Like meeting a goddess."

"You mean I'm hot?"

"No. It's totally different."

Jools made a face. "Kim, not to be rude, but would a *guy* think I'm hot?"

I smiled. I would have kissed her on the cheek, but I couldn't have reached, not even on my tiptoes. "Yes, I'm a total expert on how guys think," I said. "Not. But I guarantee they won't be able to take their eyes off you."

"I can't take my eyes off spiders," Jools muttered, "but I don't think they're hot."

"YOU'LL BE AS HOT AS A VOLCANO," I ASSURED HER "We'll all be supermodels, and have such rock-hard abs we'll crack walnuts with our belly buttons." I ran my fingers dramatically through my brush cut. "Tomorrow morning, I'll be a six-foot-tall redhead."

"That's not what your wish fulfillment wants," Jools said. She looked at me thoughtfully. "Actually, I'm hella curious what your wish-fulfillment look turns out to be."

"You and me both." I felt a stab of discomfort talking about such matters, even with Jools. Not good at sharing, our Kim. "Did you want something?"

"I wanted you to tell me I looked hot," Jools said. "Instead you went all weird."

"Sorry. Your Halo hits like a battering ram."

"Well, good; then I'll knock guys off their feet."

"Wayne Gretzky, but with thirty-six triple-Ds," I said. "The total guy-magnet package."

"You really *don't* understand guys," Jools said. "If I want action, I'd be better off rubbing myself with bacon."

"Instead of smelling like vodka?"

The words came out without a thought—as if someone else had said them. I gasped and covered my mouth with my hand. I *never* said things like that.

"Ouch," Jools said. "Busted."

"Oh, Jools," I said, "I'm sorry. I don't know what got into me."

Green light flashed around her head. "Personality changes are common when people become Sparks. Especially increased impulsiveness." She tried to smile. "Maybe my personality will change and I'll stop drinking."

My face was burning. I didn't know what to say.

"Kim," Jools said, "I'd rather get hassled by you than Shar or Miranda. And now that I'm a Spark, maybe everything will be great. Olympic-level willpower. Olympic-level common sense."

I nodded, not saying the obvious: that despite her superpowers, Jools had raced to belt back a drink the moment she got home. I mumbled, "Do you want to talk about this or something?"

"Fuck, no," Jools said. "But," she added after a moment, "I'll help you make a costume."

"What makes you think I need help?"

"Three years of looking at your wardrobe." She smiled. "Dude, I know why you wear what you do, and I'm a fan, truly. I admire you for going your own way. But you don't have the kit for the costume thing. I do. I have my own sewing machine, tons of thread, stuff I can use for lining—all that shit. And on top of that . . ."

"You're an Olympic-level costume maker?"

"Preee-cisely. And a big part of that is knowing what the customer wants and needs. I promise not to deck you out like a cheerleader. I'll be sensitive as fuck to who you are—"

"I don't know who I am," I said. "If my personality is changing . . . if my body is changing . . ."

"Blah fuckity blah," Jools said. "Have your identity crisis after we're done. Right now, Zircon needs threads."

I hesitated, but I wasn't really thinking it over. Kim 2.0 (or maybe Zircon) was simply having a knee-jerk bout of ego.

"All right," I said when the resistance subsided. "Come in. Make me look super."

"FIRST THINGS FIRST," JOOLS SAID
"We have to know the constraints. Put on something different and see if it shrinks when you do."

"I told you," I said, "I have an omnimorphic field. It includes my clothes and anything I'm holding."

"First rule of science, dumbass: Hypotheses don't mean shit until you do the lab work." Jools tapped the side of her head. "I've checked for info on Sparks who change size, and let me tell you, they aren't all omnimorphic. There's this chick in Denver, grows ten stories tall. (Calls herself Mile High. Inevitable, but yuck.) When Mile High gets big, her clothes rip to shreds unless she's wearing exactly what she had on at the moment she got her powers. Every day, she has to squeeze into the same pair of jeans and Diet Sprite T-shirt. Otherwise, when she grows, she ends up naked. And ten stories tall."

"I don't grow," I said. "I shrink."

"Same difference," Jools said. "If your costume has to be made from what you were wearing in the lab, let's find that out now, okay?"

Grumbling, I pulled a shirt at random from the closet. I put it on over what I was already wearing and tried to shrink.

The transition wasn't easy—like when you think too hard about swallowing and your throat cramps up. I forced myself to relax, and swish! I was ant-sized on the floor. The new shirt shrank exactly as much as I did. Omnimorphic field FTW!

"Whoa!" Jools said. She squatted for a closer look, towering above me like King Kong.

"I told you my clothes would shrink." At least, that's what I tried to say. It was the first time I'd spoken while miniaturized. My throat and larynx were ridiculously small, so the vibrations had proportionally tiny wavelengths. (Basic Physics 122: fundamental frequencies.) My voice was so high it was way past dog whistles. Even my minuscule ears couldn't pick up the sounds. It made me wonder how I could have a normal human hearing range no matter how small my ears were. Maybe my omnimorphic field shrank incoming acoustic wavelengths to match the size of my eardrums. I mentally kicked myself for not claiming that omnimorphism would adjust my voice to an audible pitch, whatever size I was.

But that boat had sailed. If I was right about how Spark powers worked, my too-high voice had just gotten locked in.

How big did I have to get before I could speak comprehensibly? I started repeating, "Testing, one, two, three," while growing. I reached six inches high before I finally became intelligible. My voice still sounded like Pikachu, but at least I wasn't past the end of the piano.

Jools stared down at me. "You're so adorable! I want to cuddle you and make you play with my Barbies."

"Ick!" Completely as a reflex, I shot back up to normal size. Unfortunately, Jools was still leaning over me with an "Aren't you precious?" expression on her face.

My head clocked her jaw and knocked her out cold.

I WAS AS TOUGH AS STONE AND COMPLETELY UNHURT

Jools, on the other hand, had essentially been smashed in the face by a fast-moving rock. She sprawled unconscious on the ground.

I rolled her onto her back and checked her over. She'd lost her two front teeth. If I hadn't been so horrified, I might have laughed. Jools had kept her teeth intact through hundreds of hockey games; *I* was the one who'd finally wrecked her streak.

The teeth had snapped off at the gumline, leaving jagged, bloody stumps poking out. I couldn't see where the teeth had gone. Down her throat? Where she'd choke on them?

It was for times like this I'd learned to swear in Mandarin.

I COULD SEE JOOLS'S MISSING TEETH BY SLIDING MY VIEWPOINT DOWN HER THROAT

The teeth were too deep to reach with my fingers, so yes, I had to climb in and get them.

When you're the size of an insect, carting a tooth up someone's esophagus is like carrying a lightweight but awkwardly big box up a hill made of meat. *Slobbery* meat. The glamorous life of a superhero.

And all the time I was clambering up Jools's tongue, I kept thinking, "She regenerates, she regenerates, she regenerates."

I shoved the first tooth out between her lips and saliva-skied back to get the other. As I tried to haul the second one up her throat, the tooth began to glow green. I quickly dropped it, asking, "What fresh hell is this?"

Hairline fractures spread across the tooth's surface, like mud developing cracks. The enamel made twig-snapping sounds as the fractures grew wider. Simultaneously, the broken roots on Jools's upper gums began extending into full teeth again—as if the enamel and pulp from the detached teeth were teleporting back to where they belonged. Erosion, deposition. The new teeth grew at the same speed that the old ones decayed. Both the old and the new shone soft green, like Christmas lights.

JOOLS GROANED

I was still in her mouth. I hurriedly pushed past her lips. By the time her eyes opened, I was back to full size and kneeling beside her.

"Ow." Jools sat up. "Illegal body contact."

"Sorry," I said. "How do you feel?"

"Like someone head-butted me." She gingerly fingered her face. "You're lucky you didn't break something."

"I broke two of your teeth, but they fixed themselves. Better than before: I think they're straighter."

"They may be fixed, but they still hurt like hell."

"Negative reinforcement," I said. "So you won't completely ignore injuries, even if all of the damage heals."

Jools grimaced. "Does the Light think I'm so fucking stupid, I won't be careful unless it makes me feel like shit?"

I didn't answer.

"Yeah, okay, the Light knows me." Jools laid her head on her knees. "Ow." She glanced at me. "I seriously want a drink."

"A drink likely won't make the pain go away."

"It would make the wanting go away," Jools said. "For a while."

"STAY HERE," I SAID; "DON'T MOVE"

I ran downstairs, and came back with a dozen cookies. "These are better than liquor," I said.

"No, they aren't. But give 'em here."

Jools took the plate of cookies. Chocolate chip. I watched as she tried to eat one; she chewed with the side of her mouth so she wouldn't have to use her tender front teeth. "Got anything to wash these down?" she asked.

I looked at my desk. "A liter of three-day-old Diet Coke."

"I was thinking of something that rhymes with Smirnoff."

"Not gonna happen." I took one of the cookies for myself. "I'm surprised that drinking affects you. If you recover from injuries so fast . . ."

"Then my body should purge itself of foreign substances?"

"Right," I said. "You should be immune to poisons, disease, parasites . . ."

"As it happens," Jools said with a sly grin, "I have my own omnimorphic field. It neutralizes toxins and infestations, but it knows that alcohol is medicinal. So booze has its usual effects on me until it dissipates naturally."

I winced. "You're going to regret saying that."

"Probably," Jools admitted. "But aren't all Sparks supposed to have some Achilles heel?"

I said, "I have no Achilles heel."

Immediately, I thought of Nicholas.

And Elaine.

And my general obsession with Darklings.

Shut up, brain.

"CAN WE TALK ABOUT SOMETHING ELSE?" I ASKED

"Your costume," Jools suggested. "How ambiguous do you want it?"

"Ambiguous isn't the point," I said. "Ambiguous can just be a tease. I want out of the game completely."

"Got it," Jools said. When she saw I wasn't sold on her ability to pull this off, she said, "Seriously, Kim, I won't jerk you around. You're my roomie. And my friend. I'll do this right."

I felt the sting of tears . . . which felt so stupid, almost crying just because someone said something nice to me. "Okay," I told her. "Use any of my clothes. Cut them, sew them, whatever you need to do."

I practically ran from my own bedroom.

I WENT TO HIDE IN THE BATHROOM

The basement bathroom, where the others wouldn't hear me sniffling.

Jools had called me her friend. She probably meant it.

I thought of Ninety-Nine's Halo: that inspirational goodness. I knew it was just a trick—Jools herself couldn't live up to such an aura of sainthood. But if Spark powers were wish fulfillment, Ninety-Nine's Halo showed who Jools aspired to be.

I was terrified of what Zircon's Halo would say about me.

AFTER A WHILE, I WIPED MY TEARS

My eyes were still red and I didn't want to be seen. Besides, I couldn't do anything else until the costume was finished, so I took off my clothes to see if I had changed.

With Spark-o-Vision, I could examine myself in ways I'd never done before: ways *no one* had ever done. I may be the first human who's ever seen their own back directly. I could inspect parts of me I'd only looked at in mirrors and badly-aimed selfies, and I could do it without having to twist like I was auditioning for Cirque du Soleil.

As far as I could see, nothing was different. Same face, same body, no edits.

Except my hair. I've mentioned I dyed it white, and had recently sprayed it pink. The pink was gone. So were the tiny bits of black at the roots. Considering how long it had been since I'd touched up the color (too busy studying for exams), I figured my wish-fulfillment changes included permanently white hair.

I could live with that.

And yes, of course I've sometimes dreamt of being taller. I've sheepishly imagined being some jaw-dropping *package* whose life would be full of open doors. Maybe a blond Caucasian bombshell like Miranda, or dark-skinned perfection like Tigresse. In the summer between high school and university—between Kimmi and Kim—I mulled over dozens of options.

I knew what wasn't working. It took time to get my head around what would.

I've read about people who "just know." I would have loved to be like that. But self-knowledge is not my strong point. I was all about denial.

Blame it on my obsession to get good grades. For seventeen years, I'd worked my tail off doing all the extra assignments and getting top marks. That's what good girls did—they mastered what they'd been taught. They did *not* drop the course. They definitely didn't think about chucking the whole curriculum.

If not for Nicholas and Elaine, I might have stayed stuck for a long time. But between the two of them, they kicked me off a cliff. Being in free fall can give you a wide, clear view of everything.

I chose what I finally chose because it felt like the true, honest me. It still feels right. But it's thought-provoking to see yourself from a point outside your body, and know you could transform with a simple "I wish." I was still in the Spark transition stage; if I wanted to be different, I could be. An omnimorphic adjustment.

But.

I hadn't run crying into the bathroom because of my body. Or my hair, or my clothes, etc.

Don't fix it if it ain't broke. Quietly, I got dressed again.

MOST OF MY CLOTHES FIT LOOSELY

But good socks are snug—you don't want them slopping around in your boots. Snugness, however, makes them a chore to put on. As I was struggling, I had the brilliant idea to shrink just a little and make my feet smaller so the socks would go on more easily.

Nope. The socks got smaller too. (Omnimorphic field. Duh.) But the important discovery was that my skin turned to the same polished rock I was made of when I was insect-sized. Useful information! At full-size I was normal flesh and blood, but experiment showed I went rocky even if I only shrank a millimeter down from normal. I could be 99.9 percent of my usual height, but armored up . . . and since mineral me was the same color and shape as the bio-version, Zircon could pass for human, at least in bad lighting.

This discovery made me wonder about other aspects of my powers. Like how small could I go?

ALOUD I SAID, "MY SHRINKING HAS NO LIMIT."

Then I proved it.

THE EXPERIMENT WENT SHAKY AS BROWNIAN MOTION KICKED IN

Brownian motion happens because of imbalances in the random movements of molecules, like if a trillion molecules in the air hit you from the right side, but a trillion and ten hit you from the left. Slight differences like that happen every millisecond, but they have no effect when you're a gazillion times the mass of those extra ten molecules. On the other hand, if you're small, those differences in impacts can make you jiggle. (Have a look at dust motes in water; you'll see them dancing.)

I did indeed get small enough to jitter like a flea on a vibrator. Getting battered by all those molecules didn't hurt a bit. I was still as hard as stone and couldn't feel the tiny smacks. Their effects on Spark-o-Vision were more of a problem; if I kept my viewpoint centered in my eyes, my perception shook as badly as I did. I had to shift my viewpoint out of my body and position it on some external point. That stabilized what I saw. My body continued to bounce, but since I couldn't feel it and it didn't affect my senses, it made no difference.

I SHRANK

And shrank.

And shrank.

I could have tried to shrink instantly to the size of a quark, but I was being hypercautious. I'm in geology, not physics, and my knowledge of quantum mechanics is limited to a couple of lectures in first-year chemistry. Beyond that, my notions of quantum weirdness are hazy. I knew the world worked differently down at nanoscale, and I had no idea if I might suddenly get sucked into another universe, ripped apart by quantum forces, or turned into a Kim-shaped black hole.

I came close to chickening out and growing back to normal. The reason I didn't was that I was sure it would establish my lower bound forever: "This far but no farther." So I pressed on slowly, through ever-diminishing scales, until I was too small for visible light. (Once you're tiny enough, you can't reflect light because its wavelength is so big in comparison. Essentially, you fall between the electromagnetic cracks; the waves slop around you rather than bouncing off. It's the same reason long waves like radio go through solid objects as if the objects weren't there.)

My Spark-o-Vision adapted, moving into smaller wavelengths, but always letting me see my surroundings . . . which were increasingly more unrecognizable. I was still in the basement bathroom, nominally on floor tiles, but really inside a dust speck that had become electrostatically attracted to me when I was bigger and had swallowed me when I got small enough. The speck was biological, but don't ask me what it was. Some ridiculous percentage of dust is either flakes from human skin or feces from tiny critters. All I saw were long-chain molecules and fast-moving geometric blobs. I was just starting to make out individual atoms when suddenly the light changed.

THE WORLD WENT ZEBRA

Interference patterns sprang up on everything I saw: shimmering lines of black and white wherever I looked. I thought I'd passed some size threshold that conflicted with my Spark-o-Vision, but to make sure, I tried growing back bigger. The zebra pattern persisted: moiré on every molecule. Even on my own stony skin.

I grew more, but the effect refused to go away. *All right,* I thought, *I could still keep shrinking; I haven't hit a limit. But I'd better check the normal-sized world to see if anything needs my attention.*

Slam! I shot up, to almost full height. But I held back a titch so I'd stay rock instead of flesh. If something weird was afoot, I wanted to be impervious.

I saw no threat in the bathroom, but the lighting seemed odd—infected by some color that shouldn't be there. Cautiously, I sent my viewpoint through the closed door, up the basement stairs, and into the kitchen.

Ah. Oh.

I COULD SEE THE OUTSIDE WORLD THROUGH THE KITCHEN WINDOWS
The stars were still in place, but the stellar background had changed. Previously, it had been an unexceptionable black; now the empty sky displayed the zebra pattern I'd seen at molecular scale. The pattern was dim, like when I turned down the brightness of my computer screen so faint I could barely see it, but the pattern persisted across the entire sky.

I moved my viewpoint outside the house and high enough to clear the rooftops. I could see the stars, and the full moon climbing, but everything was set against that faint black-and-white background.

AS I WATCHED, SNOW BEGAN TO FALL
There were no clouds for the snow to come from. Nothing blocked my view of the stars. But the snow fell anyway: big flakes drifting down sedately.

This wasn't supposed to happen. Every write-up about the eclipse had said *perfect viewing conditions, no clouds*. The weather forecasts might have been wrong, but this had *violation of natural law* written all over it.

I RAN UP TO MY ROOM
At the last second before going through the door, I realized I was still in slightly shrunken rock-form. I stopped and grew one more millimeter, changing back to flesh; then I threw the door open and said, "Jools, what do you see outside?"

She glanced out the window. "It's snowing."

"What color is the sky?"

She gave me a look. I said impatiently, "I don't see normally anymore. What color?"

"Uhh . . ." She went to the window. "The sky is black. Well, grayish—the city lights reflect off the clouds."

"You see clouds?"

"Yes. Don't you?"

"No." I scowled. "I wish I knew which one of us was seeing the truth."

Jools laughed. "See, this is the fun of being a Spark: when things go shit-ass crazy and you can't tell if it's you."

"Yeah, I'm loving it." I glared out the window. "This snow is a very bad sign."

"Of course it is," Jools said, way too cheerfully. "Epic shit is hitting the fan! Four n00b Sparks are all that stand between the world and destruction!"

"Why does it have to be world destruction?" I asked. "Why can't we start small? Like rescuing kittens from trees. I could totally rescue a kitten from a tree."

"How? Your powers are shrinking and not seeing normally. You suck for rescuing kittens."

"I'd say, 'Miranda, please rescue that kitten.' Miranda likes me; she'd do it. And that, my dear Ninety-Nine, is what we call teamwork."

"Speaking of teamwork," Jools said, "I'm trying to make your damned costume. Go away and let me work."

I LEFT
And for the better part of an hour, I parked myself on the couch and did what I do best: I studied.

Specifically, I started filling the gaps in my knowledge of Sparks. I knew the basics like anyone else, but had never dug down into details.

Not that there *were* a lot of details. Oh, it was easy to find flashy stuff: photos of fights and stuff like that. But only a handful of Sparks were *out* in a public way. Few ever talked to the press, and they almost never breathed a hint about their private lives.

Instead, what we got were fantasies. Fiction was full of Sparks, just as it was full of spies and private investigators. Everyone knows the life of a spy is nothing like James Bond, and private eyes don't solve locked-room murders—they take grotty pictures of cheating wives and husbands. I suspected the stories about Sparks were equally inflated and inaccurate. There might be hundreds of books about what super-people did in their civilian lives, but they all sounded like, well, wish fulfillment.

I pressed on, reading at random: about heroes and villains, cosmic and street level, quasi-gods and Mad Geniuses.

I read about Grandfather.

I read about the Inventor.

I read about Stonewall, the only hit on Google when I searched for "genderqueer Sparks." (No good photos, but I liked the "stone" part.) Then I started reading Wikipedia articles on mineral-based Sparks (including that douchebag Diamond who'd preempted my name) until Jools's voice spoke inside my head: *«Yo, Zirksie, time to come back to Zircon Central. Let's see if this costume fits.»*

WHEN I GOT BACK TO MY ROOM, JOOLS GESTURED TOWARD THE BED She'd laid out an outfit on it. The shirt I recognized: a plain white one I'd pulled from the men's rack at Value Village. Everything else was unfamiliar . . . except something about the pants . . . their fabric . . .

I suddenly laughed. The pants had been made from the white lab coat I'd been forced to buy for first-year chemistry. I'd forgotten I owned it; Jools must have found it stuffed in a dresser drawer. I was surprised the coat had had enough fabric for a pair of trousers; then again, Jools might have cut up her own coat too. Both were the same tough cloth, and I could imagine how much satisfaction Jools would get from destroying her coat. She'd hated that class.

One thing for sure: Jools was a kickass seamstress. The pants looked elegant, not hacked together from pieces of something else. If I hadn't known better, I'd have guessed they were new from some upscale store. Then again, maybe this was some of that "plausible deniability" Grandfather had talked about. If you could argue that a good seamstress might have made a nice pair of pants from those lab coats, maybe the Light would bend reality to produce something slick.

Next to the pants lay a white silk vest. It was Miranda's; I'd seen her wear it. But beside the vest was a white frock coat, and I hadn't a clue where it came from. It was a sweet morning jacket with tails that would hang low on me, maybe all the way down to my ankles.

Put the whole ensemble together and it was fit for a cross-dressing bride at a wedding: shirt, tie, vest, tails, all in brilliant white. There were even white gloves, a white leather belt, a white bow tie, and a white silk top hat.

I said, "Where did you get all this stuff?"

"Vest, tie, and belt are Miranda's," Jools said. "The coat is Shar's—at some point in her travels, she was apparently a cricket umpire. Who knew? But I can totally picture her ordering cricket players around. Anyway, cricket umpires wear white jackets. Considering the difference in your sizes, I had enough extra cloth to make tails. The gloves are Shar's too; she has, like, a dozen pairs, going back to when she was a kid, so that pair should fit you. I got the top hat myself at Oktoberfest. I don't remember buying it, but I woke up the next morning and the hat was all I had on." She grinned. "Ask if I was in my own bed."

"No." I picked up the frock coat. "Linen. This feels expensive."

"You're lucky," Jools replied. "Most umpire jackets are frumpy, but that particular coat came from some special charity match. Old money Darkling kids from private schools, playing against each other—even the umpires were dressed to kill. Shar told me all about it." Jools fanned her mouth while faking a yawn. "But wait! I haven't shown you the pièce de résistance."

JOOLS KNELT AND REACHED UNDER THE BED

Clearly, she'd kept this final element hidden so she could make a showy reveal. "Ta-da!"

She pulled out a white silk cape. She drew it across her arm to show how smoothly the silk slid. "It used to be a slip—Miranda's, of course. But I've opened it up and given it a collar. It's wide enough to billow, and on you, it'll reach the floor. It'll be fabulous."

"Uhh . . ."

Jools said, "Yes, I know you're not into fabulous. But that's Kim. Why shouldn't Zircon be a bit flashy? Didn't Grandfather talk about establishing a separate identity?"

To tell the truth, I liked the look that Jools had put together. After years of dressing down, I could handle some up. I also had the feeling that Zircon would *love* showboating. But as Kim, I felt obliged to say, "A cape? People will laugh at me."

"You're forgetting your Halo," Jools said. "Everybody will ogle you the way you drooled over Ninety-Nine." She gave me a don't-try-to-deny-it smile.

I felt myself blushing. "My Halo will likely make people curl their lips and whisper behind my back."

Jools gave me a look. "Get dressed and see how fucking wrong you are."

I SHOOED JOOLS OUT OF THE ROOM WHILE I GOT CHANGED

Before she left, she took my mirror: It hung on the inside of my closet door, and Jools yanked it off its fasteners. "No peeking!" she said. "I want to see your reaction the first time you look at yourself."

I said, "I hate to tell you, but I can look at myself without a mirror."

"Don't," Jools said. "Let it be a surprise." Tucking the mirror under her arm, she left.

I CHANGED FROM KIM'S COSTUME INTO ZIRCON'S

It wasn't a fast process. I wondered how other Sparks managed.

Let's say I saw a school bus heading for a cliff. I could never change my clothes in time to do anything. Not that I could do anything anyway—as Jools had said, my powers sucked for rescuing. But what about those heroes who *did* save people in the nick of time? Did they go around all day in costume?

Maybe. Now that I thought about it, Jools was in the same boat as me. Strapping on fiberglass armor took ages. Even worse, how would Jools carry her stuff around? Me, I had it easy: I could put on my costume, shrink down, undress, then grow back to full size. Voilà! My costume would stay small and I could carry it in my pocket. I could do the same with street clothes. Carry my whole wardrobe if I wanted.

And I could change while I was shrunken to the size of an amoeba—I didn't have to worry about prying eyes. Jools, on the other hand, would have to carry her stuff in a duffel bag. When she needed to change, she'd have to scoot into an alley and hope no one wandered by while she was making herself Ninety-Nine.

Admittedly, Jools would be an Olympic-level quick-change artist. But still.

I FINISHED CHANGING

The costume fit surprisingly well. I couldn't imagine how Jools had made it in an hour; it would have taken me days. But that just shows that you should never judge super-stuff by ordinary standards. Once the Light gets involved, you have to scrap normal expectations.

The shirt was mine to begin with, but everything else had been tailored by Jools without even taking my measurements. The frock coat, for example: Anything Shar-sized was way too big for me. But Jools had reduced the coat's height and width to hit my size bang on. The cape draped beautifully, flowing around me. And the hat was a perfect fit; it had originally been bigger, but Jools had padded the inner band exactly enough for my smaller head. I put the hat on, then made fast jerky movements to see if it fell off. The hat clung like magic, not slipping a millimeter. Either Jools had worked miracles, or my omnimorphic field automatically adjusted the clothes to make them just the perfect size.

Final touch: my own running shoes, originally black but spray-painted white. (Jools was, of course, an Olympic-level spray-painter. The paint was still damp.)

I WENT TO THE DOOR AND OPENED IT

Jools sat in lotus position on the floor outside. Her eyes were closed and her head glowed green. I wondered if she was accessing information or simply meditating. (Hard to imagine Jools meditating, but now she had to be as skilled at it as the Dalai Lama.)

I said, "So what do you think?"

She was on her feet in an instant. She looked at me critically. "Nice. Except . . ." She whipped off the bow tie and started retying it. "You need practice your knots."

"*You* try tying a bow tie without a mirror." I was proud I could tie one at all. But Kimmi occasionally wore big black neck bows, and she'd spent an embarrassing amount of time getting them right.

"Better," Jools said, finishing the tie. "Now we're ready for the most important part." She reached around her back and pulled out something she must have had tucked into her waistband. "The mask."

SHE HELD UP A WHITE PASHMINA SCARF

I caught my breath. It had been a gift from Nicholas: the first thing he ever gave me.

On the day of Banff's first snowfall, in the year we were together, Nicholas had asked me to kneel by his chair. Snowflakes on our eyelashes. He said, "This is for you," and he'd tied the scarf around my neck. The snow was quiet as it fell around us, shutting out the world.

I hadn't worn that scarf since Nicholas left me. I hadn't wanted to wear it ever again. Yet I'd brought it with me on the plane from Banff to Waterloo, despite the limited space in my luggage. I'd kept it folded in the back of my underwear drawer, where I saw it every day.

Jools moved the scarf toward me, obviously planning to tie it around my eyes. I shrank back—literally. Down to paramecium size.

Jools stared at me in surprise . . . or rather she stared in my general direction, since I was too small to see. "What?" she said. "What?"

I forced myself back to normal, making sure I didn't head-butt her when I grew. "Sorry," I said. "Bad memory."

She gave me a questioning look. I didn't explain. I just took the scarf from her. "You want me to wear this for a mask?"

"What's wrong with it?"

Pause. "Nothing." I held it in front of my eyes.

"And the best part is," Jools said, "you won't need eyeholes. Right?"

"Right."

"It'll look so amazing: like a blindfold, except not. Tie it on."

She was itching to tie it for me, but that wasn't going to happen. I could barely imagine doing it myself. I lifted it to my face, thinking, *If I start crying, at least Jools won't see the tears.*

But actually, Jools had closed her own eyes. After a moment, I understood. I was about to become Zircon for the very first time. Jools didn't want to look at me until she could get the full impact.

WITH BUTTERFLIES IN MY STOMACH, I TIED THE SCARF AROUND MY EYES

My vision didn't change. Everything else did.

Butterflies gone in an instant.

A moment earlier, I'd felt kind of fake. Kim wasn't used to the top hat and tails, or most other parts of the costume. Zircon, on the other hand . . . these clothes were home. From the hat to the cape to the gloves to the mask, each piece was so natural I could barely feel it.

As if a weight had been lifted from my shoulders: a weight I'd carried all my life without noticing.

I shifted my viewpoint out of my head so I could see the new me.

The. New. Me.

ZIRCON SHONE LIKE A DIAMOND

Kim Lam was the one who'd put on a stagy white costume and tied a scarf around her eyes like Pin the Tail on the Donkey.

Kim wasn't with us anymore. Zircon was.

Ninety-Nine had exuded the height of human potential. An achievable hero: everything you wanted to strive for.

But Zircon wasn't human. As I put on the mask, I'd unconsciously shrunk just a bit to turn from flesh to stone. The result was something more ancient than *Homo sapiens*. More ancient even than the first living cell.

Zircon was what I could feel when I held a rock in my hand: four and a half billion years of existence made solid. Majestic. Powerful.

Me.

"HOLY FUCK," JOOLS WHISPERED

She had opened her eyes. "Holy fuck. Holy fuck."

"JOOLS," ZIRCON SAID, "STOP BABBLING."

Zircon's voice was higher than Kim's. Was that a trick of the Light? The same way it warped a Spark's fingerprints?

No, I thought, *it's just Zircon.* Kim's voice was pitched low, trying to sound exactly half-and-half between male and female. Zircon didn't play that game. Zircon was outside male/female distinctions.

When you look at a rock, do you ask its gender? The question never crosses your mind. Zircon didn't think about voice pitch, or the hang of shirt and pants. If (heaven forbid!) I developed thirty-six triple-Ds, it wouldn't matter. On Zircon, no one would care or notice.

At least that's how my Halo appeared to me. Maybe Jools felt something different. She was still gaping.

"Jools, focus," I said. "Put on your helmet. Turn back into Ninety-Nine."

She didn't move. She'd hung the helmet on my bedpost when she started working on the costume. I grabbed it and tried to hand it to her. She flinched away.

"Don't be ridiculous," I said. "Hold still." Jools froze, almost in fear, until I plunked the helmet onto her head.

JUST LIKE THAT, SHE BECAME NINETY-NINE

Her Halo flamed into life, but this time it didn't awe me. It was warm and familiar. We smiled at each other as she adjusted the helmet and did up the chin strap. "Fuck, you're intimidating," she said.

"Nah. Same as ever."

Suddenly, we were hugging as hard as we could squeeze, like

friends who hadn't seen each other in centuries. "A zircon?" she said in my ear. "Yeah, right."

I laughed. "Says the person who calls herself Ninety-Nine. Couldn't even go for a hundred?"

"Adaptive coloration."

"Same shit, different day."

I gave Ninety-Nine one last squeeze, then let her go. "Do you think the others are ready?"

"You know how it works," she said. "Always right in the nick of time."

She gestured toward the door. We exited into the hall just as Aria and Dakini emerged from their rooms.

THEY WERE WEARING THEIR COSTUMES TOO

Aria's came straight from the Carnival in Venice: a golden gown trimmed with lace on every possible hem. The dress was not a full-blown Madame de Pompadour outfit, but it still flounced with multiple petticoats. I knew exactly how Miranda got it—she'd sung a noon-hour recital for the chamber music society and had commissioned a suitably operatic costume. Miranda couldn't conceive of dressing "just good enough"; her clothes always had to be perfect.

The costume included gold lamé gloves and calf-high golden boots. The entire seed-pearl output of a clam bed lined the sleeves and décolletage. But the costume's most dominant feature was the huge feathered headpiece, serving as both mask and crown. Like many Carnival masks, its nose was a bird beak, sharp enough to look lethal. Black feathers fanned out around the face, contrasting dramatically with Aria's blond hair. Gold wires ran through the hair to keep the headpiece in place; the wires also framed the mask's blackness in bright gold filigree.

I'd seen the headpiece before. As Miranda had said, she'd worn it at Halloween—not with the gold dress, but with long black robes. The ominous robes had been spooky, but the gown worked even better for intimidation. There's something daunting about a beautiful woman dressed so extravagantly out of everyone else's league.

Add the bird-of-prey mask, multiply by Aria's Halo, and the impact would stop mortals dead in their tracks.

NO SUCH EDGINESS WITH DAKINI

Blingapalooza. Dakini jangled with every movement, like a dancer who made her own musical accompaniment.

Her costume was predominately violet: the same color I saw when Dakini used her powers. But dozens of other colors were splashed in too. Perhaps the violet simply stood out more because of what I'd previously seen.

The basic outfit was a choli blouse (short-sleeved, baring the midriff) with a gauzy chiffon skirt over pajama-style pants. The clothes were accessorized with uncountable silver bracelets, anklets, and necklaces; elaborate jeweled piercings in ears, nose, and navel; and a foot-high silver crown that resembled Angkor Wat. The bottom of the crown extended around Dakini's eyes, circling them with whorls of silver wire. It was scarcely a mask at all, barely more than wire-rimmed glasses. But it was enough to change Shar into a goddess.

Not a stately goddess: a dancing, easygoing divinity who mocked religious pretension. Her Halo laughed and whispered, "Don't take yourself so seriously! Just let go."

I thought, *She's the most dangerous of us all.* The one you forgot to fear.

Then again, I was Zircon. I had nothing to fear from anyone, least of all my teammates.

"WE RULE," NINETY-NINE SAID

"That we do," Aria agreed.

"Ready for action?" Dakini asked.

"Let's rock," Zircon said. *I* said.

We left the house. As we crossed the parking lot through snow that shouldn't have been falling, I shifted my viewpoint ahead of us. I saw exactly what I expected: four superheroes doing the slow walk, backlit by snow-steaming streetlights.

*Unconformity**

I'VE MADE A DECISION

Up until now, I've been talking about Miranda, Shar, and Jools. Suddenly, they're Aria, Dakini, and Ninety-Nine. Should I keep using their civilian names to avoid confusion? Or should I switch to who they actually are?

If you could see their Spark identities, the answer would be obvious. Sparks simply aren't the same as their human counterparts. Their bearings are different, their voices are different, even their body proportions seem different. Your brain's fusiform gyrus says, "Totally not the same person." In the abstract, I know that Aria "is" Miranda, but it feels ridiculous: like claiming that a sweater is the sheep that produced the wool.

Then again, I'm the one who believes Kimberley, Kimmi, and Kim were all different people.

Which they were.

You might prefer me to stick with the names you know. But if I say "Miranda" when I'm talking about Aria, it's a lie. I don't mind lying for a good cause, but when I changed from Kimmi to Kim, I promised myself I'd stop lying just to make things easier.

Besides, you know us super-folk: We'd rather punch problems in the nose than dance around them.

So I'm going to call Aria "Aria" and Miranda "Miranda." Et cetera.

Using the wrong names would piss them both off. I don't need that. My life is complicated enough.

* The contact zone between rock layers of substantially different ages, e.g., much younger rocks lying on top of much older rocks. Unconformities indicate significant change points in a place's geological history.

10

Bedrock Exposure

WHEN WE WALKED PAST THE VAN, IT MADE ME THINK OF RICHARD
I cast my Spark-o-Vision back into the house and saw him in Shar's bed, sleeping off the sedative from the tranq dart. If Invie's memory wipe worked, Richard would eventually wake up with no clue what had happened. I wondered if Shar had left him a note to explain; I wondered what the note would conveniently not mention. But unlike Shar, I didn't pry into other people's privacy.

Said Zircon while peeking into Shar's room.

"SO WHERE ARE WE GOING?" ARIA ASKED
Ninety-Nine answered immediately. "Adam Popigai's office. Czerny Center, room 5040."

"Do you think we'll find anything?" Aria asked. "Whatever Popigai is up to, he'd be crazy to leave anything incriminating in his office. That's the first place anyone would look."

"Of course it is," Ninety-Nine agreed. "But if we don't look there at all, we're idiots. Besides, who knows? With all our powers and senses, we may actually find something."

Dakini said, "The Light is paving our way. It will ensure we aren't stopped by dead ends."

Aria made a disgusted sound. "You think some *deus* will *machina* us just because we're Sparks?"

"Yes." Dakini smiled. "Aria, dear, you still haven't grasped the concept of plausible deniability. We can't wait for information to fall into our laps, but if we take reasonable steps to search for evidence, the Light will have the excuse it needs to help us."

"That doesn't make sense," Aria said.

"It never does," Dakini replied. "And please keep questioning it. Once in a while, it will truly be bullshit. The Light has to keep us honest."

NINETY-NINE SAID, "SEE YOU AT POPIGAI'S OFFICE."
She took off running. Aria yelled after her, "You think you'll beat me? I can fly at the speed of sound!"

Ninety-Nine didn't bother to reply; she ran damned fast for someone wearing bulky hockey equipment. But of course, Aria was faster. She took to the sky and shot off like a bullet, including a gun-like crack of sonic boom.

I looked at Dakini. "Sooner or later, we'll learn to stick together." I smiled. "But not right now."

I shrank to wasp size and jumped into the air. The cape looked great as it billowed behind me; it helped hide that I was once again clutching my coattails and flapping like a fool.

THE SNOW CONTINUED TO FALL
I was small enough to be missed by most of the flakes, but I did collide with a few on my way to campus. When you fly like I do, in jerky fits and starts, you just don't have enough control to avoid every flake in the air.

After a few such collisions, my costume was soaked with snowmelt. I was cold but not *cold*. I could feel the chilly dampness, but it didn't affect me. I was, after all, a rock; and while rocks aren't 100 percent impervious to low temperatures, they aren't in danger unless they get super-cold (below -100° C) or they're whipsawed back and forth, cold-hot-cold-hot (which can make them crack and exfoliate). The fear that I'd felt in the alley, when I worried about freezing to death, had been misplaced: Small mammals may be subject to hypothermia, but sand grains simply don't care.

So when I reached the Czerny Center, I was soggy but serene. I headed for the nearest doorway—a back door with a wide concrete overhang—but I stopped when I saw it wasn't empty.

A guy and a girl were glued to each other under the overhang, making out as thoroughly as a couple can possibly do while fully clothed and vertical. Both had unzipped their coats so they could press together more tightly. They had the look of people who would stay where they were for hours, until their lips and jaws were so sore they absolutely had to stop.

I could have sneaked past them—they wouldn't have noticed a rhino, let alone wasp-sized me. But temptation. Curiosity. Which I rationalized as concern for their safety.

I GREW TO ALMOST FULL HEIGHT

I stayed a millimeter shorter than Kim, so my skin stayed stony instead of flesh. Call it my "Maximum Zircon" height. Then I sauntered toward the couple.

Neither Kimberley, Kimmi, nor Kim would have considered bothering those people. Zircon was less deferential, and I wanted to test my Halo. How did it affect normal humans? Would a couple with their minds on each other even notice me?

They did. I had barely taken a step before they detached from their kiss and snapped their heads toward me. Their arms stayed around each other, but they stopped squeezing. Their grips loosened as if they'd gone numb. The guy gaped; the girl did too for a fraction of a second, then closed her mouth quickly.

Neither spoke. After a long moment, I said, "I'm Zircon. I'm a Spark."

The guy said, "You sure are," then dried up for words.

The girl said, "I've never seen a Spark before."

She smiled at me. I can't describe that smile. It wasn't shy, but it also wasn't a come-on. She didn't seem flustered or in awe, like she might be when meeting someone important, but I'm sure she didn't smile that way at very many people.

The guy seemed more nervous. He pulled the girl closer, not protectively, but as if he needed to hug someone. "Is something bad happening?" he asked. "Like aliens or something?"

"Not aliens," I said, "but something. This snow isn't natural, and there've been several strange events on campus in the past few hours. If I were you, I'd go home and stay inside."

"Okay," the girl said.

The guy looked at her with a bit of surprise, then looked back at me. "Okay."

They didn't move. They just kept staring.

After a strange little silence, I shrank out of sight and stayed that way until they left.

THE ENCOUNTER MADE ME FEEL WEIRD

Kim didn't like affecting strangers so strongly. First, because Kim was wary of drawing attention; that seldom worked out well. Second, because Kim didn't know what to do after drawing attention. (Hence, Kim's celibate lifestyle.) And third, because it seemed wrong to overwhelm people for no good reason.

I was hitting them with a superpower: basically, controlling their emotions. I hated when Shar had done that to me, and I decided I hated doing it to others. As I slipped into Czerny Center, I thought, *Does this mean I have to avoid normal people? That I can only be Zircon around folks who resist my Halo? Maybe I'll never be comfortable except with Sparks and Darklings.*

I continued to ponder that question as I flew toward room 5040, right up to the moment when I ran into Nicholas.

HE LOOKED DISTRACTED

Eyes closed, utterly motionless. He had pressed himself into a recessed doorway, and he must have been there for some time—the door behind him had cobwebs in all the corners.

Nicholas seemed to be concentrating hard on something; perhaps using a supernatural power. But I saw no glow around him. Nicholas was just as I'd first seen him in the police station: ashen, transparent, and dwindling below the waist. The only difference was his eyes. They were now dark pits with nothing eyelike inside them.

I wondered if this was what he actually looked like. Perhaps when I'd seen him before, he had consciously made himself have eyes, the same way he could look like a tennis star if he exerted himself. He might have dressed himself up with real eyes because he'd heard that a Kimmi Lam was in the station.

Or perhaps he was dressed up now, with his eyes deliberately deleted. After Sparks arrived in the world, many Darklings began to copy them: wearing costumes and adopting codenames, especially among plebeians. Maybe the hollow-eyed look was Nicholas's version of a mask. But unlike Sparks, Darklings had no superpowers to give themselves anonymity. I recognized Nicholas instantly, despite his lack of eyeballs.

Perhaps he was hiding in shadows—all the building's lights were off except for the EXIT signs. But to me, the Czerny Center was as bright as day, and Nicholas stood out like a black-and-white photograph against a colored background.

I WAS STILL SOME DISTANCE AWAY WHEN I SAW HIM

I'd been flying with my viewpoint centered far ahead, the better to spot trouble before I reached it. With that much advance warning, I could have avoided Nicholas entirely. Kim might have done so, but I couldn't say for sure. I was losing my sense of how Kim would react. I was Zircon, and Zircon was confrontational.

I liked the idea of sneaking up so microscopically small that Nicholas wouldn't know I was there. Then I'd shoot to Max Zirc size, go "Boo!" and scare the ghost.

But as I approached, Nicholas jerked his head in my direction. I didn't think he could see or hear me, but who knows how keen a ghost's senses are? Still hoping to take him by surprise, I snapped up to Max Zirc height so quickly it would seem that I'd appeared out of nowhere. "Don't worry," I told him, "I'm just saying hello."

Despite my reassurances, Nicholas went more misty—his instinct was obviously to desolidify in the face of unknown threats. But he didn't take any other visible action. He looked tense but under control. "Guess I'm not as invisible as I thought."

"Guess not," I agreed. I resisted the urge to disguise my voice. Either my Spark anonymity would work or it wouldn't. If it didn't,

Nicholas would recognize me even if I talked funny. He'd seen me only an hour earlier, and a top hat wasn't nearly enough to make me look like a different person. Even worse, my eyes were wrapped with the scarf that Nicholas himself had given me; he would know it in a flash, unless my superpower clouded his mind.

It did. No recognition. After a moment, I said, "I'm Zircon. And you?"

"Wraith."

"Inventive name. What are you doing here, Wraith?"

"I could ask you the same question."

"And I'd give the same answer as you," I said. "We're both here to search the office of Professor Adam Popigai. Correct?"

He hesitated, then said, "Correct."

"Because we're worried about what happened in a lab that he controlled. Six Darklings, a portal, an explosion, and more."

Nicholas nodded.

"Then the only question," I said, "is why we've made this our business. And to show I'm a good sport, I'll answer first. My teammates and I consider ourselves Waterloo's guardians. We're investigating this mess because it looks like the start of something bad."

"Sparks," Nicholas said, shaking his head. "Why are you all so territorial? You're worse than were-beasts."

"Good question," I said, and I meant it. Sparks are amazingly focused when it comes to geography. Take New York City, with its ridiculously high density of superheroes and villains. If you wanted to commit super-crimes, why wouldn't you go elsewhere? You could rob every bank in Cleveland without superpowered opposition.

But no. Almost every supervillain in the entire US of A operated in metro New York: the one place where there were enough heroes to foil every villain's plans. Crazy! But villains never seemed to consider leaving what they saw as their turf.

And what about me and my teammates? Mere minutes after discovering our powers, we'd told Grandfather we were claiming Waterloo as our protectorate.

Strange. And strange how natural it felt. "That's how it is," I told

Nicholas. Or should I say Wraith? No. I might have to call him Wraith to hide my identity, but inside my head, he would always be Nicholas.

I said, "I'm involved with this because I'm concerned with any trouble in the region. And you?"

"I can't say," he replied. "I signed an NDA. That's a nondisclosure agreement."

"I know what an NDA is," I snapped. I didn't mention that Nicholas himself was the one who'd explained the concept to me—particularly the special NDAs Darklings often signed in blood or whatever effluent their bodies could produce.

If Sparks had a thing about territory, Darklings had a thing about contracts. They couldn't just say, "Let's work together," they had to draw up formal legal documents. When I was with Nicholas he was only seventeen and physically restricted, but he'd still been forced to sign multiple agreements with his family, dictating what he would and wouldn't do. Some of those agreements were only on paper and therefore unenforceable—he was still a minor, so anything he signed wasn't legally binding. But some of the contracts were "special" and far more inviolable than mere Canadian law. If he tried to defy them, he might go blind or catch fire. Now that Nicholas had come of age as a full-fledged creature of the Dark, he had undoubtedly signed even more pacts, probably all of them "special." Nicholas might be lying, but if the NDA was real, either he'd literally be incapable of going against it, or he could do so but would face a severe magical backlash.

"What *can* you tell me?" I asked. "What do you know about Popigai?"

"A professor in chemical engineering," Nicholas said. "Recently hired, Russian background, and he's covered with metal. Either flexible skintight armor, or his body is actually metallic."

"Darkling or Spark?" I asked.

"He's not in the Darkling Index."

I kicked myself for not checking the index on my own. It was a public list of everyone who'd signed the Dark Pact since 1982.

Darklings had a love/hate relationship with the index. On one hand, they got off on the status of being listed, like making the *Forbes* list of the world's richest people. At the same time, rich people had a knee-jerk aversion to being on public lists of any kind. Many tried to cut deals with the Elders of the Dark: "If I pay you double, can I be Converted without anyone knowing?" But as far as anybody knew, no one could stay off the index. The Elders had sworn an oath to maintain a true and complete account of every Darkling they created, and they laughed at the idea of breaking their oath just to please some whiny wannabe.

The only unlisted were the Elders themselves.

And the Unbound.

And whatever offspring the Unbound chose to sire outside the Pact.

"SO POPIGAI IS LIKELY A SPARK," I SAID

"That's the only alternative," Nicholas replied.

"No, it isn't."

Nicholas said nothing. When he was still human, he'd told me about the Unbound. Now that he was a Darkling, he was less forthcoming. After a moment, he said, "What do *you* know about Popigai?"

"No more than you." But I could now hear voices in the quiet building. My teammates were out of sight but not far away. "Shall we check Popigai's office?"

Nicholas gestured down the hall. "Lead the way."

I WALKED; HE FLOATED

It was eerily like when he was in the chair and rolling beside me through Banff. His head drifted along at the same height as mine, and I walked a fraction slower than when I was alone.

Old patterns in new containers.

As we walked, Nicholas's face surreptitiously aged from seventeen to thirtyish. He must have wanted to seem more mature when dealing with Sparks. It made me smile; so many second-gen Darklings went through Conversion as soon as they came of age, then spent the rest of their potentially endless lives trying not to look like kids.

Darklings yearned for respect more than they yearned for blood or flesh. With one another they vied for status; with mortals, they wanted deference, admiration, and acknowledgment of their greatness. However, once Sparks had arrived, the hero worship that Darklings saw as their due switched over to the folks in tacky costumes rather than the Beneficent Bestowers of Prosperity.

Now I was a Spark myself: on the same level as Nicholas and all the Vandermeers. Three years ago, if Zircon had been in that room with Elaine instead of poor powerless Kimmi . . . well, we'd already seen that Zircon could handle vampires.

I thought about that. Had I beat up Lilith as a subconscious stand-in for Elaine? No. If I had equated Lilith with Elaine, I might have done things I'd seriously regret.

But the real Elaine was still out there. So were the other Darklings I'd met when I was with Nicholas: the ones who had bullied and belittled me. Now I had the power to . . .

No. Just no. Wish fulfillment is a pleasant fantasy, but when you suddenly aren't shooting blanks, you have to be more responsible.

Maybe the real purpose of Darklings is to show Sparks who not to be.

WE TURNED A CORNER AND FOUND MY TEAMMATES
Dakini and Aria were watching Ninety-Nine fiddle with a lock on an office door. I wondered how Ninety-Nine happened to be carrying lockpicks. Maybe thinking ahead was another one of her talents. (That proved, by the way, Ninety-Nine ≠ Jools.)

Dakini saw us coming. "Look, Zircon has found a friend."

"This is Wraith," I said. "A Darkling. He's interested in Popigai too."

"Why?" Aria demanded.

"I can't say," Nicholas replied.

"Can't or won't?" Aria asked.

"Let's not be adversarial," Dakini said. "If Wraith wishes to help us, we should welcome his support."

She smiled at Nicholas. I wondered how soon it would be before her violet tentacles were rummaging through his brain.

NICHOLAS SAID, "I DIDN'T KNOW THIS CITY HAD SO MANY SPARKS." "Waterloo is a quiet place," Dakini told him. "We've had no reason to show ourselves."

"Towns with Sparks don't stay quiet," Nicholas said. "The presence of Darklings makes no waves, but as soon as Sparks arrive . . ."

Aria bristled. "Are you blaming us for something?"

"Just making an observation. By the way, if you want to keep Waterloo quiet, I recommend you stop picking that lock."

"Why?" Ninety-Nine asked.

"It might be booby-trapped."

Ninety-Nine stopped working the picks. "Really?"

"I don't know what Popigai is up to," Nicholas said, "but he might be a bad guy, correct?"

"Possibly," Aria said. She obviously hated to agree with a Darkling, but until we knew what was going on, we had to treat Popigai as a potential villain.

Maybe a supervillain.

Maybe a Mad Genius.

"In that case," Nicholas said, "he might have rigged that door to go Gothic on intruders. A bomb. Poison gas. You name it."

Ninety-Nine carefully withdrew her picks from the lock. "Zircon," she said, "tag, you're it."

I SHRANK I did it slowly, and kept my gaze on Nicholas's face as I got microscopic. Since he didn't have eyes, I was denied the satisfaction of seeing them go wide, but it was gratifying to see his mouth gape in surprise.

I tried to move my viewpoint into Popigai's room, but Spark-o-Vision went dead halfway through the door. Crap: a blinder wall.

If Popigai was a Spark, how on earth did he get a blinder? They're created with magic. But perhaps a Spark with engineering cred could build something similar to a blinder using Cape Tech. Besides, Popigai had Darkling acquaintances; any of the six Darklings I'd seen might have cast a blinder spell on Popigai's behalf.

However the blinder got there, it meant I had to enter the office without advance reconnaissance. Not good. But if I shrank really small, I probably wouldn't set off traps.

Probably.

I grew back to full size and told the others, "Back off a bit. There's a blinder wall down through the middle of the door. I can't see if anything will go boom when I enter."

"I could likely dispel the blinder," Nicholas said. "They're usually easy to break."

"And breaking the blinder wouldn't set off a trap?" I asked.

He looked sheepish. "Actually, it's pretty common to set booby traps on blinders so if anyone tampers with them . . ." He shrugged.

"Move down the hall," I said. "I'll call you when it's safe."

I SHRANK IMMEDIATELY

Otherwise, Aria might have argued at being told to back off. Once I was gone, however, she and the others grudgingly put some distance between themselves and the door.

When I thought they were far enough away, I shrank to virus size and flew under the door. I could easily see the blinder ahead of me, reaching down into the floor. Just short of the black curtain, I landed, then jumped forward with all my strength. I worried I might get trapped in the black neural nothingness, but I cleared the blinder's breadth with millimeters to spare. That's huge when you're the size of influenza.

Past the blinder, I stopped. I was still underneath the door, but now my Spark-o-Vision could check out what waited inside. It was a mess much akin to Popigai's lab after the explosion.

At one point, the room must have been a normal office: bookshelves, desk, computer, etc. But something had tossed everything around like a whirlwind, emptying the shelves and heaving the computer so hard the monitor screen was embedded edge-on into the wall. The place looked like it had been hit by an artillery shell. Strangely, however, the air smelled of spice, not smoke: some herb that was sharp and sweet. I had no idea what the spice was. On my very best day, my nose is hard-pressed to identify anything more exotic than soy sauce. But Dakini would know the smell immediately, so I didn't waste time guessing.

The only question I cared about was whether it was safe to open the door. I examined it with Spark-o-Vision. The door was standard university issue: a wooden core covered with white plastic laminate. The plastic was charred and melted, baring the wood beneath. A patch of damage showed a curlicue pattern. I suspected that a glyph had been painted on the door, and had surged to plasma heat in the blink of an eye. The glyph's combustion might well have caused the hurricane that tore up the office. I wondered if the glyph had been designed to hurt intruders, or just eliminate any evidence the room might hold.

Whatever its purpose, the glyph had gone off and spent its energy. I saw no other traps. I finished crawling under the door, grew to Max Zirc height, and let the others in.

MY TEAMMATES AND NICHOLAS TROOPED INTO THE ROOM
The office didn't have space for five full-grown people, so I shrank to Barbie size. I stood in one corner of the room and let my Spark-o-Vision roam, searching for "clues" that hadn't been destroyed by the glyph's incineration.

My companions did the same. Ninety-Nine searched methodically, Aria sang her searching song, and Dakini "attuned herself psychically to serendipitous forces." As for Nicholas, does a ghost have powers that help in searching? If you survey world folklore, you can find ghosts with any power imaginable. Some ghosts seem able to do almost anything as long as it's creepy. Others are virtually powerless, like the ones trapped in loops washing their hands or trying to open a door.

Nicholas likely had a large ghostly repertoire, but for now, he just turned intangible and backed partly into a wall so he wouldn't interfere with my teammates. Even so, I could tell he was concentrating: His expression was distant, and he'd gone as motionless as a vampire. Watching and gathering intel on how we operated.

"LOOK AT THIS," DAKINI SAID
She dragged a corkboard from under a pile of books. A lot of offices had corkboards, usually covered with *xkcd* cartoons, takeout menus from nearby restaurants, and reminders about deadlines that had already passed. Typically, such papers are held up with thumbtacks, but the winds that Cuisinarted the office had torn off anything merely tacked on. The only things remaining were two items stuck on more securely with staples—a white business card and a color brochure.

I zoomed in my Spark-o-Vision. The card bore nothing except the name C. G. *Rossetti* in an elegant handwriting font. The brochure had a generic sun-sea-and-swimsuits photograph with the title *Fabulous Caribbean Escapes!* Aria snorted when she saw it: "Can you *get* any more lowbrow?"

"I believe that's the point," Dakini said. She made a *V* with two fingers and laid them on the card and the pamphlet.

Immediately, both the card and the pamphlet changed. "Psionic illusions," Dakini said smugly. "They can fool weak minds."

Aria glowered, then leaned in to look at the newly revealed items.

THE CARD WAS STILL A CARD AND THE BROCHURE STILL A BROCHURE
But the card now had a lurid purple background, against which a cartoonish face had been drawn as if in white chalk: a huge grinning mouth full of sharp jagged teeth . . . pointed ears lined with dozens of earringed piercings . . . gigantic eyes with cat-slit pupils. As we stared, one of the eyes winked.

The brochure had also turned purple. It was covered with writing in a script I didn't recognize, all squiggles and geometry. I can read Chinese pictograms (very, very slowly), and I know the basic look of Cyrillic, Greek, Arabic, and Klingon. This wasn't any of those. I suspected it was "Enochian," a name that Darklings used in front of rubes when they talked about the language of spell incantations. All I knew about "Enochian" was that its true name was something different, and Darklings hated outsiders catching a glimpse of it.

Nicholas tried to snatch the brochure. His movement looked involuntary, as if his hand moved without his brain's involvement. But Aria had speed-of-sound reflexes and caught Nicholas's wrist in midair. "Problem?" she asked.

"No." He let his arm turn to steam and diffuse from her grip.

"You recognize this brochure?" Aria asked him.

"Not at all," he replied. We knew he was lying, and he knew we knew, but it didn't matter. Unbeknownst to Nicholas, thin violet tendrils had run up the wall beside him and inserted themselves into his brain. We'd find out what he was hiding soon enough.

IN THE MEANTIME, I CONTINUED TO STUDY THE BROCHURE

I couldn't read the writing, but the brochure's layout reminded me of a restaurant menu: headings in large type, followed by lists in a smaller font. I didn't want to think what kind of food items might be on offer.

"I know every human language in the world," Ninety-Nine said, "but I can't read that. Wraith, are you sure you don't recognize it?"

"It might be a sorcerous language," Nicholas said, still feigning ignorance. "Centuries ago, there were dozens of Darkling factions—the Hermetic Order of This, the Secret College of That—and they were all deadly rivals. Each group invented its own secret language, deliberately hard to decipher." His fingers twitched. "If you let me show that around, I might find someone who can read it."

Aria said, "If Popigai was a Spark, why would he have something written in a sorcerous language?"

"He was working with Darklings," Nicholas said. "That's more common than you might think. Lots of people on both sides want to combine the Light and Dark. They want to build sorcerous computers. Laser-guided golems. And the ultimate prize: finding a way to let Sparks cast magic or give Darklings superpowers."

"Has anyone ever succeeded?" Aria asked.

"If they have, they aren't blabbing it around," Nicholas said. "The Elders say the Dark and the Light are non-overlapping magisteria: If you have access to one, you're absolutely cut off from the other, period, full stop. But that hasn't stopped people from trying."

"Especially the Unbound?" Aria asked.

"The Unbound are a myth," Nicholas said, as automatically as a politician saying, *No comment*. "And if they *did* exist, they wouldn't conduct such experiments. The Unbound refuse to change with the times. They'd be horrified at the thought of getting into bed with the Light."

I found myself blushing. I shrank even smaller.

"LOOK," NICHOLAS SAID, "THIS OFFICE IS A DEAD END"
"Whatever trashed the place was designed to eliminate evidence. Not to mention that someone got here before us—that's what set off the trap. We won't find anything useful."

"And this brochure?" Aria asked.

"If you let me take it, I'll see what I can find out."

"You think we'll let you walk off with the only clue we've found?"

"Can any of you read it?" Nicholas asked. Nobody answered. "See? It's useless to you but maybe not to me."

"Why should we think helping you is a good idea?"

"The Dark and the Light don't have to be enemies," Nicholas said. "We come from different backgrounds but often have common interests. Why not extend professional courtesy rather than being dogs in the manger?"

Aria bristled, but Dakini said soothingly, "Let him have the brochure. A gesture of goodwill. Someday, he can return the favor."

Nicholas's eyes flashed. "Favors" mean a lot to Darklings—more like business obligations than casual generosity. He said nothing as Dakini detached the brochure from the corkboard and handed it to him. "Let us know if you learn anything," she said.

"How can I contact you?"

"I'm sure we'll bump into each other. Soon." Dakini smiled. Her tendrils retracted from Nicholas's brain and slithered out of sight.

"All right," Nicholas said. He sounded wary but couldn't figure out why Dakini seemed so smug. "Thank you," he said. "Good night."

He sank through the floor. The brochure went with him, turning as insubstantial as he was. Apparently, Nicholas had an omnimorphic field. Or, since he was a Darkling, it likely had a magicky name: "sympathetic evanescence" or "phantasmal contagion."

Losing solidity from being right next to a ghost. I could empathize.

WE WAITED IN SILENCE FOR AT LEAST TEN SECONDS
Finally, Aria turned to Dakini. "Well?"

"He wasn't easy to read," Dakini replied. "As if he was barely there."

"He *was* barely there," Ninety-Nine said. "But I assume you got something, or you wouldn't have been so cooperative."

"I got surface thoughts," Dakini said. "That brochure was an auction catalog for the Goblin Market."

Ninety-Nine said, "Aha!" She tapped the business card, still stapled to the corkboard. The name on the card had reverted to C. G. *Rossetti*. "Christina Georgina Rossetti," Ninety-Nine said, "1830 to 1894. English writer who wrote a children's poem called 'The Goblin Market.' Want me to recite it?"

"Absolutely not," Aria said.

"But," added Dakini, "I'd like to know what the poem was about."

"A girl buys magical fruit from a bunch of goblins," Ninety-Nine said. "She wastes away from eating it and nearly dies, but she's saved by her sister. The power of love over magic."

"Are goblins real?" Aria asked.

"Probably," Ninety-Nine said. "The Dark Conversion loves making creatures from myth and folklore. Considering all the stories about goblins, there are bound to be some out there."

"But running a market?" Aria said. "Selling fruit? Remember who Darklings are. If they were selling financial derivatives, okay. But fruit?"

"What about GMO fruit that costs five times as much as normal and gratuitously kills bees?"

"Better," Aria said, "but still a stretch. Imagine you're rich. You spend years learning sorcery to become a hotshot wizard. Are you going to waste your time making apples? Which you sell at a grungy fruit stand tucked between a woman who butchers pigs and a guy who churns his own butter?"

She had a point. A modern-day goblin would have been a multimillionaire before joining the Dark. Multimillionaires don't get their hands dirty for small change. They might enjoy making things as a hobby—plenty of wealthy people paint landscapes in their spare time. But that's only to relax and feel creative, not as a serious career.

Then again, what about dot-com Darklings? Many techies made fortunes, bought themselves fangs, then wondered what to do next.

Some refused to change their lifestyles: They still stayed up all night pumping out code. But others had shifted from C++ to sorcery. Magic demanded the same mental gymnastics, but it was even more demanding than high-level hackery.

Being a wizard made you elite. Whipping up complex magic creations was a way of proving your intellectual superiority. I could imagine a community of sorcerous hackers who made glamours for the glamour. Like the group Anonymous, except with necromancy.

I grew to Max Zirc size so I could join the conversation. "Look," I said, "there are plenty of reasons that goblin Darklings might start a magical market. Maybe goblins need to make fruit the same way vampires need blood. Maybe they even do it for the cash; no matter how much they have, some people never can have enough."

"If goblins can make wondrous things," Dakini said, "like Aladdin's Lamp or the Dagger of Time, that would surely be worth their while. They'd gain status in the eyes of their fellow Darklings, and they could make a great deal of money selling their wares."

"Fine," Aria said, "let's say there's a Goblin Market. Why would Popigai have their brochure?"

Ninety-Nine said, "Because he wants to buy something?"

"Like what?"

"How should I know? But if he's a bad guy, we should stop him getting it."

"So we should go to this market?" Dakini asked.

"Sure," Ninety-Nine said. "When you were pillaging Wraith's mind, did you see where it was?"

"He didn't know," Dakini said. "The market is held irregularly, and only for a single night from dusk to dawn. It's taken place in dozens of sites around the world. However, Wraith suspected that tonight it would be set up in some location where the lunar eclipse reaches totality. An eclipse that occurs on the winter solstice has great occult significance; many Darkling festivities are being held where the eclipse will be seen."

"The totality region is a thousand kilometers wide," Aria said. "A shit-ton of people can see this eclipse—the whole eastern sections of North and South America. There's no reason to believe this Goblin Market is anywhere near Waterloo. Why not New York? Miami? Rio de Janeiro?"

"Actually," Ninety-Nine said, "Rio is too far to the east. They aren't in the totality region."

"Shut up," Aria explained.

"Wraith believed the market would be nearby," Dakini said. "He intended to phone an acquaintance to find the exact location, but he thought it wouldn't be far."

"It'll be close," I said. "That's how this works. Now that we're entangled in the situation, we won't discover that the trouble is actually going down in Argentina. This is *our* problem, and the shit will hit the fan in our backyard."

"Why?" Aria demanded. She sounded genuinely angry. "Why assume this will stay in a neat little package? This isn't a story. There's nothing that says, 'It would be convenient if our heroines don't have to go too far, so that's how it's going to be.' *It makes no sense!* And don't give me crap about, 'That's how it works.' If there *is* some force of Fate trying to pull our strings, the smartest move is to jump off the merry-go-round. Sleeping Beauty should get a shotgun and blast the damned spinning wheel. When something wants you to play its game, you win by saying no."

She glared at us all. Silence. Then Ninety-Nine said, "If someone builds a Death Star, you don't win by saying Death Stars are a stupid waste of resources. You win by blowing the damned thing up. And we're the only Jedis in town." She put her hand on Aria's arm. "If we walk away, the Death Star doesn't collapse from its own ridiculousness. It does its Death Star thing."

"Well, it shouldn't," Aria said.

"I know."

"It doesn't make sense."

"I know."

"And I hate that we'll probably end up storming some trumped-up evil stronghold and having a mega-damage fight, as if that's the only way to solve problems."

Ninety-Nine gave Aria's arm a squeeze. "Picture yourself as Sleeping Beauty. We're blasting the spinning wheel. Now let's go."

"Where?"

"To the Goblin Market."

"You know where it is?"

Ninety-Nine tapped the side of her head. "I know things."

She pried the goblin-faced business card off the corkboard, then headed outside.

THE UNNATURAL SNOW WAS STILL FALLING

It was wet aggregate snow: the fluffy kind that sticks on surfaces. It was slowly, gently burying the campus under a stratum of white. Hard edges were vanishing; even though I saw the world lit brightly, I couldn't tell the exact line of separation between the ring road and its curb. Snow feathered the boundary into a delicate blur.

The campus and city were being erased. Police would soon be

dealing with dozens of accidents. Anyone who had planned to watch the eclipse would have given up and gone to bed.

The phrase "No witnesses" popped into my mind. Curtains of snow would reduce visibility and muffle sounds. Whatever anyone did, no one else would see or hear. It was Canada's version of a pea-soup fog—silently, it said, "You're on your own."

"WHERE ARE WE GOING?" ARIA ASKED
"To the Market," Ninety-Nine replied.

"I know," Aria said, "but where?"

"To. The. Market," Ninety-Nine repeated.

"But . . . oh." Aria smacked her forehead. "Duh. I can fly there in less than a minute."

"No," Ninety-Nine said. I can't describe how she said it. Not loud, not commanding, but Aria had been about to zip off and Ninety-Nine's single word stopped her. The voice of leadership. "You're faster than the rest of us," Ninety-Nine told Aria, "but let's not get in the habit of you zooming ahead on your own without backup."

"I can be Aria's backup," I said. "I'll piggyback on her. I'll be so light, Aria can fly full speed and not even feel I'm there."

"We'll *all* piggyback," Dakini said. "I have this figured out." She gestured to Aria. "Would you hover, please?"

Aria gave her a look.

"Please," Dakini said.

Looking sour, Aria rose a meter off the ground. "Now what?"

"Now we hitch a ride."

A violet cord reached out from Dakini's forehead, looping around Aria's shoulders and under her armpits, rapidly weaving a harness. Another strand emerged, spreading out into a sheet that wrapped Ninety-Nine in a cocoon from chest to knees. "Hey!" Ninety-Nine protested. Clearly, she could feel something enveloping her, but couldn't see it; apparently, "normal" people didn't see Dakini's violet emanations.

Dakini's cocoon left Ninety-Nine's hands free. Ninety-Nine pulled at the rubbery invisible violet, trying to get free. "Stop," Dakini said. "Don't make a fuss." Violet light shimmered down Dakini's own body, forming a cocoon much like Ninety-Nine's. Before Dakini tried to wrap me too, I shrank to wasp size and flew to Aria. I crawled into her hair. Somehow that felt less intrusive than clinging to her gown.

"Are we set?" Dakini asked. I wasn't going to answer, since my voice would be hypersonic. Then I remembered the rings Grandfather had given us. I focused my thoughts and projected, *«I'm good.»*

Ninety-Nine and Dakini looked startled. Ninety-Nine said, "Whoa!"

"Whoa what?" Aria asked.

Dakini said, "Zircon is using her communication ring. She was speaking inside our heads."

«I have to,» I said. *«When I'm small, you can't hear my real voice.»*

"Aria, stop being paranoid and put on your ring," Ninety-Nine said. "It's the only way you'll hear Zircon. She's, like, ultra-ultrasonic when she's shrunk."

"I can hear ultra-ultrasonic," Aria said. "Sound powers, remember?"

"Oooh," I said aloud, "nice grab."

Aria smiled, so she must have heard me. "I can hear any acoustic frequency," she announced, just to make sure the Light knew what new power she was claiming.

"LET'S JET!" NINETY-NINE SAID

"But please be careful with acceleration," Dakini put in quickly. "Your powers, dear Aria, no doubt protect you during high-G maneuvers. We may be more vulnerable."

"I hope so," Aria said. "I'm desperate to believe that something still obeys Newton."

She headed skyward. The violet strands attached to Dakini and Ninety-Nine snapped taut, but held solid. I caught my breath, wondering if Aria could lift the weight of two additional people. She did it easily. I wondered just how strong Aria was. She probably couldn't juggle SUVs, but I suspected she was well beyond normal human limits.

We slowly gained altitude through the falling snow. We gained speed too; within seconds, all I could see was a hurtling blizzard of white. "Dude!" Ninety-Nine yelled over the wind. "Can you even see where you're going?"

"Sonar," Aria said. "And a sense of magnetic direction. Like carrier pigeons."

I said, "So your motifs are birds and sounds?"

"I fly. I have a bird mask. It's a no-brainer."

Aria put on a burst of speed. Ninety-Nine and Dakini clapped their hands over their ears. In the shelter of Aria's hair I couldn't feel the wind, but out in the open, the gale must have lashed my teammates like a cat-o'-nine-tails.

Oh well, I thought, *Dakini has a force field. And Ninety-Nine regenerates. They'll be fine.*

Rifting

WE FLEW NORTH

Waterloo's city limits can be hard or soft. At the hard limits, stores and houses can sit directly across the road from active farmland. At the soft, the city boundaries are only visible when modest three-floor office buildings for tech start-ups give way to hotels and big-box stores. Along Weber and King Streets (which supposedly run parallel, but actually interweave like the snakes on a caduceus), the city's edge is populated with shops that will fix your motorboat engine or sell you cedar fencing, until suddenly, you get Outside and there's an eruption of factory outlet stores.

Then the Market.

St. Jacobs Farmers' Market bills itself as Canada's largest year-round market. Every Thursday and Saturday, it's full of farmers selling produce, fresh meat, and homemade knickknacks. It's big, it's busy, and it smells. New UW students are told it's an important rite of passage to drag yourself out of bed at 6:30 AM and drive to St. Jacobs "before all the good stuff gets bought." This is hazing, pure and simple; unsuspecting frosh end up squashed in with hundreds if not thousands of other people, lining up to get preservative-free zucchinis. Through such experiences, they learn the Market's business plan: three times the price and ten times the hassle for food that goes bad twice as fast.

(Grandma Lam once came for a visit, so I took her to the Market—it *is* Waterloo's foremost tourist attraction. After a glimpse of the hubbub, she dragged me out of the building and said, "Kim, dear, we left China to get away from this sort of thing.")

"THIS SORT OF THING" IS INTENTIONALLY RUSTIC

The Market consists of a big two-story main building, with half a dozen smaller ones surrounding it, plus rows of outdoor stands selling everything from schnitzel to death metal T-shirts. The small buildings were cheaply slapped together with tin roofs and siding, making them ovens in the summer and frighteningly loud in rainstorms. The main building, however, is wood, built from heavy fir timbers specially shipped from British Columbia. After decades of service, the wood is permanently imbued with the scent of raw meat, accented by fresh-grown lavender, onions, and extra old unrefrigerated cheddar.

Sorry for being so negative. I'll admit that some vendors have really good pastries; however, I've found other sources of pies, and they don't get you out of bed at zero-dark-thirty, or make you jostle with people who demand that their kale still be flecked with manure.

Still, the Market might not have been so bad if you could shop at a decent hour without the madding crowd. That made it ideal for the Goblin version.

AS WE FLEW, I SENT MY SPARK-O-VISION TO SCOUT AHEAD

My perception didn't have a hard-and-fast range, but the farther away I projected my viewpoint, the less bright-as-day it got. The focus also went blurry, the way my eyesight used to when I took off my glasses. Beyond a kilometer, my Spark-o-Vision dwindled to nothing; even at half that distance, when I tried to center my sight a long way from where I actually was, I stopped seeing with bright midday clarity. My vision was reduced to true night darkness and I could only discern big things like cars and buildings.

Speaking of cars, I was surprised by the number in the Market's parking lot. There were fewer than on a bustling market day, but more than I expected. Did Waterloo really have that many Darklings? Or did the Goblin Market draw shoppers from farther afield? From Toronto . . . maybe from Michigan and New York state . . . maybe from all over the world.

I was about to march into a hive of deadly powerful people while dressed like a blindfolded tap dancer. I thought, *My costume should be black instead of white. That way, it wouldn't show as much if I pee myself.*

ARIA SET US DOWN IN THE PARKING LOT

We landed in the lot's outermost corner, as far as possible from the buildings. In what she likely thought was a low voice, Aria said, "What now? Just walk in?"

Ninety-nine held up the goblin business card she'd taken from Popigai's office. "Let's show this at the door and see what happens."

"They'll know we're with the Light," Aria said. "We're wearing masks and costumes. And we have"—she lowered her voice for real, as if uttering a dirty word—"Halos. We're unmistakable."

"So what?" Ninety-Nine said. "The Dark won't be happy to see us, but they'll think twice about hassling us."

"Look at all these cars," Aria said. "Dozens of Darklings, and only four of us."

"This needn't get adversarial," Dakini said. "We have an admission ticket." She plucked the business card from Ninety-nine's hand. "We don't have to go in expecting a fight."

"Of course we do," Aria said. "Four Sparks plus a mass of Darklings equals disaster just waiting to happen. We have to be prepared for the worst."

I grew to full size so I could join the discussion. "Let me go in first. I can shrink so small they can't see me, then use my comm ring to tell you what I see. Maybe there won't be a need for any of you to go inside. I can get in and out without being noticed."

Ninety-Nine laughed. "Nice plan. But I bet we end up going in anyway, and eventually, fists'll fly." She held up her hands to forestall Aria from protesting. "No, I don't plan on provoking a fight. Yes, I'll behave myself: *Olympic-level* behaving. No, I don't know what will fuck up our good intentions. But yes, I believe it'll all end in bruises because the Light and Dark get along like nitro and glycerin."

Aria sighed. "So noted. But we can try." She looked at me. "Nothing but reconnaissance, as small as you can get away with. Do *not* get into trouble while you're in there alone."

Through my ring, I said, *«I'll stay in contact the whole time.»*

I took off without waiting for more discussion. Also without mentioning a glitch in our plans . . . because by then, I'd already tried sending my Spark-o-Vision into the main market building. It didn't work: yet another blinder wall. I had no idea if the Inventor's comm ring could broadcast once I was inside the wall.

Oh well. I was Zircon, fully costumed and ready for the lions' den.

I flapped across the parking lot at top speed. I didn't slow down as I shrank to the size of a bedbug and barreled through a crack in the wood-plank wall.

NOSTALGIA. HARD.

Three years had passed since I'd attended a Darkling gathering. I'd forgotten what they were like.

First, the candlelight. Darklings universally preferred candles to electric bulbs. Even the youngest, raised since birth under artificial lights, had a racial fondness for the days when humans feared the night and huddled around candles after sundown. Besides, electric lights didn't fare well when surrounded by the reality-warping power of a large group of Darklings; the bulbs flickered, fizzed, and occasionally exploded, showering glass in all directions. As a result, Dark assemblies always smelled of beeswax and flame: tealights, tapers, and fat hexagonal candles that could burn for days.

Next, the background music, in this case provided by a twelve-person chamber group of strings and woodwinds. (Live music worked better than recordings for the same reason that candles worked better than lightbulbs. By the end of an evening surrounded by dozens of Darklings, an electrical sound system would make nothing but static.) As I entered, the musicians were playing something I didn't recognize. That wasn't surprising. When I was young, I took the obligatory violin lessons, but I never got deeply into the classical music repertoire. Even if I had been a bit more knowledgeable, Darklings shied away from "populist" works like *The Four Seasons* and *Messiah.* Well-known = vulgar. Whatever the orchestra was playing, it was pretty but not catchy—something Mozart or Haydn might have whipped off for a minor noble's birthday.

Finally, there was the food. A banquet table was laid with white linen, while waiters circulated carrying trays of caviar, sashimi, and pâté. No goblets of blood, no plates of maggots (although the polished silver trays would rapidly tarnish and have to be replaced every few hours). Rumors abounded of Darkling debauches where they ate human flesh and drank from naked victims, but if that ever happened at all, this wasn't the place. Too many non-Darkling witnesses: the musicians, the serving staff, the shoppers' chauffeurs, and many more.

Besides, you have to remember that Darklings were rich before they were Dark. For them, a proper party involved gowns and tuxedos, not intestines and knives. Think charity balls. Opera galas. *The Great Gatsby*, not *Saw*.

The Goblin Market was cocktail-party chic, despite being held in a not-quite-windproof building that usually sold fresh-killed chickens and pickled beets. People perused the merchandise while holding champagne flutes, or they sat at elegant tables with centerpiece candelabra.

ITEMS FOR SALE WERE SPREAD ALONG THE BUILDING'S CENTRAL AISLE

Two other aisles were dark and unused. The Goblin Market placed quality ahead of quantity, and there simply weren't enough wares to fill the building.

Merchandise was impeccably displayed: a diverse collection of consumables, clothes, curios, and contraptions. I learned later that the majority of goods had been placed on consignment, crafted by artisans who had no direct affiliation with the Goblin Market but who availed themselves of the chance to show off their creations.

Just as olden-day families had once assigned their offspring to different seats of power—the eldest sent to the army, the next to the church, the third into government, and so on—modern Darklings often slotted their children into careers that gave the family a wide spectrum of expertise and influence. An MBA. A lawyer. A "numbers wonk." And (if the parents weren't yet bored of paying surrogates to bear their kids) a wizard to handle chores the others didn't have time for, including the production of useful magic items.

James Bond had Q; Darkling clans sired their own magic hackers to supply the rest of the family with cool toys.

Mostly, the toys were kept secret. You didn't want rivals to know that everyone in your family carried an amulet to detect lies or shoot bolts of fire. But secrets don't last forever, and once word got out, ingenious bling could win bragging rights, not to mention earning a pretty penny.

Hence, the Goblin Market had stall after stall selling privately made goods. Each item was a one-off, hand made by a very rich person who cared more about street cred than money. The goal was to make other Darklings stop in surprise and say, "How did they *do* that?"—such as a magnifying glass that translated languages (look through the glass, and printed matter turned into English) or a CD of silence (i.e., when you played the CD, it canceled nearby sounds, creating a bubble where no noise was possible).

I could have spent all night looking at goodies. (I'm a sucker for shiny things.) But I forced myself to shift my attention to the people, and there, I saw more shininess: Darklings dressed in finery, even if they were lizards or half-rotted corpses.

As many as sixty Darklings were visible—a huge gathering, considering how rare they are in the general population. Each had brought support staff, if only to lug purchases back to the car, but there were also bodyguards and shopping "consultants," easily recognized because they were dressed in business-wear rather than competing for style with their betters. Dark suits, drab haircuts, and sensible shoes.

I scanned the crowd but saw no one I recognized. No Lilith. No

Nicholas. No one who might be the all-metal Popigai. But that was only the ground floor; the building had a second story. I headed upstairs.

THE SECOND FLOOR HAD AN AUCTION IN PROGRESS

It looked like an art auction at Christie's or Sotheby's. By which I mean it looked like such auctions do in movies. I've never seen Van Goghs or Rembrandts go up for bid, but I'll bet the movies are close to the truth—these days, customers at real auctions must expect them to resemble the Hollywood versions, so Christie's and Sotheby's have to conform to expectations.

The market's auction area had six rows of straight-backed chairs upholstered in the same shade of purple as the brochure in Popigai's office. Three dozen people sat in the chairs. Some were Darklings on their own, while others were Darkling-human pairs: probably a Darkling boss and a human "personal assistant" who'd deal with administrivia once an item was purchased.

But the auction had one thing you'd never see at Sotheby's. The auctioneer was a purple-skinned creature even shorter than me. (I mean me-Kim, not me-Zircon, who was currently the size of a fruitfly.) The auctioneer's head looked exactly like the sketch on the business card. He had ears pointier than a Vulcan's and a broad mouth with too many teeth. Bald head. Yellow eyes. He wore a robe that was tailored like an academic gown, the same shade of purple as his skin.

A goblin. Or perhaps *the* Goblin. I'd seen no similar creatures elsewhere in the building. Perhaps this was the market's sole proprietor.

Was he a Darkling? Presumably. But unlike most, he didn't project an aura of intimidation. He reminded me of the Count on *Sesame Street*: an endearing version of a scary original. His yellow eyes crinkled like Yoda's. If he had a Shadow at all, it didn't say, "Fear me," it said, "Trust me."

What's worse than a Darkling that terrifies you? A Darkling you want to cuddle. Now *that's* frightening.

THE GOBLIN STOOD ON A STOOL AT THE AUCTIONEER'S PODIUM

As I arrived, the item up for sale was a stoppered test tube filled with cardinal-red fluid. The instant I saw it, I thought, *Healing potion*. A moment later, I saw a sign on the auctioneer's podium confirming that I'd guessed right. Someone had made a video game–style healing potion that supposedly worked in real life. I assumed if you swigged it, your wounds would close and your bones unfracture. Amazing.

Healing magic was rare among Darklings—too warm and fuzzy for their tastes. Besides, they healed quickly enough without artificial aids. Even so, some Darkling had spent time and effort not just to create a potion that could cure injuries but one that looked the part.

Why? Let me speculate. The purpose of a healing potion isn't just to knit up your wounds; it's to see the look on an enemy's face when you chug back a bottle during battle. Suddenly, you're as fresh as you started, and the other guy has to be saying, "Are you fucking kidding me?"

That's what was really being auctioned: that look, that priceless moment. And bidding was fierce, in a repressed Sotheby's way, where lifting a finger by a centimeter was equivalent to screaming, "It must be mine!"

One person at the auction wasn't bidding. A woman dressed in black sat in the back row, with a veil over her face and widow's weeds fashioned like a bridal gown.

THE WIDOW SAT STOCK-STILL, HEAD HIGH, BACK RIGID

Her face was impossible to see under the veil, but her manner made it clear she disdained everything around her: the auction, the bidders, the entire Goblin Market. Everything here was beneath her dignity, as if she were an aged Victorian duchess who'd doddered into the twenty-first century and deplored what the world had become.

I didn't see the others who'd been in the black Lexus—neither the tough-guy driver nor the pustule-faced demon. The Widow sat on the end of a row and the chair beside her was occupied by a nondescript young woman: no one important. I checked out the other bidders, but the Widow was the only familiar face. So to speak.

A voice spoke in my mind. *«Dude, are you dead or what?»*

«I'm fine,» I said. *«Just scouting.»*

«You were supposed to report what you were seeing.» That came from Aria, who'd apparently relented on the whole I-won't-use-the-comm-ring bullheadedness.

«I haven't seen much,» I said. *«Just an upscale market, with oodles of Darklings. But I've reached the second floor and the Widow is here.»*

«The one who was in on the first attack?» Dakini asked.

«That's her,» I said. *«At least I think so. I can't tell for sure with the veil covering her face, but the outfit is the same.»*

«This strikes me as odd,» Dakini said. *«Is it not your belief that she's related to the Bride you saw in the lab?»*

I ground my teeth, trying to stop myself from projecting angry thoughts. The only way Dakini could know what I believed was by prying into my mind. After a moment, I forced myself to sound calm as I said, *«The Widow's outfit is identical to the Bride's, except for the black/white thing. I'm thinking twin sisters.»*

«So the woman's twin sister just vanished through a rift, and the Widow decided to go shopping? Even for a Darkling, that seems disengaged.»

«Let's ask her what the fuck,» Ninety-Nine said. *«Meet you at the door so we can face her together.»*

I said, *«I'll be there in a minute.»* But I took one last look at the Widow. If she hated her surroundings so much, why had she come? Most likely, because she wanted something that was scheduled to come up for sale—wanted it so badly, she had swallowed her distaste at where she was. I stared harder, the way you do when you're trying to understand somebody: as if you could read their mind if only you looked with enough intensity.

As I stared, I became aware of a subtle influence nudging my consciousness. Not from the Widow. I looked at the woman beside her, but immediately my mind said, *No one important,* and flicked my attention away.

Damn! Another Ignorance spell, subtler than the one Nicholas had used. I knew someone was sitting in the seat beside the Widow; I just couldn't be bothered to pay attention.

I forced myself to look. Perhaps because my Spark-o-Vision had a degree of resistance against unnatural influence, I managed to break through the spell.

Sitting calmly beside the Widow was Elaine Vandermeer.

IT WAS ONE OF THOSE FIGHT-OR-FLIGHT MOMENTS

Would I fly out of the building and keep going forever? Or plunge into Elaine's ear and rupture her skull from inside?

I just froze in fear and shame. I wasn't Elaine's victim anymore—I wasn't Kimmi. But my body didn't realize I had moved on.

I nearly threw up. Kimmi had been so *breakable,* compared to Kim and Zircon. But I had moved on, damn it! I had!

ELAINE HAD BARELY CHANGED SINCE THE LAST TIME I'D SEEN HER

(Since she'd bitten my arm and licked my blood.) Her glasses still looked as if they came from an optician's poster, but the frames were smaller. They made her look less like a model pretending to be a scientist and more like a model pretending to be an executive. Her makeup was different too: paler than I remembered. This was a Darkling soiree, and at such events, vampires make a point of looking bloodlessly white. Otherwise, they're too easy to mistake for mortals.

So physically, Elaine looked much the same, but her effect on me had changed. When she'd bitten me, I had been human and under the thrall of her Shadow. She'd seemed so imposing and superior, the way queens must have overwhelmed peasants long ago. Now though, I was a Spark. Elaine's Shadow barely touched me. I could sense it trying to weasel into my mind, but it couldn't get inside.

Elaine now struck me as very, very young. Like Nicholas, she'd undergone the Dark Conversion as soon as she turned eighteen. She hadn't visibly aged a day since. In the unforgiving noon of Spark-o-Vision, she seemed like a teen whose hair, makeup, and glasses were way too old for her, like a kid all dressed up for her first job interview.

Baby-faced sadist. I hated her. I hated her.

«*YO, ZIRCON,*» NINETY-NINE SAID

«Weren't you meeting us at the door?»

«Sorry. Distracted.» I dragged my attention from Elaine and flapped my coattails back toward the stairs. *«Hey,»* I said, trying to get my mind off the woman behind me, *«how do you know I'm not down there? I might be too small to see.»*

«No,» Dakini said. *«I can't feel your presence.»*

«If I were there, you could feel my presence?»

«You're a heroine, sweet.» Dakini chuckled. *«However small you may be physically, on a psychic level, you're enormous.»*

«So psionic people can tell when I'm around?»

Dakini hesitated. *«I don't know if my psionic powers are typical, but when you're near, the air fills with the scent of vanilla, as strong as a fifteen-year-old wearing body spray. If I focus on the aroma, I can determine your exact location.»*

I scowled. That damned First Law of Dark and Light. My shrinking didn't hide me as completely as I thought.

So I was visible and vulnerable to mental powers: the most intrusive kind of magic. I couldn't even use pseudoscience double-talk to justify a degree of immunity. Dakini had already proven psionics could affect me, so the window of opportunity had closed.

Shit. With so many Darklings here at the market, some of them would have enough psychic power to turn me inside out: hurt me, dominate me, make me tell my passwords.

Maybe even Elaine. Vampires are famous for their powers of mental domination.

Shit, shit, shit.

I HURRIED TO THE MARKET'S MAIN ENTRANCE

By the time I got there, my teammates were being greeted by a fiftyish man in a charcoal gray suit. He reminded me of Pavarotti: rotund, bearded, expansive. Really though, he was a bouncer. He had the charismatic charm to deflect most unwanted visitors, but the size to get physical if needed.

As far as I could tell, the man had no supernatural powers. Why would he need them? The only people he might have to get rough with were ordinary mortals. Darklings were welcome one and all, and as for Sparks, you do *not* start a fight with super-folk when surrounded by millions of dollars of breakable merchandise.

Bouncer-Pavarotti surely knew my teammates were Sparks. If the costumes and masks weren't enough, their Halos must have sent the message loud and clear. Mr. Pseudo-Pavarotti deserved credit for not being reduced to awed silence. Then again, a greeter at the Goblin Market had to be guarded by mental shielding magic; he'd be exposed to so many Shadows, he'd go mad without protection.

"Good evening, ladies," he said. (I wasn't offended—he couldn't see me. I was naught but a drifting dust mote.) "Welcome to the Goblin Market. May I see your invitation?"

"Certainly." Dakini handed him the business card from Popigai's corkboard. The moment Pavarotti touched the card, it flared with purple light. "Excellent," he said. "I assume you're with one of the suppliers?"

Aria looked as if she was about to say something overly honest. Dakini managed to speak first. "We're here for Professor Popigai. Have you seen him?"

"I'm unfamiliar with the professor," Pavarotti replied. "However, I've seen his name on a merchandise display." He gestured down the aisle in front of us. "Fourth stall on the left."

"Does the market carry many goods made by Sparks?"

"Not as many as we'd like," Pavarotti replied. "The Goblin is eager to purvey the best from both magisteria." The man examined my teammates with a critical eye. "Would any of you have a flair for crafting items of interest?"

He meant, "Are any of you Mad Geniuses?" A handful of Sparks who created super-gadgets weren't utterly crazy—the Inventor, for example. Usually though, when superintelligence got jammed into a human brain, it was like parking an eighteen-wheeler in an ordinary-sized garage. The result wasn't pretty.

"I can make things," Ninety-Nine said. She flashed green. "Actually," she added, "I can make *amazing* things." Her face turned thoughtful. "Wow. If I just . . ."

"Stop," Aria said. "Do not. Go. There."

Dakini stepped forward quickly and put her hand on the bouncer's arm. "We'd be delighted to speak with the Goblin about business opportunities. Can a meeting be arranged?"

"I'll let him know you're interested." Pavarotti withdrew a phone from a pocket in his jacket. "If his duties permit, the Goblin will contact you soon. In the meantime, please enjoy what his market has to offer."

Pavarotti smiled as he gestured to the aisle in front of us. Inside my head, Aria muttered, *«Come into my parlor, said the spider to the fly.»*

THE STALL NEAREST THE DOOR HAD DAGGERS FOR SALE

Three slender knives lay on a purple velvet cloth: one gold, one silver, one bronze. The stall held nothing else except the three weapons, but they were so beautiful, they didn't need window dressing. Each gleamed brightly, made of solid metal; no ornamentation, just plain unmarked blades. The hilts were bleached white bone. (Don't ask the obvious question.) Beside each knife lay an unadorned belt sheath of scaly black leather—possibly from some kind of lizard, but the unspoken words "dragon hide" hung in the air.

No one staffed the stall. The weapons sat unattended.

"Want!" Ninety-Nine said. She reached toward the knives, but Aria caught her wrist.

"You don't just fondle magical weapons, especially when you can't afford them."

"How do you know I can't afford them? They don't have prices on them."

"That's how I know."

"But . . ."

Aria said, "What do you have in the bank? A few hundred dollars?"

"Um," said Ninety-Nine. "Yeah, let's pretend that."

"This market is aimed at Darklings," Aria told her. "Even if it was selling, like, off-the-shelf bottled water, the prices would be mega-inflated. A magic dagger is completely out of your league."

"Can't I just hold one?"

"That would be unwise," Dakini said. "Taking up a magical weapon is dangerous. You create a connection with something designed to kill. Perhaps these weapons *enjoy* killing. And notice the lack of a salesperson. Does that not suggest magical defenses to keep the daggers safe?"

Ninety-Nine pouted and made little puppy whimpers.

"Oh hell," Aria said. "If you really want one, I'll buy it for you."

Ninety-Nine stopped whimpering. "What?"

"You heard me," Aria said. "I've got a platinum card. I'll buy it."

"You'll buy me something that costs a zillion dollars? What's the catch?"

Aria turned away and tried to speak breezily. "No catch. We're Sparks. Everyone keeps saying we'll get into fights, and all you have to fight with are fists and feet. With a magic weapon, you'll have more to contribute. Guard my back, that sort of thing."

Ninety-Nine stared at her. "This is a trick, right? You're using psychology to . . . I don't know, but it won't work. You can't use your platinum card, cuz it would give away who you are. Welcome to the world of cold hard cash, missy."

Aria was still turned away. "So you don't want a magic weapon?"

"Of course I want a magic weapon. I'll just get one on my own."

"How?"

"I'll go Mad Genius and make one. Or steal it. Or extrude it from an orifice like any respectable superhuman."

Ninety-Nine turned her back on the daggers and flounced down the aisle. As much as one can flounce in a hockey uniform.

FOURTH STALL ON THE LEFT: ADAM POPIGAI'S

The dominant feature of the stall was a box the size of a refrigerator. It had a brushed steel surface and REPLICATOR stamped into the front face.

The only other thing in the stall was a rough wooden sales counter with its top painted white. Every stall in the Market had a similar counter, where the usual Market vendors would display their onions, doilies, and plaques with bible quotes. Tonight the Goblin had covered most of those counters with purple velvet, but Popigai's stall hadn't been nice-ified. Popigai had just laid a small chapbook on the ugly white counter, then called it a day.

The chapbook was a catalog of what the replicator could make. Each entry had a code number followed by an astronomical price. The craziest part was that the prices seemed fair. I mean, seriously: What would you pay for an honest-to-God light saber? A working one, like in Star Wars? *Lop off the hands of your enemies,* said the catalog entry. *Color determined by your moral alignment.*

"That must be a joke," Dakini said.

"George Lucas won't be laughing," Aria said. "No way these are legally licensed."

"Awesome swag," Ninety-Nine said, flipping through the catalog. "A *Back to the Future* hoverboard . . . thirteen different sonic screwdrivers . . . a voice-activated Chemex coffeemaker robot . . ."

"How much?" Aria snapped, like a drowning woman offered a lifeline.

"You can't afford it," Ninety-Nine said.

"Yes, I can."

"Can't use credit, only cash."

"Fuck."

Ninety-Nine patted her arm. "Next time we meet Grandfather and Invie, we'll ask how they buy big-ticket items. They likely route purchases through anonymous bank accounts . . ." She stopped. Glowed green. "Oh."

"Oh what?"

"I just realized how to route purchases through anonymous bank accounts." Ninety-Nine grinned. "Which tax haven do you like? Grand Cayman? Isle of Man?"

Dakini said, "Olympic-level money laundering?"

Ninety-Nine shook her head. "*Mad Genius*–level money laundering." She whistled softly. "Fuck."

WHILE THE OTHERS TALKED, I PERUSED POPIGAI'S CATALOG

I couldn't turn the pages, but I didn't have to: I could position my Spark-o-Vision *between* pages, and read what was written on them. Like X-rays, only better. Everything was clear, like reading under perfect light.

The catalog had only thirty-two pages, but I've already described what kind of stuff it offered—simultaneously astounding and trivial. Take light sabers. If Popigai could actually make thin energy fields that cut through solids, then producing toys for the idle rich was a criminal waste of technology. Why not create equipment for factories, or mining, or rescue work, or any of the other beneficial applications you could come up with, given a few seconds to think?

I'm hardly the first person outraged by the gap between Cape Tech's potential and its actual use. You invent an ultrapowerful, ultraefficient energy source and the first thing you do with it is fly around and shoot lightning? What are you, three years old?

But Sparks had tunnel vision—focused on fighting, never on more productive aspects of life.

What was *wrong* with us?

THE REPLICATOR GAVE A LOUD *CHUG*, THEN REVVED UP INTO A HUM

Aria turned to Ninety-Nine. "What did you do?"

"Nothing! It started on its own."

"Voice-activated?" Dakini suggested. "You were talking about light sabers."

"The machine can't be that stupid," Aria said. "At the very least, it should start by asking, 'Do you really want a light saber, yes or no?' "

The replicator added a descant whine to its ongoing hum. "This makes me uneasy," Dakini said.

Ninety-Nine said, "Is that ordinary nerves, or a full-on premonition?"

"Premonitions would be in keeping with my powers," Dakini replied.

"Fuck," Aria said. "What if the machine is a Trojan horse?"

"What do you mean?"

"Think about it," Aria said. "Popigai plants a device in the middle of the Market—a box that supposedly makes wonderful things. But actually, it's a weapon of mass destruction."

"What would he gain from that?" Dakini asked.

"Carnage," Aria said. "Popigai has Mad Genius written all over him. He may get off on destruction for its own sake."

Ninety-Nine glowed green with incoming knowledge. "Historically, Mad Geniuses love to target Darkling events. No point in murdering mere humans—they're nobodies. But Darklings have money and power. Kill them, and you'll make the front page of Reddit."

Aria looked at the humming replicator. "We have to turn this off."

"It's likely booby-trapped," Dakini said. "Remember how Popigai rigged his office door? Tamper with this replicator, and you may set off a bomb."

"Or worse," Aria said.

"What's worse than a bomb?" asked Dakini.

"A pandemic virus," Aria replied. "Self-replicating nanites. Something that creates a mini black hole. Stop me when you've heard enough."

"I could deactivate it," Ninety-Nine said. "I'm an Olympic-level deactivator person." She stopped. "Wouldn't that be an awesome Olympic event? Give every competitor a bomb to defuse. Fastest time wins, so you encourage people to rush . . ."

Aria said, "Can we focus? We have a problem."

"We *may* have a problem," Ninety-Nine corrected. "We don't know for sure this machine is dangerous. Maybe it just runs automatically once in a while, like a refrigerator. It looks like a refrigerator. Maybe it's harmless."

"Then feel free to keep standing in front of it," Aria said. "I'm going to find the Goblin and tell him he might have a disaster on his hands."

"For cripes' sake, we're superheroes," Ninety-Nine said. "If something is about to go kablooey, we don't run crying to Dad."

"This isn't running, it's going through channels," Aria said. "This is demonstrating to Darkling witnesses that Sparks can behave with respect, rather than acting precipitously. Zircon?" She looked around for a moment, trying to find me. Wasp-sized, I flew in front of her eyes. "Ah, there you are. Where's the Goblin?"

«Upstairs at the auction,» I said.

Aria headed for the stairs. Ninety-Nine and Dakini exchanged looks, then followed on her heels. "What do you think the Goblin is going to do?" Ninety-Nine asked Aria's back. "He doesn't know you. Why should he listen?"

"Because I'm a fucking Spark," Aria said. She flared golden, so bright that Ninety-Nine and Dakini had to avert their eyes. "My powers include an overwhelming presence," Aria continued, "because I want them to. And because I am goddamned used to people staring at me. I am perfectly comfortable raising my voice, and my voice is good at being raised. I will make the Goblin see that action is required."

"And he's going to do what?"

"This building is full of magic. There must be something that can handle a Trojan horse. Even if we just teleport it into the parking lot, that's better than nothing."

"I thought you were worried about pandemic viruses," Ninety-Nine said. "Should we teleport a bioweapon out where it's open to the wind?"

"It wouldn't be safer in this drafty old building," Aria said. "Anyway, we don't know it's a bioweapon. It could be plain old dynamite. Or something we can't imagine. One way or another, if it activates in here, a hundred people get hit immediately. Outside is better."

"And if the replicator is just a replicator, everybody labels us as paranoid wingnuts."

"My dear Ninety-Nine," Aria said, "paranoia is our friend. Paranoia is our sunscreen, our condom, our duct tape. Paranoia tells the truth nine times out of ten, and the tenth time is when you weren't paranoid enough. We will never correctly anticipate what flavor of shit will hit the fan, but we can calculate the trajectory and attempt to avoid the splatter."

"Wow," said Ninety-Nine. "Can I get all that on a T-shirt?"

"Fuck off," Aria said. "And *that* you can get on a T-shirt."

OUR GROUP ATTRACTED A LOT OF ATTENTION AS WE HEADED TOWARD THE STAIRS

Darklings dominate the public eye: Most world leaders belong to the Dark, as do financial bigwigs and A-list celebrities. The people you see in the news today are disproportionately Dark because they're the ones with national and international clout. (In the old days, it was harder to notice how much the media fawned on the rich. Now, when the rich stand out because of their fangs or fur, it's more obvious who gets to frame social narratives.)

By contrast, most Sparks stay out of the limelight. They don't do press conferences. They appear out of nowhere and fly off posthaste. Apart from Tigresse and a few others who've appointed themselves as "speakers for the Light," Sparks are mostly seen in blurry cell-phone photos snapped by people with fast reflexes.

That meant we were novelties: possibly the first Sparks anyone here had seen firsthand. Even the Darklings found us exotic. They were taking pictures, trying to start conversations. Aria ignored them—as Miranda, she'd had abundant practice giving people the brush-off.

But Darklings don't take no for an answer, and they weren't as cowed by her "overwhelming presence" as ordinary humans would be. Aria could have taken to the air, but that might have looked like she was running from the crowd; uh-uh. So she excuse-me'd as assertively as she could without actually picking people up and throwing them against walls. Even with Ninety-Nine and Dakini helping to wedge the way forward, our progress toward the stairs was slow.

I MADE MYSELF USEFUL BY PLAYING SCOUT

I nestled in Ninety-Nine's hair so I wouldn't have to fly while my eyes were elsewhere. Then I shifted my viewpoint back to the replicator to see what it was up to.

Nothing noticeable. Humming? Warming up? Whatever the machine intended, nothing had happened yet. So I moved my Spark-o-Vision upstairs to check out the auction.

The healing potion had sold. Bidding had moved on to a gadget that looked like a TV remote control. I saw no sign explaining what it was—just a card saying LOT 49. But I also saw the Widow sitting rigid with attention. This gizmo was clearly what she hoped to buy.

The Goblin, as auctioneer, said a few words. (I could only see, not hear. Memo to self: Learn to lip-read!) He held a dainty brass hammer above the podium. This looked like the "Going once, going twice" part of the auction. Nobody in the audience showed any interest except the Widow.

And Elaine.

THE GOBLIN SAID, "SOLD!"

Even I could lip-read that. An assistant wearing purple gloves carried the gadget to the Widow. The assistant held the device in both hands, as if it were an ancient and holy relic. He bowed and presented it to the Widow like handing a queen her crown.

The Widow took it and mashed her thumb on the power button.

BANG, THEN *BOOM*, THEN *SHUDDER*

The *bang* was as sharp as a rifle shot. Delicate champagne flutes shattered as if hit with bricks.

The *boom* was even louder, but it was a blunt instrument: a lead pipe in the hands of Colonel Mustard, bludgeoning our eardrums in the conservatory. The sonic impact ripped me from my perch in Ninety-Nine's hair and sent me skittering. I felt myself spinning, but my vision still centered on the Widow and Elaine, as stable as a gyroscope. I saw the two of them stagger as the market building lurched like the *Titanic* becoming a metaphor.

Then I smacked into something hard and crunchy. Ow.

My viewpoint snapped back home. I found myself embedded in the wooden wall of the building, like a pellet of buckshot blasted from a shotgun. I started to crawl out of the hole that I'd made, then decided to reconnoiter first. I peered out to see what the Widow had unleashed.

OH, LOOK: ANOTHER RIFT

It was downstairs, projected by Popigai's replicator. Or should I say "rifticator"? Either way, the machine had ripped the universe a new one.

Except that the new one was actually the old one. My view through the rift was the same as before: the brown vapor atmosphere, the multicolored fireballs swarming like angry bees, and the same six Darklings floating weightless inside the hole.

But something *had* changed. The were-beasts were stirring.

THE WERE-PANTHER WAS FIRST

She twitched, then stretched. She was in half-human feroform, but still looked like a cat waking up. I could tell the moment she became fully conscious, because she suddenly thrashed her arms like someone trying to balance on ice. The rift universe didn't have solid ground, or any apparent gravity. The panther drifted in a world with nothing but flame-bees and coppery vapor. She flailed for several seconds before getting her bearings and beginning to "swim" toward the portal that led back to our reality.

The moment the panther's head crowned through the gap, she plunged forward, either pushed by the world she was leaving or sucked through by our own. She'd barely touched the floor before she was up on her feet, mouth snarling, claws extended. Her eyes were bloodshot from immersion in the caustic brown gas, her sclerae like pools of red surrounded by black fur. Were-beasts are tough, but the damage must have stung like the smoke from a hundred campfires. The panther seethed with fury as she stood in our world once more.

She coughed and brown vapor gushed from her lungs. It surrounded her like a nimbus . . . but no, that wasn't vapor, it was some kind of energy of exactly the same color. The nimbus flared brighter in my Spark-o-Vision, and suddenly the panther was ten meters away from where she'd been. The move wasn't teleportation; it left a vapor trail between its start and ending point, as the panther ran through clouds of gas that spilled from the rift.

"Faster than a speeding bullet." It's a cliché, but how else can I describe how she moved? It was my first sight of true superspeed: faster even than Lilith's blood-augmented speed at the loading dock. I barely had time to register just how scary fast it was before the panther demonstrated why terror was the right response.

She zipped across the floor to a man lying on the ground. Darkling, mortal, I never found out—he was just some guy who'd been too close when the replicator opened the rift. The man had been knocked off his feet by the *bang-boom-shudder* and thrown into one of the wooden pillars that held the building up. The panther raced toward him and gouged her claws into his belly with .44-caliber velocity. She pawed internal organs out of the way until she found the man's liver, then buried her muzzle in the cavity and began chowing down.

I puked my guts all over my white costume.

«*DUDE,*» NINETY-NINE SAID INSIDE MY BRAIN, «*WHAT'S WRONG?*»
The comm ring must have transmitted my retching. I said, «*Popigai's machine has opened a rift. Same rift, same Darklings. The panther just came out and disemboweled a guy.*»

«*On it,*» Aria said. She took to the air.

«*Stop!*» I said. «*It's too late to help the victim, and the panther has super-speed. Spark-speedster fast. She's quicker than you are, Aria—you're better than humans, but speed isn't your major thing.*»

«*Are you sure she's faster?*»

«*Definitely. And think about it. We got superpowers from being exposed to the rift. Why not the Darklings too?*»

«*Impossible,*» Aria said. «*The Dark and the Light are incompatible. Wraith said it back at Popigai's office: They're non-overlapping magisteria.*»

«*Wraith also told us that plenty of Darklings are trying to break that barrier,*» Ninety-Nine said. «*My head is full of official reports where Darklings bathed in weird chemicals or ran naked through cyclotrons in an attempt to become super. It hasn't worked so far, but they keep trying.*»

«*Looks like somebody finally succeeded,*» I said. «*Except it seems to have driven the panther feral. She's . . . oh damn, here comes the bear.*»

THE DARKLING POLAR BEAR EMERGED FROM THE RIFT
It landed on the floor with the force of a meteor impact. The floorboards splintered and broke. They were thick fir planks that could hold the weight of market-day throngs, but they couldn't withstand the bear's landing. I didn't know the normal mass of a feroform were-bear, but this one was obviously way off the charts.

The bear glowed with the same brown nimbus as the panther, but I didn't expect super-speed. This time, I thought the nimbus implied a greatly increased mass, likely with a corresponding boost in strength and damage resistance.

«*Feroform polar bear,*» I transmitted to my teammates. «*Superdense, so probably super-strong and super-tough.*»

«On it,» Aria said, and this time I didn't stop her. If the bear had become as feral as the panther, it would attempt to rip out the guts of some unlucky bystander. We couldn't let that happen again.

«I'm on backup,» Ninety-Nine said. She leapt up onto the nearest support pillar, then swung from pillar to pillar toward the stairway. (That girl played way too much *Tomb Raider.*) Her moves kept her above the heads of the crowd, letting her make faster progress than she would have on the ground.

I gritted my teeth but said nothing. I had to stop thinking Ninety-Nine was weaker than the rest of us. In fact, I had to stop thinking of *everyone* as a weak link, including myself. Time to become the shining Zircon.

MEANWHILE, DAKINI APPROACHED THE WIDOW

She clearly trusted Aria and Ninety-Nine to handle the downstairs fuss. However, dealing with the were-beasts was only symptomatic relief. Dakini wanted to understand the roots of the problem. She thought she could do that by dumpster diving into the Widow's brain.

Dakini slid behind a pillar a few paces back from the Widow. A violet tendril extended from Dakini's forehead and snaked across the intervening distance, jabbing into the Widow's skull like a plug into a socket.

I thought Dakini's powers were only visible to me, but the Widow sensed the attempted intrusion. A black aura sprang up around the Widow's body, and a moment later, the tendril disintegrated in a whizz of violet sparks.

The Widow wheeled toward Dakini's position. She raised a finger like an angry schoolmarm. The finger aimed at Dakini. Black energy emerged, with the look of a diseased nerve cell. The cell's nucleus nestled against the Widow's fingertip and a thicket of black dendrites bristled out in all directions, but a single long axon shaft lanced straight toward Dakini.

Dakini threw up a violet barrier to stop it. For several seconds, the axon stabbed the barrier over and over, making no headway.

Then Elaine, standing beside the Widow, laid her hand on the woman's arm. Elaine whispered and, after a moment, the Widow lowered her finger. The attack on Dakini vanished.

Elaine looked at Dakini. "What do you think you're doing?"

"I could ask the same question," Dakini said. "Do you realize your companion opened a hole in the universe?"

Elaine looked at the Widow in surprise. The Widow showed no reaction. I wished I knew what secrets they were hiding; clearly Dakini wished the same, because a new violet tendril sprang out of her head and slithered toward Elaine.

The Widow pointed her finger at the tendril. Dakini backed off.

Before anyone could speak, another detonation went off downstairs.

ALL THIS TIME, I'D BEEN EMBEDDED IN THE WALL

I'd moved my viewpoint, but not my body. When the building shook under the second detonation, a shock of air blew into the mouth of my hiding place. Lucky for me, I was a boat in a safe harbor, only catching the edge of a storm.

Outside was worse. Fires had ignited from candelabra knocked over by the blasts. Mostly, the candles had just gone out, extinguished by gusts of wind. Only a handful had stayed alight, and even fewer had fallen onto anything flammable. When I'd surveyed the building after the first explosion, the fires were just getting started; with my bright-as-day vision, I hadn't even noticed that the candlelight was gone. Now the fires burned harder and were spreading in all directions, perhaps feeding on magical energies woven into the merchandise.

The people still on their feet were mostly Darklings. Non-Dark staff had been bowled over by the explosions, unless they were far removed from the double ground zero. Even those still upright had injuries: cuts from flying debris, plus damage from two consecutive concussion blasts. Blood ran from ears and noses.

The whole bottom of the building was knee-deep in vapor. Brown gas flooded from the rift, which was growing. Its top nearly reached the lower floor's ceiling, and the base dug into the ground. Where it touched the floorboards, they ceased to exist, negated from reality.

«FUCK»

That came from Aria, speaking inside my head. I needed a moment to locate her. The most recent explosion had tossed her against a wall, far from both the rift and the replicator. She'd saved herself from the impact by throwing up her golden force field, but as she got to her feet she seemed wobbly.

«What happened?» I asked.

«The fucker exploded!»

«Which fucker?»

«The bear! He headed for a woman like he intended to eat her, so I sang him in the face. The stupid bugger started vibrating like a jackrabbit. Next thing I knew, kaboom.»

«Vibrating?» That came from Ninety-Nine. *«Shit.»* She yelled out loud, "Everybody run!"

«What's wrong?» Aria asked.

Ninety-Nine didn't answer. I saw her sprinting like Usain Bolt for the stairs to the second floor. I moved my Spark-o-Vision back to see what she was running from.

The were-panther lay on the ground near the man she'd been eating. She must have caught the brunt of the blast when the polar bear exploded. Now she lay unconscious, her body quivering unnaturally. In Spark-o-Vision, she strobed like a cheap visual effect, alternating rapidly between bright white and deep black, the way that Dalek death rays used to.

Light-dark-light-dark. I had a sick suspicion what it meant. I yanked my Spark-o-Vision far back from the panther's strobing and shouted through my comm ring, *«Brace for impa—!»*

THE PANTHER BLEW UP WETLY

Under Spark-o-Vision, the explosion combined both bright and black—a moiré pattern of black and white bands fluttering stroboscopically.

The effect burst outward, smashing anything that got in the way. After the two preceding explosions, much had already been flattened, but the bulky wooden pillars holding up the building were still intact. The blast lashed into them, flaying off splinters and exposing the raw wood beneath. The fires that burned all around the ground floor seemed to feed off the explosion's energy: Flames whooshed and spread into hotter infernos. The outburst of power also fed the otherworldly rift. It dug deeper into the floor and up into the ceiling, ramming a hole to the building's upper floor.

Nothing remained of the panther. Her body had been rendered into light, heat, and fumes. Nothing to see except floorboards charred black where she'd been lying.

Spontaneous Darkling combustion. I suspected she wouldn't be the last.

«What the hell is going on?» Aria demanded. After the bear's explosion, she'd been slammed into the building's outer wall. Now the blast from the panther had smacked her against the same damaged wood, and this time, she'd gone through. She lay half in, half out of the building, sprawled on a litter of broken lumber. Snow drifted down onto her golden gown and mask.

«The super-Darklings are unstable,» Ninety-Nine said. I'd seen her racing for the stairs, but she hadn't gone up them. She'd run behind, taking shelter in the gap beneath the steps. Only her head stuck out as she surveyed the damage. *«It must be what happens when a Darkling gets superpowers. The Dark can't hold the Light. If anything hits 'em hard, they fly to pieces.»*

Aria said, *«So the polar bear . . . I was the one who made him blow up? I hit him with a sound blast.»*

«Dude,» Ninety-Nine said, *«the guy was a pimple ready to pop. And he was going cannibal, right? You had to stop him.»*

«I had to stop him, not kill him.»

«Popigai killed him,» Ninety-Nine said. *«Popigai turned him into a crazed carnivore time bomb. All you did was put the poor guy out of his misery.»*

«But . . . »

«Aria,» I interrupted, *«you'll have a second chance to see if super-Darklings can be saved. Here come the vampires.»*

I'D SEEN MOVEMENT INSIDE THE RIFT

Both vampires were on the move, flailing in zero-G toward the portal. The male made it out first, tumbling onto the floor in a cloud of brown mist. We didn't have to wait to see what superpowers he'd acquired. The moment he got to his feet, his eyes flared like furnaces and sizzling brown beams shot out.

The vampire's target was a were-eagle who'd just flown down from the second floor. The eagle might have intended to help the wounded, put out fires, or otherwise make a constructive contribution. At least, I like to think that—it's nice to believe a person's last thoughts are virtuous.

The vampire's brown lasers struck the eagle. The beams sliced through the bird's wings with surgical precision, severing both at the shoulder. The eagle's body dropped, but not as fast as you might imagine: Its bones were hollow, its body was light, and its singed, smoking feathers caught the air, slowing the descent. The eagle's wings took even longer to fall, buoyed up on the air like kites. They tumbled and twisted all the way down, until they landed in two floppy heaps.

The eagle shrieked in agony, thrashing on the ground and trying to crawl toward its wings. The vampire's face stayed deadpan. He merely scanned the area for someone else to hurt.

THE FEMALE VAMPIRE EMERGED FROM THE RIFT A MOMENT LATER

She toppled onto the male vampire, who was still standing right in front of the rift's mouth. He'd been so keen to use his laser eyes that he hadn't put any distance between himself and the portal. He turned to gaze at the female vampire, and shot her with his eye beams.

Smoke billowed from her flesh where the beams struck. She hissed in rage. Her body started strobing light-dark-light-dark, but that didn't stop her from retaliating. Her arms transformed into shining silver cleavers and slashed at her male counterpart. She didn't quite lop off his head, but she left it dangling from strands of gristle at the back of his neck.

Double strobe effect. Ninety-Nine and Aria simultaneously yelled, "Fuck!" Ninety-Nine dived under the stairs again while Aria (now outside the building) flew straight up and out of sight. Ninety-Nine shouted, "Everybody, get to cover!" just before both vampires went off like incendiaries.

I'D BEEN WATCHING THEM CLOSELY. BAD IDEA

Before, when the panther exploded, I'd pulled my Spark-o-Vision back to a safe distance. This time, I forced my perception to stay mere inches from the vampires. I thought maybe if I saw exactly what happened, I might be able to do something the next time. The Bride and the bogeyman were still in the rift, and I could guess that they'd soon be coming out.

But when the two vampires detonated, my head filled with the flash of their annihilation: Light and Dark energies bursting outward. Fire and ice stabbed into my brain; flame through my right eye, cold through my left. The stabs seemed like physical things—a red-hot poker and an icy needle. Something went *SNAP* inside my skull and I went blind.

More accurately, my Spark-o-Vision cut out. I could see, but only with my damp physical eyeballs, nearsighted and dependent on photons. I found myself in near-total blackness. Only a hint of light reached me in the hole where I'd been hiding all this time.

Even when I clambered out, I could barely see. The rift, still growing, was a ghost in the darkness. The fires throughout the building seemed dimmer than before. Had some of them been extinguished by the explosion? No. I realized that my eyes were just too small to catch much light. If they were a thousand times smaller than normal human eyes, they'd only receive a thousandth of the usual input. Or was it a thousandth squared? One way or another, everything was much much darker.

I grew to the size of a butterfly. My vision improved, yet I still felt blinkered. I'd only had superhuman perception for a few hours, but it was already the way I knew vision ought to be. Losing it hurt. I hoped the loss was just a brief overload that would fix itself as fast as Ninety-Nine recovered from wounds. But the *SNAP* in my head had been ominous—the sound of something breaking forever.

THE RIFT PULSED LIKE A DRUMBEAT

In that moment of pulsing it grew, thrusting farther through the ceiling and floor. Without thinking, I tried to shift my viewpoint to see how close the rift was to breaking through the roof. My weak mundane eyes remained stubbornly in my head.

I didn't need Spark-o-Vision to know the building was in trouble. Its timbers had taken a beating. And what about the snow? The roof slanted so that most snow would slide off, but the flakes were sticky enough that a layer would cling to the roofing. The weight would be pressing down on damaged supports.

If the building collapsed, Darklings and humans alike would get crushed. No one on the bottom floor seemed conscious except my teammates. People on the upper floor weren't badly injured, but how could they get out except through the ground floor?

I used my comm ring. *«Dakini, if you see fire exits up where you are, start everyone evacuating. If not, rip a chunk out of the wall. With all the snow we've been getting, maybe it's deep enough for people to jump into without getting hurt.»*

«I've already begun the evacuation,» Dakini said. *«What about the three of you?»*

«I'm fine,» Ninety-Nine answered. *«I'll start carrying out the wounded.»*

«But carefully!» Aria said, wherever she was. *«Some likely have spinal injuries.»*

Ninety-Nine said, *«You seem to forget I'm an Olympic-level EMT. And an MD too, now that I think of it. Whoa! I really am a doctor. I know all kinds of shit about . . . oh fuck!»*

«What's wrong?» we all said in unison.

«My brain just downloaded an entire medical library. You do not want mental pictures of every known skin disease.»

«Less talk, more action,» Aria said. *«Meanwhile, Zircon and I . . . fuck, here come the demons.»*

THE BOGEYMAN EMERGED FIRST

He was wreathed in brown vapor. It curled and eddied around him like a cape, quite possibly a result of his powers. In a movie, the effect would be pure cheese, but not with a real-life Darkling. The bogeyman's Shadow was so intense, even clichés became terrifying. With my diminished vision, I could barely see him; he was just an unfocused blur inside the vapor cloud, and he still nearly made me pee myself.

Then the bogeyman disappeared. Right from under my eyes.

«Invisibility?» Aria said. *«Are you fucking kidding me?»*

«Can you pick him up on sonar?» I asked.

«No good,» Aria said. *«His powers must work on sonar too.»*

«Then stay near the ceiling,» I said. *«He may be invisible, but he likely can't fly.»*

«Screw that,» Aria said, *«I have a force field. I'll let him grab me, then I'll fly him straight into the stratosphere. If and when he explodes, no one gets hurt except the ozone.»*

I didn't say it, but Aria was putting a lot of faith in her force field: not just that it could prevent the bogeyman from hurting her (with whatever superpowers he now possessed) but that her field would also protect her if the bogeyman blew up while he was holding her.

Still, I had no better ideas for dealing with Mr. Bogey. At least Aria's plan would avoid more injuries to people and the building.

If it didn't kill Aria herself.

I TOOK TO THE AIR, FLYING SEMIBLINDLY TOWARD THE RIFT

Ahead of me, the Bride awoke. She uncoiled from the fetal position and floated out into the Market. Brown vapor dropped away from her like a discarded amniotic sac. She shone clearly and more distinctly than the world around her—the only thing my dim eyes could bring into focus.

A vision in white. Then she began to scintillate with power. Flecks of energy shot off the Bride like sparks from a welding torch. Each spark had a different color: hot reds, blues, and greens. A burning yellow one came straight at me with the speed of a meteor.

You know those cartoons where a huge ball of snow rolls down a mountain and plows into somebody at the bottom? I had no time to get out of the way. There was only the moment of seeing it shoot toward me on a collision course. Then I was completely engulfed in yellow light.

My brain erupted in agony—sharp pain and dull throbbing, like a migraine and stuffed sinuses with a toothache on top. My eyes flooded with tears. My stomach heaved. Yet a pinprick of clarity shouted inside me. *Psionic attack. Induced nausea. Fight it.*

As Dakini had warned, it didn't matter if my body was too small to see. My psyche loomed large enough for the Bride's mental powers to target.

I could barely think from the pain, let alone move. I managed to flap my arms, more a spasm than a deliberate action. I was totally blind now, my real eyes as dead as my Spark-o-Vision. Even so, I could feel myself moving closer to the source of my torment. Pain intensified, pounding in my temples like a rock hammer. I flapped again; the pain increased. Over and over I flapped forward, barely conscious, as if something alien had taken possession of my arms.

The alien thing was Zircon, finally freed in full. Kim was in too much pain to exert the slightest control.

But even Zircon had limits. It persisted far beyond Kim's mortal endurance, but in the end, even a Spark of the Light can exhaust its strength.

Zircon shut down. It just let go. My omnimorphic field sputtered out like a lie and I exploded back up to fleshly height.

I didn't even feel my head hit the Bride under the chin. The pounding in my skull overrode other sensations. But a moment after that uppercut, all my pain went away—everything but the sudden ache at the top of my skull, in exactly the same spot where I'd slammed Jools an hour earlier.

Spark-o-Vision returned with a rush, showing the Bride starting to topple. She and I briefly stood face-to-face: both of us in white, her in her veil and gown, me in my suit, as if we were newlyweds. With Spark-o-Vision, I could see the two of us looking like the decoration on a wedding cake.

Then the Bride slumped, unconscious. She began to strobe and vibrate. I said, "Shit," and started to shrink.

I HAD ONLY GOTTEN DOWN TO BARBIE SIZE WHEN THE BRIDE EXPLODED Barbie-me nearly got blown through the rift. I missed the edge of the opening by a hairsbreadth, soaring so close that the wind of my passing sent vortices roiling through the rift's vapor. Fireball-bees swarmed toward me, but then I was past the hole, still riding the blast of the Bride's destruction.

I slammed into the Market's wall, making one of those person-shaped holes so popular in cartoons. Even with the hardness of a zircon, I got the breath hammered out of me.

For a moment, I stayed embedded in my silhouette. The pause gave me time to see what was happening throughout the building.

Ninety-Nine had been carrying someone over her shoulders in a fireman's lift. She was dozens of paces away from the blast, but she still got hurled backward into a rack of half-burnt clothes. The clothes were surrounded by a heat haze of magical energy.

Aria and the bogeyman sprawled in a tangled heap. She'd been standing near the rift, and the bogeyman had taken the bait. He'd been lurking invisibly behind her back. When the Bride exploded, it took him by surprise. He'd become visible as the explosion knocked him off his feet.

Aria's force field flickered weakly, nearly destroyed by the Bride's explosion. The bogeyman was also flickering: light, dark, light, dark . . .

Overhead, timbers groaned.

I screamed, "Everybody, run!"

In my squeaky, Barbie-doll voice.

Which only Aria heard.

ARIA BOLTED

Reflexes as fast as the speed of sound. With more-than-human strength, she shoved the bogeyman off her. Not wasting the time to get to her feet, she flew straight off the ground and shot toward Ninety-Nine. A quick grab, like an osprey snatching a fish from a stream, then the two of them shot through the hole in the wall that Aria had bashed out earlier.

Just in time. The bogeyman exploded. The roof came crashing down.

THE MARKET COLLAPSED IN A ROAR OF SPLINTERED LUMBER

Magical merchandise, Darklings, and humans were crushed under heavy fir crossbeams. I was caught in the collapse myself, still embedded in the wall. But I had just enough time to shrink to a sand grain. Like the ancient zircons that had survived four billion years, I remained intact while everything around me went to hell.

Crashing. Screams. Crunches. Wet sounds.

After the slaughter fell silent, I clambered up through debris and grew a little, using my vision to plot an insect-sized path through the shattered wood. I took to the air, wafting slowly over the carnage: blood and smashed bones protruding from flesh. Fires continued to smolder.

The upper half of the stairway had been destroyed, but the lower half was still intact. Falling timbers had hit the steps and rolled downward, leaving a patch of stairs exposed. Elaine Vandermeer lay half in, half out of that patch, her lower body smashed but her face perfectly untouched. A splinter of wood had driven itself through her chest. It must have been propelled by the explosion, on a flawless trajectory to impale her through the heart.

She was very dead.

The person I hated most in the world, killed by a fluke of bad luck.

But in a way, I was the one who'd killed her. I'd hit the Bride, and the Bride had blasted the bogeyman. He'd taken down the building.

I had killed my greatest enemy. Revenge. Triumph.

Dozens of other Darklings had died as well. Also, their human servants. I should have been happy, overjoyed. The only good Darkling is a . . .

Wait. What?

I looked down again at Elaine. Her face was twisted in pain.

Of course I'd had revenge fantasies, but never this. I'd dreamt of getting her arrested . . . of Nicholas discovering what she'd done and having her expelled from the family . . . of Elaine going bankrupt, being sent to jail, and realizing how awful she'd been.

But I'd never thought of killing her. The sight of it made me sick.

I grew back to full size and stood over Elaine in the silence of the fallen building. Some people said a staked vampire could come back to life if the stake was removed. I reached down and pulled.

SOMETHING BROKE; MY MIND CLEARED

I was back in the Market. The building was damaged, but still standing. Nothing had changed since the moment the headache had stabbed into my brain.

My Spark-o-Vision was still blind. My real eyes could barely see in the darkness. The only light came from fires, and from the ever-growing rift.

My size: small enough to float without falling. I'd barely moved since the Bride had attacked my mind. For a moment, I didn't understand how I'd flipped back in time. Then I realized how many far-fetched flukes had given me my "victory" over Elaine.

It had all been a delusion: an extended power fantasy compressed into a heartbeat.

A SHRIEK PIERCED MY HEAD

«You rejected my gift!»

The voice sounded like violin strings scraped by a badly held bow. The scraping shaped into words, conveying rage maddened by pain: a wounded animal lashing out because it couldn't find a way to stop hurting.

The Bride stared straight at me, even though I was so small I ought to have been invisible.

I said, "A hallucination isn't a gift. And what you created was ugly."

I was far too small for my voice to be heard, but the Bride had her claws hooked into my brain. *«You should be happy,»* she transmitted. *«You should be lost forever in the dream.»*

"How could I be happy about killing people?"

«Happiness comes from winning.»

"If you're a lion with a thorn in your paw, you can't make the pain go away by killing the thorn bush. You have to pull out the thorn."

«You're wrong,» said the Bride. *«I give happiness. Happiness comes from winning.»*

Her voice still sounded like a scraped violin, as if trying to make music by brute force. The other Darklings from the rift had been bestially insane; the Bride was on the edge of madness too, but she retained a sliver of self-control. Perhaps having psionic powers gave her greater mental strength. If I kept her talking and I said the right things, maybe she could keep a grip.

"The dream you gave me," I said. "Is that new? A power from the rift?"

«I give dreams of happiness. All wishes made true. All foes destroyed.»

I grimaced. I didn't give a damn about destroying my foes. My actual daydreams were embarrassingly conventional: finding a place I fit; loving someone who loved me back; becoming the most brilliant, most respected geologist of the twenty-first century.

But the Bride was a demon. Her fantasies wouldn't be so sunny.

"The rift gave your companions superpowers," I said. "Did you get some too?"

«I'm using my powers now,» the Bride said. *«Before, I could only give visions. Now I can transmit and receive.»*

"Then receive this," I said. "Happiness. Better happiness."

I WAS NO SHINING BEACON OF CONTENTMENT

I wasn't one of those sages Grandma Lam loves to talk about. I didn't do serenity, meditation, or ink-brush calligraphy, and I didn't plan on a life of celibacy. Believe me, I was (and am) messed up in the usual ways.

But I knew the happiness of reading that expanded my mind.

I knew Cherry Garcia ice cream.

I knew laughing to myself when someone obviously couldn't tell what sex I was. I knew the warmth of smiling at other people who'd received the same kind of stares, even if the reason we got those stares was completely different.

I knew breathtaking photos and viral videos. I knew *xkcd,* and hugging big dogs, and saying, "This, this, this!" when a tweet stated the absolute truth.

I knew hiking in the mountains. Seeing a fold in a wall of rock and understanding how it was made. Peering through a hand lens and finding itty-bitty garnets embedded in a stone that had previously seemed bland.

The right music at the right time. Sometimes the wrong music too. Looking at myself in the mirror just after coloring my hair and thinking, *Whoa.*

Shar's cookies. Miranda singing for the joy of it. Jools telling stories about partying with her hockey team, featuring crazy bad behavior I would never indulge in myself but loved to experience vicariously.

And Nicholas. Despite everything, there had been so many magical times when Nicholas and Kimmi were happy. I remembered those times clearly, even if they happened to a pair of people who were now both dead.

I sent all those memories to the Bride. I hoped she'd find them calming. Maybe they could ease her gnawing madness.

How could I have known it would be lethal?

SCRAPED VIOLIN STRINGS: A SCREECH, A SQUEAL, A HOWL

«Why have you made me remember?»

Keening: a word we all know, but a noise we seldom hear. The sound of a grief so bitter, it pulls a cry from the soul.

If Darklings even *have* souls. That's what the keening was about.

How much did the Dark Conversion kill? For vampires, it definitely killed the physical body. They didn't breathe and their hearts didn't beat. For other Darklings, it might be worse—like Skinless, the strangler skeleton, with no heart or lungs at all. Embers of life persisted, remnants of the original personality. But what about the soul? If such a thing existed, did Darklings have one? Or were they just dead inside?

They claimed to be as human as any mortal. But spend enough time in their company and you saw worrisome characteristics: extreme self-centeredness, lack of softer emotions, indifference to "the herd of hoi polloi." I had wondered if such traits just came from their upbringing—"the rich are different" has a history as long as the human race. But Nicholas had been raised that way too, and before he Converted, humanity had burned inside him like a supernova.

I hadn't seen enough of the new Nicholas to know how much was left. And I didn't know the Bride at all. Had she really thought happiness was synonymous with hurting those you hated? Did nothing else lift her spirits?

The Bride's new superpowers let her feel what she'd been missing. The reminders I'd sent her: not momentous thrills but everyday pleasures.

They stabbed her like a stake. The Bride's psychic powers had linked my mind with hers. I felt her grief as she realized what she'd lost.

She didn't vibrate or strobe. The Bride didn't die because Light and Dark energies warred inside her. She simply chose self-destruction rather than stay what she was. The explosion came afterward: energy released from a corpse with nothing left to hold it together.

Kaboom.

I'D ALREADY SEEN THAT BLAST IN MY HALLUCINATION

That gave me a split-second advantage. I still didn't have Spark-o-Vision, but I could see that the explosion had knocked Aria and the bogeyman into a heap, just as in my dream. As fast as I could think, I transmitted, *«Aria! Get the bogeyman outside. Now!»*

In the dream, Aria had rescued Ninety-Nine and let the bogeyman blow himself to pieces. This time, she scooped up the bogeyman in her arms and shot through the hole in the side of the building, flying at the speed of sound.

Even at Mach 1, she couldn't fly far. The Bride's explosion had sent the bogeyman into that fatal light-dark strobing. Aria only had a moment to whip him away from the building, then get herself clear.

She disappeared out of the hole in the wall. I stayed where I was and listened. The lumber around me creaked and cracked and groaned as the building teetered back and forth.

Outside I heard a distant explosion. The end of the bogeyman. I could have used my comm ring to ask if Aria was all right, but I was afraid I might get no answer.

THE RIFT GAVE A DRUMBEAT THUD

It had already broken through the floor that separated the upper and lower levels. I couldn't see how much farther it reached, but unless someone stopped it, the top of the rift would soon spike through the building's roof.

That would be bad, maybe total-collapse bad. The rift puncturing the roof might be the straw that broke the Market's back.

Luckily, I knew how to close rifts: Power down the rift projector. I jumped into the air and flapped toward Popigai's "replicator."

NOW THAT I LOOKED AT THE MACHINE, I COULD SEE SIMILARITIES TO THE ONE IN POPIGAI'S LAB

Both were the same size and shape. But there were two major differences:

I couldn't see a plug on the Market machine. Damn. It must have had a built-in battery or some other power supply.

Also, the machine in the lab had had a glassy exterior so I could see the weird components inside. The one in the market was encased in steel, hiding the Mad Genius guts.

The opaque case might also be hiding booby traps. Considering the state of the building, I didn't want to set off yet another explosion (or a pandemic, black hole, or any of the other things Aria had worried about). On the other hand, if I let the rift grow, it would bring down the building anyway.

No choice: I had to get into the machine and shut off its power. That meant dealing with any traps it might contain. Unfortunately, disarming traps wasn't my thing, especially when my perception consisted of two myopic eyes.

Just cope, I told myself. Ninety-Nine might be our Olympic-level bomb disarmer, but I was the one who could get into small places.

The glamorous life of a hero: If entering Darkling orifices wasn't bad enough, now I was going to climb inside a bomb.

I ALMOST HEADED STRAIGHT INTO THE REPLICATOR

Then I pictured myself the size of a gnat, ripping out electrical wires. Instant bug zapper! Zircon-hard skin would do zilch against electricity. The current would pass right through me, fry my tissues, and stop my heart.

I couldn't do this job with bare hands. My gloves wouldn't help at all—at this size, they were so thin, they provided zero insulation. I needed a tool.

Or maybe three tools. Yeah.

I flew back to that stall with the three magic daggers. Gold, silver, and bronze were all excellent conductors, so the blades wouldn't save me from getting jolted. The hilts, however, were bone. I had no idea how well normal bone conducted electricity, but these bones were imbued with magic.

Magic doesn't play well with electricity. The two aren't completely incompatible—plenty of Darkling wizards have developed lightning-bolt spells. But electrical conduction is a Science thing, locked into the framework of physics. Magic hates cooperating with the physics worldview; that's fraternizing with the enemy. If there's an escape clause, magic takes it.

Mark it down as another chance for plausible deniability. Everyone knows that metal conducts electricity. The magical metal blades had no choice but to follow the rules. Bone, however . . .

I grew to Max Zirc size and said in a loud, clear voice, "I happen to know that magic-enhanced bones are perfect insulators."

Then I picked up all three knives in a single sweep.

DAKINI HAD WARNED US AGAINST TOUCHING THE DAGGERS

Why did I blithely ignore her?

Because the Zircon part of me said, "I'm a Spark, and I can handle whatever happens."

Because the part of me left over from Kimmi was obsessed with magic and the Dark.

Because the part that was Kim said, "You need this. If you don't have good offensive weapons, you can't operate on your own."

Or maybe the knives just called to me, and without my teammates, I didn't have the self-control to resist.

Whatever the reason, I scooped up the knives as casually as cleaning up after dinner. Whereupon Nicholas appeared out of nowhere and said, "Are you insane?"

HE WRENCHED THE DAGGERS FROM MY GRIP

I didn't feel him touch me at all. His hands passed through mine, as if *I* were the ghost, but his grip on the knives was solid. He seized them from me, gold, silver, and bronze, and I couldn't hold on. My fingers refused to tighten. The daggers' sheaths rose up from the table and hovered in midair without support. One by one, Nicholas released the knives and they slithered into their sheaths like trained snakes. They continued to levitate in front of us both as Nicholas said, "What were you thinking?"

"I need them," I said. "To destroy the machine that's projecting the rift."

"Hard to do that when you're dead," Nicholas growled. "The Goblin puts antitheft spells on all his stuff. You're allowed half a minute to pick them up and examine them. After that . . ." He narrowed his eyes and stared closely at the knives' hilts. "I can only read the first few curses, but the knives start with stabbing you in the eyeballs. Then they get creative. I don't know what powers you have, Zircon, but you'd need a lot to survive."

"Oh," I said. "Well, then thanks, uhh, Wraith."

I couldn't meet his gaze, but I felt him glaring. The force of his Shadow pummeled me; I could resist it, but if I'd been human I might have fainted. Mortals don't do well in confrontations with angry ghosts. After a moment, I said, "Can you please stop that? You'll turn my hair white."

He gave a snort of a laugh. The pressure from his Shadow eased. "Do you really need the daggers?" he asked.

"Maybe." I gestured toward the replicator. "It's a Mad Genius machine, and it's feeding the rift. I need to shut it down, and Cape Tech tends to be vulnerable to magic."

The rift chose that moment for another drumbeat thud. The hole heaved wider and taller. The roof shrieked with the sound of wood rupturing.

Nicholas said, "Fuck!" and threw up his hands, as if he were catching something heavy coming down on his head. The daggers that had been floating between us fell with a clatter. "Fuck," he said again. "I can't hold this weight for long."

"You can hold up the roof?" I said in surprise.

He gave a strained smile. "I'm a ghost; I have a knack with wooden buildings. I can seep straight into the woodgrain and make it do tricks. Faces looming out of the wall, that sort of crap. But I can also strengthen the rafters. A bit. For maybe a minute."

The muscles in his arms bulged as if he were actually holding up a load. He'd always had great upper-body strength from using the chair. But he was sinking under the burden. His vaporous body now ended at the level of his navel rather than his hips, and his head was well below mine.

"Anytime you want to do something," Nicholas said, grunting under the weight, "please go right ahead." He nodded toward the daggers. "They should be safe now."

"You dispelled the curses?"

"Ripped them to shit." Another strained smile. "Ghosts are good with curses—putting them on, taking them off. Of course, those are still magic weapons. They'll try to corrupt you, blah blah blah. But probably not in the next minute. Which is how long you've got before my arms give out."

I snatched up the daggers, tucked their sheaths into my belt, and shrank.

OMNIMORPHISM FTW: THE DAGGERS SHRANK WHEN I DID

Getting inside the replicator was no problem. Cape Tech can thumb its nose at mundane physics, but it still needs to keep up appearances. Specifically, the replicator needed ventilation slits to dissipate waste heat. Otherwise, the machine wouldn't be Science-y enough. So I went in through a vent, at which point I realized the first glitch in my plans.

The interior was dark, and my Spark-o-Vision was still off-line. All I could sense in the blackness was the machine's incessant hum. The hum shook the floor under my feet so strongly, it threw me off like a bucking bronco and I ended up floating in the air. I needed light before I drifted into something high-voltage.

A solution occurred to me. In *The Lord of the Rings,* Frodo's sword glowed in the dark.

I drew one of the daggers (I couldn't tell which) and held it in front of me like He-Man yelling, "By the power of Grayskull!" Instead, I yelled, "Light!"

The continuing blackness mocked me.

I said, "Really? Really?" But I knew what the damned dagger wanted: the standard price for the Dark to acknowledge you. Sighing, I took off one of my nice white gloves. I touched my finger against the knife point and pushed.

My skin was solid rock, but apparently I could turn that off if I really wanted. A patch of my stone turned to flesh, and the dagger tip went in. I pictured my blood squirting onto the blade.

Let there be light.

THE LIGHT WAS TINTED BRONZE; THAT TOLD ME WHICH BLADE I'D DRAWN

The first things I saw were my finger and the knife. My finger oozed blood, but the blade was clean and dry, as if it had swallowed the blood with thirsty glee. If anything, the dagger seemed shinier than before.

"Excellent," I said. "I see no way that this can end badly." Luckily, I couldn't hear my voice, so I couldn't hear it waver.

HOLDING THE KNIFE ALOFT LIKE A TORCH, I EXAMINED THE REPLICATOR'S GUTS

Under the dagger's bronze light, my surroundings looked like a sepia photograph: out of focus, thanks to my 20/60 eyes. But I could see well enough to recognize components similar to the ones I'd seen in Popigai's lab. The wired-up lemon . . . the brain in a jar . . . the ray gun being fired by a robot hand.

Good. These were things I could slice and dice with my trusty daggers. Especially the brain.

Mind you, the jar holding the brain looked impenetrable. At my size, the glass was thicker than I was tall. Breaching it would be like cracking the wall of an air-raid bunker.

But you can't have a brain in a jar without feeding it blood, and I had already established what blood was good for.

Since I needed the bronze dagger's light, I swapped that knife to my left hand and pulled out the next one in my belt: the silver. It leapt out of its sheath and into my hand, as if it knew it was next. I lifted it and showed it the jar.

"You want that?" I asked with the sort of fake enthusiasm you use when you play fetch with a dog. "Yummy yummy blood! Do you see?"

The dagger quivered.

I touched the knife tip to the glass and said, "Go get it! Get the blood!"

I let go of the hilt. The knife fell. It lay on the floor and continued to quiver, as if writhing with desire but still on its leash.

I rolled my eyes. "Who makes up these rules?" Sighing, I retrieved the knife and squeezed my already pricked finger to get a new drop of blood. When it touched the silver blade, I swear I could hear a slurp.

"*Now* are you ready?" I asked. The dagger wiggled in my hand as if wagging its tail. I pressed the blade's tip against the jar and aimed it at the brain inside. I said, "Sic," and pushed harder.

The dagger burrowed into the glass like a piranha into a heifer. Its passage left a knife-sized tunnel. Molten glass dripped from the tunnel mouth but quickly solidified, like transparent candle wax.

Within a heartbeat, the knife had dug through the glass and into the blood. I had trouble following it after that—the knife swam and feasted, repeatedly whisking out of sight inside the scarlet murk, then reappearing as a silver flash far from where it had been. Each time the knife vanished, the brain shook from an unseen impact. Soon, chunks of detached cortex floated in the fluid like bits of cauliflower in tomato soup.

I really hoped the brain wasn't still conscious. I imagined what was left of a living person losing fragments of IQ and memory as pieces got hacked away.

But if the brain was still capable of thought, it would surely thank me for ending its awful existence.

ANOTHER DRUMBEAT THUD SOUNDED OUTSIDE THE MACHINE

Was the rift shrinking or growing? I wanted to go out and see, but I was on the clock. Nicholas would soon run out of strength.

The replicator still seemed to be running. The robot hand was still pulling the ray gun's trigger, and the gun was firing with the same frequency as when I'd first seen it. Perhaps the brain in the jar had been a computer used only in setup, deciding when to activate the rift projection mechanism. Now that the process had started, destroying the brain didn't halt the machine.

So, the ray gun. Shutting it down had to be good, right? But the gun obviously ran off a powerful energy source, and damaging that source might loose a storm of who-knows-what. It was safer to stop the hand that pulled the trigger. Doing that wasn't risk-free, but it seemed the lesser of two evils.

THE HAND WAS ENORMOUS

I was a millimeter tall. A normal hand is, what, ten centimeters across? So the hand was a hundred times my height. Attacking it would be like taking on a fifty-story building, and all I had was daggers.

If I'd still had Spark-o-Vision, I could have searched for weaknesses. Maybe laser-sighting would have homed in on a size-appropriate target. But all I had were my normal eyes and the light of the bronze dagger.

Hmm. I thrust the dagger forward. "Show me where to stab."

Brown light shot from the dagger's tip. The beam burned with the brightness of molten copper, focusing on the center of the robot hand's wrist—exactly where you'd cut to commit suicide.

Oh good, not creepy at all.

I DREW THE FINAL DAGGER: THE GOLD ONE

By the time-honored rules of fairy tales, the golden knife had to be the most badass. I wondered what it had been built to do. Maybe like me and my teammates, the weapon wasn't yet locked into a specific power set: It was ready to be what I wished for, provided I danced to the right tune.

I knew how the dance started. I grimaced and squeezed more blood from my punctured finger. Before I could dab the drop on the golden blade, the dagger moved of its own accord. It lifted its tip and plunged into one of my other fingers. Apparently, a knife made of gold was too posh to drink from another knife's wound. The blade embedded itself in my flesh and sucked like a hungry piglet feeding from its mother for the first time.

It hurt more than it should have. I had a stomach-churning flashback to Kimmi in Elaine's study, and I yanked the knife out with all my strength.

Blood erupted from the wound. In my head, I heard the dagger snicker.

"Oh, nice," I told the weapon. "Stop being a dick and get to work."

I TOOK TO THE AIR, FLYING TOWARD THE POINT ON THE ROBOT HAND LIT BY THE BRONZE KNIFE'S BEAM

I wish I could have taken a selfie because it was definitely a look: me holding my cape spread wide, with the bronze knife in my left hand and the gold one in my right. Blood streamed from my fingers as I flapped, spattering red on my white costume. Weird shadows fluttered around me as the bronze knife moved, giving me the start of a headache. When I reached the robot wrist, I glared at its polished metal surface then rammed the golden dagger into my own reflection.

The hand clenched in agony—a spasm that jerked it free from the gun and closed its fingers into a fist. It squeezed tight, then tighter. A real hand would have gone white-knuckled. Then the fist simply fell apart. The rivets, screws, and solder that held the hand together collapsed from sheer exhaustion.

Wires and circuits and ball joints sloughed off limply. They dropped to the bottom of the replicator's box like my hair when I ran electric clippers over my scalp.

Quietly, I withdrew the golden knife and slid it back into its sheath. It adjusted its hang slightly, making itself more comfortable against my hip—like a snake settling into a new home.

THE REPLICATOR STOPPED HUMMING

I could literally feel the silence. The air around me stopped vibrating, and I was becalmed enough to drift downward, like silt in a lake that only settles to the bottom when the wave action stops. Mission accomplished, I guess. I began flying for the exit.

I couldn't see outside the machine, but I could tell when Nicholas's strength gave out: I could hear the squall of nails ripping out of wood. I waited for timbers to crash, pulping everything under their weight.

But nothing happened. Either the roof was still managing to hold or someone else had taken on the burden.

Dakini might have held the roof up with telekinesis. Darklings might have stepped in too: either ones with powers like Nicholas's, or wizards who could cast appropriate spells. But I had no way to tell, and nothing to do except keep flying.

As I did, something warm and wet brushed my cheek like a dog's tongue. I flinched and shrank a hundred times smaller, but it made no difference—I could feel the slobbery thing slither down the front of my shirt. I looked and saw the silver dagger sliding into its sheath on my belt. The knife was covered with blood and whatever fluids might be excreted by a brain in a jar. It left a gory trail down my shirtfront.

"Awesome," I muttered, and kept flapping.

I EXITED THROUGH A VENT HOLE

Outside, no sign of Nicholas. When you're a ghost, I guess you like vanishing. At least the rift was shrinking. Its top edge had sunken below the ground floor's ceiling; its bottom had risen out of the hole it had dug in the floorboards. The rift hung in midair, no longer threatening to pop the building at its seams. Stinking vapor continued to dribble out of the opening, but it seemed half-hearted.

So, ten points to Gryffindor (i.e., me) and only one pressing issue left: What would happen when the rift shut completely? A final explosion, as in the lab? If so, it would bring down the building, and I had no idea how to prevent it.

«Dakini,» I transmitted. *«Are you available?»*

«I'm helping evacuate,» she answered. *«But if there's something more urgent . . . »*

«We need to get Popigai's replicator outside. It might be programmed to explode when the rift closes. Popigai probably likes to cover his tracks.»

«I'll come immediately,» she said.

«Aria,» I transmitted, *«Dakini is going to move the replicator, and when she does, she may set off booby traps. Can you surround the machine with a force field? Just till we get it outside.»*

A pause. Then, *«I'll do my best.»*

Aria didn't sound good. The last time I'd seen her, she was flying out of the building with the bogeyman. I wondered how close she'd been when he exploded. She would have had her force field up, but she sounded injured. Concussion? Internal bleeding? It scared me to hear her so haggard. Miranda had always struck me as an unstoppable force of nature, and surely Aria was more so.

Moments later, Aria appeared in the hole through which she'd left the building. She wasn't flying; she was barely walking. She clutched the edge of the hole to prevent herself from falling.

Her golden dress was tattered and burnt. I couldn't tell where the charred shreds ended and the body underneath began, because Aria's flesh had been blackened too. She clung to the broken boards and did nothing but pant.

Dakini didn't look much better as she floated down the stairs. She hadn't been torched like Aria; she'd been slashed by something with claws. Four long parallel gashes cut the side of her costume. Some were-beast must have gone crazy and taken it out on her. Dakini's skin was too dark to show blood at this distance, but any attack that hacked up her clothes must have gouged her too. She still had the energy to fly, sprawled on a platform of violet energy like a flying carpet. But her platform just limped along, barely clearing the ground.

I felt guilty asking my teammates to exert themselves more. Compared to them, what injuries did I have? Two pricked fingers. Boo-hoo. How could I ask them to exhaust themselves further when I wasn't even breathing hard?

But neither Dakini nor Aria would thank me for calling them off. They both had mountains of pride that wouldn't let them quit. They likely wouldn't back off now, even if I asked.

And the replicator might explode. So I said nothing.

ARIA SANG A LOW NOTE

Not loud, but like one of those give-you-shivers songs that start off softly, then build. ("My Body is a Cage." "I Dreamed a Dream.") The note expanded gently as it moved until, by the time it reached the replicator, it was big enough to wrap the whole machine in a golden blanket.

Gold. I could see Aria's power. Did that mean my Spark-o-Vision was returning? Yes. A ghost of it overlaid my mere eyes, faint but growing.

Dakini let her flying carpet dissipate, probably to conserve her strength. She sat down on the stairs like a kid on the front stoop. Violet light misted out of her forehead, as thin as fog on a morning river. It crossed the Market and slid under the replicator. Dakini grunted as she raised the machine just far enough off the floor to let it move. Carefully, ponderously, the cloudy forklift carried the replicator toward the hole in the wall.

Aria's voice sounded through the Market: "Ahhh." And in that golden light, Spark-o-Vision replaced eyesight and I could fully see again.

I saw the rift closing slowly like bacon shriveling in a pan. I saw Darklings from the upper floor standing on the stairs just above Dakini. They watched the replicator being borne away, and although they didn't know what it was, they realized it had to be dangerous. Tension—like watching someone in a lab coat gingerly carrying a test tube toward a disposal unit. Several people also watched from the ground floor: people who'd been far enough away from the explosions, or hardy enough to endure the blasts. Ninety-Nine was there, with a were-hyena draped around her shoulders. She and the others watched the machine's progress, like a crowd mutely lining the street for a funeral procession. The only sound was Aria's low note holding her force field in place.

The rift closed. The replicator flared, a nova inside the force field. But like a nova in the vacuum of space, it was completely silent.

It wouldn't be silent for long. Novas are like lightning: Their light travels faster than their thunder, but eventually the shock wave arrives. Aria's "Ahhh" became a growl, a rasp fighting the inferno in its grip. Aria's lips drew back in a rictus, and Dakini wore almost the same expression. She was trying to drive the machine faster, to get it outside before Aria ran out of breath.

The machine neared the hole where Aria stood, holding onto the broken boards. Aria's eyes had squeezed shut with effort; she likely didn't know how close the machine was to her. If her strength gave out, not only would the explosion rip down the building, she'd be at ground zero.

Ninety-Nine said, *«Come on, Aria, don't be a wuss.»* She let the hyena slide off her shoulders and sprinted across the room. *«Don't freak,»* she told Aria, *«I've got you.»* As the replicator edged outside, a fireball trapped in a song, Ninety-Nine wrapped her arms around Aria to keep her from falling. *«Hang on, you big doof, just a few seconds more.»*

Ninety-Nine moved Aria inside the building and around the corner of the wall. She put her own body between Aria and the machine.

At the very last instant, a sheet of gray energy spread across the hole, and the entire outer wall of the building. A Wraithly barrier, as tenuous as smoke. When Aria finally passed out and her note fell silent, the explosion broke free from its pent-up violence and shredded the ghostly barrier into a million wisps.

But it was enough. The Market stayed standing.

MY TEAMMATES, NOT SO MUCH

Aria was unconscious. Dakini slumped back against the stairs, too exhausted to move. Ninety-Nine lay sprawled across Aria's body;

she'd taken a portion of the blast, despite Nicholas's last-ditch shield. The back of Ninety-Nine's jersey was burning. The satin 99 had shriveled to ash, baring raw red skin beneath.

She regenerates, I told myself as I flew across the room. I didn't know what I intended to do; maybe just stand guard until Ninety-Nine healed and Aria woke up. But as I landed beside them and grew to Max Zirc size, my perception jerked out of my control.

It felt the same as when my viewpoint did that camera-shot tracking to the Widow's car. Spark-o-Vision wanted to show me something. It zoomed out the hole in the wall and into the sky.

High above the Market, obscured by falling snow, hovered a man coated in metal. Adam Popigai had come to survey his handiwork.

HE WAS TOO FAR AWAY TO SEE CLEARLY

My vision still wasn't a hundred percent, but I could make out his steel exterior—exactly the same surface as the replicator that had just destroyed itself. Popigai wore no clothes except his skin/armor, and his face appeared featureless. He reminded me of an Oscar statuette: sleekly anonymous.

I might not have been able to see him well, but I felt his Halo clearly. Anarchic. The gleeful Bad Boy.

Inside me, Kimmi said, "Meow." *Oh, stop,* I told her. Teenagers!

As I watched, Popigai raised his hand. His arm turned to crystal from the elbow down to the fingers. A hole opened in his palm, about the size of a quarter. Out shot a missile no bigger than a Magic Marker, heading straight for the Market.

Damn!

The missile was small, but I had no doubt it carried enough firepower to knock down the ravaged building. Clearly, Popigai wanted a bloodbath. One way or another, he intended to get it.

I SNATCHED THE SILVER DAGGER FROM MY BELT

The knife had already shown me it could move on its own. My perception automatically switched into laser-targeting mode. The sights weren't trained on the missile, but on empty air; I hoped they were showing me the trajectory that the dagger had to travel in order to intercept the missile. I held the knife in my right hand and plunged its blade into my left palm—lots of blood for fuel. Then I hurled the dagger as hard as I could.

No way was I strong or accurate enough to throw a knife and hit a rocket in midair. But the silver knife knew its business. It was also much faster than it should have been, given my pathetic throw. Even as the dagger was leaving my hand, I could feel it accelerate, pulling me forward until I released my grip.

The blade flew straight and true. It hit the missile like a hawk striking a sparrow.

Yet another explosion. But the dagger had moved so quickly, the blast was closer to Popigai than the Market. He was rocked by the detonation. His steely surface briefly transformed into shining crystal before flicking back into metal.

It was the same crystal his arm became when he fired the missile.

Crystal like the casing of the first rift machine.

Crystal like that object we'd found in the lab: the one the size of a birthday candle, steel on one end, morphing smoothly to glassy brilliance on the other.

"Oh fuck," I said. "Fuck."

FACE-PALM

For a geology student, I'd been painfully thickheaded. I should have recognized the name "Popigai" immediately. It's a place in Siberia: a meteor crater where the heat and pressure of the impact transformed local graphite into diamonds. The Russians claimed that Popigai held more diamonds than any other site on Earth.

And "Adam" . . . in Latin, "adamas" means "diamond." Mineralogists use the word "adamantine" to describe crystals with the brilliance of diamonds.

We weren't just dealing with a random Mad Genius. He'd disguised himself with a steel exterior, but "Adam Popigai" was a blatant cover name for Diamond: the most lethal, Maddest Genius in the world.

DIAMOND HOVERED IN THE SKY ABOVE ME: TWINKLE, TWINKLE

Diamond's face was inscrutable under his blank steel facade. Was he furious because his missile hadn't worked? Or just coolly assessing the situation? I couldn't tell. He hovered, unreadable.

I held out my hand. The silver dagger flew and slapped into my palm, like a scalpel being handed to a surgeon. I waited.

After a long pause, Diamond's feet transformed from steel to crystal. Flames shot out of boot-jets. He rocketed southward toward Waterloo. Within a heartbeat, he was beyond the range of my perception.

I slumped, feeling as if I'd just run a marathon. "Uh, Zircon," Ninety-Nine said in my ear, "whatcha doin' with the knife?"

I YANKED MY VIEWPOINT HOME

Ninety-Nine's back had healed from baked red to her normal color. She was in the process of tying the remains of her jersey to her shoulder pads, knotting the cloth around the fiberglass to hold her shirt up. As she worked, she said, "Did naughty Zircon do some shoplifting? Hey, have you gone deaf?"

I realized I wasn't facing her. I could see her perfectly well without turning my head, and I felt so drained I hadn't bothered to move. I hadn't even known which way my physical eyes pointed.

I had only been super a few hours, and I was already losing normal human responses. Not good. I wondered if every Spark went down a slippery slope.

I aimed my eyes toward Ninety-Nine. It felt unnatural, like when you meet someone you really don't want to look at and you force yourself to do it anyway.

I said, "I needed the knife to sabotage the replicator. I needed all the knives."

Ninety-Nine nodded toward my blood-smeared palm. "You also

need a course in knife safety. Cut *away* from your hands, not toward them."

"The daggers don't work unless . . . you know."

"Magic. Fucking magic." Ninety-Nine shook her head. "Be careful with that shit. You have no idea what those knives are drinking besides blood. And unlike me, you're stuck in the old-fashioned 'natural healing' paradigm." She nodded toward my cuts. "Sparks heal faster than normal people, but those'll still take ages to go away."

"I'll be fine," I said. "But . . ." I knelt beside Aria. She was unconscious, and her burns hadn't regenerated. As Ninety-Nine had said, Sparks usually recover more quickly than ordinary human beings, but with burns like Aria's, she still faced a long time in the hospital.

"Thanks for reminding me," Ninety-Nine said. She reached into her belt and pulled out a vial containing cherry-red fluid, just like the one I'd seen at the auction.

"A healing potion?" I said. "Where'd you get it?"

"Salvaged it off some demon made of wood who was going up in flames. While I was putting out the fire . . . uhh . . . two of those potion bottles fell right out of his pockets. Cuz, like, his pockets were burned and couldn't hold stuff anymore."

I said, "You picked the pockets of a guy who was on fire?"

"Hey, I put him out first. And if he'd been conscious, I know he would have given them to me in gratitude for saving his life." She handed me the vial. "Use that on Aria. I'll take the other to Dakini. They need this more badly than you do."

She moved quickly toward the stairs. I lifted Aria's upper body, tucked my knee underneath her to maintain elevation, and poured the red fluid down her throat.

MAGIC WORKS LIKE MAGIC

When Ninety-Nine heals, it's conventional healing on fast-forward. (By now, I've watched it several times close-up, internally and microscopically. Zircon, the human MRI!) Ninety-Nine's cells grow over her wounds and restore underlying damage. Broken bones get reset as if by invisible hands, then the fractured ends fuse together. When Ninety-Nine rids herself of a bullet, tissues around the slug slowly squeeze it out of her flesh. It looks like time-lapse photography.

But the magic healing potion didn't try to mimic normality. Its effects looked more like a transformation in old movies, where the "before" picture blurs for a moment and then you get the "after." Beast turns into a prince? Just beast-then-blur-then-man, with no attempt at joining the dots.

Aria's burns didn't heal, they just blur-morphed into health. It took at most two seconds, like in a game where your hit points rise to full and you're good to go. Apart from the wreckage to her costume, Aria suddenly looked fresh from the spa. Even her hair unmussed itself, blurring from rat's nest to salon.

Aria's eyes snapped open. I was still holding her, one hand behind her head, the other holding the vial to her mouth. She shoved the vial aside. "What are you doing?"

"Uhh, giving you a healing potion?"

She glared. "Don't be . . . oh." The classical phrase is "everything came flooding back to her," or at least that's what it looked like: Aria remembered what had happened, and how the rules had changed. "Really?" she said. "A healing potion?"

"Yep. Totes magic."

"Wow. Very suspension of disbelief." She sat up and saw the remnants of her outfit. "Damn. This was a really nice dress. I'll have to call my parents and renegotiate my clothes budget."

"No one ever mentions how much Sparks must spend on their wardrobes," I said. "Although now that I think about it, those posters of Tigresse always show her costume ripped to shreds."

Aria snorted, then looked around. "I take it we won?"

I nodded. "I also learned something important. Adam Popigai is actually Diamond."

"The Australian supervillain?"

"That's him. I'll spell out the details when there's time."

"But you sensibly shared the key fact," Aria said, "rather than sitting on it and then getting kidnapped or killed before you could pass it on."

I winced. "Let's not talk about getting kidnapped or killed. That's way past 'tempting Fate' and snuggling up to 'foreshadowing'."

WE GOT TO WORK ON EVAC

We hadn't saved the building, we had only delayed the inevitable. Snow continued to fall; the weight on the roof kept building. There was practically no wind, yet the Market's timbers creaked like the masts of a clipper ship in a storm. We could save any people still alive, but the Market itself couldn't be salvaged.

Ninety-Nine had healed Dakini, so we were back to full strength. In our various ways, we transported the injured to the parking lot, with Ninety-Nine doing triage to decide which casualties needed special handling. Those people were left to Dakini, who immobilized them inside violet cocoons, then levitated them out to a covered stable where they'd be out of the snow. (The Market had stables for old-order Mennonites, who still used horse-drawn buggies to get around.)

Ninety-Nine was as strong as an Olympic weightlifter, so she had no trouble lugging people around. Her biggest problem was keeping her damaged costume from falling off during the process. Soon she "found" (stole) a poncho to cover herself up, and, looking like Clint Eastwood, she made trip after trip to the stable.

Aria did the same, but faster. There could be no doubt now that she was superhumanly strong; the old Miranda had been in good shape, but it takes more than yoga to cradle a quarter-ton were-boar as if it's a toddler. She wasn't one of those Sparks who could uproot oak trees and use them as baseball bats, but I knew whom I'd ask when I couldn't get the lid off the pickles.

Well, okay: Ninety-Nine is an Olympic-level weightlifter. She can handle the pickles too. And Dakini's telekinesis can lift a truck, albeit slowly.

I'm the only one who sucks.

I don't like pickles anyway.

FOR PICKLE-JAR REASONS, MY ROLE IN THE EVAC WAS TO STAY OUT OF THE WAY

Pending the onset of belly muscles and an action-hero physique, I wasn't much use in carting people to safety. Instead, I searched the building for threats and bennies.

No sign of Nicholas, nor the Widow, nor Elaine. Nicholas could still be hanging around invisibly, but the Widow and Elaine must have left by a fire escape. Either that, or they'd simply used magic. I wasn't sure what spells Elaine knew, but the Vandermeers had appointed her the family's next Master Wizard if and when Grandpa Vandermeer got put in a coffin permanently. Elaine could likely toss off a teleportation spell as easily as biting a jugular.

My search did turn up the Goblin. I thought he'd be hurrying to move his merchandise before the building collapsed, or maybe he'd just be moaning with his head in his hands. Instead he sat alone near the buffet, sipping from a purple teacup.

He didn't look frantic or shell-shocked. He exuded the air of an introverted child who withdrew when the world got too noisy.

I'd never met a Darkling whose Shadow was so mild. Even ones who looked like children had a disquieting edge. When it suited their purposes, they could make a show of innocence, but they never fully committed to the deception. They always retained a tiny knowing smirk.

But the Goblin seemed truly childlike, like Piglet in *Winnie-the-Pooh*. I told myself it was only an act—he was a Darkling; he was dangerous. But I couldn't force myself to believe it. Every time I thought, *His Shadow is totally leading me around by the nose,* I looked at him and said, "Awww."

I wanted to give him a hug, and I'm not a person who hugs. I'm small and don't like feeling engulfed.

But the Goblin was smaller than me, so hugging him would be okay.

SUDDENLY, I WAS STANDING BESIDE HIM

I didn't remember deciding to approach him, but there I was. I almost hugged him, I really did. But I had enough self-control to walk around to the other side of his little table and sit across from him.

"Hi," I said. "I'm Zircon."

"Hello, Zircon," he said. "Thank you for saving my market."

"It's not saved, not really. This building could collapse at any time. You should go outside where it's safe."

"But all my stuff is here."

"I can start hauling it out; at least the things light enough for me to carry. If the building falls on me, there's no problem." I tapped a fingernail on my stony skin. "I'm tough."

"You don't have to carry anything," the Goblin said. "It will all disappear at dawn."

I should have thought of that. Of course, that's how a Goblin Market *had* to work. Probably a prearranged spell would teleport everything back to some warehouse. I said, "The building may not last till dawn."

"I know."

He sounded so sad, I nearly leapt up and hugged him. That hug loomed larger and larger in my mind, like a cookie you've sworn not to eat till you finish an assignment. I said, "Are you sure there's nothing I can do to help?"

"Not that I can think of." He brightened. "But I can help *you*. For being so brave and kind."

"You don't have to."

"Yes, I do. You're sort of messy." He wrinkled his nose. With 360-degree vision, I couldn't help seeing the blood and other effluents smeared all over my costume. "Your teammates too," the Goblin said. "They're all torn up. I'll make you new costumes. With magic. I'm good at magic."

"I'm sure you are." I was beginning to think of this childlike Darkling as a savant: a one-track mind focused entirely on making enchanted things, without the usual Darkling hunger for power and status. I said, "We can fix our costumes on our own. Ninety-Nine is an Olympic-level seamstress. She's very good at sewing."

"She's not magic," the Goblin said. "Besides, sewing takes time when you could be saving people. And what if somebody bad tries to do stuff while your clothes are in the wash? I could enchant your costumes so they mend and clean themselves. Wouldn't that be good?"

I couldn't help nodding. I was Zircon, not Kim, but both of us hated spending time on clothes. A costume that would maintain itself? So I didn't have to waste any effort, or ask for help from my roomies? No devil could have devised a stronger temptation.

It was hard for my brain to say, "There must be strings attached." The poor little Goblin wanted so badly to thank us, it was cruel not to let him.

"Okay," I said. "Go ahead."

THE GOBLIN BEAMED WITH DELIGHT

He poured four dollops of liquid from his teacup onto the tablecloth. The liquid made chalky white stains on the purple fabric. (I wondered what the liquid was. Probably not milk.)

The Goblin touched one of the stains with his purple finger. "This one is for Zircon." He touched another. "This one is for Ninety-Nine. What are your other friends called?"

"Dakini and Aria."

He smiled. "Pretty." He tapped one of the remaining blobs. "This is for Dakini. And this is for Aria."

On the tablecloth, the blobs shifted and refocused, changing into white icons. Aria: an eighth note. Dakini: three open eyes arranged in an equilateral triangle. Ninety-Nine: the number with a hockey stick threaded through the openings in the two 9s. Zircon: a classic round brilliant-cut diamond (i.e., the shape most commonly associated with diamonds set in rings—faceted on the top, pointed on the bottom).

I sighed. If the Goblin was using a diamond to represent me, he was likely confusing zircons with cubic zirconia. Why didn't anyone know the difference? But that brought something else to mind. I said, "You had a consignment here, sponsored by a man who called himself Adam Popigai. Popigai is actually the Mad Genius called Diamond. He's the one responsible for all the destruction."

"Really?" the Goblin said. "I'll put him on the blacklist."

"Can you tell me about your dealings with Popigai?"

"No," he said like a petulant child. "I hate *dealings*. My staff deal with *dealings*. I just make things."

He bent over the table and breathed on the tea-blob icons. They trembled as if they were tiny mice, not inanimate stains. The Goblin breathed again, and a purple glow misted out of his mouth. The icons soaked up the glow like humidity, then lifted off the linen and shot into the air.

The diamond flew straight at me, striking my chest above my heart. Purple energy splashed outward, covering my costume all the way to the tip of my top hat. The purple burned brightly, blazing into every piece of my outfit. Light flooded into the fibers, then disappeared, taking with it every speck of dirt, blood, and dishevelment that the clothes had acquired. My costume became an ad for laundry detergent: whiter than white, better than new, and cuddly warm as if straight from the dryer.

The other icons headed from the tablecloth toward my teammates. Just as the potion had magically healed Aria, I could imagine the purple magic restoring everyone's costume.

I felt good about that. Only later did it dawn on me: I'd accepted a "gift" just like that girl in the Goblin Market poem. Oops.

"THERE," THE GOBLIN SAID, "YOUR CLOTHES WILL BE GOOD FOREVER AND EVER"

"Thank you," I said. "You're very kind." I tried to intensify my Halo—make myself more majestic. "But I really need to know anything you can tell me about Adam Popigai."

The Goblin sighed. If he could feel my Halo, it wasn't overwhelming him. "There's nothing to tell," he said. "This man Popigai asked for a stall. He showed me samples of what he could make.

They were interesting. So I put him in contact with my staff and they arranged everything."

"How did Popigai find you?" I asked. "Or did *you* find *him?*"

"Someone I know introduced us," the Goblin said. "And vouched for him."

"Who?"

The Goblin looked uncomfortable. "That's supposed to be confidential."

"Whoever it was," I said, "either they were in league with Diamond, which means they're partly responsible for the damage here tonight, or else Diamond fooled that person into helping him, in which case, I'm sure the person would be mad and want Diamond stopped. Please help me stop him. Tell me who introduced you to Diamond."

The Goblin chewed on one of his knuckles. After a moment, he said, "It was Elaine Vandermeer."

Ouch. But not a surprise.

ELAINE WAS AMBITIOUS IN THE OLD-SCHOOL SENSE

I mean "ambitious" as the word is used in *Julius Caesar.* Not merely eager to get ahead in the world, but avidly steamrolling competitors, allies, bystanders, and stray puppies in order to wield power. Elaine might look like an eighteen-year-old with a fifty-year-old's haircut, but on a scale of ambition from one to ten, where one was a doorknob and ten was a great white shark, Elaine would use the doorknob to beat the shark to death. I had no idea how she'd made Diamond's acquaintance, but she'd do it in a heartbeat if it gave her any advantage.

Elaine's involvement allowed me to guess why her brother was in town. He could have found out what she was up to—a ghost has plenty of ways to spy on others. Nicholas could have followed Elaine to Waterloo in the hope of preventing her from doing anything crazy. It would hurt the entire family if Elaine committed some atrocity . . . or at least, if she got caught.

And who knows, it wasn't impossible that Nicholas actually cared about his sister. Perhaps the Dark Conversion hadn't completely destroyed his humanity. Perhaps something inside him was still capable of family feeling.

Or even love.

Don't go mushy, I told myself. Nicholas could also have come to Waterloo because he was in cahoots with Elaine, and therefore with Diamond. Nicholas might be part of some conspiracy that included Lilith and all the other Darklings we'd seen.

Then again, Nicholas had prevented the Market from collapsing. If he was on Diamond's side, Nicholas wouldn't have done that. Unless . . .

No. Just stop. Speculation only wasted time. I told myself to stick to the facts instead of making excuses for what Nicholas might have done.

"Where are they now?" I asked the Goblin. "Elaine and Popigai. Can you contact them?"

The Goblin sighed again. "My staff hate me giving out details like that. I'm supposed to keep everything confidential." He turned his eyes toward me. "I wouldn't be doing you a favor, helping you find this Diamond. He's a legend in our community. He's bad."

I said, "I know he's a Mad Genius. One of the worst."

"More than that," the Goblin said. "We Darklings have a system for ranking Sparks by power level. We classify Sparks like weapons. The least powerful are Daggers, then Swords, then Pistols . . ."

"What class is Diamond?"

"Hiroshima."

"Oh. Damn." I didn't know where my teammates and I ranked on the Darklings' scale—grenades? bazookas?—but even the four of us together didn't add up to a nuke.

Then again, it didn't matter. "However powerful Diamond is," I said, "we can't just walk away. Someone has to stop him. My teammates and I are the only Sparks in town."

"Sparks," the Goblin said as if he pitied me. "Whether you're heroes or villains, you have to be on some crusade." He laid his hand lightly on mine. "Oh, you kids."

Without warning, he upended his teacup onto the table. Chalky liquid splashed across the tablecloth, spelling out a local address. "That's a bed-and-breakfast," the Goblin said. "Darklings only. Elaine Vandermeer wouldn't stay anywhere else." He touched my hand again. "You can keep the knives. They like you. When you catch up with Diamond, give him a stab from me."

The Goblin smiled fiercely with all those sharp teeth. Suddenly, he didn't seem so childlike. Then he faded from sight, leaving his toothy grin behind for several seconds after the rest of him had vanished.

Apparently, the Goblin was a fan of Lewis Carroll as well as Christina Rossetti.

I SHRANK AND FLEW OFF TO FIND MY TEAMMATES

They weren't inside the building. I went out to the parking lot and saw a dazzle of flashing lights from a recently arrived fire truck.

No police or ambulances. I overheard a firefighter say that none were coming, at least not soon. No one had predicted the snowstorm, so no one had prearranged snow-removal crews. By the time any plows hit the streets, the city was impassably deep in snowdrifts. Also, impassably deep in car accidents. The mayhem at the Market was a national-level crisis—dozens of Darklings were dead, which made it front-page news. Nevertheless, Waterloo Region didn't have any more first responders available.

The firefighters had told my teammates, "We'll take it from here." In places more experienced with having Sparks, emergency services developed plans for how to use local heroes productively. However, the captain of this fire crew clearly regarded costumed freaks as crazy amateurs who ought to be sidelined. By the time I flew in, my teammates were leaning against a closed schnitzel stand and taking a breather.

I landed and grew to Max Zirc height. "All done?" I asked.

"We've rescued everyone we could," Aria said. "Only corpses left in the building. How 'bout you?"

"Spent time talking to the Goblin."

"Is he the one who fixed our costumes?" Ninety-Nine asked. She grabbed a handful of her jersey and held it up. "This hasn't been this clean since Gretzky was actually on the Oilers."

"Not just clean," Dakini said. "Our clothes are repaired." She looked at me. "The Goblin's magic?"

"He was grateful for our help. From now on, our costumes will clean and mend themselves."

"Awesome," Ninety-Nine said.

"Worrisome," Aria corrected. "Not only are we now surrounded by magic, so we're detectable by anything that can sense magical energy, but who knows what enchantments were added besides cleaning and sewing? For all we know, the longer we wear the clothes, the more we'll want to do what the Goblin tells us."

"Feel free to take off the costume," Ninety-Nine said. "Then spend a gazillion dollars buying a new one after every fight."

"Talk clothes later," I said. "We have more serious things to discuss."

As quickly as I could, I told the others about Diamond and Elaine. All I said about Elaine was what the Goblin had given me—nothing about the connection between her and Nicholas. Then again, I'd never told my roommates much about Nicholas either.

Kim: not a sharer. Zircon: ditto. Maybe for Kim 2.0, that ought to change.

I did, of course, share that I'd seen "Wraith" again, and that he'd helped save the building. Maybe I was too insistent on that point. "He must be a decent guy, right? He really exerted himself to save lives."

But I centered my talk on Diamond. Popigai = Diamond = Hiroshima-level mass murderer who'd waltzed up from Australia to plague Waterloo. It wouldn't be hard for a Mad Genius to fake credentials from distant universities—he'd just have to hack some computers, and bribe or mind control a few people. ("Why yes, I know Dr. Popigai. A brilliant researcher. I recommend him highly.") Considering how eager UW was to achieve a presence in Cape Tech, the engineering faculty would leap at any chance to hire a

Spark. And Diamond had used his Mad Genius skillz to keep from being recognized. Since he was known for his diamondlike appearance, he'd overlaid his crystalline self with steel. But I'd seen that he reverted to diamond in order to use his powers.

"Why is he here?" Dakini asked. "What does he want?"

Ninety-Nine accessed her mysterious database. "He's an anarchist," she said, glowing green. "The kind that publishes manifestos. Bottom line, he hates Darklings. Truly, madly, deeply. Most authorities think that Darklings hurt him personally. *The Dark killed my Dad!* That sort of thing. But his manifestos don't give personal details. They're all about the horror of soulless thugs seizing power, establishing a parasite-ocracy, blah blah blah.

"Anyway," Ninety-Nine continued, "Diamond's schemes always damage the Dark. *Giga*-damage. Which for Diamond means disrupting governments, crashing the financial system, et cetera. Since Darklings have power and money, you can only seriously hurt them by demolishing major targets. That's what Diamond does, and he doesn't care what happens to innocent bystanders. If blowing up a building will bankrupt some billionaire, Diamond will do it. Never mind if it also kills hundreds of ordinary people."

"Charming," Aria said.

"This doesn't make sense," Dakini said. "If Diamond hates Darklings, why did he work with them as Popigai? Not just with Elaine Vandermeer, whoever she is. What about the Darklings in the lab? They were clearly following some plan cooked up by Popigai."

"And they ended up dead," I said. "You heard what Wraith said in Popigai's office. Darklings will cooperate with Sparks on projects that aim to combine the Dark and the Light. The holy grail is to give superpowers to Darklings. That's what Diamond did; we saw the results a few minutes ago."

"I have an idea how it would work," Ninety-Nine said. "Diamond opened a rift into someplace filled with Light energy. That's how *we* became Sparks: Those little flame balls were chunks of the Light, and they powered us up. It took longer to power up the Darklings—they had to marinate in the Light for a couple of hours.

But eventually, they were ready. When they came out, they were genuinely super."

"But unstable," Aria said. "They'd gone insane, and as soon as they got jostled, they blew up." Her eyes narrowed. "Do you think Diamond knew that would happen? Could he have *wanted* them to explode the moment we hit them?"

"Probably," I said. "Think about it. He arranged for his super-Darklings to make their appearance in the middle of a big Darkling event. Super-Darkling explosions would guarantee other Darkling deaths. It would have been even worse if we hadn't kept the building intact. He could have racked up quite a Darkling body count."

"Do you think he's finished?" Dakini asked.

"Not a chance," Ninety-Nine said. "For someone like Diamond, a few dozen corpses is just an appetizer."

"He could have easily destroyed the Market," I said. "He only fired a single rocket. I'm sure he had more."

"Yes, Diamond always carries a shitload of weapons," Ninety-Nine said. "Not just rockets. Heat beams, ice cannons . . . plenty of ways to kill people."

I said, "If the Market was his endgame, he could have leveled it. But he just took a parting shot."

"He didn't want to give himself away," Aria said. "If he went all out with a dozen different weapons, someone would realize who he was."

"Anyway," Ninety-Nine said, "Diamond *can't* be finished yet. The eclipse has barely started."

"What do you mean?" Dakini asked.

"Ask yourself why Diamond came all the way from Australia," Ninety-Nine said. "Sparks almost never leave their home territories. Not even Mad Geniuses. So what does Waterloo have that Australia doesn't?"

"Ahh!" Dakini said. "A lunar eclipse on the winter solstice."

"Right," Ninety-Nine said. "It's daytime in Australia; no eclipse down there. But Waterloo is in the middle of the eclipse's maximal region. And until a few hours ago, the city had no Sparks. Perfect place to carry out some scheme tied to the eclipse."

Aria checked the time on her phone. "1:56 AM," she reported. "An hour until totality. That's presumably when the biggest shit will hit the fan."

"We should contact Grandfather," Dakini said. "Perhaps he can send additional Sparks."

"Grandfather has his hands full with that lake monster," Aria said. "It's just the sort of threat a Mad Genius would use as a distraction. It draws nearby heroes to Toronto, so they can't interfere with Waterloo."

Ninety-Nine glowed green and said, "Diamond loves creating monsters. Giant rampaging monsters. He breeds 'em by the dozen. Toronto will likely face an escalating series to keep local Sparks busy."

Dakini asked, "Does that mean *we're* going to face giant monsters?"

"Likely not," Ninety-Nine said. "Until tonight, Waterloo didn't have any Sparks who needed distracting. As for the regular cops, the snow is enough to tie them up. Impassable roads and car crashes—the police are out of the picture."

"That leaves us," Aria said. "So where are we going?"

"A bed-and-breakfast," I said. "The Goblin told me where Elaine is staying. She might not be there, but we can search her room for information."

"Fight, search, fight, search, fight," Ninety-Nine said. "How soon before we have to fetch the Mushroom of Truth from the Mines of Despair and take it to the Guild of Wizards?"

"We're superheroes," Aria said, "not *World of Warcraft* characters. Instead of fetching things, superheroes obliterate the mushroom, cave in the mines, and burn the guild to the ground."

"Much better," said Ninety-Nine. "Allons-y."

Active Faults

SAME FLYING FORMATION AS BEFORE

Me in Aria's hair. Dakini and Ninety-Nine riding a sled of psionic energy, yoked to Aria as if she were a husky.

Aria had no trouble hauling us along at frightening velocity. I couldn't tell how fast we were flying, but it beat any speed I'd ever experienced in a car (and my dad is a crazy-fast driver). Without protection, we would have been ravaged by wind and snow—flakes aren't so fluffy when they pummel you at hurricane speeds. But Aria was inside her force field, I was in the same bubble, and Dakini had erected a violet wind deflector in front of the sled. As we flew, she and Aria had a comm-ring debate about what deflector shape would be the most aerodynamic. Dakini experimented with rounded noses, V-shaped cowcatchers, and other designs while Aria kibitzed and Ninety-Nine solved fluid-flow differential equations in her head.

The thought of Jools voluntarily doing calculus was scarier than flying hell-bat fast through a blizzard. I suddenly realized that Jools now was smarter than me; if she was human-max in everything, that included intelligence. She had joined the lofty ranks of Newton and Einstein.

I felt weird about that. I didn't mind if Jools could beat me on raw facts, but if she was actually quicker, brighter, and more astute than I was, it upset the balance between us.

I was used to being the alpha IQ. If the scales had reversed, and Jools now had the edge, I felt a wall going up inside me. I knew I was being a dirtbag, but there it was.

«YO, ZIRCON!» **ARIA TRANSMITTED,** ***«ARE YOU STILL WITH US?»***

«Sorry,» I said. *«Distracted.»*

I was supposed to be navigating. Aria's sonar made sure that we didn't hit obstructions, but it couldn't chart where we were, especially through blinding snow. Even my Spark-o-Vision was hard-pressed to scope out our surroundings. Snow blanketed everything, and drifts hid many landmarks. I could still tell where the streets were—they were the flat swaths of snow lined by stores and houses. But telling one street from another was a challenge. Have you ever tried reading a street sign covered with snow as you whooshed past at ungodly speed?

At least I knew where I was going. Ninety-Nine had Google Maps built into her brain, and she'd laid out a straight-line course toward our destination.

The bed-and-breakfast lay in a neighborhood called Black Pine Dale, a part of town I'd never heard of. Darkling enclaves were like that: below the radar. Anyone in Waterloo could list the names of upscale neighborhoods—Beechwood, Eastbridge, Belmont Village—but those were only occupied by accountants and upper-middle-managers. People who lived in such districts were doing very nicely, but they would never own their own Learjets.

Darklings lived in neighborhoods like Black Pine Dale: unknown to us plebes. Black Pine Dale had a single access road whose entrance was lined with modest houses proclaiming, "This street is nothing special." You had to follow the access road farther, over a rise that shielded the view, and suddenly you were in an old-growth forest area of cul-de-sacs and yards designated as national parks. The homes weren't tasteless McMansions, but soothing chateaus designed by the best in the business. Think Fallingwater without the mildew.

The owners didn't pay for size, they paid for quality and uniqueness. The "One Perfect Rose" school of architecture. So Darkling.

IN THE HEART OF BLACK PINE DALE LAY THE B&B

It called itself Red Pine Villa. Yes, Red, not Black, although it was built from chestnut brown bricks with hunter green trim. There had to be a story behind the difference in piney colors, but not a story I'd ever hear. A private joke by the villa's owner? A feud between the owner and Darkling neighbors over the virtues of red pines versus black ones? Or just a Darkling being contrarian? It was one of those impenetrable mysteries not even Ninety-Nine's database could explain.

Red Pine Villa was surrounded by mature pines whose needles held armloads of snow from the blizzard. The trees crowded the house and must have submerged it in gloomy shadows, but I saw the place as bright as a picture in *National Geographic*.

The walls radiated a rainbow of energies: dozens of sorcerous wards and defensive enchantments. I couldn't guess what the spells did, but the implications were obvious; this place was a fortress. Anyone trying to enter unwelcomed—whether by teleportation, walking through walls, or shrinking and creeping through a crack—would suffer extreme consequences. I decided not to find out what those consequences were.

The villa had many windows, but every one looked slathered with black paint. Blinder walls. Again.

But what else would you expect? *Of course* a hideaway for Darklings would be smothered with privacy spells. And they were needed. Given any sort of opening, I'd be spying the heck out of Red Pine Villa. But the blinder spells were top-of-the-line, and their coverage was total. To see what lay inside, we'd have to go in.

WE STOPPED IN THE VILLA'S FRONT YARD

Aria hovered to avoid sinking knee-deep in the snow. "Looks quiet," she said. "See anything, Zircon?"

«Wall-to-wall blinders. Also defense spells.» I scanned more closely. *«But the front door looks safe. Nothing glowing.»*

"That makes sense," Dakini said, "They wouldn't want to vaporize the mailman."

Ninety-Nine grinned. "Front door it is. Last one in is a—"

Aria grabbed her collar. "It may be safe to *touch,* but not to throw open and race inside. Let's knock and announce ourselves before we do anything impulsive."

"How do we announce ourselves?" Ninety-Nine asked. "Do we have a name?"

"You mean a *team* name?" Dakini asked.

"Yeah. I've been trying to think of one, but I got nothin'. Four Girls from Different Science Departments is not going to fly."

«Especially the 'Girls' part,» I said.

Dakini said, "We could call ourselves Heroes of Science . . ."

"Lousy acronym," Ninety-Nine pointed out.

"Oh. Sorry." Dakini looked momentarily sheepish. "But it would still be beneficial to establish a group identity. If we've learned anything tonight, it's how much the Light cares about symbols. Costumes. Masks. A good team name would give strength to our group identity."

"Yes, but we *have* no group identity," Aria said. "We're all over the map. A soprano, a hockey player, a muse, and a rock."

«Zircon isn't a rock, it's a mineral,» I muttered.

"My point is, there's no unifying concept," Aria said. "Our powers have no common factors."

"We could take a name based on our aspirations," Dakini said. "Something like The Defenders."

"The name's taken," Ninety-Nine said. "By a group in Miami."

"The Guardians?"

"Manchester."

"The Protectors?"

"Auckland."

"The—"

Aria cut in: "Can we not do this here? There's a non-zero chance one of the worst supervillains on Earth is watching us right now. I do not want him to kill us while we're sounding like fourteen-year-olds trying to name their garage band."

"Oooh!" Ninety-Nine said. "Band names are a lot more fun than

The Defenders! You can pick any old shit. Like Streaked Silver Panties or Too Many Cooks."

Dakini said, "I like Too Many Cooks. It's fitting."

Aria groaned. "Forget what I said about knocking. I'm blasting the door down. If some magical defense blows me to pieces, it'll put me out of my misery."

ARIA STARTED TOWARD THE HOUSE, FLYING JUST ABOVE THE SNOW But she flew with deliberate slowness, giving the rest of us time to catch up and/or stop her. Me, I was still perched in Aria's hair, and desperately poking my Spark-o-Vision at the house to detect any threats we should worry about. I had no idea if my vision could do that, but what the hell: If I asked nicely, maybe the Light would download a new app into my visual cortex, and suddenly I'd see blinking red flashers on any wards about to zap us.

Alas, no new app. However, as we neared the front door, I noticed magical runes up on the lintel. The runes were the same shade of green as the lintel itself; the villa's owner must have painted the lintel first, let the paint dry, then used a fine artist's brush to dab on the runes. You'd never notice them, unless your eyes worked in the brilliant daylight of Spark-o-Vision.

The runes didn't glow. I zoomed my viewpoint to check them more closely. Nope, nary a trickle of power. *«Runes above the door,»* I transmitted. *«But they seem shut down. Or shorted out.»*

"That sounds bad," Ninety-Nine said. She and Dakini had followed Aria. More precisely, Dakini had kept her flying sled tethered to Aria's shoulders, so when Aria approached the front stoop, Ninety-Nine and Dakini got dragged along.

"Stop a second," Dakini said. She extended a violet tentacle and lightly pushed on the door. It opened with a creak. Nothing was visible beyond except a black blinder wall.

"You gotta love the classics," Ninety-Nine said. "Creaky unlocked door that opens the second you touch it. Haunted house stuff."

«Then keep an eye out for Wraith,» I said. *«He left the Market before we did, so he could have easily gotten here ahead of us.»*

If Nicholas had eavesdropped invisibly on the Goblin and me, he'd have heard where his sister was staying. He might have raced straight here.

"You think Wraith deliberately left this door ready to creak open?" Aria asked.

«I think he can't help it,» I replied. *«Darklings warp the world around them. Dust accumulates, lights burn out, and deathwatch beetles appear out of nowhere. Even if Wraith closed this door as carefully as he could, it might spontaneously unlatch and swing wide open with an ominous creak as soon as someone walked by.»*

"That must suck when you're flicking the bean in the shower," Ninety-Nine said. "Hypothetically. If that were something anyone ever did."

"Shut up," Aria said. She flew over the threshold and into the house.

AS SOON AS WE PASSED THROUGH THE BLINDER WALL, WE COULD SEE THE VILLA'S INTERIOR

The entrance was just a foyer with mats for damp footwear. I'll remind you the city had no snow on the ground until the unnatural snow started falling, yet I could see several pairs of galoshes and those silly rubber slippers you wear over your oxfords when you want to seem like a candy-ass. At one time, the galoshes and slippers must have been neatly aligned on the mats, but someone or some*thing* had tossed them around, bouncing them off the foyer's walls and scattering them higgledy-piggledy.

This did not bode well.

Beyond the foyer, a reception room had received the same tornadoed treatment. The room had originally been designed to give a cozy ski-lodge ambiance. The main part was two stories high, with polished wood stairs leading to the upper floor, and a big stone fireplace framed in white salt-and-pepper granite. (Or granodiorite. Or granitoid. Something igneous, felsic, and phaneritic. I'll shut up now.)

The fireplace had survived the upheaval. Not so the rest of the room. Furniture had been volleyed around so violently, every piece was broken . . . and it takes a lot to break an expensive leather sofa. Lamps had been smashed. Copies of the *National Post* and *Wall Street Journal* had been innovatively disrupted and the shreds jammed into corners of the room. Whatever happened had even swept away the usual signs of Darkling occupancy: dust and cobwebs had been pulverized, insects eradicated, and crumbling paint sandblasted clean.

The blinder walls on the windows remained intact. Perhaps they were extra-tough blinders, made bulletproof to guard against snipers. Whatever the source of their strength, the magic black walls had prevented the window glass from breaking despite the furor inside. It occurred to me that someone could set off a bomb inside Red Pine Villa, and no one on the street would ever know. The super-duper blinders would shut in all evidence. The blinder walls were intended to defend against external dangers, but the spells worked just as well to hide internal violence if a threat ever got in the door.

The house was silent, but that might just be another effect of the blinders. No sound could be heard from outside, and if every guest room was individually shielded, someone could be screaming under torture and we'd never hear.

«What do you think happened?» Dakini asked. She was using her comm ring, but somehow she managed to whisper.

«Looks like an explosion,» Aria said. *«And what does that make you think of?»*

«A rift opening?»

«Bingo.»

We looked around the room. With its lofty ceiling, the place could accommodate a rift almost as big as the one in E3. The floor and roof weren't visibly damaged, but that might just mean the rift had come and gone quickly, before it outgrew the available space.

Without warning, Ninety-Nine vaulted toward the stairway. It led to a mid-floor landing, then angled back to a second-floor balcony overlooking the reception room. Ninety-Nine bounced off an overturned armchair and grabbed the balcony railing. She pulled herself up, then somersaulted over the railing to land on the balcony floor. "I thought so," she said, crouching and pointing to the balcony's broadloom. "Indentations in the carpet. Just the right size for a rift machine."

"So someone brought in a rift projector," Aria said. "They revved it up and set off the usual explosion. I wonder what the other guests thought of that."

"Maybe they were all in on it," Ninety-Nine suggested. "If every guest was one of those Unbound douches . . ."

"Let's call them the Unbound Cabal," Dakini said. "That would look most excellent on a book: *Too Many Cooks Versus the Unbound Cabal.*"

"Zircon," Aria said, "how much would I have to pay you to crawl into my brain and lobotomize me?"

"Shush, I'm Sherlocking," Ninety-Nine said. "Let's say this place's owners have Unbound sympathies. That would explain all the ultramax blinder spells. They were hiding covert activities. Other members of the cabal booked the rooms so they could open a rift, troop inside, and receive superpowers. Woohoo!"

"Do they know that the rift makes Darklings unstable?" Dakini asked. "Insanity, and then detonation?"

"Depends when they entered the rift," Ninety-Nine said. "If they went in before the mess in the Market, they wouldn't know what happened to the others. If they went in after . . ."

"If they went in after," Aria said, "Diamond could have just told them, 'I've taken careful readings and I know what went wrong.' Maybe that's why they opened the first rift in a lab: to monitor the process with lab equipment and refine the techniques. Diamond says, 'Don't worry, I've corrected the problems. This time, the process will work.' "

"It hasn't been that long since the Market rift closed," Dakini said. "We only spent twenty minutes or so dealing with casualties. Is that really enough time for Diamond to correct a flawed process and start another trial?"

"Maybe," Ninety-Nine said. "If he knew what the flaws were likely to be, and just had to make adjustments, like tuning a radio."

"Especially if," Aria said, "Diamond had no intention of actually getting the process right. Given what we know about Diamond, he might just get his jollies from tricking Darklings into something that'll kill them."

Ninety-Nine said, "And the cabal took no precautions in case they were being played?" She shrugged. "Guess we'll see when the rift reopens and lets out a new crop of superpowered Darklings."

"Oh," said Dakini, "is that likely? I suppose it is. Will the rift open here?"

Ninety-Nine shook her head and gestured to the marks on the carpet. "The rift projector is gone. The cabal has bugged out. They probably worried someone would find them—if not us, then the Dark Guard."

I nodded. By now, the cabal would know that Waterloo had its own set of Sparks—Diamond had been watching the Market, so he saw us in action. And even if we'd never found our way to Red Pine Villa, the Dark Guard would. They were the Darkling MI5; mostly, they hunted Darklings who violated the Dark Pact, but they also dealt with assaults against the Dark. The injuries and deaths at the Goblin Market would bring the Guard running, as would any hint of Unbound activity. The Guard had a reputation for being ruthless but thorough. They'd wring the Goblin for information and raid the villa shortly thereafter.

"Whatever happens," Aria said, "Diamond won't open his next rift behind closed doors. When his insane super-Darklings are ready to emerge, he'll set it up someplace public. Produce maximum carnage. That's what he gets off on."

"Besides," Ninety-Nine said, "Diamond *can't* open a rift twice in the same place. The process creates a dimensional scar that messes up the continuum too much to allow another rift. You can only open rifts in unscarred locations."

Surprise. Dubious looks. Aria said, "Are you bullshitting, or do you actually have a clue how rifts work?"

"Dude," Ninety-Nine said, "I know things."

"Could you open a rift yourself?"

Ninety-Nine considered the question. "I can guess a few ways it might work. With half a million dollars and a month to experiment, I could come up with something."

"So for the cost of a half-decent condo, you could open up a hole into another universe?"

"When you put it like that . . . well, yes. But I can think of better ways to spend the money."

"Curing cancer? Perfecting cold fusion?"

"I was thinking of buying beer," Ninety-Nine said, "but curing cancer is good too."

"That's a relief," Aria said. "For a moment I thought you were serious."

"I'm serious about the rift machine," Ninety-Nine told her. "Piece of cake."

"Fuck," Aria said. "Are you turning into a Mad Genius?"

"I'm not turning into anything," Ninety-Nine snapped. "What I've become, already, is an expert in everything. My head is filled with enough for a thousand PhDs. And it's all just immediately *there*, you know? I don't have to search through lists or tables, it's just *there*. I see so many connections, I'm in this constant state of 'Eureka!' and nearly bursting into tears, because it would be trivial to make the world better. But the instant I think of a new invention, I also see how some bastard could wreck everything by abusing it, or just creating a cash cow that only the rich could afford. I see a million possibilities but not how they'll play out. So fuck it, I want a beer. My head is full of noise, and it's exhausting."

Her shoulders slumped and she turned her back on us. Silence. I had never heard such a tone in her voice; I couldn't remember her ever admitting to genuine weakness.

Apparently, it was new to Aria too. Almost at the speed of sound, she flew to the balcony and wrapped Ninety-Nine in her arms. It was so fast and unexpected, I lost my grip on Aria's hair. I was left a loose speck of dust, tossed by the wind of her passage.

DAKINI TURNED TOWARD ME

Proving once again I was mentally obvious, despite my size. *«Let's let that happen,»* she transmitted. *«You and I can search the house.»*

«I'll take the top floor,» I said. *«You've got down here.»*

«Be careful. Even if everyone in the cabal is gone, they may have left traps.»

I nodded and flew to the second floor. On the balcony, Ninety-Nine had started to cry; Aria held her, whispering. I gave them a wide berth as I headed for the guest rooms.

I DIDN'T EVEN CHECK WHETHER THE ROOMS WERE LOCKED

I just scuttled under the doors and through the blinders that kept each room private. As soon as I had a clear view of a room, I did a five-second scan for people, corpses, and ticking bombs. Nothing? Then on to the next room.

I only needed a minute for a complete circuit. Nobody home, and no blatant threats or emergencies. Good. I started again at the beginning, this time being more thorough.

For the record, the rooms were lovely. Each had a four-poster bed, a writing table, and an en suite bathroom. Oak hardwood floors with Moroccan rugs. No televisions. A many-buttoned phone on each writing table. Every room had a painting on the wall that I suspected was genuine: a Matisse, a Picasso, a Monet, and so on. (I'd have bet a nickel the management used those paintings to refer to the rooms. "Ah yes, you'll be staying in the Renoir Suite.")

Each room showed signs of occupation: clothes in the closet, toiletries in the washroom, plus the usual eccentricities one expects from Darklings. A cage full of hamsters (probably food). Oddly shaped tongs (likely for grooming). Eight Victorian porcelain dolls arranged in an asterisk on the floor (no idea what they were for, but I stayed the hell away).

The rooms *didn't* show much degeneration, despite the many Darklings who must have passed through. The paintings had to be protected by magic; otherwise, they would have faded and crumbled by now. Maybe additional magic kept the rest of the rooms clean and nice. Either that, or diligent maids visited several times a day and the furniture was replaced every week. Considering the prices people must have paid to stay in the villa, that was also a possibility.

THE FIRST ROOM I SEARCHED HAD BEEN OCCUPIED BY A MAN

Or at least someone who identified as male. Masculine business suits in the closet, male underwear in the drawers. Since I was looking for Elaine, I moved on. (I refused to entertain the possibility that Elaine might be a covert cross-dresser. That would bring her uncomfortably close to my own status as "none of the above." I didn't want to think Elaine might be anything like me.)

The next room had female clothes in the closet. It also had a handwritten letter on the writing table: gold-embossed stationery proclaiming, "Thank you for choosing Red Pine Villa," and promising courteous, discreet service for all the guest's needs.

The letter began, *Dear Lilith*. Jackpot.

I SEARCHED LILITH'S ROOM BUT FOUND NOTHING OUT OF THE ORDINARY

My search turned up a smoked-glass "water bottle" that smelled strongly of blood, but that was *totally* ordinary for vampires. They invariably carried flasks of the good stuff in case their throats got dry. Now that I thought about it, I was surprised Lilith hadn't had anything to swig during our fight in the alley. Perhaps like an alcoholic under stress, she'd chugged everything she had before the fight began.

Next stop, Elaine's room. That just meant going from room to room until I found a *Dear Elaine* letter. I hit pay dirt in the Mary Cassatt room. (No, I can't identify a Cassatt on sight, but there was a label on the frame. I noticed that none of the paintings in other rooms had labels. Maybe we were expected to recognize Monet and Degas, but Cassatt was considered obscure. The painting was a mother and daughter looking at a picture book.)

Nothing in Elaine's room leapt out at me, but I searched anyway. I grew to full size to do it—I could have relied on Spark-o-Vision, but it was more satisfying to pick things up, paw through the clothing, and toss every piece on the floor. The biggest challenge was staying on task and not ripping the clothes to shreds.

The longer I searched Elaine's belongings, the more I felt I was wasting my time. Why would she leave anything in her room apart from the same old, same old? Elaine had to expect investigators would go through her things—as I've said, the mess in the Market would have brought the Dark Guard running. The Goblin would tell all, and point toward Red Pine Villa. The Guard was guaranteed to search this room with a fine-toothed magical comb.

Elaine would have prepared for that. She'd leave nothing in the room except what she wanted the Dark Guard to find. Even if I stumbled onto a "clue," it would be deliberately planted—Elaine had the time, skills, and brains to avoid unintentional slip-ups.

I was wasting my time. Wasting my time. The feeling grew overwhelming.

DAKINI CLAIMED I HAD NO PSIONIC DEFENSES

But within the past few hours, I'd resisted Ignorance spells cast by Nicholas and Elaine, and had seen through the Bride's vision of "victory." I may not have had mental shields, but I was quick to realize when something had its hooks in my brain.

I muttered, "This is a waste of time," and stamped out of the room in a huff. I did it while staying full size. But as soon as I got outside, I shrank to the size of a virus and flew back through the gap under the door. In my head, I counted, *One Mississippi, two Mississippi, three Mississippi . . .*

Nicholas appeared in a corner of the room. He hadn't been hiding in shadows or behind an Ignorance spell; he'd learned his lesson and chosen flat-out invisibility. Now he looked winded, his stringy hair glistening with sweat. Perhaps going invisible demanded considerable effort—similar to holding his breath, even if Nicholas didn't actually breathe anymore.

I knew he could perceive me if I got too close—I'd seen that when we met near Popigai's office. So I kept my distance but flew into his line of sight. Then I shot up to Max Zirc size and said, "Boo."

Nicholas could still bring out the Kimmi in me.

HOW MANY PEOPLE HAVE EVER SCARED A GHOST?

Nicholas jumped and jerked away, backing halfway into the wall. He yelled, "Ow!" and flew forward again as if bouncing off a trampoline. He hit me square on. A moment later, we were plummeting to the floor. Being at Max Zirc size, I was still made of rock. When my head hit the hardwood, I didn't bash out my brains; in the contest between my skull and the oak floor, my skull won.

Don't ask why I didn't shrink as I fell. Usually that was my automatic reflex. This time, though . . . blame it on Kimmi. Always Kimmi.

But also Nicholas. I'd already seen that his default response to being surprised was to go insubstantial. This time, though, he stayed solid and fleshy, falling flat on top of me.

Nose to nose. With our lips almost touching. Full body, too—for once, Nicholas didn't fade out below the waist.

He said, "Ouch. You're hard."

"Isn't that supposed to be *my* line?"

Nicholas groaned and rolled off me. He lay on his back, covered his face with his hands, and groaned some more.

I raised myself on one elbow. "What's wrong?"

He didn't move. When he talked, his hands muffled his voice. "Number one," he said, "this place has enchantments in the walls to keep out incorporeal intruders. You made me back into one; it burned my ass and threw me out like a catapult. It also screwed up my ability to go intangible. Thanks so much. Number two, I landed on a shrimpy QUILTBAG Spark who's as hard as fucking marble . . ."

"Don't be insulting," I said. "Marble is only 3 on the Mohs hardness scale. Zircon is over 7."

I saw him freeze. After a moment, he lowered his hands. His eyes were wide. He levered up on an elbow and faced me there on the floor.

Once again, we were nose to nose. Nicholas stared, and I didn't shy away.

A costume and mask won't hide a Spark's identity if the Spark is begging to be caught.

Nicholas said, "Kimmi?"

I said nothing. I just waited.

I WAS SEEING IT ALL IN THIRD PERSON

My vision hovered outside my body, looking down on the two of us. We were so close, our faces almost touched.

If Nicholas had been human, I would have felt the warmth of his skin and his breath on my face. But he had no warmth or breath. I felt nothing, as if I were alone in the room.

I wondered what I'd feel if he kissed me. But he didn't. Kimmi tingled within me, but Nicholas only saw Zircon.

Or Kim.

No one he wanted to kiss.

HE PROBABLY WOULDN'T HAVE KISSED KIMMI EITHER

She was the ex. The discard.

Anyway, the real Nicholas was dead. This was just his ghost.

HE ROLLED ONTO HIS BACK AGAIN AND SAID, "DAMN"

Inside me, Kimmi seeped quietly away. Back when I was her, I'd felt so strong and bold. But Kimmi wasn't a survivor.

Zircons, on the other hand, endure. Not bold, but tough as hell.

"YES, NICHOLAS," I SAID, "I'M FINALLY IN YOUR LEAGUE"

I got to my feet. It would have been nice to do some flashy Jackie Chan–style flip, but clambering was more my style. "You have powers. I do too. At last, a level playing field."

"Was that your problem?" he asked. "You thought I looked down on you because . . ." He didn't finish his sentence.

"You dumped me," I said, "because you were going to become a Darkling and I wasn't."

I wanted to say more: all the speeches Kimmi had rehearsed in the emptiness after the breakup. The things Kimmi would have said if Elaine had actually brought Nicholas to me for one last conversation. I had muttered and blurted those speeches aloud while hiking alone in the mountains. I'd actually shouted, "I loved you, damn it!" in the Valley of the Ten Peaks, half hoping I would be barraged by a thousand dramatic echoes.

There was no echoing at all. My voice just disappeared into the empty air. At most, I scared a few tourists.

All the hurt feelings. All the things I'd wanted to say. But what was the point of venting them now? Kimmi was gone, and good fucking riddance, right? She'd been nothing but a stopover on the road from Kimberley to Kim. My first step toward the edge of the cliff, until Nicholas and Elaine kicked me all the way over.

I should have thanked him for that. But I didn't. I was pissed at that "shrimpy QUILTBAG" remark.

"LOOK," NICHOLAS SAID, "CAN WE NOT DO THIS?" He started to stand, then didn't. He just hoisted himself on one elbow to look at me. He was still completely solid—the enchantment in the wall must have really done a number on his ability to turn ghostly.

It occurred to me that maybe Nicholas *couldn't* stand. With his Darkling powers suppressed, maybe his paralysis was back. I felt a pang of pity; I wanted to help him up. But he'd hate me if I offered. Even when Nicholas had loved me, his face would turn to stone if he needed my help to do anything. He could recognize the necessity, but he would mentally shut down until the indignity was over.

Nicholas saw the way I was looking at him. He saw my pity; I saw his anger and shame. But we had practiced denial together, and the moves came back like riding a bicycle. I turned away as if nothing were wrong. With the eyes in the back of my head, I saw him relax. Marginally.

"No time for hashing out the past," I said. "We have more urgent matters to deal with: Elaine and Diamond."

Nicholas grimaced. "What diamond?"

"No, *who* Diamond. Adam Popigai is actually a Mad Genius named Diamond. Elaine may or may not know that. If she doesn't, he's using her, and he'll kill her when she's no longer needed. I've read about him; that's his MO. But if Elaine *does* know he's Diamond and she's working with him anyway . . . well, he'll still likely kill her, unless he decides to let the Dark Guard do it instead."

Nicholas closed his eyes. He shook his head and said, "Elaine."

"Do you know what she's up to?" I asked.

"Maybe. Check the nightstand."

I'd already checked the nightstand. I had, after all, searched the room, even if I'd done it perfunctorily thanks to *This is a waste of time* being forced into my brain.

But I went to the nightstand and saw papers I hadn't seen before. Had Nicholas made them invisible the first time I searched? Or had he simply stopped me from noticing them?

I hated mental powers.

THE NEWLY REVEALED PAPERS INCLUDED A GOBLIN MARKET BROCHURE

It was identical to the one in Popigai's office. No surprise; still, I wished I could read the writing to see what it said about the doohickey the Widow had purchased.

The papers also included something that resembled a wedding invitation. It was printed on expensive white card stock that glimmered in my Spark-o-Vision. The writing was done in the same incomprehensible squiggles as the Goblin's brochure—obviously, a script that Darklings used to keep things secret. In this case, the secrecy was undermined by a map on the back of the card. An X marked a spot on the shore of Lake Huron, a couple hours northwest of Waterloo.

I held up the card. "What's this? And please don't pretend you can't read the writing."

"There's a blood moon ritual," Nicholas said. "Tonight at the height of the eclipse. All Darklings are invited."

"What does the ritual do?"

"Nothing you should worry about," he said. Of course, that worried me like hell. "The point is it'll be another large gathering of Darklings. Like the Goblin Market."

"You think Diamond will attack it?"

"It's a similar target. The only place nearby where you'll find a bunch of Darklings together."

"Really?" I said. "It's three days before Christmas. Surely some Darkling must be holding a party in Toronto or Buffalo. Some city reasonably close."

Nicholas rolled his eyes. "Who spends Christmas in Toronto or Buffalo? The nearest parties tonight are in New York City. Or"—he nodded toward the card in my hand—"there."

"Okay." Getting to Lake Huron was doable. Aria could fly us there in less than an hour. But I didn't like leaving Waterloo—it didn't feel right. "Awfully convenient," I said, "Elaine leaving this invitation so easy to find."

"True," Nicholas said. "But . . ." He stopped.

"You know something you're not saying?" I asked. "Maybe something you overheard from Elaine?"

"Elaine is extremely private about what she does in her spare time," Nicholas said. "But I knew she'd been hanging out with Lilith. You remember Lilith? From that party at our place?"

"I remember," I said.

"She and Elaine hit it off that night. Father wasn't pleased—he thinks Lilith is a disaster waiting to happen. So he kept an eye on her. It wasn't difficult, considering how much Lilith likes the spotlight. When he found out Lilith and Elaine had set up a meeting in Waterloo, supposedly to shop at the Goblin Market . . ."

"Your dad sent you to spy on her."

Nicholas nodded. "When I arrived, I kept my ear out for trouble. A few hours later, I heard about an explosion that might have killed six Darklings. I started investigating. You can fill in the rest." He sat up straighter. "If you're heading to Lake Huron, there's no time to chat."

I looked at him hard, then laughed. "If your powers were at full strength, I bet I'd be racing out the door. But at the moment, you're practically human, and a human I used to know well. I think you're hiding something."

"Kimmi . . ."

"No," I said, "it's Zircon." I hit him with the full strength of my Halo.

IT WAS A CRAPPY THING TO DO

It wasn't all that different from the mental powers that had been imposed on me, from the subtle attempts to influence me all the way up to forceful domination. I'm not proud of what I did to Nicholas; especially not how quickly the idea popped into my mind. What do you do when somebody's reluctant to speak? Hammer him into submission.

A shitty thing to do. But I did it anyway. Superhero entitlement.

I DON'T KNOW WHAT NICHOLAS SAW WHEN I HALOED HIM

A goddess? An ancient force of nature? Or a monster of the Light, a Darkling's eternal enemy? Whatever he saw or felt, his powers were still at low ebb, and that included any resistance he had to my aura. He made a soft, high-pitched sound, then rolled away and tucked into a ball.

I felt like total shit, towering over a frightened paraplegic who looked like a kid I once loved.

I knelt quickly beside him. I wanted to hug him, but he shied away. To make myself less scary, I started to shrink. Slowly. When I got to half-size, I was apparently small enough not to be totally overwhelming. He suddenly lashed out and knocked me across the room. I stayed where I landed, not speaking, leaving him alone.

Time passed. Thirty seconds? Suddenly he went cloudy; his powers had come back and he could turn ghostly once more. He disappeared completely for a moment, then returned, floating upright again, dwindling below the waist. The same as he'd been when I saw him in the police station. Trying to pretend nothing had changed.

"Shit," he said. "Did you do that for revenge?"

"No. I don't want to hurt you, Nicholas."

"Just carelessness, then." He drifted toward me. "Not knowing your own strength?"

I didn't answer but grew back to Max Zirc. "I'm sorry," I said. I wanted to add something about being new and inexperienced, but that was no excuse. "Do you want me to leave?"

"No." His Shadow flared with fierce intensity. That really *was* revenge, a ghost trying to terrify me. I could feel all the horrors I'd ever run from: the dark basements, the sounds at night, the nightmares that woke me screaming. Stories I shouldn't have read at bedtime. Movies I was too young to watch.

If I'd been human, his Shadow would have broken me—maybe even that cliché of being scared to death. But I was a Spark in the fullness of power, too pumped with ego to feel a rational amount of fear.

"Sorry," I said, "I'm sorry. Sorry for what I did, and sorry I'm not as vulnerable to your Shadow as you were to my Halo. When this is over, I'll let you punch me really hard on the arm or something. For now, just tell me what you were hiding."

He made a face, then sighed. "Oh, all right."

"MAYBE YOU DON'T FIND ME SCARY," HE SAID, "BUT I'M ACTUALLY QUITE POWERFUL: SPHINX LEVEL"

I knew what that meant. Nicholas himself had explained it to me when we were together.

The Dark grow stronger as they age. A thousand-year-old Darkling is much more intimidating than a typical new convert. Being as old as the Sphinx means a Darkling is very scary indeed.

But some new Darklings are "born old." They emerge from the Dark Conversion with the same level of power as Darklings with much more experience. If Nicholas already matched Elders who'd been around since ancient Egypt, he was near the very top of the Dark-power pyramid.

I wondered how that had happened. Luck? "Liminality quotient"? Or could the Elders control the Dark Conversion and give certain candidates more power than normal? If so, why Nicholas? What did the Elders have planned for him?

I had no idea. Perhaps he was just lying to impress me.

"IF YOU'RE SO POWERFUL, WHAT CAN YOU DO?" I ASKED

"Serious ghostly things," he replied. "Practically anything that ghosts can do in any story you've read."

"That's an awful lot," I said.

"It is." Nicholas tried to look matter-of-fact.

"Why did you bring this up?" I asked.

"I can sense ghostly afterimpressions." He gave me a look. "Basically, I can reconstruct events from the past. I could show you if you'd let me."

I didn't say yes. I didn't say no.

"Let's go into that corner." He pointed to the only corner in the room not occupied by furniture. "We'll see everything from there."

I didn't know what he had in mind, but I walked to the corner anyway.

Consent.

Nicholas floated toward me. He raised his hand. His fingertips reached toward my head like Spock doing a Vulcan mind-meld.

I could think of a million reasons why this was a bad idea. Letting a Darkling inside my brain? Especially Nicholas? Did I trust him not to . . . well, anything from reading my most intimate secrets to turning me into his mind-slave?

Did I trust him? Of course not. But I took off my hat and let him touch me. Because.

HIS FINGERS DIDN'T FEEL SOLID AT ALL

His touch was like an icy wind. Then the coldness slid into my brain.

I watched it happen from a viewpoint outside my body. I *saw* his fingers go in. Then I felt them like a freezing mass of pain behind my eyes.

My perception collapsed from 360 degrees to the intolerable tunnel vision of normal sight. Colors were replaced by shades of gray: like a black-and-white movie, except that the blacks were faded and the whites were dingy. Everything seemed less solid, almost transparent.

Semitransparent chairs. Semitransparent Cassatt. Semitransparent bed with rumpled sheets.

This was how Nicholas saw the world: as if everything in it were a ghost.

I REALIZED WE WEREN'T ALONE

Elaine Vandermeer stood in the bathroom doorway.

Not the real Elaine: a ghostly reconstruction. But she was still real enough to make me squirm. I closed my eyes, but nothing changed. Nicholas was sending this image straight into my mind.

Elaine wore a gray silk bathrobe, untied. She held a blow-dryer in one hand and a brush in the other. Her hair was wet.

The sight of her nearly made me throw up: half repugnance at seeing the woman who'd hurt me, and half . . . well. There's a difference between sexual attraction and the sickly urge to submit to a vampire who once bit you; it's just hard to make that distinction when you're dizzy with approach-avoidance. I didn't want to have sex with Elaine, I wanted to fight her with the absolute abandon I'd used on Hannah years ago. I wanted to punch and scream and twist . . .

. . . but I wanted Elaine to win. And bite me again.

The relationship between vampire and victim is toxic. Vampires like it that way.

I WONDERED HOW MUCH NICHOLAS COULD SENSE

He was connected with my mind. Could he feel my nauseated reaction?

And what was *he* feeling? This was his sister, for god's sake. How could he so blithely play voyeur? Sharing her image with somebody else was even sicker.

I wanted to turn away. Maybe throw up. But the icy fingers digging into my brain held me frozen.

Elaine said, "Are you leaving? It's still early." Her voice was tinny, as if I heard her over a cheap phone. Just as Nicholas couldn't see colors, his sense of hearing seemed to be diminished.

Another semitransparent figure walked into the scene: a man coated with steel, all too familiar. Like the first time I'd seen him, he resembled the Oscar statuette—faceless, sleek and broad-shouldered, but asexual. His lack of genitals seemed odd, considering how postcoital the rest of this scene was. Then again, the steel exterior was just a costume. Popigai/Diamond was dressed up and ready to go.

"We need to check everything one more time." His voice was as tinny as Elaine's. His accent was Russian, not Australian: the Popigai persona, not Diamond. That suggested he was hiding his real identity from Elaine. I wondered what she did and didn't know.

"Why do 'we' need to check?" Elaine asked Diamond. "Can't you do it on your own?"

"Two pairs of eyes are better than one," Diamond replied. "It's easy for trivialities to mess up a plan. A mouse chews on a wire; a meddler wanders past and says, *That shouldn't be there, I'd better move it before there's an accident.* Worst of all, we have to watch for coincidences. Light and Dark can both manufacture flukes of luck, so we have to be doubly careful. Triply careful." He waved his hand toward her. "Hurry up and get dressed."

"Do you really need two pairs of eyes?" Elaine asked. "Or do you not trust me out of your sight?"

"That too," Diamond said. "Trust is for fools. Now come, we have to get to Lake Huron and back before things start here."

"Of course," Elaine said.

Diamond turned impatiently toward the door. Elaine turned deliberately toward me.

Seriously: It was direct eye contact. Nicholas and I stood in a corner where there was nothing. When this scene originally took place, Elaine had no reason to look in this direction.

But she did. Not a random glance, but a long meaningful look. Then she went into the bathroom and began drying her hair.

THE SCENE CONTINUED

But when Elaine appeared again, she was not even wearing her bathrobe. Nicholas finally seemed to realize that he was showing me his sister naked. He jerked his fingers out of my skull.

I could move again. I could see real colors. The full 360 degrees.

I allowed myself a moment of relief. Then I said, "Did you see that?"

"Of course I saw it," Nicholas said. "I was the one showing it to you."

"But Elaine looked at me . . ." I stopped. "No, she must have been looking at you. I just saw it through your eyes."

"Kimmi, I was reconstructing something from hours ago. Elaine couldn't have looked at me. I wasn't here."

"She looked where she thought you'd be later," I said. "She knows you can do reconstructions, right? She *expected* you to see this whole scene. She even guessed you'd stand in this corner to do it. It's empty and out of the way."

"She couldn't have known I'd be here."

"Couldn't she?" I asked. "She wouldn't expect you'd be sent to spy on her?"

"Look," Nicholas said, "the point is that Popigai—Diamond—he came right out and said that the conspiracy's next move will be at that ritual."

The white invitation card rose from the nightstand and floated toward me. It hovered in front of my face until I took it. Nicholas said, "That's where you and the other Sparks should go. Soon."

"What about you?"

"I'll call my father and see what he wants me to do. He might send me to the ritual, but maybe not. Elaine is obviously in this up to her eyeballs. Maybe he'll leave her to twist in the wind, or maybe he'll go and get her himself."

"Your father can get from Calgary to Lake Huron in less than an hour?"

"Yes. So I'll let him make the decision." Nicholas glanced toward the phone on the writing table, then shook his head. "Not from here. This whole place may be compromised. I'll go somewhere else."

"You're leaving?"

"I have to, Kimmi," he said.

"Zircon," I corrected him.

"Sure."

The door of the room swung open of its own volition. Nicholas hesitated. I wondered if he was trying to decide whether to kiss me good-bye. A peck on the cheek? Did he think I expected that?

A look of revulsion passed over his face.

"Someone walking over your grave?" I asked, trying to make my voice light. "Just go."

Nicholas went, turning invisible the moment he crossed the threshold.

WELL, I THOUGHT, I REALLY FUCKED UP, DIDN'T I?
I'd given away my identity to a Darkling. Who would now phone his father and deliver a full report. If Nicholas didn't say, "I ran into Kimmi, she's a superhero now," it would only be because he was too embarrassed to mention me.

I was a "youthful indiscretion." *Let us never speak of her again.*

And obviously, my queerness appalled him. That made me laugh; the secret of my identity might depend on Nicholas's discomfort at how I'd changed. "Who? No, sorry, that name doesn't ring a bell."

Well, there were worse ways to keep a secret than relying on het-male squeamishness.

I LOOKED AROUND THE ROOM ONE LAST TIME
Not much had changed since the scene I'd witnessed. The bed still wasn't made, but it had been de-rumpled: The sheets and coverlet

had been haphazardly smoothed by someone who neither knew nor cared how to produce hospital corners. Still, it showed that Elaine and Diamond hadn't dashed out the door the instant Elaine was ready.

They'd taken the time to straighten the room. Yet they'd left the invitation card on the nightstand.

It smelled like a red herring: a sign saying GO HERE NEXT, sending anyone who searched the room on a wild goose chase far from Waterloo.

But in Nicholas's reconstruction, Diamond had explicitly mentioned Lake Huron. It implied that the secret solstice ritual really was being targeted.

Unless Nicholas had faked the whole scene to get me and my teammates out of town.

Or Diamond had faked the scene for the same reason. Because he knew that Nicholas or the Dark Guard might come to this room and do exactly the kind of reconstruction I'd seen.

Diamond was a genius. He might have planned a ruse to throw off anyone who could look back into the past. Maybe Elaine's meaningful look into the corner told her brother, "Don't trust this." She couldn't say it aloud with Diamond watching, but she could hint. For that matter, she may have left other hints in the room, and Nicholas had pocketed them before I arrived.

"This is annoying," I said aloud. Too many what-ifs. Too many people with too many powers that could leave false trails.

Well, screw it. Maybe our Olympic-level Sherlock could ferret out the truth. Maybe Dakini had powers of retro-cognition, or Aria could just see through the bullshit. Let *them* take a crack at this. I sucked at playing detective.

Holding the invitation card, I headed back downstairs.

WHILE I WAS GONE, A VISITOR HAD ARRIVED AT THE VILLA

It was the pustule demon, the one from the Widow's car. Thanks to Red Pine Villa's blinders, he'd entered without knowing anyone was inside. Dakini had sensed him immediately—a stink of phenol wafting through the house. Somehow she'd kept him from bolting off into the night. (I hoped she had done it with words, as opposed to brute mental force, but I didn't ask.)

The demon said his name was Pox. It was a codename, of course, like Wraith or Zircon. Dakini had likely fished his real name out of his brain, but so what? It would be something like Nigel Smith-Hawkington III, and Pox was infinitely easier to say with a straight face.

Pox didn't look good. More of his pustules had broken open since the last time I'd seen him. He'd made a clumsy attempt to clean up, but crusts of dried blood still surrounded his buboes. Maybe scrubbing had hurt so much, he'd given up.

Even so, Pox had been lucky. He'd been at the Goblin Market and hadn't died.

He had us to thank for that. We had, of course, prevented the roof from collapsing and crushing everyone. More than that: Ninety-Nine had apparently given Pox first aid, then carried him to safety.

She hadn't known who he was. She'd never seen into the car.

Surprisingly, Pox was grateful for having been saved—not a common trait among Darklings. In fact, he was so kindly disposed toward us that he willingly revealed what he and the Widow had been up to.

(Again, I didn't ask why Pox was so forthcoming, and Dakini didn't mention any suasion she might have applied. She just smiled benignly.)

POX CONFIRMED THAT THE WIDOW AND THE BRIDE WERE SISTERS

They were identical twins, but the sort who wanted to differentiate themselves rather than mirror each other. The Bride had grown up impulsive, while the Widow became a sober counterbalance. When the twins turned eighteen, the Dark Conversion transformed them in accordance with their contrasting identities: white and black opposites.

The Bride had fallen in with the Unbound cabal. Were they truly associated with ancient Darklings who hated the Elders, or were these Unbound just wannabes? Pox didn't know. I got the impression that Pox didn't know much. Whatever he might have been before the Dark Conversion, he now seemed mentally childlike: a useful tool both sisters employed if they needed someone to read minds. It made me feel sorry for him—I have a soft spot in my heart for people treated like crap by self-absorbed Darklings. But then immediately (because I'm me) I started to wonder if this was an act and Pox was much shrewder than he pretended.

Sigh.

Pox said the Widow had received a note from her sister: "Come to the Goblin Market on solstice night. Do whatever it takes to purchase Lot 49 at the auction. Push the ON button as soon as the item is in your hands." Needless to say, the Widow viewed this message with suspicion. She sweet-talked Pox into coming with her to Waterloo. The Widow intended to find her sister before the auction began and turn Pox loose on the Bride's frontal lobes to find out what Sis was up to.

Pox and the Widow reached Waterloo early in the afternoon. Their first call was Red Pine Villa, since it was the number-one place for Darklings to stay in town. The receptionist wouldn't say whether the Bride was staying in the villa, but Pox probed the man's brain and discovered that yes, the Bride had checked in. She had gone out shortly thereafter, and the receptionist had no idea when she'd be back.

Pox and the Widow poked around town. Most of the poking was done by the Widow's driver. He was a human named Trent, an ex-policeman trained in investigation. Trent spent hours beating the bushes but turned up nothing helpful. Then, around 10:00 PM, a friend who was still on the force called Trent to say that a Darkling woman in a bridal gown had been reported in connection with an explosion at the university. Trent, Pox, and the Widow had staked out the campus police station. Eventually, on the Widow's instructions, Pox tried to read the minds of four student witnesses . . .

We knew how that went.

Pox didn't remember much, just that he was quickly knocked unconscious by a mental attack. He knew that meant Darklings or Sparks were trying to prevent anyone from learning the truth.

With Pox out cold and the Bride MIA, the Widow had run out of options. She decided the only way forward was to follow her sister's instructions: to buy Lot 49 at the Goblin's auction.

WHEN THE GROUP ARRIVED AT THE MARKET, POX DIDN'T GO IN
He was awake but still woozy from Dakini's mental attack, so he stayed in the car while Trent and the Widow went inside.

I asked if the Widow had intended to meet anyone at the auction. Pox didn't know. Either the Widow hadn't told him she'd be meeting Elaine, or else the Widow hadn't expected Elaine would be there.

I could believe that. After all, Elaine had been wearing an Ignorance spell. Obviously she didn't want to be noticed. By whom? Perhaps by the Widow.

The two likely knew each other. Canada has about three hundred Darklings, and they all jet around, attending galas, soirees, and business meetings together. If Elaine wanted to get close to the Widow but not be remembered afterward, an Ignorance spell was essential.

So the Widow went to the auction. Elaine sat beside her, but shielded herself with a spell that made the Widow ignore her. Then what?

Pox remained in the car, but after a while, he recovered enough strength to snoop around from a distance. Clairvoyance? No, he couldn't do that—the market was blocked with blinders. Pox just tapped into the Widow's mind to see what she was seeing.

Good thing Pox was just a naive kid, or he'd have *creepy* written all over him.

So Pox piggybacked on the Widow's mind at the auction. He watched her buy Lot 49. He watched as she pressed the big red button, in accordance with the Bride's instructions.

DIAMOND'S GADGET SUCKED MAGICAL ENERGY FROM HER
It nearly drained her dead. The Widow collapsed as gushers of magic pumped out of her like blood.

"Of course!" Ninety-Nine said, interrupting Pox's story. "The rift projector must need magic to start the process! That's how this whole thing connects with the eclipse and the solstice. Science doesn't depend on occult trappings, but magic does."

It made sense. When we'd first seen Popigai's "replicator," it had begun running but nothing happened. The rift didn't open until the remote-control gadget sucked up energy from the Widow. As for the rifts in the lab and Red Pine Villa, there'd been plenty of Darklings present on both occasions. They could have contributed energy to help the rift open.

"It would have to be voluntary," Ninety-Nine said. "The replicator couldn't just grab a passerby and milk 'em for magic. Sorcery only works if you play by the rules. In this case, a Darkling would have to willingly make the sacrifice to start the ball rolling."

"Was the Widow willing to get drained?" Dakini asked. "She didn't know it would happen."

"She might not have known the exact details," Ninety-Nine said, "but she pressed the button anyway. She accepted whatever would happen."

"Her sister set her up," Aria said. "The Bride sent the Widow that message, knowing that pressing the button would drain the Widow's energy. Also cause an explosion, and possibly drop a roof on her head."

Ninety-Nine shrugged. "Sisters." Jools had four of them. Their presence in Alberta was one reason Jools had picked a university far from home.

I'm glad I'm an only child.

I ASKED POX, "WHAT HAPPENED AFTER THE WIDOW PRESSED THE BUTTON?"
Pox didn't know. He had seen this all through the Widow's eyes; when the gadget drained her energy, Pox was caught by the same

magical effect. He nearly passed out before he managed to sever the connection.

"You may have saved the Widow's life," Ninety-Nine said. "You contributed some of your own magical energy. If Popigai's doohickey had taken all it needed from the Widow herself, it might have killed her."

"Really?" Pox said. "I guess that's good." He actually smiled—not a great look for him, considering the blood-rimmed sores all over his face.

Pox had no idea what happened in the time that he was reeling from energy drainage. When he recovered, he ran into the building to see if the Widow needed his help, but by then, the rift was open and the super-Darklings were loose. Luckily Pox missed most of the explosions, but he got smacked by the final one. All he remembered was waking up with Ninety-Nine tending his wounds.

Later, Pox tried to go back to the Widow's car. It was gone. He returned to the stables where other Darklings were being treated. Eventually, he found somebody he knew and begged for a ride to Red Pine Villa. He hoped the Bride or the Widow would show up there eventually.

None of us told him what had happened to the Bride. We didn't have the heart.

NINETY-NINE SAID, "IF THE CAR WAS GONE, THE WIDOW MUST HAVE SURVIVED"

"Either her or Trent," Aria said.

"He wouldn't have left without her," Dakini said.

"Probably not," Aria admitted. "If she was hurt, maybe he threw her into the car and drove her to the hospital."

"Or maybe they just ran," Ninety-Nine said. "They may have wanted to escape before anyone found out the Widow had set off the whole mess."

"She did so unwittingly," Dakini said. "Why would she run?"

"Maybe she worried no one would believe she wasn't involved," Ninety-Nine said. "Or she didn't want to damage her family's reputation by telling what her sister had done."

I said, "Maybe Elaine had something to do with the Widow leaving."

"Why do you say that?" Ninety-Nine asked.

"Elaine was sitting right there when the Widow pressed the button. And Elaine knew what was coming. If the Widow was supposed to die but didn't, what would Elaine have done?"

"Finish her off?" Ninety-Nine suggested. "Maybe that's why Elaine was there in the first place: to whack the Widow if the gizmo didn't. Tie up loose ends."

I shook my head. "Killing someone up close and personal has all kinds of mystical consequences. For one thing, it creates a connection that skilled sorcerers can trace. A wizard can try to cover the traces, but then it becomes a contest: who's stronger and smarter, the tracer or the tracee. Elaine is good at magic, but is she good enough to beat the Dark Guard at one of their specialties? She wouldn't take the risk if she could avoid it."

"So what do you think she did?" Aria asked.

"The Widow had been drained. She was weakened, maybe unconscious. Being a vampire, Elaine would be plenty strong enough to carry the Widow to a fire escape and leave the building. In all the confusion, she'd just seem like someone taking a wounded friend to safety. Then off to the car and away."

"What about Trent?" Ninety-Nine asked. "He was the Widow's bodyguard. He had to be somewhere close by. When the shit hit the fan, he would have rushed to the Widow's side."

"Even if he did," Aria said, "so what? Elaine would just say, 'Let's get the Widow out before anything else happens.' Any decent bodyguard would say, 'Hell, yes.'"

"Where would they go?" Dakini asked.

Nobody answered. I thought, *Maybe Lake Huron*. But I didn't believe it.

OUR GLUM SILENCE WAS BROKEN BY THE WORST SOUND IN THE WORLD
"I'd Come for You" by Nickelback.

Aria, Ninety-Nine, and I cringed. We knew the ringtone well.

Dakini smiled. "My sweet is finally awake." She calmly got out her phone while the rest of us tried not to kill her in front of Pox.

DAKINI SAID, "HELLO, SWEET."
Pause.

"I had to go out for a while."

Pause.

"No, you should go home. I don't know when I'll be back."

Pause.

"It's in the parking lot right behind the house. The keys are on my dresser."

Pause.

And.

Because Dakini was psionically attuned to the energy flows of the universe (which allowed her to make serendipitous discoveries, even in the midst of chaos, or a lame phone call from her boyfriend), she said, "By the way, sweet, have you ever heard of an engineering professor named Adam Popigai?"

Pause.

"Really?"

Pause.

"Really?"

Pause. By that point, Ninety-Nine and I were covering Aria's mouth with our hands to prevent her from blasting Dakini into foie gras.

"How interesting," Dakini said.

Pause.

"No, his name just came up in conversation. You go home. We'll talk in the morning. Bye-eee."

With maddening composure, she tucked the phone back into her costume. Even with Spark-o-Vision, I couldn't see where she put it—as if time and space suffered a momentary stutter. In literally no time at all, the phone wasn't anywhere in sight; it had gone to wherever people in Highlander movies hide their swords.

Ninety-Nine and I dropped our hands from Aria's mouth. Aria's eyes blazed. "What's this about Popigai?"

Dakini looked smug. "Remember what my sweet said about that surplus equipment we were supposed to carry? His supervisor tried to throw it out earlier in the day, but the e-waste drop-off area was full."

"Popigai," Aria, Ninety-Nine, and I said in unison.

"Yes," Dakini said. "Apparently my sweet's supervisor ranted at great length about a self-important professor who thought he could monopolize university facilities."

"So you're saying," Aria said, "that Popigai left a shitload of electronic equipment in the university's disposal area?"

"Yes."

Aria whipped toward Ninety-Nine. "Where would things go from there?"

Ninety-Nine glowed green. "To the regional dump. It's not just a landfill these days; it has complete recycling facilities for paper, plastic, e-waste . . ."

"Damn, Diamond is sneaky," Aria said.

"He covered his tracks beautifully," I agreed. "By now, the Dark Guard will be all over this: computer records and phone traces, scrying, clairvoyance, retro-cognition . . ."

"And none of that will turn up anything," Aria said. "Popigai shipped a ton of equipment to the landfill without ever going there himself. He didn't even leave a paper trail. He just dumped the stuff and let university services do the work. Investigators would never connect the dots. Not in the short amount of time before Popigai uses the equipment to do something mega-death-y."

I nodded. This plan made more sense than crashing some ritual more than a hundred kilometers away. It was also easier for us to check. The dump was on the outskirts of town; Aria could get us there in a minute. If we didn't find anything, at least we wouldn't end up far away and feeling like idiots for having been tricked.

But this felt like the real deal, even if it had been handed to us by an epic coincidence.

LET'S TALK ABOUT COINCIDENCE FOR A MOMENT

Sparks are creatures of drama and wish fulfillment. We're Victor Frankenstein creating new life even though he knew nothing of how biology actually worked. We're ridiculously beneficial mutations, as opposed to the 99.9 percent of mutations that are either negative or give you a slightly more efficient pancreas. We're the last-of-their-kind aliens, the experiments that only worked once, the billionaires who rejected the Dark Invitation and instead used their fortunes to Fight Crime.

Every species has an ecological niche. A Spark's niche is coincidence. We inhale luck and exhale unintended consequences. We're born in fluke accidents, die in dramatic irony, and come back to life at the precise moment it will have maximum impact.

So don't worry about that perfectly timed call from Richard. If you accept that I can shrink in defiance of every conventional law of physics, you should also accept that wild coincidences fall into our laps in defiance of sane expectations.

Besides, any lucky break a Spark receives is balanced by a steaming pile of disaster. Call it the Second Law of the Dark and Light: For every stroke of luck, there is an equal and opposite reaction.

Or as Jools says, "BOHICA."

Bend over, here it comes again.

Deformation

TO THE DUMP, TO THE DUMP, TO THE DUMP DUMP DUMP

Pox stayed behind at Red Pine Villa. He was too injured to venture into danger, and anyway, we didn't trust him enough to bring along. On top of that, the Dark Guard would show up at the Villa sooner or later; if Pox was there, he could tell them where we'd gone. Aria huffed and puffed about that, but I told her (a) we ought to welcome help from the Dark Guard because they wanted to stop Diamond from causing death and destruction, and (b) we couldn't stop them from getting the truth out of Pox even if we wanted him to keep silent.

Now that we were Sparks, we had to expect occasional "encounters" with the Dark Guard. We may as well start out on a cooperative footing. Besides, when we were facing off against one of the world's worst supervillains, we could use all the cannon fodder we could get.

STANDARD OPERATING PROCEDURES

Aria flew us from Red Pine Villa to a hill opposite gate number one of the dump. From there, I attempted reconnaissance.

It wasn't easy. First, I was hampered by the snow. It came down thickly, like the chaff used by planes to confuse radar. I wished I could place my viewpoint high in the sky and get an overview of the site, but I couldn't—wherever I centered my Spark-o-Vision, it couldn't see more than a couple of paces before the whiteness became impenetrable.

Second, the landfill was huge. On our way from Red Pine Villa, Ninety-Nine had regaled us with a quick infodump. (See what I did there?) I therefore knew that this was the only waste-management site in the entire Regional Municipality of Waterloo. It served half a million people and included a lot more than just heaps of trash. It had a center for recycling, facilities for producing compost, places for dealing with several types of toxic waste, and a generating station that burned gas from rotting garbage in order to produce electricity. According to Ninety-Nine, the station generated enough power to service six thousand homes.

But from where we were on the hill, almost all of the station was out of sight. I couldn't even see the actual garbage. The mounds were just too far away for Spark-o-Vision to perceive, especially with the snow. The landfill site was bigger than the university campus, with multiple entrances, more than a dozen buildings, and a network of internal roads.

But at least I found the e-waste disposal. The gate closest to us had a sign saying ENTER HERE FOR ELECTRONIC WASTE DROP-OFF. Additional signs appeared at intervals along the roadway, eventually leading to a prefab building labeled ELECTRONICS DISPOSAL.

For once, there was no blinder wall blocking my view. However, there still wasn't much to see. The building's door opened into a small receiving area. Behind that was open space holding assorted bins of computers, televisions, microwave ovens, etc. The back of the building had a large loading door where new drop-offs arrived and where filled-up bins were sent to other sites. Electronic junk sat near the door, presumably waiting to be sorted, but none of it looked like Cape Tech. Diamond must have already picked up his stuff and taken it elsewhere.

Did he have a truck to transport his equipment? I looked outside the loading door but couldn't see tire tracks—the snow had covered any marks that might have been there. I moved my viewpoint, looking for tracks on other roadways; I found a barely discernible trail from gate number one leading into the back of the complex.

«Got something,» I told the others. *«Someone drove through the gate recently enough for the tracks to be visible.»*

«Then we follow,» Aria said, rising into the air.

WE TRACKED THE TRACKS ALONG A TWISTING TRACK

I had to admire the skill of whoever had driven the vehicle. Following the dump site's winding roads was difficult enough (in the dark, in the snow), but driving the route without getting trapped in a snowdrift was practically a miracle. On top of that, few of the landfill's roads were actually paved. Most were just temporary, made of packed earth, and changing as the dump itself changed.

Over time, the trash heaps moved like glaciers of garbage, slowly advancing. The roads had to move in synchrony, modified by the same bulldozers that plowed through the garbage and covered it with topsoil. The edges of the ever-changing roads were marked with red plastic light-reflectors mounted on steel rods and jammed into the dirt, but the roads themselves were invisible under the snow.

Aria's voice sounded in my head. *«Are you sure we're going the right way?»*

«I can still see the tracks,» I told her. I didn't mention that they were barely visible. In another ten minutes, they'd be hidden completely by new-fallen snow.

«I can't see a thing,» Aria said. *«None of the lights are on.»*

I hadn't noticed: Spark-o-Vision. But I had seen that the landfill had security lights on the buildings, and streetlights lining the few roads that were paved and permanent. I'd just assumed that the lights were still shining. If they were out . . .

I said, *«This is a promising sign. Diamond is likely here, and cut the lights so no one would see what he's up to.»*

«Either that,» Ninety-Nine said, *«or the snow just took down some power lines.»*

«No, there's definitely something afoot,» Dakini said. *«Local wildlife are upset. I can feel them.»*

«Ugh,» said Aria. *«You mean rats, don't you. Nasty little beasts that live on garbage.»*

«Not as many rats as you might think,» Dakini said, *«because of all the predators that eat the rats. There's a forest on the property that's full of hawks and owls. Even a pair of eagles. I can also sense coyotes, skunks, raccoons, and feral cats. But most of all, I sense gulls. Many,*

many gulls, with loud squawky thoughts, even though they ought to be sleeping.»

«Can you find the center of the disturbance?» Ninety-Nine asked. *«That's likely where we'll find Diamond.»*

«Yes, by all means,» Aria said, *«let's head toward the greatest mass of agitated vermin.»* Under her breath she muttered, "I know it'll mostly be rats."

«You can't be afraid of rats,» Ninety-Nine said. *«You have a force field. And a sonic blast that can turn rats into pâté.»*

«I'm not afraid of rats, I just don't like them,» Aria said.

I sympathized. I could imagine being eaten by a rat when I was shrunk small enough to swallow. I'd be as hard as a rock, so being eaten wouldn't actually hurt, but once you're inside a rat's digestive tract, there's no good way for the story to end.

«CAR AHEAD,» ARIA SAID

«How do you know?» I asked. I hadn't seen anything.

«Picked it up on sonar,» Aria replied. *«Since I can't see for shit, I've been pinging.»*

I shifted my viewpoint far forward and found the car quickly enough. It was a familiar black Lexus. It had hit a patch of deeper-than-expected snow and gotten stuck. I reported this to the others and added, *«There's nobody inside, but I see footprints in the snow. Three sets: driver, front passenger, and someone who was riding in back.»*

Aria said, *«So, the Widow, her driver, and who?»*

«Land by the car,» Dakini said. *«Let's see what we can sense.»*

We landed. Dakini sniffed, Aria listened, and Ninety-Nine used the light from her phone to examine the tracks in the snow. I remained where I was in Aria's hair; I could see just fine from my perch, and I didn't have to worry about getting buried in drifts that were hundreds of times my current height.

After a few seconds, Dakini said in a low voice, "I can smell the third person's scent, but it's unfamiliar."

"Could it be Elaine Vandermeer?" Ninety-Nine asked.

«That makes sense,» I said. *«The Widow would only come here if she*

knew something would be happening. Who else but Elaine knew Diamond would be here?»

Now that I thought about it, who else but Elaine could guide the car along these twisty, unseen roads? Neither the Widow nor her driver would know the landfill's layout, but if Diamond had picked this site for his grand finale, Elaine would surely have gotten a map and memorized every detail.

"Where do you think they're going?" Aria asked.

"The generator station," Ninety-Nine answered immediately. "That's where Diamond will be."

Aria smacked her head. "Of course! It gives him a power source."

"An *uninterruptable* power source," Ninety-Nine said. "If he plugged into the normal grid, we could disconnect him by cutting some wires, or at worst, demolishing a transformer. But these generators run on methane from rotting garbage. The garbage will keep rotting for decades. That gives Diamond a serious number of kilowatts to play with."

"Crap," Aria said. "There's nothing I hate more than a supervillain who plans ahead."

"What about rats?" Ninety-Nine asked.

"You can shut up now," Aria replied.

WE BEGAN FOLLOWING THE FOOTPRINTS

Of course, I could do that much faster with my Spark-o-Vision. While my teammates slogged through the snow—or rather while Ninety-Nine slogged, and Dakini and Aria flew beside her, just high enough to clear the drifts—I sent my vision ahead.

As expected, the prints led to a building that had to be the generating station. Now, maybe the words "generating station" make you picture a big shiny place with turbines and Three Mile Island–like cooling stacks. Wrong. This one looked like a prefab cattle barn with aluminum siding.

It was the same size and shape as a barn—two stories tall, and longer than it was wide. It had six chimney stacks, but just small ones: bare metal pipes on the outside of the building, with fat sheaths of heat-proofing material between the pipes and the siding to prevent the aluminum from being damaged. The bottoms of the pipes connected to chunky blue exhaust fans that must have attached to furnaces inside the building. The walls of the building had many additional heat vents, each of which was pumping hot air out into the night. I could tell because they were making heat-haze ripples. The station was apparently running at full capacity, providing all the power Diamond might need.

The footprints from the Lexus led to a door at the front of the building. I shifted my vision inside . . .

. . . and immediately wanted to kill myself.

Literally.

THERE WAS NOTHING SUBTLE ABOUT IT

With Ignorance spells and the Bride's "happiness is winning" dream, obfuscation was the name of the game. I wasn't supposed to realize someone was playing with my mind. But this time, the attack made no attempt to disguise itself. A wave of crushing force gripped my brain and said, "Die. Do it now. Do it fast."

I tried to resist, but I didn't have the strength. I don't mean I was too weak. I literally didn't have any type of power I could use as defense.

It made me think of Nicholas in his chair. He told me once about reading an "inspirational" book claiming that people could use mind over matter to achieve anything. "The crippled can walk if only they believe." Nicholas had tried to get out of his chair, and of course, he collapsed. He simply didn't have the neural links to make his legs work.

I didn't have anything that could fight this mental magic. In the moments I was thinking of Nicholas, my hand moved of its own accord and drew the golden dagger from its sheath. At the same time I leapt from my place in Aria's hair and grew to full size, unable to resist the imperative. I didn't stop growing at Maximum Zircon height, but went all the way up to soft-fleshed Kim.

I lifted the blade to my throat. It happened without hesitation—

none of the straining you see in movies, where someone's arm trembles as they try to stop what their arm's going to do. I was absolutely helpless to prevent this.

But no. That wasn't true. All I had to do was overcome a lifetime of being Kimberley/Kimmi/Kim.

As the knife rose with a flash of golden metal, I whispered, "Help."

DAKINI RESPONDED THE FASTEST

Given her ability to smell mental powers, she may have already noticed psychic forces at work. She threw out a violet tendril that grabbed my wrist and stopped it from slashing my jugular. A second later, a violet globe sprang up around my head like a diver's helmet; it blocked the magic compulsion and put me abruptly back in control.

Adrenalin rushed through me, as hot and burning as shame. I started to shake.

"What's wrong?" Ninety-Nine said. She put her hand protectively on my shoulder and looked around, trying to spot threats out in the storm. I doubt if she saw anything; the generating station was only fifty paces away, but normal vision would only have encompassed the ongoing blizzard and the snow-covered road.

Dakini seemed to have senses that went beyond eyesight. She shot out another violet strand, crossing the distance between us and the generating station and stabbing through the building's front door. The door burst open and Dakini yanked the Widow roughly outside.

"WHAT THE HELL?" ARIA SAID

Whether or not she could see what had happened, she could certainly hear it. Her force field snapped into place and she flew forward toward the sound. She stopped in midair about ten meters away from the Widow. Aria's eyes narrowed, likely trying to decide whether to hold her fire or loose a sonic blast.

She opted not to start a fight immediately—probably a wise

choice, because the Widow's driver, Trent, came running out of the building. He thundered through the snow and threw himself between his boss and Aria.

He held a pistol. It wasn't a standard Glock or Walther PPK; it had *unconventional weapon* written all over it. The gun was made from some material so black it seemed like a hole cut out of reality. Even my Spark-o-Vision couldn't focus on it. The pistol was an absence, not a presence. Its silhouette had bumps and protrusions not seen on ordinary firearms. They reminded me of how the sights and stabilizer arms used in modern archery make the bows of today look Frankensteinian.

The pistol had the same Frankensteinian aura. It screamed Cape Tech with Dark magic as an add-on. If Trent pulled the trigger, I didn't know what would come out of the barrel but I'd hate to be the target. Even Aria, with her force field, might not be proof against the gun; it looked like the sort of weapon a Mad Genius might design for those times when he really, really needed to put a hole through damned near anything.

Ninety-Nine came running out of the blizzard. As soon as she saw the gun, she held up her hands and said, "Easy now. Let's not do something we'll all regret."

Trent said nothing. He held the pistol in both hands, rock solid.

WITHOUT THINKING, I'D SHRUNK THE MOMENT I SAW THE GUN

I was now too small to be seen by the naked eye, a particle of zircon clay. Silently, I flapped toward Trent and his pistol. If the situation went pear-shaped, I wanted to be close enough to spoil Trent's aim.

"No reason to get excited," Aria said, putting her hands up too. "I think we're all on the same side."

"She killed my sister," the Widow said, in a voice exactly like the Bride's: violin strings scraped too hard by a rough-handed bow.

"Who did?" Aria asked.

Dakini floated into sight. "I believe she means Zircon," Dakini told Aria. "But our friend wasn't the one responsible," she added, turning toward the Widow. "Your sister was killed by a man named Diamond. He promised her superpowers, but he changed her into a walking time bomb. Zircon happened to set her off, but Diamond was the one who made her die."

"I'll deal with Diamond when I find him," the Widow said. "But your Zircon drove my sister over the edge. I felt everything as it happened. And I can feel Zircon sneaking up on us. If she doesn't keep her distance, Trent will shoot."

I was well off Trent's line of fire, but for all I knew, his gun might be able to shoot Spark-seeking bullets. I stopped advancing.

Still, I had already closed half the gap that separated Trent and the Widow from my teammates. That meant I was near enough to ground zero when all hell broke loose.

BANG, THEN _BOOM_, THEN _SHUDDER_

Aw, hell.

A GIGANTIC RIFT TORE OPEN

It materialized on a patch of snowy ground between the generating station and a hill that was actually a twenty-story-tall mound of garbage. I don't know how old the garbage actually was, but it had been around long enough that the heap was no longer used for collection. Instead, a network of buried pipes ran through it, siphoning off methane and transporting the gas to the generators.

An instant after the rift split the night, a force-dome snapped into existence over the entire generating station. In Spark-o-Vision, the dome was a meter thick and transparent, like glass tinted a faint olive green. I was trapped inside, along with the Widow and Trent. My teammates were outside, and unless I missed my guess, none of their powers would make a dent in Diamond's hard-shell barrier.

The rift had opened outside the dome, but the rift projection machine was inside. To be more specific, the projector was inside the generator building. Diamond had cut a circular hole in the building's aluminum siding. Light from the rift projector shone through the hole, then through the transparent dome in order to keep the rift open.

If the size of the rift was anything to go on, the projector must have been several times larger than previous versions. The rift was as huge as the Eye of Sauron from the Lord of the Rings movies—if not for the blizzard, it would have been visible for miles. The rift was hot too: The instant it tore itself open, it released enough heat to vaporize a gigantic patch of snow. But I didn't have time to see more because Diamond had one trick left.

Ka-zap! Electricity flashed through the dome's interior a moment after we were shut in. It was Diamond's way of sterilizing his bell jar, like a Taser with the amperage of a lightning bolt.

Trent and the Widow collapsed, their clothes smoking. I felt the zap just as hard. It was worse than any electric shock I'd ever experienced. Parts of my costume smoldered, and my cape caught fire. But I maintained enough consciousness to flap my coattails once more, driving myself straight toward the ground.

I PLUNGED INTO THE SNOW

In a heartbeat, the surrounding flakes melted and their water put out the flames from my burning clothes. I lay unmoving in a tiny pit of snow as my head turned cartwheels.

I didn't pass out. I'd been zircon-hard when Diamond's jolt hit me, and maybe that helped a bit. I was also in the air, so I wasn't grounded. Lastly, unlike the Widow and Trent, I was relatively uninjured. The Widow probably had inhuman levels of resilience, but Diamond's trick at the auction had drained most of her energy. All the subsequent explosions had hurt her that much more.

So I doubted that the Widow would wake up anytime soon. For all I knew, she and Trent were both dead. I felt half dead myself, despite my toughness. I lay weak and dizzy, not even able to shift my point of view.

Mostly I just listened. Several times the rift gave deafeningly loud drumbeats. It was growing.

I also heard thumps against the force-dome as my teammates

tried to smash their way in. Negative results. As far as I could tell, I was on my own inside Diamond's endgame.

EVENTUALLY, MY HEAD CLEARED

By then, my partly burned costume had nearly stitched itself back together. Thanks, Goblin.

But when I tried to use my comm ring to talk to my teammates, I got no answer. Either the force-dome blocked the ring's signals, or the electric zap had fried the ring's circuits.

Well, poo.

On the one hand, I was trapped and cut off from my teammates. On the other, maybe I was better off than they were. The rift was on their side of the dome, and I could see what it contained: the were-bat, Mr. Skinless, and Lilith.

Ouch. Those three had been hard enough to fight the first time. When they came out of the rift, they'd have superpowers.

Admittedly, they might blow up as soon as they got hit. But if Diamond had fixed his process, the three Darklings might last long enough to raise unholy hell.

A MOMENT LATER, I SAW SOMETHING ELSE, MAYBE WORSE THAN SUPER-DARKLINGS

Gulls.

A flock of them emerged from the blizzard, approaching from the garbage mounds. There must have been a hundred of them: big white birds with orange beaks and gray or black markings. Dakini had called their thoughts "squawky," but these gulls were utterly silent. Not a whisper as they landed in a circle around the rift; no jostling for position, no fighting, just quietly settling down on the snow.

They were met by a flurry of fireball-bees from the portal. Each bird was immediately surrounded. The multicolored ping-pong balls ghosted in and out of the gulls, the same as the balls had done in the E3 lab. Apparently, the spheres of Sparkhood were just as interested in birds as they were in humans.

More birds arrived: not gulls, but the others Dakini had sensed. Hawks. Owls. Eagles. They landed in perfect silence beside the gulls. No aggression from the raptors, no fear from the gulls, just all of them touching down on the snow, then being enveloped in sparks.

Two raccoons hurried in. Raccoons aren't built for speed, but these ran in the awkward way that their species does when crossing a road. They stopped when they reached the outer ring of the flock of birds. They lay down. Got surrounded by fireballs.

A skunk arrived. Another raccoon. Then rats.

I DON'T KNOW HOW ARIA RESISTED THE URGE TO BLAST THE RAT HORDE
Maybe Dakini did some subtle psychic soothing. The only thing that happened when the rats swarmed in was that Aria flew higher—perhaps high enough that she couldn't see the wildlife through the falling snow.

But ignoring them wasn't an option. My teammates would soon have to decide whether to start a mass slaughter. The little fireballs had to be trying to bestow superpowers on the assembled fauna. Much as one might hate killing innocent creatures, we'd hate even more having to deal with superpowered eagles. I imagined my friends were already using their comm rings to discuss the dilemma.

I felt guiltily glad to be out of it. I could likely find a way to escape the force-dome, if only by shrinking to a subatomic level and squeezing between whatever particles the dome was made of. But I would contribute more by staying inside and dealing with "big-picture" problems: disabling the rift projector and finding out if Diamond had any more ugly surprises up his sleeve.

I HEADED FOR THE DOOR TO THE GENERATOR BUILDING
But before I went inside, I checked on Trent and the Widow. No heartbeats—I looked inside their chests to make sure. With the Widow, the lack of a pulse might not be a problem. Who could tell with Darklings? But with Trent . . .

I truly considered growing to full size and giving him CPR. But my greatest advantage was staying unseen. Diamond might not know

I was inside his dome. Even if he did know, he might think his electric *ka-zap* had taken me out of action.

Trying to save Trent would destroy my advantage. It would also take time, and likely wouldn't even work. When I'd studied first aid, the instructor stressed that CPR failed more often than it succeeded. "But don't beat yourself up," the instructor had said. "You only use CPR on someone whose heart has stopped. Technically, that person has already died. Whatever you do, you won't make them worse."

I decided not to try to make Trent better. I decided to let him stay dead.

AT LEAST I DIDN'T TAKE HIS GUN

I wanted to. Trent's pistol lay on the ground beside him: a scary-awesome weapon that was either Cape Tech, magic, or both. I could definitely use something so badass powerful.

But I left it alone. And not just because I'd have to grow to a visible size in order to pick the gun up.

Letting Trent die was bad enough. Stealing from him was worse. Since I didn't do that, I wasn't a truly awful person, was I?

Terrible logic. But I clutched at it.

I SLIPPED UNDER THE GENERATING STATION'S DOOR

I crawled out into a tiny entrance area. It was just a place to scrape the mud off your boots. But what I saw on the floor wasn't mud; it was Nicholas.

He looked more deadish than ever. His face was more ravaged, and spattered with flecks of rot. His stringy hair had fallen out in patches. The previous times I'd seen him, his clothes had been similar to what he'd worn when he was alive: nice quality, well-maintained. Now, they were rags. If I touched them, they might have disintegrated.

Two things struck me more than anything else. First, his color, gray on gray. He seemed like something snipped out of a black-and-white movie and Photoshopped onto the normally colored world.

Nothing in real life is truly devoid of color; there are always faint reflections from nearby colored objects, and hints of coloration from the light itself. But Nicholas's body simply didn't allow color to touch it. It rejected color completely.

The second thing I noticed was Nicholas's legs. I'd gotten used to him discreetly fading away at the waist. Now, his body went all the way down. He wore no shoes, and his pants were so threadbare, they ended at the knees. That made it easier to see how withered his legs were. They had the emaciated look of a famine victim: literally skin and bones.

By contrast, his arms were normal, actually quite muscular. But the Dark Conversion had given Nicholas the legs he saw in his nightmares. (He'd told me about those nightmares—the most intimate confession he'd ever shared.) For the first time, I was seeing the new Nicholas completely undisguised: changed by the Dark into the thing he'd most feared.

I FLEW DOWN AND LANDED ON HIS FOREHEAD

His flesh was just barely solid. It had the temperature and feel of cold grape jelly. Ectoplasm? Was that what he was in his natural state? He was as gooey as quicksand—his skin surface sucked at my feet. I had to flap hard to take to the air again.

I could see that he wasn't breathing. When I looked inside his chest, I saw a heart but it wasn't beating. So what? Nicholas was a ghost. This wasn't death, it was deathiness, just like truthiness is to truth. Eventually Nicholas would regain consciousness—I was absolutely sure of that. If he were really, truly dead, I'd feel some emotion, wouldn't I? I mean, something more than just being mad at him.

But I had to wonder how he got this way. Unconscious. Burned out.

Drained.

Ah.

Opening a rift required magic. I didn't know how many ways there were to acquire such energy, but Diamond liked draining magical power from unsuspecting Darklings. The extra-large rift that had just opened must have required an extra-large dose of energy, maybe from an extra-powerful Darkling. Sphinx level.

Somehow, Nicholas had gotten suckered. Probably by his sister. She must have laid a trail of bread crumbs that he followed to the station. Perhaps she left telltale hints at Red Pine Villa: things that Nicholas found in her room before I arrived. All the time we'd been talking in that room, Nicholas had known that the real action would happen in Waterloo's landfill. He'd still done his best to send me on a wild goose chase.

Bastard.

A voice in my head said, *He got what he deserved.* The judgment was cold but not unjustified. If Nicholas had asked for my help instead of lying . . .

But asking for help was something Nicholas never did. That was one reason we were simpatico.

Nicholas, I thought, *you've set me such a good example. You're the person I have to stop being.*

I HAD NO IDEA HOW TO HELP NICHOLAS, OR IF THAT WAS EVEN POSSIBLE I left him where he was and headed deeper into the station.

A security door blocked the way forward. It was solid steel, requiring both a keycard swipe and a passcode punched in with numbered buttons. I wondered if those buttons could be booby-trapped. Suppose Elaine had "conveniently" left a passcode in her room. Suppose Nicholas had tried punching the number in. That might have been what drained the magic out of him.

Not that the details mattered. Elaine had tricked him. The specifics were irrelevant.

I crawled under the security door and into a nondescript corridor. To the right was a break room for the station's workers; it held a fridge, microwave, and coffeemaker, plus tables and chairs from IKEA. The left side of the corridor had two washrooms—unlabeled, not gender-specific. My kind of place.

Except one of the washrooms had a dead guy on the floor.

He was dressed in green coveralls. Fortyish. Shockingly pale. His pallor told me all I needed to know, but I checked his throat anyway.

Two puncture wounds on the jugular. It was one of those sights we were never supposed to see—not in movies or on TV because "inflammatory" images were a hate crime, and not in real life because our good and noble Darklings didn't do such heinous things. But the marks were still painfully familiar. I'd seen look-alikes on my arm for months after that night with Elaine. If I rolled up my sleeve, I'd still see the scars.

I was willing to bet that the marks on my arm matched exactly what I saw on the dead man. Made by the same teeth.

"GOOD EVENING! I'M CALLED DIAMOND. WELCOME TO MY GRAND FINALE!"

The words boomed from above my head. Oh crap.

I was already as small as a bacterium, but I shrank by another order of magnitude. Then I zipped to the wall and put my back to it. Even if I could see 360 degrees, it still felt better not to be out in the open.

"Surprised you, didn't I?" Diamond said with a chuckle. The voice didn't come from the corridor. I shifted my viewpoint through the ceiling and saw loudspeakers mounted on the roof.

Sigh of relief: Diamond was speaking to my teammates, not me. He still might not know I was inside the dome.

"Before you go getting ideas," Diamond went on, "this is a prerecorded message. Being a genius, I can do almost anything, but I can't resist a soliloquy. Besides, I have to respect the Third Law of Dark and Light: If you want to break the rules, you need to sell it with a story. Say I want to set off a doomsday device. I can't just push the button; I have to start by making a big brass-balled speech about why what I'm doing will work. Otherwise, everything fizzles. Believe me, I've tried some bloody ingenious stuff in places like Antarctica—no muss, no fuss, just mucking up reality where no one will ever find me.

"It doesn't work. The Light and Dark want drama. Public spectacle.

"On the other hand, I know not to waste my time on oratory when I ought to be . . . oh, committing mass murder, something like that. Whenever I start a speech, there's always some beetle-browed hero who can't be arsed to listen. I say, 'I'm going to blow up the city of—' then boom, the bugger blasts me. His teammates are all, 'Couldn't you have waited one more word?' but for some of these yobbos, it's a point of pride not to let me finish my sentences.

"So now I record everything in advance. It's fun sitting in the studio, blathering on without time pressure. I make sure I cover all the pertinent information, and edit out slips of the tongue. I used to add background music, but I got into copyright trouble. Seriously. I load all my soliloquies onto YouTube once the dust settles, but if I put in soundtracks, BMI and ASCAP get the video yanked. Cheeky bastards. Not coincidentally, BMI and ASCAP are run by Darkling shitheads. (Note to self: Fill their headquarters with anthrax.)"

At the risk of being a yobbo, I didn't wait till the speech had finished. The corridor I was in led up to a fire door: the hefty kind of door you'd put on a place where gas-fired boilers were heating up a storm. The door was well-fitted, with almost no clearance space between the door, its frame, and the floor. That was probably great for shutting in fires, but it meant I had to shrink very small to get under it.

I eased myself down and began belly-crawling. At my current size, I had a long, long way to go—the proportional equivalent of at least a hundred meters. And the floor was a jagged landscape of concrete. To someone of normal height, the surface might have looked smooth, but for me, it was a nightmare of cliffs and craters. My Spark-o-Vision let me chart the easiest route forward, but it was still slow going.

Meanwhile Diamond prattled on. "Now to business," he said. "I'm the world's greatest expert on the Light, which makes me pretty damned clever about the Dark too. You can't truly understand one without the other. As you may have seen, I can give Darklings superpowers, but rest assured, they'll never be more than temporary. The Dark and Light are like matter and antimatter; if you're brilliant, you can bottle them briefly together, but the key word is *briefly*. Then, like matter and antimatter, things go downhill with extreme prejudice.

"Why? Because Darklings are dead. D.E.A.D. Even the ones with a heartbeat. An entity produced by the Dark Conversion may believe it's still alive, but that's a delusion. Darklings have the same brains as the humans who previously occupied their flesh, so their thoughts and memories are similar to the originals. However, for lack of a better word, they've lost their souls. Their stories have ended and they're just too self-absorbed to take the hint.

"So Darklings can never play host to the Light. The Light will only fuse with the living. Any life will do—right now, rats and other vermin should be racing toward my portal, drawn by an urge to merge with the Light. Just be thankful this type of rift can only be opened on winter solstice, when insects aren't active. Otherwise, you'd have mobs of superpowered mosquitoes and horseflies buzzing the countryside.

"But insects will come eventually, drawn out of hibernation. Because the Light calls to life. All life. Including humans.

"Any human within ten klicks will feel driven to embrace the Light. They may resist for a while, but the compulsion will grow. People are likely sleepwalking in this direction already. You might want to deal with that somehow; if not, some of those sods will die of hypothermia. Unless you Canucks can handle the cold as well as you claim. Furthermore, anyone who gets close enough to the portal will become super, at which point, they should be able to withstand the cold even in their nighties.

"Actually, I tell a lie: A lot of them *won't* become super. Believe it or not, there's such a thing as destiny. Some people aren't cut out for greatness, even when it's thrust upon them. My rift is the best chance anyone will have to get supered up, but nine out of ten people just can't handle it. They'll flame out and die deader than Darklings. Sorry about that."

I thought about my own experience of getting powers. I had faced the worst moments in my life. Was it a test of mental strength? If I hadn't been able to change what happened between me and Elaine, would I have died? The Light was ruthless—this I knew. It might subject each potential Spark to an ordeal and kill anyone who didn't pass.

"But," continued Diamond, "let's not dwell on the negative. Most of the rats and other vermin will die too. And my rift may kill ninety percent of the local human population, but there's, what, three hundred thousand people living nearby? So I'll add thirty thousand Sparks to the world.

"And that's just the start. What'll happen once word gets out? Hopeful idiots from all over the world will flood in like a bloody gold rush, each one certain they're special enough to become super. And some will be right! A cracking great lot of Sparks will be injected into the world, until they outnumber all the damned Darklings.

"Then the feces will *really* hit the flabellum, because the Dark and the Light can't coexist. Live and let live is a lovely idea, but that's not how the story goes. Dark versus Light, to the death; anything else is wishful thinking.

"So congrats to any Sparks who might be listening. You're about to get reinforcements in the war. But only if you keep the portal open. If you try to shut it down—and with enough Sparks on the job, I'm sure you'll eventually succeed—then you're closing off a source of useful troops for Armageddon.

"Because trust me, Armageddon is coming. Dark versus Light for all the marbles. If you're smart, you'll walk away and let my portal generate an army. If not, you're siding with the Darklings, however noble your intentions. You really don't want the Dark to win this war. Walk away."

I DIDN'T WALK AWAY

Nor did I think Diamond expected that to happen. If he seriously wanted us to leave his rift alone, he wouldn't have mentioned killing

90 percent of the local populace. Eventually we'd see people dying, but until then, we might have said, "More Sparks . . . what's wrong with that?" The average person on the street could be trusted with superhuman powers at least as much as the people who bought the Dark Conversion.

But Diamond wanted us to know that hundreds of thousands of people would die. He was taunting everyone within earshot: "Stop me or else."

Diamond enjoyed killing. Darklings might be his number-one targets, but humans were in solid second place.

Bastard.

I FINALLY EMERGED INTO THE GENERATOR ROOM

The place divided in two. On one side, six generators produced electricity. They were boilers that heated steam to turn turbines: not fancy, but I'm sure they worked well. Still, they weren't slick-looking machines. They were built to give bang for the buck. The public was never intended to see this equipment, so it looked cheap and off the shelf.

On the other side of the room was a different type of machinery, made to refine raw trash-gas into something that burned more evenly. Pipes came up through the floor, bringing untreated gas from the garbage mounds. After the gas had been processed, more pipes carried it across the aisle to feed the generators.

Close beside the refiner sat steel drums with scary warnings on the side—chemicals used in the refining process. A forklift stood in front of the drums with its lights still blinking. I suspected dead-guy-in-the-washroom had been driving the truck shortly before his encounter with Elaine.

The room held one more machine, smack in the middle of the floor: a rift projector ten times the size of the others I'd seen. All the usual elements were present, except that *this* robot hand was the size of one of those foam hands that people wave at football games, and at least a dozen brains shared an oversized glass jar. Electrical cables snaked out the back, hot-wired into all six generators.

Disconnecting the wires by hand would be dangerous, but why bother? Each generator had an emergency shut-off switch; I could simply grow back to full size and throw the switches. The projector would shut down and the rift would close.

Unless, of course, Diamond had booby-trapped the switches. Which I figured was a no-brainer.

I scanned the room. Nobody in sight. Diamond must have set up his gear and then run off, leaving the projector on a timer or radio-controlled trigger. But no way would he leave his handiwork unguarded. There had to be gun turrets, robots, or something equally dangerous.

I kept looking. Then I stopped and tried to notice where my eyes didn't want to look.

Yep: an Ignorance spell. It was good, strong but subtle. On the other hand, I now had experience in seeing what I wasn't supposed to. I forced my mind to ignore the Ignorance.

Hello, Elaine.

SHE STOOD IN THE MIDDLE OF THE FLOOR, HER BACK AGAINST THE PROJECTOR

Elaine wore loose black clothes, including a hooded cloak. Very "Shadowed Stalker of the Night." Yet another Darkling with Light-envy dressed in a Sparkish costume.

Elaine's creature-of-evil look was enhanced by a dark wet patch down her shirt. It may be possible to drink a man's blood without spilling any on your clothes, but it must take practice. Elaine usually drank from a wineglass or Wedgwood, so she'd made a bloody mess. She likely stank like a slaughterhouse, but I was far enough away not to have smelled it yet.

Elaine's hood was thrown back and I could easily see her face. The skin was surprisingly pale, considering she'd recently consumed all the blood from a full-grown man. But her body was surrounded with an aura glowing in multiple shades of red. After filling herself with blood, she must have used all that juice to envelope herself with spells—probably both offensive and defensive.

This wasn't the same as the Blood Burn that Lilith had used in the alley. Blood Burn was crude, fast, and ruinous, an all-or-nothing tactic. Elaine had used the blood's energy much more strategically, carefully weaving enchantments. Oh yes, she'd be strong, fast, and resilient for as long as the spells lasted, but they'd last much longer, and she wouldn't crash into a coma when they ended. She might even have enough surplus magic to cast additional spells as needed.

So the costume was appropriate. Elaine had abandoned her usual buttoned-down guise and had transformed herself into a full-on vampire sorceress, ready to wipe the floor with any opposition.

No matter how small I shrank, I likely couldn't get near her. Some part of her scarlet aura would surely be a force field I couldn't penetrate. She might also have a spell to sense my presence. Since Elaine was expecting trouble, she had likely cast something to sniff out hidden enemies. She might already know I was in the room. If not, I didn't want to give myself away by getting too close.

But nothing I saw answered the jackpot question: What was Elaine doing here? Was she supporting Diamond's scheme to make thousands of Sparks? Waiting to fight any Sparks or Dark Guards who managed to get inside the dome? That was crazy. What did she have to gain from a brazen last stand that would end in her being captured or killed?

It made no sense. Even if Elaine were an Unbound fanatic eager to overthrow the Dark establishment, why would she help Diamond create a Spark army?

Was she insane? Mind-controlled? Or was I missing something?

I DECIDED TO ASK HER

I know. It violates the traditional Spark approach to solving problems. I should have escalated straight to violence.

And I'll admit, part of me longed to give Elaine a good hard shake. Maybe slap her face.

But my mere human strength wouldn't hurt her. Besides, hurting Elaine wouldn't make me feel better. I didn't want an eye for an eye, I just wanted to hear her say she was sorry for what she'd done to Kimmi. To me.

And I wanted her to mean it.

That wasn't going to happen, not even under the influence of my Halo. In our world, impossible things happen every second. But other things don't. Even wish fulfillment has its limits. The best I could do was prove to myself I was a better person than she was.

So I grew to Max Zirc size and said, "Elaine, we have to talk."

I WAS READY TO BE ATTACKED

I was also prepared to shrink and jump if Elaine blasted me with fire, ice, lightning, or worse. (Elaine once told Kimmi, "Here are all the ways I could kill you in the next two seconds." That was Elaine's idea of making chitchat with mortals.)

No attack came. She said, "I was wondering when you'd stop hiding. Who are you?"

"Zircon."

"Oh, darling, rethink that name."

"No."

Elaine shrugged. "Only trying to help. What did you want to talk about?"

"What you're doing here. Why you're helping Diamond."

"You think I'm helping him?"

"You tricked your brother into coming here, then drained his energy to open Diamond's portal. That sounds like helping to me."

"My, you *are* well informed." She tried to say it breezily, but looked unsettled.

"What I don't know," I said, "is why you're doing this. What do you get out of it?"

"Freedom," she said. "From the status quo. The Dark Consensus."

I said, "I thought the Dark Consensus was a Taboo Truth."

"Taboos were made to be broken."

As taboos go, speaking of the Dark Consensus was pretty tame. Still, Darklings were never supposed to utter the phrase, even in whispers. The Dark Consensus didn't exist—not at all. The

Darklings who ran one country absolutely didn't conspire with the Darklings who ran other places in the world. Canada was run by Darklings, the US was run by Darklings, China was run by Darklings, Russia was run by Darklings, and so on down to even Haiti and Burkina Faso, but heaven forbid that anyone suggest there was a global master plan. Each country's leadership focused faithfully on their own nation's interests. There was no Consensus: nope, nope, nope.

"So you're rebelling," I said. "Becoming Unbound for the good of the world."

"Yes."

I knew she was lying.

I. Knew.

As if her thoughts were slopping over into mine.

WAS ELAINE DELIBERATELY PROJECTING IDEAS INTO MY HEAD? She could do that if she wanted, with the right kind of spell.

And maybe she had good reason to say one thing but communicate another—if she wanted to hide the truth from somebody watching.

Of course! Diamond *had* to be watching. I felt stupid for not realizing. Diamond would plant cameras here in the generating station to watch whatever happened. He was spying on Elaine, and she was pretending to be a loyal coconspirator.

What was she really?

Dark Guard.

That was another mental spillover. Knowledge that sprang into my mind as soon as I asked the question.

Elaine belonged to the Guard. She'd been assigned to take Diamond down.

Now *that* made sense. Elaine was a talented wizard with impeccable self-control. She'd make an excellent Guard recruit. And Diamond had killed so many Darklings, of *course* the Guard would go after him.

Elaine was a covert agent pretending to be a rebel. Somehow

she'd ingratiated herself with Diamond and infiltrated his scheme. As soon as she found an opening, she would move to destroy him. In the meantime, she played a fanatic, ruthless enough to sacrifice her own brother.

Well, shit. In the "enemy of my enemy" sense, Elaine was one of the good guys.

HER EYES WIDENED, THEN NARROWED

One of the good guys? Not so fast.

"You're *reading* me?" she said. Her face turned even more pale as she summoned her blood to cast a spell. "You're—"

She stopped. Then broke out laughing. "Oh, perfect! You're one of *mine*."

I opened my mouth to ask a question, but she made a gesture and I froze. Not from fear—from the force of some magic that had abruptly paralyzed my muscles.

"You're one of my minions," she said, still chuckling. "One of my crumbs cast upon the waters. We share blood, you and I."

Oh crap.

"Do you know how vampires acquire blood?" Elaine walked slowly toward me. "Of course you know: We buy it. From donors who willingly bleed in exchange for the trickle-down. Our donation centers are run like the Red Cross. Except we pay, and the Red Cross doesn't."

She smiled. Her teeth thrust out in a gleeful fang-on. "One more difference: The Red Cross keeps each donation separate, but Darklings mix them together. We throw ten donations into a pot, stir well, then parcel them out again. Do you know why?"

Elaine waited for me to answer. I couldn't. She smiled more broadly.

"We mix them in batches of ten," she said, "because that gives us blood bonds with all ten of those people. We did experiments—too little blood and the bond doesn't work, but one tenth of a liter will do. Every time I feed, I gain a perfectly legal blood bond over ten complete strangers. Isn't that fabulous? All those teens desperate to buy the right lipstick . . . university students sick of Kraft dinners, who just *have* to have a good restaurant meal . . . single mothers who can't afford diapers . . . elderly cat ladies running out of Whiskas . . . the drunks, the street kids, the long-term unemployed . . . every greedy damned taker who wants a free lunch rather than work for a living. They snatch a quick buck from the trickle-down, then think they can walk away with no strings attached. Ha! I can drive down any street and feel the blood connections: 'He's mine, she's mine, all four of them are mine.' If I snapped my fingers, they'd throw themselves at my feet."

She lifted her hand and rubbed her fingers together teasingly. But she didn't actually make her fingers snap. If she had, I don't know what I would have done.

"Blood calls to blood," Elaine said, "and my blood is stronger than yours. As simple as that. A Spark like you normally has a high degree of resistance to vampiric influence. Say I used the Voice on you: Maybe it would work, maybe it wouldn't. But you willingly gave me your blood before you became a Spark. That wasn't a one-time purchase—you sold me an option on your future. Now I'm going to exercise that option to the fullest."

She had finally reached me. She brushed my cheek with her hand. I wanted to flinch away, but I couldn't. In my head, I heard her voice: *«Pretend to resist me. You can't, but pretend. Diamond will just think your mind is stronger than I thought.»* She leaned in, mouth aiming for my throat. *«Break away and destroy the generators,»* Elaine said inside my brain. *«Never tell anyone I work for the Guard.»*

Her cold lips touched my skin, then I felt the tips of her fangs. Inside my head, she said, *«Do it!»*

I did.

TO DIAMOND'S CAMERAS, IT MUST HAVE LOOKED LIKE I HAD SUMMONED SOME HEROIC LAST-MOMENT RESISTANCE TO BEING BITTEN

I shriveled from Elaine's grasp like a deflating balloon, vanishing to the size of dust. I was immediately caught on an updraft caused by the heat of the generators. I took advantage of it and flapped toward the ceiling.

Elaine yelled, "Get back here!" but mentally sent, *«Ignore what I'll be saying. You have your orders.»* No doubt she would put on a song and dance for Diamond's benefit, making a show of attempting to control me. But that was just maintaining her cover. She'd pretend to be trying to break me, but I was already broken.

The hell of it was that if I tried to defy Elaine, I'd only make things worse. I *wanted* to destroy the generators, and the sooner the better. I wanted to close the rift before Lilith and the others emerged; before innocent people died and birds of prey got superpowers.

But if I obeyed Elaine's orders, resisting would be harder the next time. Compliance strengthened her hold on me. If I didn't fight now, it would be like accepting captivity. Slippery slopes, and all that.

HOW TO RESIST?

I yearned to attack Elaine. Even if I just kicked her in the shin, it would have symbolic weight. With magic, symbolism mattered.

Too bad that she was so shielded, my foot would bounce off her like kicking a boulder. If I could actually hurt her, that would be better, both symbolically and for bolstering my mental defiance. The major question was if I had anything that could touch her.

When in doubt, ask an expert. I drew my bronze dagger.

THE DAGGER HAD CHANGED

Its plain bone hilt was now carved with a pattern of eyes framed by a hexagon grid. The eyes were all the same: that stylized Egyptian eye you see in hieroglyphics. The eye with the curlicue beneath. On the knife's bronze blade, the word *Scout* had been engraved in cursive script.

Apparently I had determined the dagger's essence, changing it from *tabula rasa* into what it was now. *«All right, Scout,»* I thought, *«good knife, pretty knife. Show me where Elaine is vulnerable.»*

I took off the glove on my other hand and attempted to prick the same finger as usual. The knife tip balked, deflecting away like a bar magnet when you force it toward the wrong pole of a stronger magnet.

«Come on, Scout, be good.» I tried again. Another deflection, more forceful than the first.

More willful.

Was the knife doing this because of Elaine's blood bond? Was her magic affecting the blade? Or was Scout being finicky about drinking from the same finger? The gold dagger had refused to drink from the same source as the bronze and silver. Maybe now that Scout had a name, it was a prima donna too.

I tried to stab a pristine finger. (This was getting ridiculous.) Nope. Scout turned away like a baby rejecting puréed asparagus.

Damned dagger, I thought. *Damned Elaine. Damned blood bond.*

I tried once more, this time aiming the knife tip at the juicy pad of flesh on my palm just below my thumb. If Scout refused to drink from such an enticing piece of meat . . .

It sank in. It drank.

It hurt.

WHAT ELSE COULD I EXPECT FROM DARKLING MAGIC?

Supply and demand. Scout knew it was needed, so it had upped its asking price. I foresaw escalation from all three knives: Each time I asked for their help, I'd have to cut deeper in some spot that hurt me more. How long before I had to hack off a finger, or worse?

I'd worry about that later. I told the knife, *«Just show me Elaine's greatest vulnerability.»*

Copper light shone from Scout's tip. The beam wove erratically over Elaine, crisscrossing her body, back and forth, up and down. Then it zipped clean away and across the room. It stopped on the machine that refined swampy trash-gas into powerful methane.

Sigh.

I didn't doubt the knife was highlighting the greatest point of weakness. The coppery dot lay on the seam of a pipe fitting—likely where the seal was a tiny bit less than perfect. If I rammed a dagger into that spot, flammable gas would gush out at high pressure. One spark and the gas would ignite. The explosion would shred other pipes and release more gas, until, with a great fireball, all of the building's generators would blow themselves apart.

Yes, fine, that was my primary mission. But first, I wanted to attack Elaine!

Scout practically laughed at me. Did I want to try again? Stab myself in an even more damaging place? How sure was I that a second try would have different results? Maybe I myself was the reason Scout hadn't targeted Elaine. Maybe beneath the level of consciousness, I couldn't hurt my "master." Instead, I'd obeyed her command: I'd found a way to destroy the generators.

To hell with it. I wasn't going to skewer myself in ever worsening places just because I didn't like the initial answer.

Besides, if I torched the generators, maybe Elaine would fry too.

I DREW THE SILVER DAGGER

It too had changed. The bone hilt showed a hexagonal grid similar to the bronze dagger's. Each hexagon held another Egyptian hieroglyph, but this time, the hieroglyph was a bird of prey. Inscribed on the silver blade was the word *Falcon*.

That fit. The silver dagger could fly on its own and attack.

Optimistically, I poked Falcon at one of my unbloodied fingers. The knife refused, just like Scout. I wondered if Falcon would demand to drink from a different place than Scout; but when I pressed Falcon's tip to the same pad of thumb-muscle, the silver blade drank deep.

Note to self: Falcon was a follower. Or maybe it had a crush on its bronze companion. Hmm. Either way, Falcon took the blood bribe and vibrated in my hand.

I took aim at the weak spot marked by Scout's beam. My Spark-o-Vision changed to laser sights, zooming in. I was about to throw when I realized I was still as small as dust.

Crap.

Falcon would be much too tiny to damage a metal pipe. Even if the dagger rammed all the way up to its hilt, it wouldn't penetrate more than a nanometer.

Crap, crap, crap. I didn't want to grow to appreciable size. Elaine was still putting on a show of casting spells, demanding obedience, and all that BS. She didn't know where I was (or at least, that's what she pretended), but if I became visible, she'd be forced to attack me with magic. That wouldn't be good.

"Okay, Falcon," I said aloud, although I couldn't hear my own voice. "When anything leaves my omnimorphic field, I can choose whether it stays small or returns to its true size. This time I choose that you'll grow, Falcon, old buddy, old pal."

I hurled the silver knife with all my strength. It stayed small.

Well, poo.

FALCON FLEW AND HIT ITS TARGET; IT JUST DIDN'T DO MUCH

The knife buried itself exactly where Scout and my laser-sights pointed. However, since Falcon could be measured in angstroms, the pipe wasn't pierced at all.

So much for pseudoscience double-talk about my omnimorphic field. Clearly, the honeymoon was over. The Light wouldn't let me keep inventing new powers for myself. I couldn't complain—I'd already pushed my luck outrageously far. But maybe that sense of overreach was what restricted me. As soon as I'd started thinking I was getting away with too much, I had set my own limit.

I reached out my hand, exerting my will and demanding that Falcon return to me. I felt the knife respond, trying to pull itself out, but it was wedged too tightly. It had spent so much magical energy going in, it didn't have enough left to drag itself free.

Reluctantly, I reached for the golden dagger. These things had to come in threes, didn't they? Two knives would never be enough. Magic demanded a three-act structure: beginning, middle, and end.

Stupid magic. This is why Science kicks magic's butt. You don't have to flick a light switch three times to get the bulb to work.

THE GOLDEN DAGGER HAD ALSO TRANSFORMED

Another hexagonal grid. Another hieroglyphic on the hilt. This time, it was a snake and the blade bore the word *Asp*.

How not-at-all ominous.

I didn't even bother offering Asp a drink from the same place as Scout and Falcon. I rolled up my sleeve and touched the gold blade to the back of my forearm. I just laid it there lightly. I expected Asp to bite me of its own accord, but that was too easy. The knife wanted commitment; it wanted me to actively draw its sharpness across my skin and make blood spurt.

I'm not a cutter. I know people who are, and they've told me that cutting gives them relief. If that's how it works for them, fair enough, but I'm not wired that way myself. The thought of deliberately slicing my arm turned my stomach.

That's likely why Asp demanded it. The knife got off on revulsion.

I pressed and pulled. My blood flowed. The dagger drank.

ASP LIT UP IN MY GRIP, SHINING GOLDLY

It knew what I intended. It was eager to blow shit up.

Elaine's gaze snapped upward and stared directly at me. Either she'd sensed Asp's blaze of power, or the knife radiated so brightly it was visible to the naked eye. That simplified my next move—since Elaine had already spotted me, I didn't need to debate whether to grow.

One moment, I was a dust mote, drifting near the ceiling. The next, I was Max Zirc–size and beginning to fall as I hurled the gold knife toward its target.

Asp flew faster than I fell. I was only being pulled by gravity; Asp had gravity on its side, plus my throwing strength, plus its own magical lust for destruction. It struck with perfect accuracy on the weak spot chosen by Scout, but Falcon was already there.

And Falcon was no longer miniaturized. As soon as I grew, Falcon did too. (That old omnimorphic field!) In fact, Falcon did the best thing possible: Its blade remained in the pipe, penetrating deeper as it grew.

Asp rammed into Falcon like a hammer hitting a nail. Falcon ruptured the pipe and released the gas within, under such high pressure that it burst outward with a whistling scream. Asp blazed even more brightly, blossoming with golden radiance, making a spark that ignited the gusher of gas.

FIREBALL

I hadn't hit the floor yet, nor did I. The explosion blasted my body straight through the building's wall. Booyah, a win for me. It meant I wasn't at precise ground zero when everything else blew up too.

The generators. The rift projector. Pipes carrying methane and other flammable gases. Those barrels of chemicals used for refining. They went up in a chain reaction, each one setting off its neighbors. *Boom, boom, ba-boom,* with shock waves to match.

Jagged remnants of machinery went flying. I was pelted with hot metal shrapnel. It hurt like flaming darts even if they didn't pierce my rocky skin. *Ow, ow, ow!* Then I hit the ground face-first, hard enough to plunge through the covering layer of snow and grind into gravel beneath.

I lay aching for long, loud moments as fragments of junk whizzed overhead. I hurt, but I wasn't damaged. Which was more than I could say for my costume—it was hanging on by shreds. But at least the melting snow extinguished the parts that were on fire.

WHEN THE BARRAGE OF DEBRIS PETERED OUT, I SHIFTED MY VIEWPOINT INTO THE WRECKAGE TO SEARCH FOR ELAINE

Fire is lethal to vampires. Their dead, dry tissues go up in smoke much faster than those of ordinary mortals. Unless a vampire can extinguish her flames before she lapses into unconsciousness, she'll keep burning until her body is consumed.

But Elaine wasn't anywhere I looked. Nor did I believe she'd been totally cremated—when everything exploded, she'd been shielded by defensive spells. Maybe her shields had ruptured and Elaine got vaporized, but I didn't think so. Darklings and Sparks can certainly die, but more often, they just go missing, only to return at the worst possible moment.

I *did* find Nicholas exactly where I'd left him. He looked unchanged. Since he'd been sprawled in front of that fireproof door, it had protected him from the hot bangy destruction. I still couldn't tell if he was "dead" or "alive" (whatever those mean for a ghost), but he didn't look worse than before.

I decided to consider that a good thing.

THE FORCE-DOME COLLAPSED ABOVE ME

I could tell the exact moment it happened. All the snow that had accumulated on top of the dome plummeted onto me as if someone had dumped a shovelful over my head. Apparently, the dome had been powered by the generators, just like the rift projector. Once the generators were destroyed, the dome had lasted mere seconds before going poof.

As for the rift, it would start shrinking too. Unfortunately, that would take time. It had grown as tall as a skyscraper and cast its lurid brown light across the snowy landscape, all the way to the looming mountains of garbage.

Closer in, corpses littered the ground: birds, rats, and raccoons, slaughtered in front of the rift. My teammates had dealt with the ugly necessity. I was so, so glad I hadn't had to participate, and so grateful they'd done what was needed.

My Spark-o-Vision could see my friends' faces clearly. One reason Sparks wear masks is so nobody knows when you're crying.

I PULLED MYSELF OUT OF THE SNOW AND FLAPPED TOWARD THE OTHERS

I transmitted, *«How's it going?»* trying to sound gentle and soft.

«God-awful,» Ninety-Nine answered. *«How 'bout you?»*

«Comme ci, comme ça,» I said. *«I—»* I stopped. My mind refused to communicate anything about Elaine. Bugger. Whether or not

Elaine was alive, her blood bond was still in effect, preventing me from saying that I'd seen her. *«Things got sticky, but mission accomplished. You heard Diamond's soliloquy about his master plan?»*

«Loud and clear,» Ninety-Nine said. *«But thanks to you, the plan's mostly history. We'll just stand guard until the rift closes. And of course, we'll fight Lilith and the gang, because no way we'll be so lucky that the rift shuts before they wake.»*

«Keep an eye out for Diamond too,» I said. *«He's likely watching from a distance. At the very least, he'll shoot a few missiles at us just to be a dick.»*

«I'm scanning with sonar,» Aria said. *«I'll notice any incoming projectiles.»*

«Unless they move faster than the speed of sound,» Ninety-Nine said. *«Would you like me to explain the physics?»*

«Bite me,» Aria said.

«I'm picking up mental activity inside the rift,» Dakini said. *«The Darklings are waking up.»*

«Can you put them back to sleep?» Ninety-Nine asked. *«Or telepathically tell them not to attack?»*

«I'm attempting to do so,» Dakini replied, *«but it's like blowing into a plugged-up straw. I can't feel anything getting through.»*

"Yo, dudes!" Ninety-Nine yelled aloud. "You Darklings in the hole! I know you want to hit something, but if we go all *Reservoir Dogs* on each other, you'll end up exploding. Chill, and maybe I can find some way to help."

"*You're* going to help them?" Aria asked under her breath.

"Like it or not, I'm the team's Mad Genius," Ninety-Nine replied. She yelled into the rift, "What about it, guys? Play nice and live another day? Cuz seriously, there's nothing to gain from busting heads anymore. If you want a big, pointless fight, let's all go to a sports bar and watch wrestling."

The were-bat leapt to his feet and screamed.

Aria murmured to Ninety-Nine, "I *told* you nobody else likes to watch wrestling."

THE WERE-BAT HURTLED OUT OF THE RIFT, SCATTERING TINY FLAMEBALLS AS HE FLEW

He wasn't as fast as the panther we'd seen in the Market, but the bat was much, much faster than he'd been in the alley. Perhaps as fast as Aria, though I couldn't tell for sure.

And when he screamed, it was serious.

SOUND IS A WAVE; THE BAT'S SCREAM WAS A TSUNAMI

A wall of noise slammed into everything. Snow blasted off the ground; debris rattled in the ruins of the generator building; my teammates were knocked off their feet.

As for teeny-tiny me, I went spinning head over heels like a tick in a tornado. Even after air resistance stopped me, my head kept whirling—the bat's cry had made me dizzy, and not just from tumbling around. My Spark-o-Vision reeled, continuing to gyrate even though my body had stabilized.

The bat's screech wasn't just a sonic blast; it induced vertigo. *Pew double-pew.*

I couldn't make my brain stop loop-the-looping. I saw movement, lots of movement, but couldn't make sense of it. Wobbling streaks of color and blurry light. It took a full five seconds before my Spark-o-Vision righted itself. When it did, I saw Ninety-Nine perched on the were-bat's back, her legs locked around his waist.

Her left arm pressed hard against the bat's throat, reefing in on his windpipe. That explained why the bat hadn't produced any more screams. I couldn't help noticing that Ninety-Nine's position was almost identical to the way she'd been ridden by Skinless in our previous fight. The only difference was that Ninety-Nine didn't have the patience to wait for the were-bat to pass out from lack of air. Instead, she was whaling on the bat's head with her free hand.

Her hand was a bare fist. Either she'd lost her hockey glove or she had deliberately tossed it aside so her hits would have no padding. Weightlifter-strong and boxer-fast, Ninety-Nine punched like

Chuck Norris and Muhammad Ali. Blows like that would break a normal person's bones—Ninety-Nine's own knuckles had to be fractured by now. The bat, however, only seemed angry, not hurt.

Mostly though, it was just berserk.

Like the Darklings in the market, the bat's brain had snapped. His eyes were feral and he frothed at the mouth. Bonding the Light to his Darkness had driven him insane.

Unlike the Darklings in the market, the bat wasn't strobing despite the punches Ninety-Nine was dishing out. Diamond had promised these super-Darklings would fly to pieces, but they sure weren't as fragile as the previous batch.

Damn.

GIVEN TIME, NINETY-NINE MIGHT HAVE PUMMELED THE BAT UNCONSCIOUS

But her opponent could fight back. A bird's wings take the place of arms, but a bat's wings are basically hands with the fingers webbed and extended to ridiculous lengths. For the were-bat in feroform, each "finger" ended in a claw as big as a meat hook. They weren't as dexterous as human hands, but they were good enough to deal damage to anything within its grasp.

The bat reached back and raked its claws across Ninety-Nine's head. She pressed her face into the bat's fur to protect her eyes, and her helmet offered a measure of defense. Still, the helmet was designed to deflect hockey pucks, not sharp, lethal attacks. One of the bat's claws stabbed through the helmet's fiberglass and into Ninety-Nine's scalp, making a deep, bloody divot.

Even worse, inside the rift, the strangler demon lurched to his feet. The fireball-bees of the Light shied away from Old Skinless—something they'd never done before. The demon wobbled forward, then shuddered as if hit by a seizure. He managed to stop himself from falling and wobbled forward again, only to be wracked by another spasm. This one was stronger than the first: so ferocious, his fleshless skull rocked wildly, as if it might come off his neck.

Then the skull *did* come off.

As did the demon's right arm.

And his left.

Within seconds, his entire skeleton had shaken into individual bones: a whirling cloud like an osseous dust devil, a tornado of knuckles, ribs, and vertebrae. They clacked against each other like castanets in a gale.

The skull remained at the top. It produced a familiar cackle that made my flesh crawl—a visceral revulsion beyond normal fear. I grimaced and rolled my eyes. This was another mind-fucking mental power, chilling my brain and making me want to run. At the same time, my muscles would barely move, clenched too tight to let me get the hell out of there.

Aria had better luck resisting the effect, possibly because she'd surrounded herself with her force field at the first sign of trouble. As Bone-Tornado Skinless emerged from the rift, Aria delivered a sound blast at point-blank range. It shot from her mouth in a cone of golden force that encompassed the entire bone cloud. Individual bones shuddered under the impact, but most of the golden energy passed through, blowing harmlessly in and out of the cloud.

The demon continued to cackle. He aimed himself toward Aria and gusted straight toward her at top speed. Within a fraction of a second, the cloud enveloped her. Bones clattered on her force field, 206 high-velocity projectiles trying to break her defenses.

I wanted to help, but how? If I tried to get close to the bone tornado, its wind would drive me back. Even if somehow I got inside the vortex, what could I attack? This time, I couldn't pull a tooth—the teeth were already detached into thirty-two biting bullets. And within that bone barrage, how long would my stone skin protect me?

«Dakini,» I transmitted, *«hit Skinless with something psionic. I'll try to help Ninety-Nine.»*

AS I FLEW TOWARD NINETY-NINE, THE WERE-BAT LOOSED ANOTHER SCREAM

Ninety-Nine was apparently weakening. Her arm on the were-bat's throat was no longer strong enough to choke off his screeches. Once more my senses reeled. I tried to keep flying forward but felt cold wetness a moment later as I plunged to the ground and into the snow. I had no choice but to stay where I was until my perception cleared.

Before that happened, the bat screamed again.

And again.

«Sober up!» said a voice in my head. *«I mean it. You're making me sick.»*

As if things couldn't get worse, Elaine was back.

BAD NEWS, GOOD NEWS

The bad: Elaine was still alive and could still speak to my blood.

The good: My dizziness was contagious through the bond.

Take that, mistress bloodsucker. I hope you puke.

Elaine could surely have shut down the mental connection if she wanted. Considering what she'd told me, she must have thousands of minions, and at any given time, some would be sick, some in pain, and so on. Elaine couldn't possibly handle such a distracting mental barrage. More likely, she could establish a small number of active connections and ignore the rest.

But she wanted to keep her hold on me. That meant she inherited my nausea.

Unless she used magic to fix it.

My vision went crimson for a throbbing moment: like when you're asleep and your mother suddenly turns on the lights and you squeeze your eyes shut but the horrible blinding shine still burns through your eyelids. Then my senses clicked back into perfect focus and Elaine shouted in my brain, *«Wake up and kill that fucking bat before my antinausea spell wears off!»*

I FELT INFINITELY BETTER

Except about the prospect of killing the bat.

Yes, according to Diamond, the bat would die soon. Was it really so bad if I hastened the inevitable by a few minutes?

But that question had become irrelevant. If I murdered the bat now, I'd be following Elaine's orders. No, no, a thousand times no. I wouldn't become her mind-controlled assassin, even if I actually might have whacked the guy on my own.

On the other hand, my *no, no, no* might not matter. I was already moving forward. Part of my mind was weighing my options: whether to fly into the bat's pointy ears or up his ugly flattened nose. Once I was inside, I could stay in his skull and rupture his brain, or head down into his chest and burst his heart. Either way, if I grew from the size of a microbe into my usual four-foot-ten, I would pulp so much of his innards, the bat would be dead before he could blink.

I didn't want to do either, but Elaine-infected blood pounded in my ears, demanding obedience.

Surrendering would make everything easy. I wouldn't even have to take responsibility; I could blame it all on Elaine. And I'd have to give in eventually; mental resistance wasn't one of my powers. No shame to concede a fight I couldn't win. Save the effort, save the pain, and just accept the inevitable.

If it had been anyone other than Elaine, I might not have fought so hard. I wouldn't have had the depths of emotion bolstering my defiance. But Elaine? I had fought and refought her every day for three years. This was *personal*.

I COULDN'T COMPLETELY REFUSE ELAINE'S COMMAND

This time, I wasn't strong enough to say, "Get fucked, this is over." But I could twist on the hook. I could choose my own method of compliance.

So instead of a cold-blooded instant kill, I flew up to the bat and clobbered him.

THE "FAST-GROW UPPERCUT" TECHNIQUE

I landed on the ground under the bat's nose. Ninety-Nine was holding him relatively still, so I trained my laser sights on a sweet spot under his jaw, made a fist, and held it over my head like raising my hand in class. Then I grew to Max Zirc, ramming the bat's chin with a fist as hard as the Rockies.

The punch hurt me too. It stung my knuckles and sprained my wrist. I'd tried to keep my arm straight, but even when turned to stone, I'm no stronger than usual. I don't know how fast I was actually moving at the moment of contact, but it felt like punching a wall at a hundred kilometers an hour.

Still, it didn't hurt me as much as it hurt the bat. It lifted him off the ground, with Ninety-Nine still clinging to his back. The bat went up in an arcing trajectory, his wings instinctively spreading to slow him down. As soon as he did that, Ninety-Nine slithered around him like a kid climbing monkey bars, using her weight to push his wings back against his sides. By the time the bat began the downward half of his arc, his wings were pinioned and Ninety-Nine was perched on top.

The bat slammed the ground nose-first. Snow padded the impact but not enough. A moment after the face-plant, Mr. Bat finally started to strobe.

"OFF!" I TOLD NINETY-NINE

Before I finished the syllable, she was moving. She could see the strobing as well as I could.

She was lucky she moved fast. The bat made a grab and might have caught her, except that (being who she was) she'd done a flamboyant backflip dismount just to show off.

Almost without thinking, I threw myself onto the bat. I could do that—I was still Max Zirc size. And the bat might be strobing, but he wasn't unconscious. If I didn't keep him busy, he'd go after Ninety-Nine again.

Ninety-Nine may have possessed tremendous powers of healing, but there had to be a limit. If she was wrestling with the bat when he exploded, she might be blasted to shreds. If I was the one who was wrestling, I'd be hit hard too, but in zircon-form I had a better chance of surviving than Ninety-Nine's human flesh.

The bat had no intention of going quietly. With yet another scream, he heaved himself off the ground. I was lying right on top of him, but he lifted full-size me as if I weighed no more than a snowflake. I tried to shift into the piggyback position that Ninety-Nine had used, but I didn't have her dexterity. I'd barely begun to move when the bat grabbed me in a bear hug and tried to sink his teeth through my rocky skin.

«*WHAT ARE YOU DOING?*» ELAINE SNAPPED INSIDE MY HEAD; «*JUST SHRINK AND GET AWAY!*»
I didn't answer.

«Shrink!» Elaine snapped again. *«He might be strong enough to bite through your skin. And when he explodes . . . »*

I tried to shut out her voice. The bat made that easier—it's hard to hear someone kibitzing when a huge damned monster is gnawing on your throat.

«Shrink, damn it!»

Red light flashed, and I shrank a few centimeters before I could stop myself. Elaine had somehow amplified the influence of her blood bond. But if I shrank from the bat's grip, he'd grab Ninety-Nine, still standing right by my side.

I yelled at Ninety-Nine, "Back off before he explodes." She didn't budge. Belatedly, I realized she was staring at my face as if trying to see something. My eyes were completely covered by my mask, but she was silently trying to make some sort of connection.

Then I got it. She could hear Elaine inside my head. My comm ring must have been transmitting Elaine's blood-bond voice. Every command echoed from my brain to Ninety-Nine's. Ninety-Nine had no idea who was trying to give me orders, but she was asking what I wanted her to do.

I mouthed the words, "Help me."

Then the were-bat hurled me onto the ground.

THE BAT PRESSED DOWN, HIS TEETH SCRAPING MY FACE
The pain was bad, but the sound was worse, like chisels trying to carve into my rock by sheer brute strength. Inside my head, I recited, *Teeth: made of apatite, hardness 5. Me: made of zircon, hardness*

7 and a half. When his teeth gnashed my skin, they'd abrade and I wouldn't.

I could take this. His bites hurt, but I wasn't actually being injured. And the guy was a lightweight bat, even if he looked as big as a bear. He wasn't nearly heavy enough for his weight to crush me. I could just let him gnash till he blew up.

Despite claustrophobic memories of that long-ago fight with Hannah, this wasn't the same. I could escape anytime, just by shrinking. It was my choice to stay, just to keep the bat busy. And I didn't feel smothered—for the first time, I realized I didn't need to breathe. I was litho, not bio. Respiration was for squishies.

More importantly, however, I could see. My gaze wasn't blocked by the bat on top of me. I could let my viewpoint float out of my body, watching the world.

Aria and Dakini had hit the bone-cloud demon hard enough to start him strobing. I didn't know how they'd done it, but two on one, they had done the trick. Now Aria had the demon bubbled inside a force field, just as she'd done at the Market with the bogeyman. She and the bubble were heading into the sky at high speed. With luck, she'd release him and run before he detonated; this time, she wouldn't get hurt.

Closer to earth, Ninety-Nine was skulking. She was likely keeping to the shadows (as if I could tell!) but her major source of concealment was the ever-falling snow. I wondered where she was going, until I saw her stop and sniff.

An Olympic-level sense of smell. I could guess what odor had caught her attention.

I SEARCHED UNTIL I LOCATED NINETY-NINE'S TARGET

Elaine crouched beside the ruins of the generator building. She too must have been hiding in shadows, but she couldn't hide the stench of the dead man's blood on her clothes. Ninety-Nine homed in on it. Like any skilled hunter, she sneaked up on her prey from behind.

Elaine was no longer surrounded by glowing defense spells. They must have been blasted to smithereens when the generators exploded. Still, they'd done their job; Elaine's clothes were crispy around the edges, but Elaine herself seemed uninjured.

Could Ninety-Nine really fight a vampire mage? I didn't know. I could call Dakini to lend a hand—she was only a short distance away. Dakini looked winded after fighting the bone-cloud demon, but even a weak mental attack would distract Elaine from Ninety-Nine.

Unfortunately, if I talked to Dakini with my comm ring, Elaine would hear my thoughts and find out Ninety-Nine was creeping up on her. I had to stay silent . . .

Wait. Even mental silence wasn't enough. The blood bond gave Elaine access to my thoughts, even when I wasn't using my comm ring. She must already have known Ninety-Nine was coming for her. That's why Elaine had stopped yelling at me to shrink and escape from the were-bat. She was lying in wait for Ninety-Nine, pretending to be oblivious while really preparing an ambush.

I shouted mentally, *«Ninety-Nine, it's a trap!»*

Then it was out of my hands.

NINETY-NINE JUMPED BACK AN INSTANT BEFORE ELAINE LASHED OUT Elaine's fingers had sprouted claws. They missed Ninety-Nine and slashed into what remained of the generator building's wall. Aluminum siding shredded like paper. Elaine tore out a handful of the tattered metal and threw it at Ninety-Nine's eyes.

Ninety-Nine ducked her head sideways, letting the scraps fly past her ear. For a moment, she and Elaine simply faced each other, a short distance out of each other's reach.

Elaine smiled, her fangs fully extended. Thanks to the blood bond, I could hear her speak. "I've read Zircon's mind," Elaine said to Ninety-Nine. "I know you have no powers. Human strength. Human speed. You have nothing that can hurt me."

Ninety-Nine smiled back. "Zircon doesn't know everything. But I do."

Green light flashed between Ninety-Nine's hands, like an electric spark arcing between two conductors. An instant later, something long and thin slapped Elaine's face, knocking her back a step. Elaine hissed: the sound of a Darkling dropping the pretense of being human.

Ninety-Nine held a hockey stick made of blazing green energy. She'd summoned it out of nothing, or perhaps the collective unconscious. A hockey player made no sense without a stick. Since Ninety-Nine hadn't included a stick with her costume, the Light had been forced to create one.

It was a thing of power like Excalibur, imbued with inevitability. A super hockey player must have a super stick.

It made me wonder if Jools had chosen to be Ninety-Nine as a way of making this happen. Had she really thought that far ahead? If so, what else did she have planned? What would she get when she finally summoned skates?

The possibilities made me shiver. Or perhaps I was only shivering at the sight of the ensuing battle. Ninety-Nine vs. Elaine . . . and I was beginning to believe Elaine was at least as high-powered as her Sphinx-level brother. Lightning-fast and elephant-strong, she would have torn Ninety-Nine to ribbons, except for the glowing stick.

Each touch of the stick seemed to hurt her. It was like a crucifix, a Holy Weapon of the Light. And Ninety-Nine used it like a world-class martial artist: attacking, blocking, and twirling it as a distraction in order to land kicks.

Elaine was no slouch at martial arts either. If I'd had any doubts whether she truly belonged in the Dark Guard, they were dispelled.

No ordinary Darkling fought like that. The Dark were bankers, politicians, and trust-fund babies. Like Sparks, they used their powers with instinctive skill, but they seldom trained for combat. Physical fights weren't the Dark's forte; they devoted their time to mastering magic and manipulation, not indulging in fisticuffs.

But Elaine had trained *hard*. She must have done so in secret—in my time with Nicholas, Elaine had always been a merciless mental bully, but I'd never seen her get physical. Now she hissed and struck like a viper. Several times she drew Ninety-Nine's blood. But Ninety-Nine struck just as hard and fast, hacking with the edge of the stick, smacking with the flat, and jabbing with the end. A normal wooden stick would have been smashed to splinters in the first few seconds, but the burning green energy seemed unbreakable.

Slashing, tripping, spearing, and other unsportsmanlike conduct: Ninety-Nine racked up penalties that would be measured in weeks, not minutes. And everything took place at Jackie-Chan speed—not even my Spark-o-Vision could follow the details. (I was also distracted by the were-bat continuing to gnaw on me. The experience was like lying on a couch and trying to follow a conversation while an attention-hungry cat pawed all over me.)

So I can't tell you exactly what ended the fight: just that suddenly, Elaine was falling, and the stick clubbed her head at least three times before she hit the ground. She lay unconscious, her face burned by multiple contacts with the stick's "holiness." Red-and-black bands across her cheeks were already beginning to blister.

NINETY-NINE LAID THE BUTT END OF THE STICK AGAINST ELAINE'S STERNUM

"Yo, Zircon!" she called. "This stick isn't wood, but I'm sure it'll do. You want me to stake her?"

With the were-bat on top of me, I couldn't answer right away—I had to do some squirming to get my mouth free of its fur. That delay was a good thing; it gave me time to think.

I could have told Ninety-Nine to finish Elaine off. A vampire's bondslaves usually can't hurt their master in any way, but the blood bond had dwindled when Elaine went unconscious. I was sure the respite was only temporary; when Elaine woke, she could reactivate the bond whenever she chose.

If Elaine woke. Her death would erase many problems.

But it would cause others. The Dark Guard swore vengeance on those who killed one of their own. Nicholas might do the same, and he knew enough about me to do unimaginable damage.

Besides, I didn't want Elaine to make me a murderer. Nor did I want Ninety-Nine to kill on my behalf.

«Dakini,» I transmitted, *«can you erase memories like Invie did in the alley?»*

«I believe so,» she said. *«I paid close attention to the technique.»*

«I thought you might have.»

Fuck, we were all so ick.

«Do that instead of killing her,» I said. *«Erase the whole of tonight if you can.»*

A moment later, the were-bat finally blew up.

THE EXPLOSION SMUSHED ME DEEP INTO THE GROUND

The ground itself got cratered by the blast. (Ooh, a geological shock structure! I wanted to look for shatter cones. But that was craziness talking: displacement. If *you* ever have a person blow up on top of you, just see if your mind doesn't grab at stupid random thoughts to avoid processing what happened.)

I lay in the middle of the crater, shoved into a divot in the dirt. I hurt as if my skin had been flayed with a rusty jackknife, then burned before my eyes. But when I examined my body from above, I saw no damage to my rocky hide . . . and I had an unobstructed view, because the detonation had incinerated the front of my clothes.

Bloody hell. Letting the Goblin enchant my costume may have been rash, but I suddenly felt pretty good about the deal.

The back of my outfit was intact, having been shielded from the blast by my body (and having regrown in the few short minutes since the *last* time it had been trashed by an explosion). As I lay in the pit, I could feel threads beginning to creep over my shoulders, around my sides, and up my crotch as the back of the costume worked to reconstitute the front.

It was pretty damned arousing. Or maybe that was just more crazy-desperate displacement. Either way, I shrank fast so no one would see me wriggle.

***«SKINLESS IS GONE,»* ARIA TRANSMITTED**

She was descending from the sky after disposing of the skeletal demon. I hadn't heard him explode, so she must have taken him so high, his demise was out of earshot. Now he was just bone dust scattered across the jet stream.

«The eclipse has reached totality,» Aria went on. *«It's lovely and red: a real blood moon. Too bad you can't see it for the snow.»*

«The snow will stop soon,» Ninety-Nine said. *«That's a given.»*

Ninety-Nine stood with her hockey stick planted against Elaine's chest. Dakini had joined her and was crouching over Elaine's unconscious body. Violet tendrils snaked from Dakini's head into Elaine's. It wouldn't have broken my heart if Dakini erased years of memory instead of just minutes, but I didn't say that.

«How do you know the snow will stop?» Aria asked Ninety-Nine.

«There's no point to it anymore,» Ninety-Nine said. *«The snow was intended to cause accidents and keep the po-po busy. Also to conceal what was happening out here until the portal opened.»* She gestured toward the rift, which was closing, though not quickly. *«If Diamond wanted people to enter the rift and get superpowers, the snow would be counterproductive. People couldn't reach the portal as easily. Besides, what Diamond really wants is the big dramatic reveal.»*

«Reveal of what?» Aria asked.

At that moment, the snow stopped falling, like a tap being turned off. It must have stopped minutes before, but only now were the last of the flakes reaching the ground. What was left was indeed a reveal: the gigantic rift, tall enough to be seen for miles, and the bloodred moon shining luridly above it.

«Oh,» Aria said. *«That.»* She paused. *«Is it horrible to think that whatever gets people out of bed to see an eclipse is a good thing?»*

Inside the rift, Lilith screamed.

«Okay,» Aria said. *«Just checking.»*

LILITH HOVERED AWAKE AMIDST THE RIFT'S BROWN GAS

Despite the scream, she looked composed. She stared at us without blinking. One of her eyes was a normal blue, but the other was utterly black: no white, no pupil, just a flat black sheen.

That would be the eye I'd splattered with the tranq dart. Whatever superpowers Lilith had acquired, I did not expect good things from that eye.

THE LIGHT'S FIREBALL-BEES SEEMED SCARED OF THE EYE TOO

They pulled quickly away, leaving a broad gap between themselves and Lilith. Like backing off from a rabid dog.

Aria met Lilith's half-black stare. "You'd better come out," Aria said. "We've destroyed the machine that keeps the portal open. If you don't leave the rift soon, you'll be trapped."

"If I come out, you'll attack me," Lilith said.

"We won't," Aria said. "Why would we?"

"Because you're Light and I'm Dark."

"That's no reason to fight."

"Of course it is. The Dark and the Light are enemies. Order and chaos."

"Which is which?" Aria asked.

Lilith sneered. "See, there's another reason to fight: You're clueless."

"Then enlighten us," Dakini said. She had finished mind-wiping Elaine. Dakini and Ninety-Nine came to stand shoulder to shoulder with Aria.

Lilith sighed dramatically, although I'm sure she relished the chance to speak. Monologuing: It never fails. "The Dark embody order. Organizers. *Leaders*. We manage sources of prosperity to maximize their return. We bought our powers legitimately, through a mutually beneficial, clearly defined agreement. Sparks, on the other hand, are nobodies. They didn't get their powers through accomplishments or character. They just won the lottery and didn't even buy a ticket. Is that fair? Is it right? Why should *you* have godlike abilities when the person next door doesn't? Because you got hit by lightning? How does that make you special?"

"What makes us special," Ninety-Nine said, "is that we came here to stop a villain and save lives. As opposed to you, who conspired with said villain because you were bugfuck with Spark envy."

"I don't envy Sparks, I hate them. And I hate Diamond. He's a mass murderer, and now that I have both Dark and Light powers, I'm going to tear him to pieces. But despite all that, I paid for his services. He set a price to make me super, and I paid him, fair and square. I didn't just fluke my way into undeserved privilege. I *paid*."

"You gave Diamond money," Aria said, "which means you helped bankroll everything he's done here. He hoped to kill hundreds of thousands of people. Such an admirable investment, especially since it's going to kill you too."

Aria waited for a reaction. She didn't get it. Lilith was a vampire, and vampires are good at deadpan. "Guess you haven't heard," Aria continued. "Diamond's process has killed every Darkling it touched. He must not have told you about the mess in the Market, and you missed seeing what happened to the others who were with you. But look around. They disintegrated. A few minutes ago, Diamond bragged that the Light and the Dark are like matter and antimatter: Lock them into a single body, and *kaboom*. That's what your money bought you. A quick, ugly death."

Lilith shrieked and shot out of the rift. The Dark and the Light really can't avoid useless fights.

LILITH FLEW WITH THE SPEED OF A "BURST PHENOMENON" AUGMENTED BY SUPERPOWERS

She was fast enough to break the sound barrier, sonic boom and all. If Lilith had gone for Ninety-Nine or Dakini, she might have killed them instantly. Their mere human reflexes couldn't have reacted quickly enough.

But Lilith targeted Aria. Thanks to our Halos, all four of us looked like legends made flesh; even so, Aria was the center of attention. I'm sure it's one of her superpowers. Miranda claims to be fed up with people gawking at her whenever she walks into a room, but when she became a Spark, her wish fulfillment included a strong urge to stand out. Miranda-slash-Aria might not have craved attention, but she totally assumed she'd get it.

Ergo she did. From Lilith and damned near everyone else we met. Aria was our designated Attention Magnet.

Luckily, she had the reflexes to handle that role. She could throw up her force field in a nanosecond. By the time Lilith reached her, Aria had surrounded herself with a golden barrier three times thicker than I'd ever seen before.

She was still bowled off her feet. Lilith hit Aria like a three-hundred-pound football player: one who could run a thousand miles an hour and punch through bank-vault doors. Lilith rammed Aria back a good fifty meters, at which point they hit a garage full of dump trucks and front-end loaders.

The attack didn't stop there. Lilith and Aria went through the garage's brick wall and slammed into an earthmover twice the size of a dump truck. The impact knocked the vehicle sideways; it toppled onto the garage's floor with a thunder of metal on concrete. Then and only then did Lilith and Aria stop.

For a moment, Lilith just lay on top of Aria's fat force field as if it were one of those big rubber exercise balls. Then her dart-damaged eye vomited hideous black bile over the field's golden surface.

THE BILE SPLASHED OVER THE FORCE FIELD

Its effect was like acid. It ate at the golden energy, making black pits in the smooth protective shell. Immediately, Lilith followed up with her fists. She pounded on the damaged surface with the force of an avalanche, fists hammering so hard and fast it sounded like a drumroll on timpani.

Maybe it was my imagination, but beneath the thunderous booms I thought I could hear the force field making soft eggshell cracks.

NINETY-NINE RACED FORWARD, HOCKEY STICK IN HAND

The stick glowed a gleeful green.

Right up to the moment when Ninety-Nine swung it at Lilith's head.

The stick didn't break, but neither did the head. Lilith didn't even notice. The stick, on the other hand, bent as if made of rubber. It folded double under the force. Ninety-Nine yelled, "Ow!" and let go; the stick unbent and boomeranged away, clattering into the shovel of a front-end loader.

Ninety-Nine shook her hands, trying to flick out the pain. I remembered the sting of hitting a baseball full strength with an aluminum bat. I didn't envy Ninety-Nine the sensation.

Dakini reacted more slowly, but she didn't have to move. A sheet of violet light swept from her head toward Lilith. The sheet wrapped Lilith's face in its folds, enveloping eyes, nose, and mouth. Lilith was still a vampire and didn't need to breathe, so blocking her airways wouldn't do much. On the other hand, covering that bile-puking eye was definitely commendable; even if the violet blindfold couldn't withstand the bile's effects, it gave Aria another layer of protection. I thought it might also make it harder for Lilith to hit her target, but that didn't seem to be true. As Aria tried to dodge Lilith's fists, the punches remained 100-percent accurate—as if Lilith could see through the blockage.

Super-speed, super-strength, super-sight, and an eye that shot deadly emissions. Who did that remind me of?

If the Light bestowed powers according to wish fulfillment, I could tell what Lilith had been wishing for, ever since that night in the wheat fields. I wondered if there was a rank of Sparks worse than Hiroshima.

I AIMED MYSELF TOWARD THE FRAY

What did I mean to do? I don't know. Murderous things.

But before I could flap my coattails, I spotted movement above me. Normal vision wouldn't have seen it—the motion was high overhead, and it shed no ordinary light. But Spark-o-Vision saw the glimmer of superhuman power: an armored figure hovering backlit in front of the bloodred moon.

Diamond had discarded his Popigai identity. He was no longer pretending to be steel. Instead, he was covered in colorless crystal, with thousands of glinting facets. It was his famous battle suit made of actual diamond, but hardened even more, thanks to Mad Genius technology, and outfitted with an arsenal of Cape Tech weapons.

As I watched, the glow surrounding his body increased until he shone with a pure white brilliance. I don't know what he looked like in the visible spectrum—maybe still as dark as night—but in Spark-o-Vision, Diamond blazed with power, all of his energies activated.

While Lilith distracted my teammates, Diamond intended to attack.

I FLAPPED HARD IN HIS DIRECTION

I wondered if I should warn the others. No, not yet. I didn't know how the comm rings worked, but Diamond was a Mad Genius. He might have a way to spot our communications. If I transmitted anything, it was possible he could pick me up as a source and know I was moving toward him. Better to maintain radio silence; I'd only have one chance for the element of surprise.

DIAMOND SHOWED NO SIGNS OF NOTICING ME

He raised his hand, as he had above the Market before loosing that missile at us. The coin-sized hole that I'd seen before appeared once again in his palm.

He aimed at the scrum, where Lilith beat on Aria while Ninety-Nine high-sticked Lilith. A single missile would hit all three. Maybe it would also hit Dakini; she stood nearby, trying psionically to make Lilith stop.

Without any better ideas, I shrank to microscopic size and propelled myself into the hole in his palm. As soon as I was inside, I grabbed my knees, curled into a fetal ball, and grew as big as I could in order to clog the missile tube.

I hoped I was as tough as I thought.

ZIRCONS ARE SURVIVORS

The oldest things on Earth.

Earth is four and a half billion years old. Almost every pebble in the crust has been bashed to fragments, melted, and metamorphosed under furious heat and pressure.

But zircons endure. They don't go to pieces when everything else falls apart.

Diamond fired his missile. I blocked its way.

Spectacularity ensued.

THINGS WENT ASPLODY

Diamond's armor protected him from external threats, but when his missile detonated against me, the blast was still very much internal. The hull of a Sherman tank does no good when a shell goes off inside. It only contains the force and makes it all the more lethal for the tank's occupants.

Diamond was just lucky the explosion took place around his hand. The resulting discharge vaporized everything up to Diamond's wrist and continued along his arm, charbroiling flesh as it went. It only stopped when it ran into some kind of seal at the shoulder joint. The seal choked off most of the blast, but a squirt of hot gas still got through. Diamond's chest received second-degree burns, but the major damage stopped at the shoulder.

Meanwhile, the armor's "sleeve" ruptured into diamond shards. Diamond's arm went with it, flayed into minced meat and bonemeal. Other weapons housed in the glove self-destructed in jets of acid, shrapnel, and Freon.

BY THEN, I WAS FAR AWAY

The explosion propelled me out of the missile tube. Since Diamond had been aiming at Lilith, that's where I went. Still tucked in fetal position, I was the size, shape, and weight of a musket ball. It would have been useful if I'd bulleted into Lilith herself, but I was far from a perfect sphere, so I instantly went off target. I might have ended up hitting the ground, but instinct kicked in: Rather than fly like a badly shaped ball, I shrank out of sight. At the size of an aphid's eyebrow, I was soon stopped by air resistance.

The air didn't resist much against someone the size of Diamond. The missile blast slammed him sideways with the strength of a wrecking ball. His trajectory turned into a classic parabola, as he fell under pure Newtonian gravity. His boot-jets did nothing—they must have gotten pwned by the explosion. Diamond basically became a first-year physics problem, destined to accelerate until he hit the ground.

It's likely impossible to lose your hand and flambé your arm without passing out. Even if you manage to stay conscious, you stop paying attention to your surroundings. Besides, what could Diamond do to stop his fall? His battle suit was toast. His only true superpower was hyper-intelligence. With his armor reduced to deadweight, he became a really, really smart crash-test dummy.

Diamond fell. He hit the pavement outside the garage with a *thunk*. The sound was made even louder by the extra mass of his armor. It was the sort of impact you'd call a sickening *thud*, except if you weren't already sickened by what happened to Diamond's arm, a noise wouldn't likely do it either.

ONE THREAT DOWN, ONE TO GO

Make that *two* threats to go, because the rift produced an ear-popping *whomp* as it shuddered and contracted.

The earth shook. All over the landfill, holes opened in the ground as buried junk shifted and subsided. Every time I'd seen a rift close, the consequences had been seismic. This rift, so much bigger than the rest, might be more deadly than Lilith.

And Lilith appeared plenty deadly. Ninety-Nine lay sprawled on the garage's concrete floor. Lilith must have smacked Ninety-Nine hard before returning to wallop on Aria. Aria had gone into complete defensive mode: She pumped everything she had into her black-pitted force field, no energy left for attack.

Lilith hammered on the force field, screaming, "Fuck you, fuck you, fuck you!" Inside the rift, she had seemed more lucid than the other super-Darklings. Now her sanity bubble had popped and she was playing for Team Berserk.

Surprisingly, Lilith hadn't attacked Dakini, even though Dakini now had dozens of violet tentacles embedded in Lilith's brain. Maybe Lilith was ignoring Dakini *because* of those tentacles. Dakini might have made herself invisible to Lilith's frenzied mind. That would give her more time to stop Lilith cold, but so far, nothing in Dakini's psionic repertoire had had a noticeable effect.

Aria's force field was weakening. Lilith's fists moved as fast as hummingbird wings, drumrolling on Aria's bile-damaged protection. Unlike Aria, Lilith showed no signs of tiring.

HOW COULD I TURN THE TIDE?

Fly into Lilith's ear and hemorrhage her brain? Considering that Lilith could have been as tough as the Big Blue Farm Boy, I might not have had the strength to hurt her even if I kicked her in the gray cells.

Use Scout, Falcon, or Asp? No. The blades might break against Lilith's skin. Even if they could hurt her, they'd demand a high price for doing so. More blood. Greater sacrifice. Every use of the knives was a downward step. I knew what lay at the end of that road.

That left me with only one option.

I flew to where the Widow and her driver lay unconscious. I grew up, got what I needed, then shrank. Flew back to Lilith. Went to Max Zirc size.

I shot Lilith in the head with Trent's pistol.

I DIDN'T KNOW WHAT THE PISTOL WOULD SHOOT

Fire? Gamma rays? Poisonous spiders? I was pretty darn sure it wouldn't be bullets. As I've said, the gun screamed Cape Tech with a side order of magic. It practically had its own Halo. I hoped it would shoot something that would rock Lilith back on her heels without actually killing her.

That's what I told myself.

THE GUN EMITTED A BEAM OF BABY PINK LIGHT

Soft and ridiculous: a color even ten-year-old Kimberley would have thought was too Hello Kitty. It enveloped the screaming Lilith in its pastel embrace, then blinked out.

Lilith's fists didn't stop moving. They just started passing through Aria's body.

"Ooo-kaaaay," I said. "Did not expect that."

Lilith had become intangible. It was actually a brilliant way of neutralizing an opponent. Lilith could no longer hurt us, yet she wasn't damaged herself. In her crazed condition, she didn't even realize what had happened. Her fists kept flying, moving faster than before but without effect.

Nice. And eminently defensible in court. You could even turn the gun on yourself, become intangible, and run. Preferably through a wall, so your enemies couldn't follow.

Aria said, "I've got to get me one of those." She rose shakily to her feet, with Lilith still hammering ineffectually at her.

"I could probably build one," Ninety-Nine said. "Just let me see how it works."

She tried to take the pistol. I backed away. "Do not dissect the wonder-gun."

As I ducked out of Ninety-Nine's reach, I noticed an LED display on the back of the weapon, just above where my hand held the pistol butt. If I'd had normal vision, I would have seen it immediately; the display was designed to be seen from the shooter's point of view. But my Spark-o-Vision had centered itself near the garage's ceiling, as if I hadn't wanted to be inside my own head when I pulled the trigger.

Huh.

THE LED READ *23*

A second later *22*. Then *21*.

I said, "Twenty seconds till she rematerializes. Ideas?"

"Keep shooting as needed," Ninety-Nine suggested. "Eventually, she'll get the shakes and self-destruct."

"In the meantime," Dakini said, "I'll keep working on her mind. I can do it, even when she's in this form. I think I'm making progress."

"Keep your eye on the timer!" Aria said, pointing at the gun. "I don't want her solidifying when her fists are inside me."

I said, "Three . . . two . . . one . . ."

Aria leapt backward. Lilith closed the gap a moment later, her fists suddenly making solid contact with Aria's force field until I pulled the trigger again.

"Your reflexes are slow," Aria complained. "Just FYI, it hurts like hell when she hits my force field."

I made a grumpy face, then handed the pistol to Ninety-Nine. "You're faster than I am. But do *not* take the gun apart."

"Not right now," Ninety-Nine said.

I glared at her.

"As I was saying," Dakini said, "I'm making progress on Lilith's mind. I've augmented her obsession with hitting Aria. That's why she hasn't tried the eye thing again. I've got her totally fixated on punching. Apart from that, her psyche is hard to penetrate. If I find some vulnerability, I'll try to whittle her down."

"You whittle," I said. I pointed to Ninety-Nine. "You shoot." I pointed to Aria. "You be the obsession. I'll see if I can deal with loose ends."

"Like what?" Aria asked.

"Peeling Diamond out of his armor before he wakes up. And—"

The rift gave a thunderous *whomp* as it jerked smaller.

"And," I said, "making sure nobody is near the rift when it closes."

"Yeah," Aria said, looking at the rift through the hole in the garage's wall. "Let's not be here anymore."

She headed out of the garage and away from the rift. Lilith followed, still pounding with her insubstantial fists. Ninety-Nine and Dakini trailed behind.

I SHRANK AND FLEW BACK TOWARD DIAMOND
He lay sprawled where he'd landed. The stump of his damaged arm was exposed burnt flesh, but the rest of his armor was intact.

The armor was glowing. It had gone dark when he'd first crashed down, but obviously it had rebooted and was attempting self-repair. Damn.

I had no idea if Diamond or his battle suit could see me, but I had to assume the worst. His suit would have all kinds of sensors—maybe ones that could pick me out no matter how small I got. The sensors might not be working yet. After a reboot, the first systems to be powered up would be damage control and life support. Defending against insect-sized threats would be farther down the list.

But anti-shrinker defenses would wake up eventually. I had to reach Diamond before his suit erected a force field or something else that would complicate my life. I flew straight at him, shrank a bit more, then entered a burn hole in his arm.

Welcome to a supervillain's bloodstream.

I STARTED BACTERIUM-SIZED AND SHRANK DOWN TO A VIRUS, THEN EVEN SMALLER

I approached a red corpuscle that in my eyes looked as big as a football stadium. I slid inside its outer membrane and let it carry me through veins and arteries, like a submarine shooting through the circulation system. Long chain molecules inside the corpuscle hurtled past me on unknown errands. If I survived this, I'd have to find a way to show it all to Jools. She didn't excel at classwork, but she genuinely loved biology.

Think about that later. Dealing with Diamond was Job Number One.

I scaled up my Spark-o-Vision and scanned what his armor was doing. Not much to see: Everywhere I looked, computer circuitry had to be processing like mad, but all I saw were faint glows of power doing nothing visible. Intravenous feeds ran from the armor into Diamond's body, pumping him full of chemicals. I had no idea what the chemicals were doing; presumably stabilizing his health and waking him up.

So what to do? I wanted to prevent the man from hurting my friends. I could grow big inside him and rip him apart, but I preferred to use that as a threat rather than actually doing it. Unfortunately, I couldn't threaten him if he couldn't hear me.

Hmm.

Using my comm ring, I transmitted, *«Diamond, what are the odds you've hacked into the Inventor's comm system?»*

No answer.

«You're a Mad Genius, Diamond. Hacking is what you do. As Adam Popigai, you've been in Ontario for months. In that time, I bet you applied yourself to tapping the local Spark chat line.»

No answer.

«I'm inside you, Diamond. In your bloodstream. If you don't respond, I'll have to find other ways to communicate. Invasive ways.»

A chuckle, strained but clear. I had to admire the drugs his suit was pumping out. If he could laugh in his condition, the painkillers must be awesome.

«You'd be Zircon, correct?» Diamond's voice sounded exactly like the prerecorded soliloquy.

«That's me,» I said. *«Right now, I'm»*—I did a quick scan—*«running through the lining of your large intestine. I think. Studying Gray's Anatomy is on my to-do list.»*

«Skip the book,» Diamond said. *«I recommend dissecting the real thing. Preferably a living subject. More fun that way.»*

«You realize I could kill you at any time, right? Saying things like that doesn't improve your chance of survival.»

«Ah, I'm just doing PR,» he replied. *«I have to maintain my reputation. After tonight's fiasco, my rep will take a hit.»*

«You certainly aren't going to get thirty thousand new Sparks. Or three hundred thousand corpses. Not even superpowered rats and gulls.»

«You surely don't think you destroyed all the vermin,» Diamond said. *«They're survivors. Super-survivors. And Dark versus Light still applies. All those super-rats and gulls will feel compelled to attack Darklings. So this project hasn't been a total waste.»*

«Why do you hate Darklings so much?»

Diamond didn't respond right away. After a long pause, he said,

«My dear Zircon, are you familiar with Rapa Nui? More commonly called Easter Island? The place with those giant stone heads?»

«I've seen pictures.»

«Then you know the island once supported a prosperous culture. So prosperous, they could afford to spend time and resources on erecting big stone heads instead of day-to-day subsistence. But eventually things went to hell. You know why?»

I said, *«They used up all the trees. Chopped them down until nothing was left, and the environment collapsed. Nearly everyone died.»*

«Ha!» Diamond sounded triumphant. *«That's the morality tale everyone likes to believe. What really happened had nothing to do with morality. Some boat arrived with rats on board, and the rats got loose on the island. They ate the seeds and seedlings of every damn plant they found. The humans probably realized what was happening and tried to wipe out the rats before it was too late. But like I said, rats are survivors. They destroyed the ecology, and took the island with them.»*

I said, *«Why are you telling me this?»*

«Because Darklings are society's rats. They'll keep eating till everything's gone. They won't stop, they won't slow down, they won't hear the word 'no.' They'll keep eating-eating-eating till the world goes to hell.»

«Darklings are intelligent,» I said. *«They can understand the consequences of their actions.»*

«They can, but they never bother. They assume the consequences will fall on someone else. They think they're too special to end up dirty and starving.»

He almost spat the word "special." I said, *«They're not that bad—»* but he cut me off.

«They are! They're dead inside. They are literally and spiritually dead, killed by the Dark Conversion. They can't change even if they want to. Which they don't. They believe they're the pinnacle of merit, and anyone who doesn't aspire to be exactly like them is either jealous or stupid.»

«Okay,» I said placatingly, *«okay.»* His rant had the sound of someone ramping up to do something extreme, like a madman with a knife talking himself into a frenzy. I didn't know what killing power

his battle suit still possessed, but I didn't want Diamond running amok in Waterloo. «*One way or another,*» I said, «*this is over. Your rift is closing, and your cover is blown. Go back to Australia. Write this one off.*»

«*Or else you'll kill me?*» Diamond demanded. «*If you had the balls, I'd be dead already. I'm a big bad supervillain, and if you don't punch my ticket, I'll keep murdering Darklings and innocent people. But you'd rather let people die than sully your conscience by killing me directly.*»

«*Which is why Zircon has friends to fill the gap,*» a voice said.

Aria. Who apparently had been listening.

I'D KEPT MY POINT OF VIEW SMALL, WATCHING INSIDE DIAMOND'S BODY AS I TRAVELED THROUGH HIS BLOODSTREAM

Now I widened my perspective to see the outside world.

Aria hurtled toward Diamond and me, flying scary-fast. Lilith was right behind, flying just as fast and trying (in midair) to punch Aria into golden goo. Diamond started to say, "Sh–" but by the time the "—it" came out, both Aria and Lilith had arrived.

Aria jerked to a stop inside Diamond's body, superimposed on him like a ghost. Ohh-kay. *She* was now the one who'd become insubstantial. Which meant . . .

Lilith lashed out, her fists as solid as granite, but much higher on the Mohs hardness scale. Harder even than diamond.

Heh.

With Aria incorporeal inside Diamond's body, and positioned so Lilith still had a good clear view of her, Lilith's super-hard punches slammed Diamond instead.

It would have made me laugh, except I was too busy banging around as the lightning-fast blows rocked Diamond's body.

DIAMOND'S ARMOR SAVED HIM FROM BEING BASHED TO A PULP

But it didn't prevent him rattling back and forth inside the armor like dice in a backgammon cup. I don't know how Diamond's head stayed clear enough to fight back against the pounding, but let's chalk it up to superintelligence: His brain was all kinds of special. It had let him survive all those battles with Australian heroes. Even when a super-team attacked with everything they had, Diamond had managed to escape.

Wait. I had read about Diamond in Wikipedia. The article had mentioned how he always escaped. *«Aria,»* I transmitted, *«he's going to—»*

«I know,» she said. *«Ninety-Nine told me about his final defense. Get out of there!»*

I shoved my way out of the blood cell I'd been riding and raced for the outside world. No time for finesse: Like that scene from *Alien*, I took the most direct route. I grew to the size of a pinhead, leaving a needle-sized trail as I clawed through the wall of Diamond's large intestine, into the abdominal muscles, and on toward the epidermis. Even that "easy" route took time and effort. With my full normal strength, it was simple enough to stab my hands through every tissue I encountered. (My friend, the thumbtack principle.) But dragging myself forward was a gooey business, made more difficult by the tossing and turning of the ongoing fight.

Lilith punched, still obsessed with killing Aria. Diamond fought back, emptying his suit's remaining arsenal into Lilith at point-blank range. Missiles. Napalm. Liquid nitrogen. When he released a stream of lava straight into her blackened eye, she began vibrating and strobing, but she didn't even notice. Lilith kept hammering so hard and so fast, Diamond was vibrating almost as quickly as she was.

Any moment, I expected to see Diamond's final defense: teleportation. Wikipedia said that a fail-safe device inside his armor could teleport Diamond's body out of the battle suit and off to some unknown place of safety where he could recuperate. Meanwhile, the suit would remain behind, then explode with a force beyond any conventional explosive. It wasn't a nuclear blast, but over the years, a dozen heroes had been killed by Diamond's lethal getaway, including Sparks noted for super-toughness.

I seriously didn't want to test how much my zircon skin could withstand.

I CLAMBERED OUT THROUGH THE SURFACE OF DIAMOND'S SKIN
But I was still inside Diamond's battle suit. The space between his flesh and his armor smelled strongly of Diamond's spilled blood.

The only way out of the armor—at least the only one I knew about—was the hole by which I'd entered, where the battle suit's arm had blown off. I grew as big as I could, given the clearance between the armor and Diamond; then I scrambled up his body like a cockroach, digging my fingers and toes into his flesh as I went. (Three cheers for experience climbing in the mountains around Banff!)

To see where I was going, I brought my vision back into my head rather than watching what happened outside. My first clue that something had changed was Aria shouting in my head, «*Stay back!*»

«*Can't,*» I heard Ninety-Nine answer. «*You turn solid in five . . . four . . . three . . .* »

I shoved myself out of the hole in the armor just in time to see Aria rise high enough to get clear of Diamond's body. Lilith rose with her, still punching. Aria's force field offered some protection, but it had thinned to the width of a dime. Even worse, Diamond raised his remaining arm as soon as Aria left him. He clearly intended to shoot her with some weapon the instant she became solid.

I couldn't let that happen.

I leapt toward his outstretched arm. As I jumped, I grew. By the time I reached my target, I was Max Zirc size and full weight.

I may not be big or heavy, but I caught Diamond by surprise. Besides, he'd taken a hell of a beating. Usually, his armor gave him superstrength, but after all the damage his suit had suffered, Diamond only possessed his own muscle power. Long story short: When I grabbed his arm, my weight dragged it most of the way down.

The attack he'd been aiming still fired, but it wasn't pointing at Aria. It wasn't pointing at anything. It did, however, have a targeting mechanism that apparently homed in on the nearest suitable victim. Unsurprisingly, Diamond had programmed it never to target him, so who was next closest?

Starts with Z.

I WAS HIT WITH HIGH-VOLTAGE ELECTRICITY

Lucky for me, I wasn't grounded. I was shorter than Diamond, and with my two arms wrapped around his one, I dangled with my feet not touching the ground. So what was the path of least resistance for a few million volts desperately eager to reach Earth?

Starts with D.

DIAMOND LIT UP LIKE THE TIME RICHARD TRIED TO REPAIR OUR TOASTER

I took a fraction of the shock myself, but only in my zircon arms.

Zircon isn't a very good conductor.

Normally diamond is also a lousy conductor, but Diamond's armor was *special*: super-hardened by Cape Tech and chock-full of electronic circuits. When the voltage zapped out at me, it fed straight back into Diamond's suit and ran toward the ground, frying much of the circuitry as it went. The glow that surrounded the armor blinked out, and high-voltage current stopped shooting through me.

I was still alive.

As for Diamond, I didn't know. But if the teleportation/explosion was going to happen, it would kick in any second. "Ninety-Nine!" I shouted. "Shoot me, then shoot yourself!"

She didn't hesitate. In the time I'd been hanging off Diamond, Ninety-Nine had already shot Aria and restored her to safe intangibility. Now she turned the gun on me. The baby pink beam surrounded my body like a Halo. The world went instantly silent—being insubstantial, my ears no longer intercepted sound waves. My arms lost their grip on Diamond and I slid through his body, drifting gently downward. I felt nothing as my feet touched the ground, but my descent stopped anyway. I could think of no good rationale for that happening, so I decided it was magic.

Hurray for magic! I wasn't going to keep sinking into the ground, then suddenly become solid when surrounded by buried garbage.

Meanwhile, Ninety-Nine turned the gun on herself. She pulled the trigger and became ephemeral. The pistol didn't. It clattered to the ground.

«Well, crap,» Ninety-Nine transmitted. *«But of course, it would have to be impervious to its own—»*

FLASH
Diamond's armor silently blew up.

FLASH
Lilith strobed out.

FLASH
The rift closed.

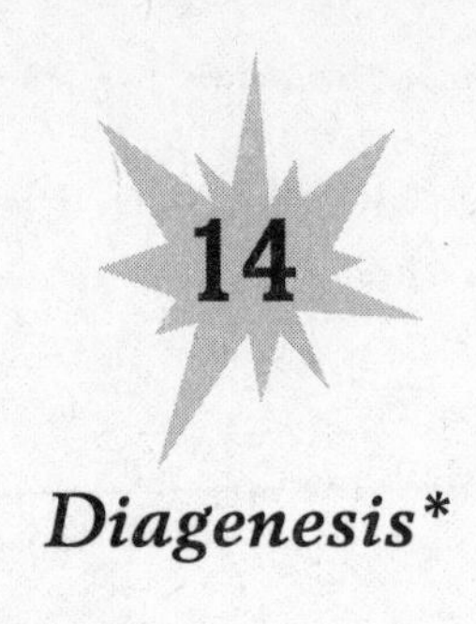

*Diagenesis**

THE EXPLOSIONS WERE SILENT

Also hyper-amazingly bright to those of us at ground zero. But the crushing blasts of superheated air went straight through us without making the least impression on our eardrums.

Yay fucking yay.

By the time we turned solid again, the fuss was over.

IF ANY SUPER-VERMIN REMAINED NEARBY, THE TRIPLE EXPLOSION MUST HAVE FINISHED THEM OFF. I THINK

Conceivably, my teammates had missed a few animals during the great extermination. The survivors may have gotten powers and escaped before the grand finale. If so, however, they kept a low profile in the days that followed.

Possibly even now, a Mad Genius rat is plotting revenge on the humans who slaughtered its brothers and sisters. Possibly, a well-fed eagle is scooping up field mice while flying at Mach 10. Possibly, the rat and the eagle are archenemies, having daily super-battles without humans ever knowing. At some point, the rat may set off a doomsday device and we'll all be like, "What the—?" just before Earth collapses into a black hole.

But I hope not.

AS ARIA, NINETY-NINE, AND I RETURNED TO CORPOREALITY, DAKINI ARRIVED, FLOATING ON A VIOLET FLYING CARPET

She was wise to stay off the ground. Anything that could possibly burn was on fire. This included all the vehicles in the garage, plus

* Creation of new rock by loose sediments cementing themselves together.

the asphalt road connecting the garage to other parts of the landfill. The tar in the asphalt made a stinking smoke that would seriously drop the property values of houses downwind. Still, the breeze blew the smoke away from the city, so that was something. (Provided you didn't live on a nearby farm.)

Another thing that was burning: the gun that had made us de-solid. The weapon had been sturdily built, but it couldn't survive being inches away from three stupidly huge explosions. Trent's pistol was now a flaming lump of metal and plastic mush. There wouldn't be enough left to analyze, not even for someone as smart as Ninety-Nine.

She nudged the burning remnants with her toe. "Damn. It would have been nice to have a dozen of those."

"Trent must have bought it somewhere," I said, then stopped. I sent my Spark-o-Vision to search where I'd last seen Trent and the Widow.

Trent was still there, extremely dead after all the flames and furor. I didn't see the Widow. Not even a corpse. That might mean she was dead—some Darklings crumble to dust when they die. Alternatively, she might have woken up and slipped away during all the commotion.

I turned to Dakini. "Can you pick up the Widow's brainwaves?"

Dakini shook her head. "I've already checked for survivors. There are none nearby. Speaking of which, that woman you asked me to brainwash—you may be pleased to know Wraith saved her."

"Wraith?" I said.

"I was watching from a distance," Dakini said. "Just before the explosion, Wraith appeared out of nowhere, picked up the unconscious woman, and ghosted away."

"Of course he did," I said.

Sparks and Darklings had Fate on their side. For every Lilith who was truly obliterated, there was always a Nicholas who seemed to be as good as dead but who recovered just in time to rescue his sister. I had to give him credit for saving Elaine, even though she'd tricked him and drained his energy . . .

Wait. Did she really trick him? The Dark Guard had assigned Elaine to ingratiate herself with Diamond. That was part of a scheme to remove Diamond once and for all. Could Nicholas have been in on it too? The Dark Guard consisted of high-powered Darklings. If Elaine was already in the organization, she might have recruited her Sphinx-level brother to be a ghostly James Bond.

That would explain why Nicholas had been covertly scoping out the campus police station. And why he wanted to search Popigai's office.

Pieces began rearranging themselves in my mind.

NINETY-NINE SURVEYED THE SWATH OF DESTRUCTION WE'D SLASHED THROUGH THE LANDFILL

"Dudes," she said, "our work here is done."

Aria looked around and nodded. "We've discovered the most important reason for maintaining a secret identity. It's not to protect loved ones, it's to avoid being sued for massive property damage."

"Just to be sure," Ninety-Nine said, "we should hide most of our cash in anonymous bank accounts. There's a financial Mad Genius in the Virgin Islands who caters to Sparks. Privacy guaranteed, and he never invests a cent in Darkling enterprises. First Bank of the Light. Very discreet."

"Yes," Aria said, "our foremost concern at the moment is definitely where to conduct our offshore banking."

"You can joke about that now," Ninety-Nine told her, "but once I start building inventions, we're all going to be rich. What do you think: Too Many Cooks Enterprises?"

"If the inventions are yours," Dakini said, "the money should be yours too. All of it."

"Nah, we're in this together," Ninety-Nine told her. "I'm the brains, you're my muscle. My gun molls."

"I'm unfamiliar with the term 'gun molls,'" Dakini said, "but it has a nice ring. Could we call our team Gun Molls? Is the name taken?"

"Shoot me now," Aria said. "I mean it."

"I'm not a moll," I said. I put one arm around Aria's waist and the other arm as far as it would go around Dakini. "I'm . . . oh, let's get out of here before I say something maudlin."

WE WENT HOME

We ate chocolate-chip cookies till dawn, thereby delaying the arrival of our rock-hard belly muscles by three days.

THE BELLY MUSCLES SHOWED UP ON CHRISTMAS

It's true. I'm as ripped as if I do a thousand crunches a day.

Same with my arms and legs. I'm glad that nothing in my wardrobe is tight-fitting. My lean mean physique will go unnoticed. But if I ever decide to wear a T-shirt and shorts, I'll look like a small, queer, Chinese Arnold Schwarzenegger.

No thirty-six triple-Ds, thank the Light. Nor other major changes to primary or secondary sexual characteristics.

Although I think my voice has changed. As Kim, I had to take care so my voice wouldn't pitch up too high. Now I'm an alto without even thinking about it.

And my hair is permanently white. I mean, *seriously* permanent. I've tried spraying on color, but it vanishes within seconds. Pink, green, blue, nothing stays.

I see this as a sign that Kim is over. Kim was a stepping stone, like the brittle-ductile transition zone, where rocks change from breaking under stress to flowing smoothly.

I'm planning to get out more. Take these muscles for some test drives.

I'm also going to stop calling Jools, Miranda, and Shar my roommates or my teammates, and start calling them my friends.

Maybe I'll call myself K. Kimberley, Kimmi, Kim, K: That

feels like progress. And it'll make things even harder for people who narrow their eyes behind my back and try to pigeonhole me.

I won't have to turn around to see them staring.

Acknowledgments

Many thanks to all the people who've had a hand in this book, including my wonderful agent, Lucienne Diver, and my equally wonderful editor, Greg Cox. Also thanks to first reader/editor Kat Howard, copy editor Melanie Sanders, and Tor staffer Christopher Morgan.

For indirect but ongoing support, I'd like to thank Robert J. Sawyer for many years of friendship and for hosting "Rob's Write-Off Retreat" where some of this book was written.

I should also mention the various role-playing game systems I've followed over the years. In particular, White Wolf and the Onyx Path have had a great influence on my interpretation of various Darklings, while *Champions* from Hero Games has influenced my take on superheroes.

Also, let's not forget DC, Marvel, and all the other companies that have spent many decades developing and refining the tropes of superheroes as we currently understand them. I grew up on comic books, and they'll always have an important place in my heart.

A tip of my hat to Wikipedia and the Comic Book Database (comicbookdb.com), which I frequently had to consult to make sure I wasn't usurping superhero names from existing characters.

Finally, thanks to various people, places, and things around the city and region of Waterloo, especially the University of Waterloo and its Faculty of Science. None of them gave me permission to write any of this, but I'm sure they'll be delighted by seeing themselves repeatedly blown to shreds.

(By the way, I should note that I've changed many details from how these places are in real life. In a world where Darklings and Sparks exist, differences have to be expected.)

Turn the page for a sneak peek
at the next book in the series

THEY PROMISED ME THE GUN WASN'T LOADED

Available November 2018

Deimatic Behavior

I'm the smartest actual human on the planet.

Also the strongest. And the fastest.

But despite my best efforts, I'm not the drunkest. This stupid airplane hasn't stocked enough booze to do the job.

It doesn't help that I'm competing for alcohol with three Darklings up in first class. My hearing is (of course) the best a human's can be, and I can hear quite clearly that they're having a drinking contest.

I saw the Darklings when I got on the plane: a vampire, a werewolf, and a demon one-off whose hide is a patchwork of human skin, mammal fur, bird feathers, and insect chitin. That's only what I could see on her face and hands; under her Armani, she likely has an entire zoo's worth of integument. Fish scales. Tortoise shell. *Cnidaria* jelly. Maybe tree bark and vegetable rinds too. Even stuff from extraterrestrials.

I should ask if she'd let me examine her—I need a project for Biology 399. But she'd likely tell me to go to hell. I've never met a Darkling who wasn't a mean drunk.

All three drunk Darklings sound like assholes. They're loud enough that even the normal people around me can hear them. At this moment, the Darklings are hassling the cute guy who's playing air host for first class.

On major flights like New York to London, the airlines *know* that first-class attendants will have to deal with obnoxious Darklings, so every attendant gets an amulet or psi-shield to defend against black-magic mind-stomps. But gadgets like that are ungodly expensive;

on pissy little runs like this one from Edmonton to Waterloo, the staff are expected to resist through sheer force of will.

Yeah, right. Even back here in sub-sub-economy, I can feel the Darklings flaring their Shadows. Every passenger on the plane is staggered by the effect—faces pale, hands trembling. A couple folks have started puking into their sick bags.

The first-class air host has probably shriveled into a paralyzed fetal ball. But I can't tell that for sure—the curtain is drawn between the first-class cabin and ours. Still, it pisses me off.

Oh look, I'm up on my feet.

I'm not immune to the mental force of Darkling Shadows, but being a Spark, my superpowers give me some measure of resistance. On a scale from zero to totally shitting myself, this is on par with what I felt when my academic adviser told me I was close to flunking out. Or maybe more like before a hockey game, when our team is up against strong opposition: I just tell myself that getting scared won't improve my game, so I set the fear aside and go on offense. Just like I'm doing now.

I force myself forward rather than running back to the bathrooms, partly because a crowd is already stampeding to bathroomland, but mostly cuz I'm a heroine, fighting fuckery wherever I find it.

Also I'm partly drunk and making bad choices. So there's that.

I push through the curtains and enter first class. It's empty except for attendant-dude and the three Darklings. Two other seats have a lived-in look, with their TVs set to a business channel and with hastily discarded copies of the *Financial Post* covering damp spots on the upholstery. The occupants of those seats are nowhere in sight—probably locked in the up-front washrooms.

Good. I don't have to worry about bystanders. I just have to figure out what I'm going to do.

Aw, fuck this, I'm drunk. I'll wing it.

"Yo!" I say. "What's holding up my drinks?"

The Darklings turn their eyes on me: vampire red, werewolf green, and the demon's one-brown-and-one-composite. The werewolf is already furry. Good. Actually seeing a werewolf change is enough to make your bladder crawl into your panties. If that part is out of the way, the worst is over.

I'm assuming, of course, that the Darklings won't actually fight me. That's a reasonable assumption: the Dark are always as rich as fuck, so they usually pay for other people to do their dirty work. Besides, they probably own stock in this airline, so they won't want to cause costly damage. On the other hand they may be drunker than me, if only because they can afford more of those outrageously small bottles of hooch that we rely on to dampen our aviophobia.

After a moment of silently staring at me and wondering, "Who the fuck is this bitch?" all three Darklings amp up their Shadows in an attempt to turn my brain into pudding. In Bio 370, we called this deimatic behavior: attempting to intimidate other creatures by physical displays, like cobras hissing or poison frogs inflating their butt cheeks. Most normal humans would collapse under the psychological onslaught. However, it's common knowledge that alcohol sometimes makes you insensitive to Darkling Shadows. I won't endanger my secret identity if I pretend I just don't feel their mental mugging.

More interestingly, the hottie air attendant doesn't seem too crushed either. His skin is a perfect black—I mean really totally black, and also perfect, making me want to rub my face all over his body—so he's never going to go pale, no matter how scared he gets. But despite being here at ground zero of the Darklings' auras, the dude is only a teensy bit shaky, and he hasn't even retreated behind his coffee cart.

Maybe the airline *did* give the guy a defensive talisman. Or maybe he's the one-in-a-million human with natural resistance to magic. Or maybe, like me, he's just numbed himself with C_2H_6O, which makes perfect sense if you know you're going to spend a three-hour flight rubbing elbows with the Dark.

"Miss," he says, "please return to your seat."

I say, "I will, but not empty-handed." I'm surprised that the words actually come from my mouth, because I'm leaning strongly toward strategic retreat. I came forward because I thought a trio of Darklings were making waves without adult supervision. Now that I see Mr. Hottie isn't jabbering in panic, I'm okay with letting him deal with the situation. It's his job, after all; and while I happen to be the most tactful, diplomatic human on the planet, and therefore a better smoother-overer of Darkling jackassery than Mr. Air-Host Cutie-Dude, I'm also hella respectful and would never undermine his hunky authority by trying to do his work for him. I'm also not so completely in the bag as to ignore the chance of me and the Darklings ending up in a brawl if diplomacy fails. Since a three-on-one Darkling-slash-superhero fight is a bad idea at thirty thousand feet, I'm prepared to retire graciously without further ado.

As soon as I get another shot of tequila.

Or gin.

Or Johnny Walker whatever-color-is-cheapest.

"I'll have what they're having," I say to Cutie-Boots, as I point to the row of single-shot bottles in front of the Darklings. "They have way way more than they'll ever need. Consider this redistribution: Down with *r*, up with *g*, one for you, and three for me. Or else I'll just drink these three job-creators under the table and prove that a real human's tolerance for alcohol poisoning beats candy-ass magic every time."

The three drunks stare at me for a long long moment. Then the demon with the patchwork skin gives me the Morpheus-Matrix hand gesture. *Come on, little girl. Show us what you got.*

"You want to join the contest?" the demon asks. She sets an unopened bottle on the little tray in front of her. "Okay, we'll deal you in."

"About fucking time," I say. I plop myself down in the big comfy chair at the end of their row. "Hi," I tell them, "I'm Jools."

About the Author

JAMES ALAN GARDNER (Jim) started reading comic books near the beginning of the Silver Age, and never really stopped. Eventually, he picked up a couple of math degrees from the University of Waterloo, after which he immediately started writing fiction instead. He has published numerous novels and shorter works, including pieces that made the finalist lists for the Hugo and Nebula Awards. He has won the Aurora Award, the Theodore Sturgeon Memorial Award, and the Asimov's Science Fiction Magazine Readers' Award. In his spare time, he teaches kung fu to six-year-olds and collects interesting rocks. He is currently working on another book in the Dark/Spark universe.